Till We Meet Again

Till We Meet Again

LESLEY PEARSE

LONDON NEW YORK SYDNEY TORONTO

This edition published 2002
by BCA
by arrangement with MICHAEL JOSEPH
an imprint of the Penguin Group

CN 107210

Set in 13.75/16.25 pt Monotype Garamond
Typeset by Rowland Phototypesetting Ltd,
Bury St Edmunds, Suffolk
Printed and bound in Germany by GGP Media, Pössneck

For all parents who have lost a child to meningitis.
My heart goes out to you all.

Acknowledgements

To two wonderful men, without whose help and support I could never have written this book: Inspector Jonathan Moore for his input on police investigative procedures, and John Roberts, Criminal lawyer in Bristol, for insight into the world of law. You both gave your help so unstintingly and offered me encouragement and support when I needed it. I loved your humour, your lack of pomposity and patience. Bless you both. Any mistakes or blunders are mine, not yours, and my excuse is that I couldn't hope to gather up all your tremendous experience and knowledge without spending at least a month or two in your shoes. Should any of my readers fall in love with Detective Inspector Roy Longhurst in my book, then it is because I was inspired by the characters of these two sweethearts.

To Harriet Evans, my editor at Penguin Books. How anyone so young can have so much wisdom and diplomacy beats me. I'll have you know I didn't once throw your notes across the room in disgust, or say 'What does she know!' You do know. You are clever, intuitive, sweet-natured and a joy to work with. Thank you, Harrie, and not just for your expertise in editing, but for the comfort when I was unsure of myself, and for the many laughs along the way.

Finally, a very special thank you to the Spencer Dayman Meningitis Laboratories in Bristol for giving me so much invaluable information about meningitis. While meningococcal B remains a serious threat to society countrywide, this charity's sterling work in providing funds for the research and development of vaccines against meningitis and associated diseases is of vital importance. If you would like to help in fundraising or to make a donation to the charity, please contact The Spencer Dayman Meningitis Laboratories, 25 Cleevewood Road, Downend, Bristol BS16 2SF.

Chapter one

October 1995

Pamela Parks glanced up from the appointment book at the sound of the street door opening. It was quarter to ten on Thursday morning, and the waiting room was full of patients. To her shock, the person coming in was the unkempt woman who spent most days sitting on a bench in the square outside the medical centre.

Pamela was not a tolerant person. At forty-five, with two grown-up children, she prided herself on her trim figure, her elegance and her efficiency. She had no time for anyone who didn't share her own exacting standards. She certainly didn't have any time for this woman, whom one of the nurses had nicknamed 'Vinnie'. The nickname had been given because Vinnie was often seen swigging from a bottle of cheap wine, and the general view was that she was an ex-mental patient who had been released out into the community without proper supervision.

It was raining hard outside and Vinnie paused on the mat by the door, pushing her stringy wet hair away from her plump, red-tinged face. She wore a torn see-through plastic mackintosh over a short coat, and old plimsolls on her feet.

Bristling with indignation, Pamela slid back the window beside the reception desk. 'You can't come in here,' she called out. 'Not to get out of the rain, or to use our toilet. Clear off now or I'll call the police.'

Vinnie took no notice, instead she took off her plastic mac and hung it up on a peg by the door. Incensed that the woman was ignoring her, Pamela leaned across the reception desk to get a better look at what she was doing. She appeared to be getting something out of her coat pocket.

'I said, you can't come in here,' Pamela repeated. She felt slightly panicky – there were at least ten people waiting for appointments, two doctors had been delayed on emergency calls, and Muriel, the senior receptionist, was in the adjoining room getting patients' notes from the files.

'I came to see you,' Vinnie said, walking deliberately towards her.

Pamela stepped back from the reception desk, suddenly frightened by the woman's eyes. They were a pale greenish-blue colour, very cold and hard. Close up, she didn't look as old as Pamela had assumed, in fact she was probably around the same age as Pamela herself.

'You don't remember me, do you?' the woman went on to say, a faint smirk twisting up one side of her mouth. 'Of course I've changed, I suppose. You haven't, you're just as rude and callous as you were then.'

Suddenly Pamela's memory was triggered by the voice. But before she could say anything, the woman's arm came

2

up above the level of the reception desk. She was holding a gun in her hand and pointing it right at Pamela.

'Don't be ridiculous,' Pamela said instinctively, backing away in fright. But it was too late for flight, a shot rang out, and simultaneously she felt a searing pain in her chest.

In the adjoining office, Muriel Olding had heard Pamela ordering someone out, but she couldn't see who it was for the room had no windows on to the hall. Although shocked by Pamela's brusqueness, and curious to know who it was directed at, at that precise moment Muriel was supporting a precarious pile of files on the open drawer of a cabinet.

But on hearing a woman's voice say quite calmly, 'You don't remember me, do you?' rather than hurling abuse at Pamela, Muriel pushed the files more securely on to the cabinet and went over to the door which led into the hall to see who it was. She had just opened the door when there was a deafening bang.

Muriel didn't even think of it being a gun shot. She thought it was a firework, for it was nearly the end of October and young louts had been letting them off for days all around the centre. As she opened the door and saw Vinnie standing there, a gun in her hand, the smell of cordite thick and pungent in the hall, she was rooted to the spot in disbelief.

For just a second the woman's eyes locked into hers, but as Dr Wetherall flung his surgery door open, Vinnie spun round towards him as smoothly as if she were on a turntable.

'What on earth!' the doctor roared, but the woman halted him by firing again, hitting him in the chest.

Muriel couldn't believe what she was seeing. Blood instantly spurted from Dr Wetherall's chest, he made a sort of agonized moan, his hands coming up towards the wound and his eyes wide with shock, and he took a few staggering steps backwards into his consulting room.

It was pure instinct that made Muriel leap back into the office, slam the door and lock it behind her. Only when she realized that the screaming she could hear wasn't just from herself, but from the patients in the waiting room as well, did she become fully aware that this was real, not some kind of nightmarish illusion.

Then she saw Pamela. She was spread-eagled on the floor of the adjoining room, blood pumping out of a hole in her chest.

With one leap Muriel managed to grab the phone, and taking cover beneath the desk, feverishly dialled 999.

Some four hours later Detective Inspector Roy Longhurst was sitting beside Muriel as she lay wrapped in a blanket on the couch in one of the upstairs consulting rooms. Downstairs the forensic team and police photographers were doing their work. All the other staff and patients who had been in the building at the time of the shooting had been in shock when Longhurst arrived, and a few were hysterical, but as none of them had actually witnessed what happened, almost all of them had been taken home now. Muriel had witnessed everything, however, and he was deeply concerned for her. She was close to sixty, and her grey hair and lined face reminded him of his own mother.

Taking one of her hands in his two large ones, he chafed it gently between them. 'Now, Mrs Olding,' he said. 'Take your time and try to tell me exactly what you saw and heard this morning.'

Longhurst was forty-five, six feet two, and sixteen stone of sheer muscle. Even in civilian clothes, or on the rugby field, he still managed to look like a policeman, something that amused his mother who had always said he was born to be one.

Whilst not handsome, Longhurst was an attractive man with thick dark wavy hair, olive skin and soulful dark eyes. He belonged to the old school of policemen, scrupulously honest, but with fixed opinions. He had no patience with thugs who pleaded a troubled childhood. He'd had one himself and survived without resorting to villainy. He would bring back hanging and the birch if he could and he thought prisons should be much harder than they were. Yet for all this he was a compassionate man by nature, saving his sympathy for those who deserved it, like victims of crime. Mrs Olding, even though she wasn't physically hurt, was a victim to him, for she was clearly devastated by what she'd seen that morning.

Dowry Square in the Hotwells area of Bristol had been built in the 1800s for wealthy merchants wishing to live away from the stink of the city's docks. But unlike neighbouring Clifton, which had mostly managed to maintain its select image for two centuries, Hotwells had floundered. A huge network of busy roads, including a massive flyover, had turned it into an undesirable area several decades ago. But since the mid-1980s, when smart new complexes of flats and townhouses had been built along the river, it had been on the up-and-up.

The property which now housed the medical centre reflected all these changes. First an elegant family house then a disreputable boarding house and finally a surgery, it had seen a vast variety of owners and tenants. The patients of the practice ranged from down-and-outs in bed-and-breakfast accommodation to the owners of houses valued in excess of half a million, with students, council tenants, old hippies and young yuppies in between.

The centre still maintained its private-house image, however, with the consulting, waiting and treatment rooms all leading off a long central hallway. There were further consulting rooms upstairs too. From the reception desk with its sliding-glass windows to the front door was a distance of some fifteen feet.

When the firearms squad had arrived that morning, they knew that two people were already dead and there were some ten people in the waiting room, plus doctors and nurses. They had anticipated a hostage situation and were keyed up for it. They assumed, because they hadn't been told otherwise, that the person who had carried out the shooting was male, and they expected it to be drug-related.

Yet when Longhurst had arrived a little later, he was told by the firearms squad that they had found the front door wide open, and a woman sitting on the hall floor. Their first thought was that the gunman had already fled, and this woman was too deeply shocked to move or speak. But after staring silently for a moment or two at the armed police officer in the doorway, she finally spoke. 'It was me who shot them,' she said, and indicated the gun on the floor beside her, partially concealed by her coat.

The officer ordered her to move away from the gun, which she did by shuffling sideways. After the gun was retrieved, she stood up of her own volition, pointing out where her two victims lay. When asked why she'd shot them, her cryptic reply was, 'They know why.'

Longhurst had been responsible for arresting and cautioning the woman before she was taken to Bridewell. Although he was only with her for some ten minutes or so, he found her puzzling. She didn't react at all to the hubbub just the other side of the door of the room she was being held in. Whilst she again admitted it was she who had shot the two people, she refused to give her name and address, and her down-and-out appearance was curiously at odds with her soft voice and dignified bearing. The gun, according to one of the armed squad, was a service revolver, almost certainly a relic from the Second World War.

'I didn't see her come in,' Muriel said, her voice quavery with shock. 'I was in the room beside the reception desk, well, it's not so much a room, more a cubby-hole. The door through to the hall is in there, but there's no window. All I heard was Pam raising her voice to whoever it was.

7

She said, "You can't come in here out of the rain, or to use the toilet, so clear off or I'll call the police."'

'Who did you think she was talking to?' Longhurst asked.

Muriel shrugged. 'I didn't really think about it, though I suppose I imagined it was some kids or something. I did think that it was no way to speak to anyone, though, whoever it was.

'Then I heard a woman's voice. She said something like, "You don't recognize me, do you?" She didn't sound rough or anything. I was curious, and that's why I opened the door to the hall. Just as I did, I heard the bang. I thought someone had let off a firework.'

'What did you see in the hall?'

'Vinnie, that's what we called her.'

'You knew her then?'

'Yes, she sits outside in the square almost every morning, she has for at least eighteen months. But she's never come into the centre before, at least not as far as I know.'

She finished telling Longhurst what she saw, and how she ran back into the office and called the police. 'I was so scared,' she said, beginning to cry again. 'I've worked here for fifteen years, and nothing like this has ever happened before.'

Longhurst had been told that when the armed squad came into the centre, Muriel was still cowering under the reception desk, just feet away from the other woman's body. She was rigid with terror, and deeply ashamed of herself for not thinking of the patients in the waiting room while she'd been taking cover.

It took some little while for the policeman who found her to convince her that immediately ringing the police and staying put had been the right and sensible thing to do. He had reassured her that none of the patients were hurt, as a nurse in the treatment room on the other side of the waiting room had ushered them all in there to safety. But Muriel still seemed to think she should have done more.

'How long had Pamela Parks been working here?' Longhurst asked.

'About eight years, I think,' Muriel said, and fresh tears sprang into her eyes. 'Her poor husband and children! What are they going to do?'

Longhurst patted her hand again and waited for the tears to subside. 'Were you and Pamela friends?' he asked. 'I mean, aside from working together.'

'Not really,' Muriel said, looking up at him with brimming eyes. 'We didn't have much in common. She was very smart, not a bit like me.'

Longhurst had already been told by one of the nurses that there was some friction between Muriel and Pamela. According to her, the older woman had been pushed on to the sidelines by Pamela because of her superior knowledge of computers. The nurse had said that Pamela was a little too officious, she wanted to streamline the whole running of the practice.

He had seen the dead woman before her body was taken away. She was very attractive, in her early forties, with blonde highlights in her hair and carefully manicured nails. He had already discovered that she lived in an expensive townhouse in Clifton, drove a BMW, and that her husband Roland Parks was a successful businessman. Very different to dumpy, middle-aged Muriel.

'Was this woman you all called Vinnie a patient?' he asked.

'I don't think so,' Muriel replied. 'She might be actually registered with us of course. Lots of people are that we never see as patients. We only get to know the regulars. But she's never come in here before as far as I know.'

'Tell me, then, when you used to see her sitting out in the square, what did you think of her?' he asked.

Muriel shrugged. 'Nothing much, only to wonder why the poor soul sat there every day. She did sometimes have a bottle of wine with her, so I suppose she was a drunk, but she wasn't ever weaving around or shouting or anything.'

'Did Pamela ever pass any comment on her?'

'Yes, she was a bit hard on her.' Muriel sighed. 'She would say the woman ought to be put away somewhere. I suppose she was right after all.'

'Might Pamela have had a run-in with her before this then?' Longhurst asked.

Muriel frowned as if trying to remember. 'I don't think so, well, she never said that she had. Anyway, if it was that, why did the woman go and shoot Dr Wetherall too?'

'Perhaps that was just because he came out of his room,' Longhurst said.

'Well, I came out too, but she didn't shoot me.'

Longhurst had already pondered on that one. He couldn't make up his mind whether Muriel was just lucky or if the gunwoman had set targets.

'Tell me what you know about Pamela,' he asked gently. 'Anything. How she was with people, with you, the doctors, her interests, that kind of thing.'

'I told you, she was smart.' Muriel sighed. 'In her appearance and her ways. Expensive clothes, she got her hair and nails done every week. She didn't need to work, she did it because she liked to. She and her family went on holiday to places like Africa and Japan, they live in a posh house. I don't know about her interests, other than cooking. She was always having dinner parties, she'd talk about stuff like sun-dried tomatoes as if I was supposed to know what they were.'

Longhurst guessed by the bleak note in Muriel's voice that she considered she and Pamela were at the opposite ends of the social scale.

'So tell me about you then,' he suggested.

'About as different to Pam as you could get,' Muriel said dourly. 'Me and my hubby, Stan, live in a council place in Ashton. Stan works for the railways. Only time we've been abroad was to Spain, none of my four kids even got any GCEs, let alone places at university like Pam's.'

'I expect you are more understanding with the patients though,' Longhurst said, trying to draw her out more.

'I try to be,' she said, her eyes full of anxiety. 'I know what it's like when you're worried about your kids being ill, you want to see the doctor straight away. Pamela could be a bit sharp with folk, especially the poor ones and the old people. But then she really wanted to make this practice the most efficient in Bristol, and she did manage to cut down on some of the time-wasters, and weeded out people who didn't really need home visits. She was doing a good job.'

Longhurst looked at Muriel, noting her grey skin colour and that she was still shivering despite the blanket around her. She wasn't up to any further questions today.

'I'll get someone to take you home now,' he said. 'I'll have to come and get a statement from you in a day or two. Perhaps you'll remember more once you've got over the shock.'

'I don't think I ever will get over it,' Muriel said sorrowfully. 'I've seen the practice grow from just two doctors to the busy place it is now, it was a safe, nice place. I never thought I'd ever see something like that! It's like something you hear of happening in America, isn't it?'

Chapter two

Heavy rain battered the windows of the offices of Tarbuck, Stone and Aldridge, criminal lawyers, as Beth Powell sat at her desk dictating letters to clients on to tape. It was almost dark now at nearly four in the afternoon, and the desk light shed a golden glow over the papers and files in front of her.

People always described Beth as striking. She was almost six feet tall, with curly black hair twisted up and secured carelessly with a spring clip, ivory skin, green eyes and a wide mouth. As a girl she had hated that label, believing it was a polite way of saying 'weird-looking'. But now, at forty-four, she no longer cared what people meant by it, or that they said she was haughty and cold. Better to be striking than insignificant, and she didn't think it was a solicitor's role to be a gossip, a mother figure or a femme fatale.

Privately she was quite satisfied with her appearance. Her height gave her an advantage and she knew she wore her clothes well. She'd come to appreciate the dramatic contrast between her dark hair and pale skin. There were times when she looked at her wide, sensual mouth in the mirror and hated it, but she was a realist and as she knew she couldn't change it, she accepted it.

She also accepted that most of the people she defended in court were guilty of their crimes, and that if she succeeded in winning their case for them they would be re-offending at the first opportunity. But then she loved criminal law: the constant challenges, the variety of cases, and the extraordinary characters she met daily.

Beth had only been in Bristol for a year. She had spent her entire adult life in London, and for the last twelve years of that she'd been with the same law practice in Chancery Lane.

The idea of moving away from London came to her after her flat in Fulham was burgled three times in the same year. Buying somewhere more secure in London would have been prohibitively expensive, so she applied for jobs in several cities, thinking a change of scenery might also bring her a change of luck in her personal life.

The interview with Tarbuck, Stone and Aldridge in Bristol was one of many, in cities as far-flung as York, Glasgow and Exeter. Beth chose this law practice purely because she was attracted to the position of its offices in a gracious Georgian building at the corner of Berkeley Square in Clifton, the most elegant part of the city. It was spring then, and the gardens in the centre of the square were bright with blossom and daffodils. Beth had noted that the interior of the building was drastically in need of decoration, yet it hadn't felt claustrophobic like the offices in Chancery Lane. Then there was the added bonus that property was much cheaper in Bristol. She had managed to buy a secure third-floor flat just five minutes' walk from the office, with a glorious panoramic view of the city.

Bristol had turned out to be a far more fascinating and cosmopolitan place than she'd expected. Its long and colourful history as a port which once ranked next to London had left a legacy of astounding old buildings and a character all its own. She loved the way the city hadn't forgotten its sea-going past; the revamped dock area was a delight to wander around in, with a museum, art gallery and dozens of bars and restaurants. The main shopping area had everything one could wish for, and in Clifton there were dozens of intriguing, quirky little shops that often surpassed anything Beth had found in London. But it wasn't a formidable concrete jungle, there was space, parks, and the open countryside very close by. She knew too from her clients and conversations she'd overheard amongst the younger staff in the office that Bristol's nightlife buzzed. But that wasn't something Beth had explored. She told herself she was past the age for discos, night clubs and trying out every restaurant, pub or wine bar, but the truth of the matter was that you needed friends for that. And friends were something she didn't have.

'You don't need them,' she muttered to herself, the way she always did when this thought sprang up. 'You are perfectly happy the way you are.'

Suddenly Beth's office door opened and Steven Smythe, one of the other solicitors, burst in, his face alight with excitement and red with the exertion of running up the stairs.

'You've been called to Bridewell,' he gasped out. 'Duty solicitor.'

Beth knew this meant it was her turn to offer legal advice to someone who had been arrested. If the police found the arrested person hadn't got a solicitor of their own, they would consult the duty rota and call in whoever was next on the list. This time it was Beth, but it could just as easily have been Steven, or any other solicitor. It was just the luck of the draw.

'Are you the errand boy today?' she said sarcastically. The receptionist downstairs could have rung to tell her. But Steven was always looking for an opportunity to speak to her, she didn't know why because she was invariably off-hand with him.

He seemed to have the idea that they should be buddies. He had said soon after she arrived at the firm that he thought they had a lot in common. Whilst it was true they were the same age, had the same love of criminal law and similar backgrounds, Beth didn't like the way he seemed to hang on her every word. He was also married with two small children, so she had no intention of encouraging him.

She supposed part of his problem was that he was a misfit. He was neither one of the lads nor a ladies' man. She suspected he'd been a bit of a swot at school. And though he was quite nice-looking, tall and well-built, with a strong jaw-line and attractive blue eyes, his clothes were always rumpled, and he badly needed a decent hair-cut.

'I came up to tell you myself because it's the woman who shot those two people down at Hotwells this morning,' he said.

Beth instantly experienced the same surge of excitement Steven must have felt to run up three flights of stairs to tell her himself. But she wasn't the kind to admit to such things.

'Really!' she said in a cool voice, getting up and reaching for her briefcase. News of the shooting had reached the office at noon, causing great shock and much speculation. No one could remember ever hearing of a woman shooting anyone in Bristol before. It was even more incredible that it had taken place in a busy medical practice.

'I expect she's mad,' Steven said. 'Apparently she won't even give her name, hasn't said one word since she was arrested.'

'Well, even madwomen are entitled to legal advice,' Beth said crisply, wishing he'd push off and let her go.

'Have you ever defended a murderer before?' he asked, seemingly unaware she wanted to leave immediately.

'Yes, I have, Steven,' she said, giving him a starchy look. 'Now, I must go. I'll see you tomorrow.'

Beth stopped downstairs in the hall to put on her raincoat and take an umbrella from the stand. She always left her car in the garage beneath her block of flats during the day, as both the police station and the courts were only fifteen minutes' walk away and parking was difficult. But the rain was so heavy she hoped she could get a taxi today. It was a faint hope, however – taxis in Bristol seemed rarer than hen's teeth.

After a few words with the duty sergeant at Bridewell, Beth paused outside the interview room where the accused woman was being held, to look at her first through the small window in the door.

For a brief moment she felt a flash of recognition as she looked at the woman sagging in her chair, but looking closer she realized this was probably only because she was so very ordinary. She was short and plump, with a round, red-tinged face and straggly brown hair. She wore navy polyester slacks and a shapeless sweater, both very worn and snagged. She was indistinguishable from count-less other worn-down women who queued for buses, shopped in supermarkets or scuttled off to office-cleaning jobs, except perhaps for the plimsolls on her feet. Beth guessed she wasn't that much older than herself, and she certainly didn't look as if she was capable of killing two people in cold blood.

The door was unlocked for Beth and she went on in. 'I'm Beth Powell, the duty solicitor,' she said crisply. 'I've been called to advise you on your legal rights.'

The woman jerked her head round, her look of shock and surprise throwing Beth for a second.

'Have we met before?' Beth asked. She looked harder at the woman's face, but even though there was something terribly familiar about it, she certainly couldn't say from where or when.

The woman shook her head, and Beth had to assume

18

that her surprised expression was merely the result of being suddenly offered legal representation. Maybe she hadn't fully grasped what she'd done yet.

Beth sat down at the table and began explaining more fully why she was there. The duty officer had already filled her in with everything that was known about the shooting. The accused had freely admitted she was responsible but wouldn't say anything more, not even to give her name or address. While there was nothing unusual about her silence – a great many people when arrested refused to say a word – it was strange to admit the offence, then clam up.

The police were out now trying to discover who she was and where she lived, for she had nothing on her to identify her. But the gun she'd used was almost the most curious aspect of the crime. The police had said it was a very old weapon which had been carefully cleaned and maintained.

'Now, come along,' Beth said a little impatiently after she'd explained what she already knew. 'I need to know your name. I can't help you if I don't know anything about you.'

The woman lifted her eyes to Beth's. They were a pale greenish-blue, with no light in them. 'I don't want any help,' she said.

'But you'll need someone to defend you when you go to court,' Beth said, thinking the woman still didn't understand the enormity of what she'd done, or perhaps was simple. 'You killed two people. You are likely to spend the rest of your life in prison because of it.'

The woman looked up again and her eyes had just a faint spark in them now. 'It was worth it,' she said.

Beth was jolted again by the woman's voice. It too had a ring of familiarity. She scrutinized her face, mentally flitting through women she'd questioned in the past or seen waiting for other solicitors at the office. But although she could remember other equally shabbily dressed women of her age, the voice didn't match up with any of those faces.

'Well, whether or not you don't care if you get a life sentence, you could at least tell both the police and myself who you are, where you come from and why you killed those innocent people,' she said tartly.

'They weren't innocent,' the woman snapped back. 'They deserved to die.'

'Why?' Beth asked. 'What had they done to you?'

'Go away.' The woman turned her head towards the wall dismissively. 'I've got nothing more to say to you. They knew why, that's all that matters.'

Beth sat silently for a while, studying the woman and wondering what she should do next. She had defended people from all walks of life for all kinds of crimes. Almost all of them had claimed to be innocent of their charges, even when it was patently obvious they were guilty. Sometimes they told her too much, sometimes not enough. Some she had grown to like, however bad their crime had been, some were so unpleasant she was almost glad when the case was lost. She thought she had a well-rounded view of criminals and the justice system. But whilst this wasn't the first time she'd been confronted with someone who openly admitted their guilt and showed no remorse, it was the first time a client hadn't wanted to explain themselves or try to convince her they were right in what they'd done.

One of the police officers had said the woman was a drunk. The red flush to her face seemed to bear this out. Yet to the officer's knowledge she'd never been taken into custody for being drunk and disorderly. Her nails were bitten down to the quick, and Beth didn't think her hair had seen a brush or comb for days. Yet she didn't look, or smell, as if she slept rough. Then there was the matter of the gun.

How would a woman like this come by a service revolver?

Guns were not a feminine weapon. While Beth believed that almost any woman under pressure could point one and fire it to defend a loved one, it was extremely rare for a woman to use one in cold blood.

Again she thought about the voice which had sounded so familiar and came to the conclusion that it was only because it was similar to her own: well-modulated, correct English without plummy overtones or traces of a West Country accent. She probably came from a middle-class background, and maybe that included hunting and shooting.

Pleading wasn't normally in Beth's nature. Had this been any other kind of crime, she would just have got up and left, saying she'd see the client in court the next day. But she was curious now, and so she was inclined to unbend a little.

'Please, tell me your name, if nothing else,' she begged. 'The police will find it out soon enough, but I want to know it so I can address you properly. Please!'

The woman kept her head down, and at least a minute passed before she spoke. 'Okay, it's Fellows, Susan Fellows. But that's all I'm going to tell you. I know you probably mean well, so get me to court and let me be sentenced. I did it. They can punish me. There's nothing more to say.'

The woman's gentility shone through, touching Beth in a way she hadn't expected. Almost all the female clients she'd defended since she'd been in Bristol had been from working-class backgrounds – shop-lifters, prostitutes and drug addicts in the main. She didn't ever attempt to identify with them, rarely even truly sympathized with them either, however harshly life had treated them. Beth had always believed this was why she was so good at defending, for she could look at their cases coldly and dispassionately and plan her strategy to win at all costs. For the first time in many years she just didn't know how to tackle this one.

She got up, but she paused before leaving the room, putting her hand on the woman's shoulder. 'You will be taken to court tomorrow, Susan, but only so the police can hold you for another twenty-four hours while they find out about you. Then you'll be back in court again. After that you will be remanded in custody, which means prison. You'll spend a long time there before it comes to trial. The doctor you shot left a wife and four children, the receptionist had a husband and two children. Those people have a right to know why you did this. Then there's me. I need to know too if I'm going to represent you and get you a fair trial. So I want you to think about that tonight and I'll talk to you again tomorrow.'

Susan looked up and her eyes were still cold and expressionless. She merely nodded and Beth couldn't tell if that meant she agreed, or whether she was just acknowledging the request.

Beth felt deflated as she walked away from the interview room. The media were going to be howling for information about this shooting, it was going to be of nationwide, maybe even worldwide interest, and Beth was aware she was going to be right in the spotlight. She had to know more about this woman, it wasn't going to help her own reputation one bit if she had to admit complete failure at her first interview with her client.

As she was let out of the last door into the reception area of the police station, she suddenly thought of Detective Inspector Roy Longhurst. He had been the arresting officer, and as she had met him fleetingly on a couple of occasions before, maybe he could tell her something she could use to persuade Susan Fellows to open up.

Beth enquired at the desk whether Detective Inspector Longhurst was still on duty, and the young policewoman told her he was about to go home. She offered to ring his office and see if he was still there.

When the policewoman nodded and smilingly held out the phone to Beth for her to speak directly to the detective inspector, she had to think fast.

'It's Beth Powell,' she said, hoping firstly that he'd remember her, and secondly that the rapport she thought she'd struck up with him at their previous meeting wasn't just in her imagination. 'I was called in as duty solicitor for the woman arrested for the shooting.'

'I hope she said a little more to you than she did to me,' he replied, his voice tinged with weariness.

'I'm afraid not,' Beth admitted. 'Except her name. It's Susan Fellows.'

'Well, that's a start,' he said.

'I wondered if you fancied an after-work drink with me,' Beth said, hoping she wasn't being too transparent.

'Now, that's the best offer I've had all day,' he replied, his voice suddenly lighter. 'I'll be right down.'

He was grinning as he came through the door. 'It's not only my charm, is it?' he said, his dark brown eyes twinkling. 'You just want to pump me for information on the shooting.'

'I cannot lie,' she said with a smile. 'But it was your charm that made me dare to ask.'

'I'm glad you did.' He ran his fingers distractedly through his thick hair. 'After the day I've had, I'd sell my soul for a pint.'

They walked round to The Assizes, a pub in Small Street which was popular with the legal profession at lunch-time. It was quiet now, just a few people having a drink before going home.

The first time Beth had met Longhurst had been while waiting at Bristol Crown Court. They'd had a fairly brief chat about criminals in general and he'd struck her as being a 'hang-'em-high' type. He had told her a story about two young men who were killed in a car crash. As it turned out, they were on their way home from robbing the house of an old age pensioner. Longhurst had been quite gleeful that they were no longer at large to terrorize anyone else.

Whilst no one in their right minds would mourn the passing of two such vicious thugs, Beth didn't meet many people who would openly admit to such delight. Longhurst told the story with such humour as well, and it was refreshing to meet someone who didn't bow to political correctness.

Over the last few months she'd had clients who had mentioned him too. It was interesting that although they were afraid of him, they also admired him too for being 'straight'. One serial offender had said he'd rather be arrested by Longhurst than by anyone else because he didn't fabricate evidence.

Over a pint Roy Longhurst gave Beth his view of the events at Hotwells that morning. 'I'm not easily shocked,' he said with a frown. 'But a bloody wino wiping out two people, leaving six children in total with only two remaining parents, makes my blood boil. I wish the armed squad had mown her down too. Now she'll have to be tried and kept in prison at the tax payer's expense. For what? She's worthless.'

'Actually she doesn't strike me as a wino,' Beth said sharply. 'And she must have had some grievance to do what she did.'

'Spare me the bleeding-heart bit,' he exclaimed scathingly. 'She's got to be mad, probably let out of some mental institution. Anyone else with a grievance against a medical practice complains through the proper channels.'

On the way to the police station Beth had thought along much the same lines as Longhurst. Even though Susan had given her nothing to make her change her mind, Beth automatically began defending her.

'Maybe she did and no one would listen to her,' she retorted. 'Look at you, Detective Inspector Longhurst, sitting there over your beer convinced she's worthless just because she's shabbily dressed. You mark my words, there's going to be a bloody good reason why she did it.'

He just laughed. 'I've never met anyone yet with a real grudge who didn't insist on telling you about it, chapter and verse. She hasn't said a word, hasn't even cried.'

They argued for a little while, but to Beth's surprise she found him funny rather than truly bigoted. He made sweeping statements – he thought thieves should have their hands cut off, and wanted castration for paedophiles and the birch for young offenders – but as Beth had also thought some of these things with certain clients, and he said it in such an amusing way, she stopped trying to argue and laughed with him.

'Well, Susan Fellows doesn't strike me as a real loony,' she said eventually. 'Maybe a little simple, but despite the way she looks and dresses, there's something quite refined about her. I had this odd feeling I'd met her before too!'

'Really?' Longhurst looked at her in surprise. 'Any idea where?'

Beth shook her head. 'Not one. I came to the conclusion it was just the way she spoke. I mean, I'm surrounded every day by Bristolian and West Country accents, so hearing someone without one tends to pull you up.'

Longhurst grinned. 'We don't get too many posh voices in the cells,' he admitted. 'Then there's the question of the gun. I think we'll find it belongs to her. Left to her by her father, something like that. Of course anyone could get a direct hit with that one, especially at such close range, but I'd say she'd handled guns most of her life.'

'What about the victims?' Beth asked. 'What do you know about them? Or have I got to wait till tomorrow and read it in the papers?'

'Both of them straight-"A" types,' he said. 'Doctor Wetherall was fifty-six, lived out in Long Ashton, played golf, good father and husband. Much what you'd expect from a family doctor. The receptionist was much the same, comfortable home, two kids at university. About the only detrimental thing we did pick up about her is that she was something of a dragon, curt with patients, a bit domineering with the other staff. Don't think she was very well liked at work. But that's no reason to shoot her, doctors' surgeries always have their fair share of dragon ladies.'

There was little more Longhurst could tell Beth, except about the actual arrest and what he'd been told by other staff at the medical centre, and after buying them both a second drink, he moved on to ask her how she was settling down in Bristol, for at their first meeting she hadn't been there very long.

'Pretty well,' she said. 'Calmer, beautiful scenery, and it's great not to have to suffer the Tube any more. If I could just get someone reliable to do a few jobs in my flat, I'd say everything was just about perfect.'

'You haven't got a man then?' he asked.

Beth bristled. It always infuriated her when people fished to know if she had a partner. 'Is that what you think a woman needs a man for?' she snapped at him. 'Just to put up a few shelves, build some cupboards? Is that all your wife values you for?'

'I haven't got a wife.' He shrugged. 'At least, not any longer. And even when we were together I was no great shakes at DIY anyway.'

Beth felt slightly chastened. 'I'm sorry,' she said. 'I just assumed you were being patronizing. Because I'm single I get that sort of line all the time and it irritates me. I also assumed you were married.'

'I certainly didn't mean to sound patronizing,' he said, and looked crestfallen. 'I just assumed a good-looking, smart woman like you would be spoken for. So much for assumptions.' He laughed. 'But at risk of having a knife stuck in my gut, may I enquire whether you are alone by choice or circumstance?'

He was on dangerous ground, but for some reason Beth found it amusing this time. 'A bit of both, I guess. I'm too involved with my work for most men.'

'That was my ex-wife's excuse for leaving me,' he admitted, and he smiled at her. Beth found herself smiling back.

Beth walked home about two hours later. Roy, for he had insisted that was what she must call him, had offered to drive her home, but she used the excuse that it was quicker to walk up Christmas Steps to where she lived in Park Row than to be driven. It wasn't really quicker, and in the dark and the heavy rain it wasn't a pleasant walk, but Beth rarely allowed any man to do anything for her. She had found to her cost in the past that even something as simple as a lift or a cup of coffee could lead men into thinking she owed them something.

Yet perhaps she'd been foolish to turn down Roy's offer, she thought. After all, it had been nice having a drink and chat with him. He was the first man in a very long time to intrigue her. On one hand he was almost a stereotype policeman, macho, opinionated, a man's man. Yet there had been moments when he'd revealed a much gentler, sensitive and thoughtful side. She liked his sense of humour too.

Beth didn't know why that should interest her. Men were nothing but trouble to her. While she still half hoped that there was a man out there who was as independent and intelligent as herself, loving and sensitive, without a lot of emotional baggage, she was too jaded really to believe such a man existed. Being alone wasn't the same as being lonely. She enjoyed having the freedom to do exactly as she liked.

Walking into her flat on the third floor, she felt a rush of pleasure at seeing the panoramic view of the city lights from her windows. The flat itself was quite ordinary and boxy, but the view had sold it to her.

She'd turned it into a snug little retreat now. Almost everything was cream, from the walls to the carpets and curtains, and that way it appeared bigger. The only colour came from her collection of pictures, vivid modern art, mostly originals by little-known artists which she'd bought in small galleries and craft fairs all over England. Her favourite one was a slice of cherry pie with custard. It amused her to imagine what her father would have said about it. He was such a snob, he had clung on to all the hideous old paintings that he'd inherited from his grandfather purely because he thought their age made them valuable. He would never have understood her view that you should have a picture because you loved looking at it, and that its monetary value was unimportant.

After kicking off her shoes and hanging her wet coat on the hall door to dry, she flopped down on the settee. The comfort of it made her think of Susan Fellows again. Had she spent a night in a cell before? Would it frighten her into explaining herself tomorrow?

It was frustrating knowing nothing about her, and she wished she could stop thinking she'd met the woman before. What could have happened to Susan to make her sit outside a doctor's surgery in all weathers? And what turned her from that into a killer?

Beth recalled a woman she'd defended a couple of years ago in London. She'd been having an affair with a married man who had strung her along for years telling her he was going to leave his wife. She had jumped on him one night as he was leaving a pub and stuck a carving knife in his back. The only explanation she could give at the time she was arrested was that she'd seen him earlier in the day buying curtains with his wife.

It had sounded so trite, so entirely irrational, yet once Beth got to know the woman better, she began to understand. Curtains, her client had pointed out, were something usually bought by a woman alone. Just the fact that her husband was there with her, engrossed in choosing the material, was evidence they were a couple who shared everything, cared equally about their home, and he wasn't intending to leave it, or his wife, ever.

Beth doubted Susan would turn out to have been the doctor's mistress. Or that the receptionist was her lesbian lover. So what did that leave?

Maybe she'd been turned away from treatment at the surgery at some time? Sectioned perhaps by Dr Wetherall when she didn't think she warranted it?

But Roy had said that one of the receptionists had told him Susan wasn't a patient there. So maybe they had done something to someone she loved?

Could the two victims have been having an affair, and one of their partners was a friend or relative of hers? It appeared to be a strong possibility. They were in the right age group for affairs, both attractive, personable types by all accounts, thrown together daily. Yet killing them for it was a bit extreme.

Beth switched on the television to see the news. The

shooting would undoubtedly be on there, and perhaps some of the journalists would have already discovered things she and the police didn't know.

Chapter three

While Beth was puzzling over why a woman would shoot two people, Susan Fellows was lying on her bed in the prison cell, trying to make her mind go blank. That was the way she'd got through bad periods of her life before. She felt it ought to be easy here as there were no distractions. Impersonal, shiny green painted walls with surprisingly little graffiti, nothing but a toilet bowl and a small basin to look at.

But the green walls reminded her of Beth Powell's eyes.

She wished she could convince herself that it was pure coincidence the solicitor had the same name as her childhood friend – after all, Beth hadn't recognized her. Besides, surely fate couldn't really be that cruel to bring her back to her at such a time in her life?

Yet even at ten, her Beth had been very tall, her green eyes, black hair and pale skin making her remarkable. Susan was pretty certain that if she'd dared snatch that comb clip out of the woman's hair, she would have seen those curls she'd so often envied come tumbling down to her shoulders.

She knew it was her Beth, but why didn't she recognize her? And why was she here in Bristol?

Still quivering from the shock of the meeting, Susan turned her mind back thirty-four years, to the day she and Beth met for the first time. A hot day in August 1961, when she was ten. Her father had come home for lunch that day and he'd offered to drop her in Stratford-upon-Avon for the afternoon so she could go to the library and look around the shops, then they could come home together when he closed the office.

Susan soon got tired of looking in the shops because it was so hot, so she went down to the river and sat on the grass watching people coming and going on the pleasure cruises. There were people all around her, having picnics, dozing in the sun, families, old people and many foreign tourists. She didn't know much about William Shakespeare in those days, and it had always baffled her that people came from other countries just to see where this man was born. She had once asked her father if he was like Jesus, and he'd roared with laughter.

She had been sitting there for some little while when she saw another girl standing under a tree, staring down at her. Susan was very shy, and her first thought was that there had to be something very wrong with her to make anyone look at her like that. She thought the girl was much older than her too, because she was tall, and she envied her curly black hair and the white shorts and pink blouse she was wearing. Susan always wore dresses – her mother made them, and some of the girls at school laughed at them because they looked babyish with smocking and puffed sleeves.

'Do you know where the boats go?' the girl asked suddenly.

'Nowhere special, just up and down the river,' Susan replied.

'Have you ever been on one?' the girl asked, moving closer to her.

Susan shook her head. 'They're just for visitors and people on holiday,' she replied.

'Well, I'm here on holiday, but I haven't been on one,' the dark-haired girl said almost indignantly. 'Can I sit down with you? I'm fed up with being on my own.'

Susan knew only too well how it felt to be alone. She didn't have any real friends as she couldn't invite them home to play because her grandmother was ill. She was delighted that this girl appeared to want to be friends with her.

'I'm Beth Powell,' the girl said. 'I'm ten, and I've come up from Sussex with my mother to stay with my Aunt Rose. We only got here on Saturday afternoon.'

'I'm Suzie Wright,' Susan had said, since in those days she was always called Suzie, even at school. 'I'm ten too, and we live in Luddington, that's a village further up the river. I'm waiting for Daddy to finish work so I can go home with him.'

Susan couldn't remember exactly what they talked about that afternoon, only how quickly the time flew by. She supposed she must have told Beth that her father was an insurance man, that her granny who lived with them was sick, and her brother Martin was away at university, but she had no recollection of it. What she remembered most was the two of them taking off their socks and sandals and sitting on the edge of the river bank dangling their feet in the cold green water and giggling about anything and everything.

Susan had said at one point in the afternoon that she thought Beth looked like Snow White, with her black hair and white skin. Beth giggled and seemed really pleased; she said everyone else told her she was too tall and skinny, and that she wished she could be small like Suzie and envied her lovely pink cheeks.

Susan hadn't known then that Beth was going to colour her whole adolescence, or that their friendship would become so important to her. All that mattered that day was that Beth loved Enid Blyton's Famous Five books, and *What Katy Did*, just like her, and that they both liked riding bikes, and Beth appeared to want to spend the whole of August with her.

That August, and the four following ones, were all spent with Beth. So many long, sunny days exploring the countryside on their bikes, damming up small streams in the woods, going to the pictures on rainy afternoons, and listening to the Top Ten in Woolworth's. Every memory was a golden one.

It was awful when the end of August came and Beth had to go home to Sussex. They both cried and clung to each other, vowing to write and be best friends for ever.

They had spent five summers together, a hundred letters exchanged in between, so many hopes and dreams shared. They believed that by being best friends, they knew everything about each other. Looking back as an adult, Susan realized that was an illusion. She had hidden a great deal that was important from Beth, so it was almost certain that Beth did the same.

The last shared holiday was in 1966, when they were fifteen, perhaps the most memorable one of all because it was when their minds turned to makeup, boys and dances.

'The wallflowers,' Susan murmured to herself, remembering their first dance in Stratford, with all the balloons in the net above them. She'd bought a red dress that same afternoon without her mother's approval, and put it on at Beth's Aunt Rose's house. It had seemed perfect in the shop, sophisticated, slinky and daring. But when they got to the dance and she saw that all the other girls were in the 'Mod' fashion, with long pencil skirts, high-necked blouses and 'granny'-type shoes, it had felt too tight, too revealing, and she thought everyone was staring at her.

Aunt Rose had said as they left her house for the dance that the best way to avoid being a wallflower was to look boys in the eye and smile. Also, they shouldn't sit down, but dance together if no one asked them. That way it would look as if they had only come for the dancing and boys didn't matter much to them.

They did as Aunt Rose said, and they were astounded that so many boys did come and dance with them. Susan wondered if Beth remembered the two boys who grabbed them for the last dance and walked them home. They were brothers, both skinny and spotty, but as Beth said at the time, they were nice enough to practise on.

'She'll have forgotten all about you long ago,' Susan whispered hopefully to herself. 'She was always prettier, cleverer and more outgoing than you. Her life's got to be too full to look back at anything.'

Susan didn't want to look back either. She'd learned many years ago that it was better to live only in the present, for thinking about the past only brought pain with it. But the present wasn't a good thing to think about either. Not when Beth might suddenly recognize her, and Susan would be forced to try to explain how she had come to this. She had to make her mind go blank.

Imagining the sea was her tried and tested way of blanking out all thought. A shingle beach empty of people, huge green grey waves crashing on to it. She pictured herself standing with bare feet on the wet shingle, running backwards each time a wave crashed in. Sometimes it caught her feet, and when it did, she got the sensation of being sucked back towards the sea along with the ebbing wave.

Yet this time, instead of seeing nothing but the water, with the frothy white crests on the waves, and hearing the sound of moving shingle, she saw herself. Not as she was now, a worn woman of forty-four, with a flabby body and lack-lustre hair, but as she was in the early summer of 1967. Almost sixteen, her birthday only a week away, she was plump even then, but she had shiny brown hair, clear skin and sparkling eyes.

She was on holiday with her parents at Lyme Regis in Dorset. It was, for all of them, their first real holiday in years, and it was also, although none of them admitted it openly, a celebration of her grandmother's death.

Susan had no memory of a time when life wasn't dominated by the old lady, for she had come to live with Susan's parents, Margaret and Charles, at their house in Luddington when Susan was just a baby. Her earliest memories of Granny were of seeing her sitting in a high-backed chair in the kitchen, with a shawl around her shoulders, complaining. Cold, heat, food, her medicine, bad legs or stomach troubles – anything could start off a litany of grouses. Susan couldn't remember ever hearing her laugh.

Her brother Martin used to claim Granny was a demon, her purpose in life to create misery. He used to stand behind her chair where she couldn't see him and mimic her pursed lips and disapproving wagging finger. But Martin was lucky enough to be away at Nottingham University when Granny became senile.

Susan was about nine when it started to get really bad. She had to take her turn watching that Granny didn't burn herself on the stove, let the bath run over, or wander down to the river at the bottom of the garden and fall in.

It was as though an ever-thickening dark cloud had come down on their house. All family outings stopped, her mother became increasingly harassed and edgy, her father seemed to withdraw to his office or study, and Susan often felt very alone and even neglected. Having other children round to play was out of the question, as her parents seemed fearful of anyone else finding out that Granny was slowly becoming barmy.

If it hadn't been for her father taking her out shooting at weekends, Susan wouldn't really have had anything in her life except school and helping with the chores. She wasn't all that keen on shooting, it seemed cruel to kill birds and rabbits, but she was a surprisingly good shot, and she liked hearing her father boast about it to friends he met while they were out shooting.

That was probably why Beth became so important to her in the next few years. Writing to her and thinking about her filled the void left when her mother no longer had time to take her out, play board games with her, and teach her to sew and cook. When the other girls at school left her out of things because she never invited them to her house, she could tell herself they'd all be green with envy if they had a friend like Beth.

But Granny's dementia accelerated very quickly, and soon she was unable to remember anything. She took to wandering around at night shouting, throwing food on the floor and talking gibberish. Then finally she became doubly incontinent too. Father seemed to stay longer and longer at the office during the week and he stopped taking Susan shooting with him at the weekends because he said her mother needed her help. By the time she was thirteen she was doing all the shopping, the cleaning and the ironing. She hated Granny for making all their lives so miserable.

Susan could appreciate now that her grandmother was actually suffering from Alzheimer's disease. But back in the Sixties, if it even had a name, no one used it, or had any real understanding of the problems that went with it, or even appreciated it was a disease. People suffering from it were either whisked away to a mental asylum, or hidden away by their families because of the stigma attached to it.

Without any explanation from anyone, as a young girl, Susan felt nothing but disgust and irritation that one old lady could create so much havoc. She could remember gagging at the smell in the house when she came in from school, feeling revolted when Granny spat out the food her mother spooned into her mouth, and wondering why her mother didn't agree to put her into a home as her father so often pleaded with her to do.

Martin seldom came home any more, he said he had better things to do than spend weekends in a lunatic asylum. He had always been nasty to Susan, her whole childhood had been overshadowed by his bullying, but she remembered being very shocked that he should say something so cruel to their mother. After all, she couldn't help how Granny was. Yet all the same she agreed with Martin in some respects, she would have given anything to have been packed off to boarding school so she could escape too.

From fourteen onwards Susan had no time to go to the library, for walks or bike rides; as soon as she got in from school there were too many other jobs to do and all weekend there were more. Sometimes she was even kept home from school when her mother felt she couldn't face yet another day on her own with Granny.

She remembered how one afternoon she was sitting with Granny while her mother quickly had a bath. The old lady was rocking backwards and forwards in her chair, making terrifying noises, and Susan wondered how she could possibly get away to see Beth that summer. She wished she felt able to admit in her letters just what was going on at home, but both her parents were adamant it was something not to be spoken of.

Yet her mother did seem to understand how much Susan needed her friendship with Beth, and for the last two summers she managed to persuade Father to get a nurse in to help for a few hours each day so that Susan was free to go out. This was quite an achievement because Father didn't like parting with money, but Mother stood up to him for once and insisted Susan must have a break from chores so that she could go back to school in September refreshed for the year ahead.

But then in February 1967 Granny died, and almost overnight, the gloom, anxiety and bad smells were blown away. Susan could remember helping her father carry two armchairs and a mattress Granny had soiled out into the garden, to burn them. They stood around the bonfire that cold, windy afternoon, laughing as Susan's mother brought armfuls of clothes out to add to it.

'We shouldn't be so cheerful,' her mother had said reprovingly at one point, although she too smiled as she said it. 'She couldn't help the way she became.'

Susan could picture that afternoon as clearly as if she were looking at a photograph. Margaret, her mother, was short and plump, with grey hair. She wasn't exactly lined, but her skin was going soft, like an apple that had been kept too long. She was wearing navy-blue slacks and a hand-knitted Arran sweater with a blue and white spotted scarf around her neck. Susan had remarked in the morning how nice her mother looked without the overall she always used to wear. Margaret had laughed and said no one would ever get her back into one of those again, and she might even get her hair permed too now she had some time to herself.

Charles, Susan's father, was very distinguished-looking, six feet tall, slender, with keen dark eyes and bushy black eyebrows, his hair still thick and dark even though he was fifty-eight. He had a boyish look that day, eagerly poking at the bonfire, soaking the old clothes in paraffin before hurling them on.

It was often said by relatives that Susan was a replica of her mother at the same age. Susan could see it for herself when she looked at the girl in the wedding photograph standing on the sideboard. She had long dark hair, girlish dimples and plump lips then. But as Margaret had been forty when Susan was born, and was already greying and plump, it was hard for Susan to equate that pretty girl with her mother.

Her parents had married at the start of the war in 1939, Charles dashing in his Army Captain's uniform. Martin was born early in 1941. Susan had often wondered about the ten-year gap between her and her brother's birth. But she never asked about it.

All through that spring and early summer of 1967, everything was wonderful. She could remember writing to Beth and asking her to come and stay with them at their house instead of at her aunt's, and how great it was not to have to creep around for fear of waking Granny, and that they were able to go out to the pictures and for walks as a family.

But she never told Beth about the transformation of their lives. How Mother would turn the wireless up loud to hear *Round the Horn* on Sundays, and how the house would resound with Father's laughter. Or how sometimes Mother would tickle him and they'd chase each other down the garden like children. She thought Beth wouldn't be able to understand that, not when she didn't know how grim it had been before.

Everything was topsy-turvy for a while because her mother wanted to spring-clean and redecorate. Furniture was piled up on the landing and the smell of disinfectant, polish and paint permeated the whole house. Father brought fish and chips home for supper, and they often ate it while watching television, something they'd never done before.

It was during those months that Susan began to notice how attractive their house was, or maybe it was just because Mother kept saying jokingly that she was going to restore it 'to its previous elegance'. Of course Susan had always known it was very old and must have been built for someone grand, by the carved oak staircase and the wooden panelling in the hall. But she had always wished they lived in one of the pretty Tudor thatched cottages in the village, or even in one of the modern bungalows and houses on the road into Luddington, for people often said The Rookery was creepy, because of the way it was hidden behind trees.

Suddenly she found herself looking at it then with new eyes, admiring the mellow red brick, the lattice windows, the tall chimneys. It was great to be able to run down the garden and watch boats coming through the lock, to see early-morning mist rising over the weir. She could hardly wait for Beth to come and stay because she had a feeling she would find it all magical.

The house had never seemed that big while Granny was alive, for all the four main bedrooms were in use, and the two attic rooms were full of junk. But now, as the wheelchair, old trunks and pieces of furniture Granny had brought to the house with her were disposed of, suddenly there was space and airiness.

'I never wanted all her clutter here,' Mother said one day as she added a couple of ugly chairs to an already large pile of furniture in the front garden which was due to be collected for a jumble sale. 'But she insisted, even though they were all worthless. My goodness, it's good to see the back of it all.'

Downstairs there were three reception rooms, plus the kitchen. The drawing room had French windows opening out on to the garden which sloped down to the river Avon and the lock. Susan had always loved the garden, the many fruit trees and flowering shrubs, the winding paths she played hopscotch on, the little pond always full of frogs.

She could see the drawing room so clearly in her mind's eye as it was on sunny afternoons: flowery chintz-covered settees and armchairs, the pink and green patterned carpet with a cream fringe which had to be brushed straight.

Her mother's collection of Worcester porcelain figurines was displayed in the glass cabinet, and an embroidered screen stood in front of the empty fireplace during the summer.

They seldom used the dining room, and the furniture there had come from Father's family. Susan used to run her fingers along the lovely rosewood table, examine the pie-crust effect around its edge, admire the vast china cabinet and the graceful chairs, and wonder at their value because Father said they were antique.

The third room was Father's study. It was lined with books and there was a huge oak desk under the window. Susan did her homework in there until they had central heating installed in 1964. Her mother used to light a fire in the big stone fireplace just before she got home from school, as she always said it was a nice quiet place where Susan could concentrate on her work. What her mother never realized was that Susan mostly just sat in Father's leather armchair and stared into the fire, glad to be in warm isolation, well away from Granny.

Susan found herself smiling. It was so long ago now, and so much had happened since, but that was a good memory. Like all the ones in the four months after Granny's death.

It seemed to her, looking back, that that was when she broke out of the gloom she'd been wrapped in for so long, looked around her and saw how much she had. Not only did she live in a lovely home in a pretty village, but her parents were good to her and shared things. Suddenly her mind was alight with possibilities. During the last summer she and Beth had spent together they'd talked of sharing a flat in London one day. That seemed possible now. Susan was going to go to secretarial college, learn to dance, find a boyfriend. She would overcome her shyness, she would be somebody.

A year earlier, when things were very bad at home with Granny, Susan had overheard a conversation between two teachers, and realized to her horror that the girl they spoke of as being 'plain, lumpy and dull as ditchwater' was in fact her. Yet after Granny's death, the jollity and sense of liberation at home gave her new hope. Her parents often spoke of the dark cloud they'd been under, and how they all needed to make radical changes, so Susan made up her mind she was never going to be labelled as 'dull as ditchwater' ever again.

Then they went on holiday in June. Susan had just sat her GCE's, and her parents let her take a week off school. Fortunately Martin couldn't come too – he was twenty-six then, with a job and a flat in London. Even leaving home hadn't made him any nicer to Susan. But of course in those days she thought all brothers were like that to their sisters.

They stayed in a hotel right on the sea front in Lyme Regis, with sea-view rooms. The weather was cold, windy and wet, but that didn't spoil it: the hotel was warm and comfortable, and they'd put on their rain coats and go for long walks, despite the weather.

Mother did complain about the rain one day, and Father laughed at her. 'It could be very much worse,' he said, giving her a cuddle. 'We could have Granny with us.'

Then, on the last day, the sun came out and they spent all day on the beach. Father went searching for fossils along the cliffs, Mother lay down on some towels and fell asleep, Susan just splashed in the sea.

She could still feel the glow of that day even now – her arms and legs prickly with sunburn, the icy cold of the water, the sharpness of the stones under her bare feet. It had seemed then that their family had walked through a gateway into a whole new realm where they could laugh, enjoy themselves, go where they wanted, when they wanted. The restrictions they'd lived under for so long were now gone for ever.

Susan sat up sharply. She didn't want to think about what happened after that, for it was so cruel and unfair that it didn't work out as she'd expected.

On the very night they got home from holiday, two days before Susan's sixteenth birthday, Mother had a stroke.

She said she felt strange as they went into the house. Susan went to make her a cup of tea, and when she got back Mother was slumped over on the settee in the drawing room, and Father was phoning for an ambulance.

The details of the months her mother spent in hospital were hazy to Susan now. A blur of rows of white-faced, sick old ladies in hospital beds, shiny floors, flowers and unpleasant smells reminiscent of Granny, that was all she could recall. She remembered how she hated to go in there, yet she did go, almost every afternoon on the bus, praying to herself that today Mother would be better.

She had to write and tell Beth she couldn't stay at the house after all. But Beth didn't come to Stratford anyway, she wrote back saying she'd got a summer job in a shoe shop in Hastings. In the back of her mind, Susan thought that meant Beth had found new and more exciting friends back home, and had been glad of an excuse to back out of the holiday.

Mother didn't get any better, she just lay there with her face twisted up in a grimace, unable to speak or move. Father kept on saying that she could see and hear and her mind was as active as always. He said she would get better, they just had to be patient.

He went to see her every night after he'd come home from the office, and he noticed even the slightest improvements. He seemed to understand what her grunts meant, he could get her to respond to his questions by blinking. His belief gave Susan hope.

He explained to Susan what he thought had caused the stroke. 'It was because of the sudden release of pressure when Granny died,' he said. 'All those years of looking after her, the endless washing, feeding, worrying about her. It took its toll, like a pressure cooker building up steam. The lid had to blow.'

Susan couldn't understand that explanation then. Granny had been dead for four months, the house was lovely again, Mother's worries were all over. Yet it did make sense to her now after all these years. Her own lid had blown. She'd shot those two people to relieve the unbearable pressure inside her.

Looking back to 1967, she could see now how simple it would have been then to divert her life from the channel it was beginning to run into, if she'd only been a little less willing. Martin didn't allow their mother's stroke to interfere with his career and ambitions. Even her father hung on to his job, his home and his hobbies of shooting and golf.

If Susan had been a couple of years older she would already have had a job; if she'd been a couple of years younger, she would have had to go to school. But she was in limbo at that time, having sat her final exams, and her only career plan was a tentative one about going to college in Stratford-upon-Avon in September. She had nothing to excuse her from housekeeping duties.

She got what might be called the thin end of the wedge. But of course at sixteen she wasn't able to predict, or even guess, what might be on the fatter end, or that once the wedge was driven in, there was no escape. She loved both her parents, she was devastated by her mother's illness, she was only too anxious to do whatever was best for everyone. And of course she had no real ambition then beyond hoping for marriage and children of her own.

Loneliness was what Susan could remember most about that summer. She would think back to all the fun she and Beth had had in previous years, and end up in tears. Sometimes she would stand in the garden watching the pleasure boats in the lock, and the sound of people's chatter and laughter made her feel even more lonely.

During August she got the results of her GCEs. To

her shame she'd failed everything but Domestic Science and Geography, and that made her feel even more despondent and useless. The holidays ended, and the days seemed even longer then with no school to go to. The only callers at the house were the odd neighbour dropping off some fruit or flowers for her mother. Sometimes, going home on the bus from the hospital, she'd see a couple of girls from her old class, yet much as she longed to go and sit next to them, and explain what had happened and ask them round, she didn't feel able to.

So she filled the days with jobs – cleaning, dusting, washing and ironing, cutting the grass – striving to do them as well as her mother would have. She undertook the bottling of plums and blackberry and apple for the same reason. She had been helping her mother do it for years; the fruit trees in the garden always had a good yield and it was an annual ritual they'd both enjoyed, like Father digging the trenches for runner beans in the spring. That year it seemed even more imperative to do it alone, to show how adult she was.

Susan could remember going out into the garden early each morning, picking up the fruit that had fallen before the wasps and other insects could get to it. She'd shake the tree to loosen more ripe fruit, and start on the bottling almost as soon as Father went out. There was a bumper crop that year, especially plums, and there was something incredibly satisfying about filling the larder shelves with the full bottles.

By that time Mother was getting a little better. She could move her right arm slowly, and her hand was just strong enough to hold a pencil and write down a few questions. Susan had never felt more proud than when she visited and could announce she'd just bottled another twenty jars of plums and ten of blackberry and apple. 'Such a good girl,' Mother wrote one day, and Susan floated home on a cloud of pride, forgetting about being lonely.

Yet she set her fate with it. Had she made a hash of it, burned herself, made the bottles explode, her father might have viewed her differently. But her success showed him how capable she was.

When Father asked Susan if she thought she could take care of her mother when he brought her home, it never occurred to her to think of what this would mean for her. She loved her mother, she wanted her home where she belonged more than anything. She certainly didn't want a stranger coming into the house.

Besides, Father made it seem quite inviting. He would pay her a wage, and a nurse would call in for an hour each day to help with bathing and physiotherapy. He said Susan could have Saturdays off so she could go out if she wanted to.

'Don't blame them,' Susan said aloud. 'You weren't forced into it.'

Yet she couldn't help but feel they ought to have thought of her future more. Surely they knew that she had let herself be nudged down that path just because she was timid of the outside world?

A couple of years later Martin said with his usual sarcasm that she thought she was going to be another

Florence Nightingale, so it served her right. He also said Father had more than enough money to pay for qualified staff, and Mother wouldn't have had the stroke in the first place if he'd put Granny in a home.

Martin was right about the last two things, Susan had realized that herself already, and she hadn't expected him to take her part because he'd always despised her. But then, how was she to know at sixteen what caring for an invalid meant? Or that her mother would never make a full recovery? Father had always said she would.

Chapter four

Beth had just got in from work at six o'clock the following evening when her phone rang.

Susan Fellows had made a brief appearance at Bristol magistrates' court that afternoon while the police applied for permission to hold her pending further investigation. Beth had hoped a night in the cells might have made her feel like talking, but it hadn't, she was even less co-operative. She had stubbornly refused to answer any questions and wouldn't even look at Beth.

'Hullo,' Beth said, wearily, but brightened a little when she realized it was Roy. She had given him her home number on an impulse, just in case he had any further information about Susan and couldn't contact her during the day.

'You sound ground down,' he said sympathetically. 'Had a bad day?'

'A frustrating one,' she admitted. 'Susan Fellows still wouldn't tell me anything. You'd think with the whole of England outraged by what she's done, she'd welcome someone in her corner.'

It had of course been on the television news the previous evening, and on the front page of every national that morning. In Bristol it was the major subject for discussion in the streets, in shops and offices.

'Well, maybe my news might make you feel more cheerful,' he said. 'First, she's got no record, and we've found out where she lives. The boys have been going through her place this afternoon.'

'Great.' Beth's spirits instantly lifted. 'Where is it? Did you find anything helpful?'

He gave a little chuckle at her enthusiasm. 'It's just a room in Clifton Wood. Very little in it.'

'Come on!' she said. 'How did she live? Was it a pig-sty of rubbish and empty bottles? Give me something to work on!'

'Not at all, very Spartan,' he said, laughter in his voice. 'I rang because I thought you might like to see it for yourself.'

Beth was taken aback by such a suggestion. The police never invited either defence or prosecution lawyers to scenes of crime, or the homes of a defendant, unless there was some very special reason to do so.

'I'd like nothing better. But won't it get you into trouble?' she asked.

'Not if you keep it to yourself.' He chuckled again. 'You'll have to understand, if you breathe a word about going there, at any time in this case, I'll have to deny it. Okay?'

Beth was puzzled now. 'Of course,' she agreed. 'But why are you prepared to bend the rules for me?'

'I think you need to see it,' he said simply. 'You'll understand why when we get there.'

55

'Okay,' she said, her curiosity aroused.

'Right, I'll pick you up in about ten minutes,' he said. 'Wait outside in Park Row.'

On the drive there, Roy explained that Belle Vue was a terrace of large Georgian houses. He said that when he first joined Bristol's police force, some of the houses were virtually slums, but gradually property developers bought them up and now many had been converted into luxury flats.

'There's still a few dodgy ones left though,' Roy said as he squeezed his car into the only parking space left in the street. 'The one Fellows lived in is one of them.'

A street lamp outside number 30 gleamed down on rubbish sacks left by the railings, the contents oozing out on to the pavement. Huge weeds were sprouting out from the basement area and it smelled fetid.

The front door was open. A couple of young girls looked out at them with interest from the lighted first-floor window.

'How did you find out where she lived?' Beth asked as they went in, side-stepping a pushchair and a couple of bikes in the hall.

'A man rang in,' Roy said. 'He'd heard on the grapevine that it was the woman who sat in Dowry Square who did the shooting, and he knew she lived in this street because he lives three doors down.'

The staircase grew dirtier the higher they went, and the lights on a timer switch kept plunging them into darkness. The last few stairs which led to the attic rooms were bare boards. Susan's room was at the front of the house.

The staircase was good preparation for the room. It was cold, damp and grim, with ancient wallpaper peeling away from the walls and sparse, rickety furniture. A sagging double bed that looked like a relic from the war years had all the covers stripped from it, presumably in the police search. A naked bulb swung in the draught from the window, illuminating the grimness. Beth shuddered, thinking of the stark contrast between this and her comfortable, warm flat.

'We haven't taken away anything yet, other than a box of ammo,' Roy said. He handed her a pair of plastic gloves. 'Put those on and have a poke around. I'd like your opinion on what you feel about it.'

Beth looked around her first. 'What is there to poke into?' she asked, staggered by the bareness of the place. 'There's no personal possessions. Not a radio, ornament or anything.'

Roy made no comment, so she opened a cupboard by the sink. 'Even the crockery and stuff looks as if it was supplied by the landlord. Yet it's all very clean and tidy,' she said with some surprise.

She turned to a chest of drawers and opened it. It contained a few very shabby clothes, yet they were clean and neatly folded. In fact the whole room was clean, at least as clean as it could be, given that the window frames were rotten and the carpet threadbare.

She opened the wardrobe and found only an old coat hanging there. 'It's quite remarkable,' she said, surprise registering in her face. 'Not what you'd expect from a deranged wino.'

Roy nodded. 'We expected it to be a slum,' he said. 'But there were no empty bottles. No mess anywhere. She'd even emptied the rubbish bin.'

'I'd say then that she knew she wasn't coming back,' Beth said. 'Interesting! She was planning murder, but she either had too much pride to leave a mess for you to find, or she cleared out everything that might incriminate her.'

'I think the first,' he said, 'or she wouldn't have left the ammo. Now, take a look at this!' He bent down and pulled out a small battered brown suitcase from under the bedstead.

Beth bent down and opened the lid, rifling through the neatly packed things on the top. A wash-bag, slippers, a nightdress, underwear, and three books.

'It reminds me of a case packed to go into hospital,' she said, looking up at Roy and frowning. 'Perhaps she was intending to do the shooting, get back, grab this and make a run for it?'

'I think that's unlikely. If that was her plan, she'd have left it somewhere nearer the surgery,' he said. 'I'd say she packed it ready for prison. Look further down.'

Beth carefully lifted out the top things. She saw a photograph album beneath, a large pink plastic padded one, similar to the kind people put their wedding photographs in.

'This?' she asked, looking questioningly at Roy.

He nodded.

The first page had many pictures of a new baby, and

as Beth turned the leaves, she saw that the whole album was devoted to the same child, a little dark-haired girl. The pictures were arranged chronologically, showing her from birth to about four.

Beth looked at them hard, disturbed by the same odd feeling of familiarity she'd had when she first saw Susan in the cells. 'Her daughter?' she asked, looking up at Roy.

'I reckon so,' he said. He pointed to one of the last ones where the child had a plump round face surrounded by dark wavy hair. She was wearing a paper crown. 'I can see a likeness in that one.'

Beth studied it. The child wasn't exactly pretty, but she had a very appealing face, full of character. She couldn't see a real likeness to Susan herself, only that they both had round faces. But there was something about the child's sweet, somewhat shy smile that affected her. 'It could be just a niece, or even a godchild,' she said. 'There's no evidence that a child ever lived here, thank heavens. It's hardly fit to keep an animal in.'

'There's a date printed on the back of one of the earliest pictures,' Roy said. 'It's 1987. That would make her eight now. Why do you reckon the pictures stop when she's about four?'

Beth's skin came up in goose bumps. She looked sharply at Roy. 'She died?'

'Well, that's my hunch,' he said thoughtfully. 'Of course, she could have had the child taken away from her, either by her husband or the authorities.'

Beth nodded. It could have been through Susan's drinking, she thought, or maybe she began drinking after having the child taken from her. Yet somehow she thought it was more likely that the child had died.

Beth glanced through the pictures again and noted that the background to all of them looked like an ordinary home. There were homely things like a fireguard, a Christmas tree, a birthday cake, flowers in a vase, even a Renoir print on the wall behind the child. 'If she was married,' she mused, 'why aren't there any pictures with the father? Or some with Susan, that he'd taken? I get the impression they lived alone. The kid looks bonny and well cared for too.'

'We think alike,' Roy said, taking the album and putting it back in the case, and replacing the clothes on top of it. 'We're making enquiries about the child now. I wouldn't mind putting a bet on it that she was seen by Doctor Wetherall.'

Suddenly Beth saw why he'd brought her here. He was not only touched by the photograph album and the ideas it suggested to him. He also saw a motive for the shooting emerging.

'Have you got any children, Roy?' she asked.

'I did have a little boy, ten years ago,' he said, turning away from her, his voice low and hesitant. 'He died too, of a heart disease when he was three.'

Beth looked at him in consternation. 'Oh Roy, I'm so sorry,' she said. 'And this album brought it right back?'

He looked round at her, chewing on his lower lip. 'Yeah. Yesterday, I thought Susan Fellows was a madwoman. Today, I see a different picture emerging, one I can understand. If anyone had been responsible for my son's death, I might have gone gunning for them.'

Beth gulped. She was no stranger to sad stories, yet somehow this one, bluntly told by a tough and forthright man, struck her to her core.

They left the room then, Roy taking the case and locking the door behind him. He didn't speak again until they were down in the street.

'Strange how just a little bit more information can change your opinion about someone,' he said suddenly. 'Yesterday, I would have brought back hanging for that woman. Now,' he shrugged, 'well, you know!'

'You're a good man,' Beth said softly, all at once seeing his motive for bringing her here. 'I'll do my best for her. Will you let me know what you find out about the child?'

'Of course,' he said, and although it was dark in the street, she thought the glistening in his eyes was tears.

That night Beth couldn't sleep. Each time she closed her eyes she was back in that cold, miserable room, imagining Susan crying over that album. Beth had never been maternal, she'd never played with dolls, babies bored her. But she could imagine the pain of losing a child, and she knew what it was to be truly alone. She thought the two things together were likely to send anyone over the edge.

She was dressing for work the following morning when Roy rang again. 'It was her child,' he said simply. 'Annabel Lucy, born 18 April 1987 in St Michael's Hospital, here in Bristol. Died 12 May 1991, shortly after being admitted

61

to the Children's Hospital. Cause of death, meningitis. The GP was Doctor Wetherall. Susan was a single mother and at that time she was living at a different address in Clifton Wood.'

Beth hardly knew what to say. As a lawyer, it was exactly what she wanted to hear, something meaty to build Susan's defence on. Yet as a woman, her heart would have been lighter if she'd heard Susan had escaped from a mental home, and the child was just a distant relative.

She managed to thank Roy for letting her know so quickly. He said they now had enough information to charge Susan formally, and she would be appearing in court later that morning.

'I must warn you,' Roy said, his voice suddenly a little stern, 'there isn't any sympathy here at the nick for her, or out on the streets, the general view is that she's a monster. On top of that, Roland Parks, the receptionist's husband, is in the *Mail* today. I only glanced through it quickly, but it's what you'd expect, schmaltzy stuff, pictures of the couple and their children. There will almost certainly be a crowd at the court waiting to catch a glimpse of Fellows, the press will certainly be there in force. It could be nasty.'

'Then I need to find out why Susan shot her too,' Beth said. 'You know what they say about fighting fire with fire.'

Beth found it hard to concentrate on either of her two appointments that morning. One was with a man of thirty who was accused of date rape, and the other was a woman serial shop-lifter, who knew she faced a prison sentence this time round. Under normal circumstances Beth would be listening carefully to them, and even if it was patently obvious that they were guilty, she would be looking for an angle to build her defence case on.

But it was virtually impossible even to like either of these clients, let alone believe in their innocence. The date rape man was particularly offensive, as he appeared to imagine that buying a girl a couple of drinks and a kebab entitled him to have sex with her. His victim was just sixteen, a virgin until he forced himself upon her. For once, Beth wished she was on the prosecuting side. She'd enjoy making mincemeat of him.

But even as she went through the motions of listening to what her clients had to say, her mind was on Susan and her court appearance later in the morning. She must have been in her mid-thirties at least when Annabel was born. Did she choose to get pregnant when she wasn't married because she knew her biological clock was running out? Or was it the result of a relationship that collapsed? What was she before she became a mother?

Before leaving for court, Beth scanned through the article in the *Mail* about Roland Parks. She was always suspicious of anyone who talked to the papers, especially this soon after a tragedy, and Parks's remarks made her feel nauseated. 'Pam was one in a million,' he gushed. 'She helped everyone, cared about everyone. My life is over now she has been taken from me.'

Beth wondered what prompted him to go public. It

would be understandable if the killer hadn't been apprehended – anyone harbouring the guilty person might turn them in after an emotional statement from the victim's family. Maybe what he said was all true, but real grief was a solitary, dignified thing. She wouldn't mind betting that the marriage wasn't a particularly happy one at all. Perhaps Roland Parks was even covering up something?

But at least Mrs Wetherall wasn't making flowery statements, not yet anyway. Was that because she had recognized Susan's name as one her husband had mentioned at home? Or was she just naturally dignified?

Beth wished she could cancel all afternoon appointments so she could go down to the library and check in their archives for newspaper reports on Annabel's death. A death from meningitis would be reported on and Susan might have aired her views then if she felt her doctor was at fault.

But Beth had to remind herself that it wasn't her job to be some kind of private eye. She only had to liaise with the accused, get as much information as she could from them, produce witnesses, and then pass it all on to the barrister who would put his defence together for the day of the trial. Until Susan agreed she needed help, and started talking, Beth couldn't really do anything.

Susan was still saying nothing at all, both before her brief court appearance and after she'd heard she was to be remanded in custody and would be taken to Eastwood Park Prison outside Bristol. Beth didn't try to make her open up by telling her she knew about Annabel, she thought she would save that for their interview at the prison on Monday. But she got the idea it wouldn't have made any difference if she had. Susan seemed to have shut her mind down and didn't care what happened to her.

The weekend seemed endless to Beth. It rained almost solidly and for the first time in months she felt desperately lonely. She had always hated this time of year. Damp, foggy days, the light gone by five o'clock, soggy leaves on the pavements, and the shops all trying to create a feeling of false optimism with their tacky Christmas present ideas. But this time her melancholy seemed worse than usual. She found herself dwelling on the past, unable to settle to anything which would take her mind off it.

The previous Christmas was one such memory which kept coming back to her. Every Christmas was torture to her; long before it came she dreaded all those cheery questions from her colleagues about what she would be doing. She used to lie and say she was going home to her family. Let them think she got the kind of Christmas portrayed in glossy magazines. A holly wreath on the door of the family home, an eight-foot tree, dozens of tastefully wrapped presents beneath. Carols and log fires, small children in party clothes, eyes wide with wonder. The dining table laid with candelabras, silver and crystal.

In the far-off days when Beth felt compelled to go home for her mother's benefit, Christmas was something to be endured, not enjoyed. Her mother a nervous wreck, her father waiting for her to make one slip up so he could humiliate her. Her brother and sister strained because they knew their partners didn't want to be there, and their children like little stuffed dummies, not daring to say a word because they were afraid of their grandfather.

Even after her mother was dead and her father in a home, Christmas had remained something to be dreaded. Of course she could have gone and stayed with either Robert or Serena and their families, they always invited her, but by then a family Christmas was synonymous with bad times. Mostly Beth booked into a country hotel, politely, but without enthusiasm, joined in the organized festivities, and escaped as often as possible for long walks on her own.

Last year had been truly awful though. Because she hadn't been in Bristol very long, she quite relished time alone in her new flat. There was an office party in the afternoon of Christmas Eve, and as it was such a short walk to her flat, she drank far more than she would normally have done. As she went rather unsteadily up the stairs to her flat, she fell and broke her arm.

It was bad enough having to wait over six hours at the Royal Infirmary down the road to get it x-rayed and put into plaster, but then she spent the next four days in pain, totally alone and unable to do the simplest thing for herself. She didn't know anyone in Bristol well enough to call them for help or just some comfort. That was when she discovered what it meant to feel suicidal.

As Beth drove out through Bristol, she thought how often her clients had remarked with some pique, 'It's all right for you, born with the silver spoon in your mouth.' It was laughable really that people jumped to such conclusions, just because she was a solicitor, and well spoken. She knew it would never occur to a battered wife from a council estate that domestic violence could also lurk behind solid oak doors and tree-lined drives. Nor would a burglar imagine that there could be poverty in a seemingly grand house.

But Beth knew better, for she had experienced both these things at first hand. Her father was a bully, a fearful snob and a charlatan. He always implied that he came from an illustrious background, but the reality was that his great-grandfather, Ronald Powell, was just an illiterate working-class man who had made good by buying cheap land and building little terraced houses in London's Kentish Town, then selling them on at a vast profit. He repeated this again and again, shrewdly buying land no one else wanted, then building little houses that were just what people did want.

Ronald was already quite wealthy when he married in 1870, but his wife Leah came from a more aristocratic family. Perhaps it was her influence that made Ronald build Copper Beeches, the house in Sussex where Beth grew up. It had the classic style and elegance of Georgian country houses, and Leah and Ronald planted the avenue of beech trees which now lined the drive.

They had three boys, two of whom were killed in France in the First World War, but Ernest, Beth's grandfather, survived, and came home to take over the thriving family business and to share Copper Beeches with his now ageing parents and his wife Honor. Beth's father, Montague, was born in 1920.

Beth had been brought up with tales of the big parties they had at Copper Beeches when her father was a boy, of the stables full of horses, the servants and the fine gardens. The stables were still there, though empty, and what had once been extensive lawns were now pasture, sold on to a neighbouring farmer. But there had been no money since long before Beth was born in 1951. The house was in dire need of repairs, it was always cold and damp, and there wasn't even any help for her mother with the cleaning.

Beth had never been able to find out why her father hadn't managed to continue making money after his father died. She knew that the post-war years, right up to the Sixties, were boom times in property development. She could only suppose it was incompetence or laziness, because her sister Serena, who was ten years older than her, said she couldn't ever remember their father working. He was always at home, sitting reading the paper, pottering around in the garden, checking their mother's household accounts and berating her for extravagance.

Beth had asked her mother, Alice, to try to explain the mystery of it to her, some fifteen years ago, but all she'd got was the same pathetic excuse she'd heard so many times before: 'Monty was brought up to be a gentleman, he was never taught how to run a business. It isn't his fault.'

'Gentleman!' Beth muttered to herself. 'The truth of the matter is that you are a pompous, nasty bastard!'

She hated him. If it hadn't been for her mother she

would never have gone back to the house after she started university. Monty even took the credit for that, boasting about the sacrifices he'd had to make to give his three children such a good education.

The truth was, it hadn't cost him anything, they'd all gone to grammar schools. When they went on to university they all got grants, and took part-time jobs to keep themselves. Monty had never given any of them anything – not money, not time, nor even affection. Now he liked to take the credit for their successes.

But Beth had loved her mother. She was a quiet, gently brought up woman who did her best for her children and stoically put up with her overbearing bully of a husband, believing that marriage was for better or worse. But it couldn't get much worse than she had it. She might have lived to a ripe old age if Montague had agreed to sell the house and move somewhere dry, warm and easier to look after.

'I wonder if you'll tell me what your parents are like?' Beth said to herself, thinking again of Susan.

Beth liked to know her clients' family background. She found it often held the key to what made them turn to crime. It certainly wasn't an infallible guide, though – there had been enough trauma and provocation in her own family for her or her two siblings to go off the rails. But none of them had.

Robert was a hard-working doctor, kind, thoughtful and with more patience than she'd ever known in a man. Serena had her mother's sweetness, but she was no doormat. She ran her accountancy practice from home, while looking after her three children too, and she was always unfailingly glamorous.

Beth couldn't claim to share her brother's and sister's gentle natures. She had always been fiery, self-sufficient, and hard-hearted too.

She had just got on to the M5 when the ringing of her car phone broke off her reverie. It was Steven Smythe. 'I know you are on your way to visit Fellows,' he began. 'But we got some information about her this morning, and I thought it might be useful to you.'

'Well, thank you, Steven,' she said, assuming he was only going to tell her about Annabel.

'She was born in 1951, in Stratford-upon-Avon. Born Susan Wright, she changed her name by deed poll to Susan Fellows in December of 1986 in a solicitor's office in Bristol.'

Beth was so astounded that her hand slipped on the steering wheel and the car veered dangerously towards the middle lane of the motorway. She dropped the phone, straightened the wheel and then pulled over to the hard shoulder, badly shaken.

'Steven?' she said as she picked up the phone again. 'Are you still there?'

'Yeah, what happened, did you drop the phone?'

'Something like that,' she gasped out. 'Where did this information come from?'

'Your chum at Bridewell. He left a message for you on the answerphone before the receptionist got in.'

For the first time since Beth had met Steven she had the urge to talk to him properly, to share with him what that name meant to her. But she suppressed it. She had to think this one through carefully.

'Thank you for letting me know,' she said, aware her voice was shaky. 'I'll be back in the office by lunch-time. See you then.'

'Are you all right?' he asked curiously. 'You sound odd.'

She looked at the cars streaming by her on the motor-way and realized she was lucky not to have caused a serious accident. 'I'm fine,' she lied. 'It's just the reception on this phone. I'll see you later.'

But she wasn't fine. She felt as if she'd been hit by a thunderbolt. Now she understood why faint bells had rung in her mind when she looked at Susan and heard her voice. And why Susan had reacted as she did when Beth first met her at Bridewell.

Her childhood friend, that tubby little girl with hair the colour of ripe conkers whom she envied for the normality of her family! Beth had loved Suzie too because she had told her she looked like Snow White!

'Oh, Suzie,' she gasped aloud, leaning forward on to the steering wheel. 'I thought you of all people would be happily married with a parcel of kids.'

Memories came flooding back to her, the pair of them whooping with glee as they free-wheeled down hills on their bikes. Paddling in the river with their dresses tucked into their knickers. Making a den in the woods, and practising hand-jiving as they listened to the Top Ten in Woolworth's.

Everything that had been good in her childhood was shared with Suzie. Not just the fun they had, for it was far more than a casual friendship. Beth had lived for August so she could be with Suzie, for it was only there in Stratford that she felt free from oppression. It was Suzie who made her believe she was clever. The way she used to rush to hug her when she arrived each summer made Beth feel loved. The two of them had complemented one another in every way. Maybe if Beth hadn't allowed their friendship, which had been for so many years the most important relationship in her life, to fizzle out and die, she wouldn't be such a cold fish now?

Her eyes prickled with tears as she remembered that one of the excuses she'd made to herself for not writing back to Suzie the year they were both seventeen was because Suzie kept telling her about what it was like being stuck at home looking after her mother. After what had happened to Beth that year, taking care of someone you loved, and who loved you, didn't seem so very awful. She thought Suzie should be grateful that she could sleep without nightmares. That was more than Beth could do.

The sudden realization that she was dangerously close to allowing the terrible events of 1968 to surface in her mind made her feel irrationally angry. She opened the car window and took some deep breaths to try to calm herself. She couldn't stay on the hard shoulder, it was a dangerous place to be, but how could she face Susan Fellows now she knew who she really was? She couldn't handle her defence objectively, nor could she deal with the memories she knew would be stirred up.

She started up the car again, signalled and pulled out. It was very tempting to call the prison and say she couldn't make it today, then drop Susan as a client later.

As Beth drove on, she saw that was out of the question. Susan would know immediately it was because she'd found out who she was, and Beth would be left with cowardice on her conscience. The very least she could do now was go and talk to her. Whatever she'd done as a grown woman, Beth owed her for their happy times as children. Maybe Susan would rather have a different solicitor anyway. But it had to be her decision.

Beth shuddered as she turned off by the pub and on to the road that led to the prison. Eastwood Park wasn't anywhere near as grim as some other prisons she'd visited clients in. It was small, housing only some 140 women, and it was set in beautiful Gloucestershire countryside. But once inside the wire fence, past the neat gardens and the first of the locked grilles, there was no mistaking it was a real prison, with all that entailed.

Maybe Suzie *had* changed beyond recognition in the last thirty years, lived through hardships Beth couldn't even imagine. Yet there would still be enough of that carefully brought up little girl inside her to be horrified by the harsh regime, the bullying, the other vindictive prisoners, the dreadful food and lack of fresh air.

As Beth was led by a prison officer to the interview room, she felt decidedly shaky and unsure of herself. Nothing she'd planned to say before she got that phone call from Steven was appropriate now. She didn't know whether to launch straight into what she knew or wait to see if Susan was intending to tell her.

But as the door opened to the interview room and she caught sight of Susan sitting at the desk waiting for her, Beth felt as if the years had been stripped away. She was far more identifiable as Suzie now, for her hair was newly washed. Maybe it didn't shine and bounce the way it used to, there was no full fringe either, but it was Suzie's hair. Even the redness of her face seemed to have subsided. She was wearing a navy-blue sweatshirt over the same navy slacks she'd been wearing when she was arrested, and she appeared slimmer than at their previous meeting.

'How's it going?' Beth asked awkwardly, hovering in the doorway, even more unsure now of how to proceed.

Susan shrugged. 'Not that bad,' she said.

'Are you ready to talk now?' Beth asked as the door closed behind her, leaving them alone.

'No,' Susan said, looking defiantly the other way and folding her arms across her chest.

Beth saw no point in playing cat and mouse any longer.

'Okay, Suzie,' she said. 'I'm sorry I didn't recognize you straight off, because I know you did me. But you weren't someone I ever expected to turn up as a client.'

Susan's mouth dropped open, shut and fell open again like a fish. 'I didn't –' she began, and faltered. 'I couldn't –'

'God moves in mysterious ways, so they say,' Beth said archly, wishing she could stop trembling. 'Not that I'm much of a believer in God these days. But fate, call it what you will, seems to have stepped in.'

'If they'd told me your name before they called you I

74

would have asked them to get someone else,' Susan said in a croaky voice. 'I couldn't believe my eyes when you arrived.'

'Well, I did turn up, so you'd better stop all this nonsense of refusing to talk,' Beth said firmly. 'You see, I know about Annabel now, I've seen your photographs of her. I know she died of meningitis and that Doctor Wetherall was your GP.'

Susan's eyes widened and the red flush came back to her face, her expression so much like ones engraved on Beth's heart. Suzie had always blushed furiously when shocked or nervous.

'I'm so very sorry about Annabel,' Beth went on, moving a little closer to her. Part of her felt she should hug her old friend, show some of the emotion she felt inside her. But Beth didn't know how to be spontaneous any more, and her lawyer's mind said she must keep her distance. 'Losing a child is the worst thing that can happen to a woman, and it does throw a very different light on what you did,' she added.

She thought for a moment that Susan still wasn't going to talk. Her face tightened, she was twisting her index finger with her other hand, and her eyes were fixed on her lap.

'Do you remember what you shouted to me when I was on the train going home that last summer?' Beth asked after a minute or two.

She could see the scene so clearly, Suzie in a pink dress, running alongside the train as Beth leaned out the window to wave and blow kisses.

75

'It was "Till we meet again,"' Beth said and heard her own voice waver with emotion. 'That's what you shouted. I could never have imagined meeting up like this, then.'

Susan still didn't speak. Beth wasn't even sure if she'd really heard what she said.

'Look, Suzie,' she began again, 'I'm sorry we lost touch. But we were young and we both had so many other things going on. Please talk to me. If not as a solicitor, then just as an old friend.'

There was a moment or two of silence, and Beth could almost read Susan's thought processes in the agonized expression on her face. She was probably relieved she'd been found out, she wanted to trust her old friend, yet she was very much aware Beth was a solicitor and therefore on the other side. Was it best to stay silent, or tell her everything?

'That bastard sent me away from the surgery twice,' she burst out suddenly, her eyes sparking fire. 'The second time Annabel had a rash, she was like a floppy doll, but he said it was nothing more than a touch of flu and to give her Calpol. I argued with him, I showed him how the rash didn't disappear if you put a glass on it, but he said I was a neurotic mother and to stop wasting his time.'

Beth sat down, very relieved that the tide appeared to have turned. 'So you took her to the Children's Hospital yourself?' she asked.

'Yes, and she died not long after I got her there.'

'I'm so sorry, Suzie,' Beth said, and even though she

had always believed she was incapable of being really moved by any tragedy, she found this time she was. 'Did you report him?'

'Yes, but a fat lot of good it did me,' Susan spat back, her pale eyes flashing like pieces of flint struck together. 'They all stick together, don't they? Cover up for one another. I was just a single mother, they didn't care about what they'd done to me.'

'And Mrs Parks, the receptionist – what did she do to you?'

'She wouldn't even give me an emergency appointment, much less let me have a home visit,' Susan said, her voice rasping with hatred. 'I rang three times altogether, and each time she said to put Annabel to bed and give her plenty of fluids. She spoke as if I was a halfwit. A mother knows when her child is seriously ill.'

'Were these phone calls before or after the visits to Doctor Wetherall?'

'Two before the first visit, then I went to the surgery anyway because I was so frantic. She didn't like that at all, and kept me waiting ages before I finally got to see the doctor. The next morning when Annabel was much worse, I rang again, insisting on a home visit immediately. She was really snotty with me, she said a home visit wasn't necessary, but that if I brought Annabel in she'd squeeze me in somewhere.'

'So you took Annabel to the surgery twice as an emergency?' Beth needed to clarify that. 'What did Doctor Wetherall say the first time?'

'That it was just a bad cold, or maybe flu,' Susan said.

'He was so dismissive, he hardly even examined her.'

'And the second time?'

'Anyone could see how ill she was then.' Susan's voice rose in agitation. 'I told you already, she was all limp like a doll, she had the rash. I said I thought it was meningitis, he said mothers always imagined that and he told me to take her home.'

'What happened then?'

'I went back out to reception, and I begged that woman to call an ambulance, but she said if the doctor thought Annabel needed hospital he would have arranged it. I was holding Annabel in my arms, for God's sake! She was a four-year-old, not a baby, barely conscious, any fool could see there was something badly wrong.'

Beth's heart contracted at her obvious pain.

'And that's when you took her to hospital?'

Susan nodded. 'I didn't have any money on me for a taxi. I had to carry her home again and ask a neighbour to take me.'

'Why didn't you take her to the hospital straight after the doctor sent you away the first time?' Beth asked.

'If only I had.' Susan sighed and slumped down in her chair. 'I suppose I thought he had to be right, and I was over-reacting. I'd always trusted doctors.'

'Where did you learn to fire a gun like that?' Beth asked after a momentary pause.

Susan lifted her head a fraction and she half smiled. 'I could do it when I knew you,' she said. 'Dad started teaching me with a shotgun when I was about eight. I was really good at it.'

'How come you never told me?' Beth asked curiously. 'I'd have been dead impressed.'

Susan shrugged. 'A lot of people used to think it was weird. Martin, that's my brother, said it was a freaky thing for a girl to do. I suppose what with having a crazy granny, I expected you'd think I was loopy too.'

Beth had forgotten until then that Suzie had often made what seemed at the time little jokes about her granny being barmy. Back then, Beth thought it just meant eccentric behaviour. Now, looking back as an adult, she suddenly realized the old lady was probably suffering from dementia, with all the horrors that entailed.

'So where did the gun come from?' she asked, intending to come back to the grandmother later.

'It was Daddy's.'

'Is he still alive?' Beth asked.

'No, he and Mummy both died ten years ago, first Mummy and then him, six weeks later.'

'I'm so sorry,' Beth said. 'But tell me, Suzie –'

'Don't call me that,' the other woman interrupted the question irritably. 'I hate it, it's a stupid little-girl name, not one for a grown-woman. I'm Susan.'

Beth raised an eyebrow questioningly. 'Well, Susan, I can see why you felt murderous towards both the doctor and his receptionist. I think any woman would. But why did you wait four years to get your revenge?'

Beth knew this would be an important issue in Susan's trial. If she had shot the doctor within weeks of her child's death she would have gained everyone's sympathy – the public's, the jury's and even the judge's.

'Revenge?' Susan looked at her questioningly.

'Yes. That's what it was. Wasn't it?'

Susan grimaced. 'I didn't see it that way. I just knew I had to do it to set myself free.'

'Explain?'

'No, I won't,' Susan said.

'But I can't help you unless you tell me everything,' Beth said.

Susan suddenly smiled and it made her look very much younger. 'You don't get it, do you? I *am* free now. I've done it and for the first time in four years I've got something to feel glad about. I don't care if I have to stay in prison for the rest of my life. There's nothing outside for me.'

Beth sighed deeply. 'Okay, I understand why you wanted to do it. But didn't it cross your mind that you'd be leaving the doctor's four children without a father, the receptionist's two without a mother?'

'I thought of killing one child from each family,' Susan said, her face darkening. 'I wanted them to know the agony of seeing your own child in a coffin. But I watched them, day after day, and I knew those two bastards cared about no one but themselves, not even their own kids. So it was them I went for.'

Beth wasn't easily shocked but the force of Susan's statement took her aback completely. She wondered how on earth she was going to be able to put together a defence for her.

'Tell me about the years before Annabel was born,' she asked.

Susan looked at her coldly. 'Why? Do you hope you might hear something which will make you feel sorry for me?'

'Not at all. I just want to know. I want to help you.'

'I don't want your help, nor your bloody sympathy,' Susan snapped back. 'I deserve to be in here. It's the right place for me because I can't hurt anyone else ever again. Forget little Suzie Wright, the kid who wouldn't say boo to a goose, she doesn't exist any more, she disappeared years ago.'

Beth faltered. It was obvious the Suzie she knew had disappeared, but there had to be a good reason for her to vanish. 'I'd like to help Susan Fellows,' she retorted. 'I think she might need a friend, if nothing else.'

Susan gave a hollow laugh. 'I've got friends in here now. We're all ground-down, chewed-up and spat-out people here. I feel right at home.'

Beth was alarmed at that bitter remark. There was so much more she wanted to know, had to know, if only to get a broad picture of why her gentle childhood friend had turned out like this. But Beth was in shock too, her pulse was racing, she couldn't be entirely professional, or just take the role of friend. And as her time was nearly up, she thought it best to leave things as they stood for the time being.

'I have to go now anyway,' she said, getting up. 'But I'm not giving up on you, Susan,' she said, looking down at her.

Susan just shrugged. 'Please yourself,' she said sullenly. 'But don't expect me to change my plea, or give you any sob stuff. I did this with my eyes wide open, I'm not mad. I want a life sentence, like I said, I deserve it. Have I made myself clear?'

Beth nodded. 'All too clear,' she said softly, and for the first time in her career as a solicitor she felt like crying for her client. 'But just remember, Susan, it was you who inspired me to want to be a lawyer in the first place. I'm going to do the best I can for you, whether you want it or not.'

Icy rain splattered on Beth's face as she was let out of the prison gates and walked to her car. Her whole body was trembling as if she was going down with flu. She got into her car and started the engine, but for a brief moment she couldn't put it into gear and drive away, because she was eleven again and riding up through Luddington village on Aunt Rose's bike to meet Suzie.

At the start of the second August it was raining hard, and she was afraid a year apart had been too long and Suzie wouldn't want to come out and play after all. She was wearing a plastic raincoat which rustled as she pedalled – the hood had blown off and her hair was dripping wet. But as she went round the slight bend by All Saints church, Suzie came hurtling out from the trees surrounding her house, waving her arms and yelling.

'You've come!' she screamed jubilantly. 'You've come!'

Beth remembered how she flung the bike down as Suzie embraced her, and she was glad it was so wet so her friend wouldn't see she was crying. She'd waited all year for this, yet she hadn't known until that moment that Suzie had been longing for it just as much.

'Aunt Rose said only ducks go out in rain like this,' Beth said, as Suzie led her to the shelter of the trees.

'Mummy said I needed my head examined thinking you'd come.' Suzie grinned, and got a handkerchief out of her coat pocket to dry Beth's face. 'What do grown-ups know? I knew you'd come.'

'It's a bit too wet to do anything,' Beth said, looking up at the sullen sky.

'Not too wet to talk.' Suzie giggled. 'Let's go in the church porch, it'll be dry there. I've got us a picnic.'

They sat on the hard narrow bench in the porch for what must have been at least two hours, talking and talking as the rain streamed down outside. Beth couldn't remember now much of what they talked about, only the joy of being together again, the taste of the fish paste sandwiches and the bottle of lemonade they shared.

'This rain isn't going to last,' Suzie said confidently. 'Daddy said it would blow itself out by tonight. Shall we meet in Stratford tomorrow? I want to get some notebooks and stuff from Woolworth's for our secret club.'

Beth found herself smiling as the seriousness of the rules they made up for their club that afternoon came back to her. They had to invent a code to write in, so no one else would read their messages to each other. They made solemn promises never to divulge to anyone what they did at club meetings. They made up a password, and there was a kind of pledge which they had to recite together as they crooked their little fingers together.

'Friends forever, whatever the weather,' Beth murmured as it popped back into her mind.

'Better to die than to betray. That is my pledge to you today.'

As far as Beth remembered, the club fizzled out very quickly. They did buy notebooks in Woolworth's the next day, and invented their secret code, but they rarely wrote to each other in it as it proved so laborious. They built a club-house, a den in the woods, and Suzie smuggled out old plates, cutlery, even a kettle and an old rug from her house to make it cosy. In fact, now that Beth was thinking back on it, she realized Suzie was a real homemaker – right through their friendship it was always she who thought of practicalities, of what they were going to eat and what clothes they should wear. A little mother even then.

Chapter five

'I have to tell someone or burst,' Beth blurted out suddenly after two gin and tonics with Roy.

It was Friday evening, five days since she'd visited Susan, and for all of them she'd been in a state of nervous confusion. Part of her ached to confide in someone about her dilemma, but the other part insisted it was something she had to tackle alone. Then this morning a letter had arrived from Susan, dismissing Beth as her solicitor.

It had been a sensible, forthright letter, in which she said she was touched that Beth wanted to defend her, but she didn't think it was a good idea in light of their childhood connection. She asked if Beth would recommend someone else.

On one level it was a welcome relief. Every way Beth looked at the case she saw problems. She felt trapped by her own sense of involvement, and by poignant memories which kept surfacing.

Yet at the same time she felt she must do right by Susan. It seemed to her that the twist of fate that had brought both of them to Bristol to meet up under such extraordinary circumstances couldn't be walked away from.

So when Roy had rung her this afternoon and asked her out for a drink after work she was only too pleased to agree – anything was better than spending another evening alone with her anxieties.

They had met in Auntie's bar, which was just a couple of minutes' walk from her office, and maybe it was the gin on an empty stomach, or just Roy's friendly, interested manner, that made her feel compelled to share her troubles with him.

'Better to tell me, the soul of discretion, than anyone else,' he said with a grin. 'You're expecting a baby? You intend to run off with a hunchbacked milkman?'

'No,' she said, and laughed. 'Neither of those, but it's almost as unlikely. You see, it's turned out Susan Fellows and I were friends as children.'

'Good God!' he exclaimed, turning towards her, brown eyes wide with surprise. 'That's incredible. I think I'd be fit to burst too, with that on my mind.'

Beth explained how it all came about. And that Susan wanted a new solicitor before she made a full statement to the police about the shooting.

Roy was a good listener. 'I think it might be for the best,' he said thoughtfully as she finished. 'I'm sure there will be parts of her life she wouldn't want to admit to you. And it would be hard for you to be objective if you feel personal involvement. You don't strike me as someone who likes that.'

Beth was a little surprised that he'd sensed that about her already, after all they hardly knew each other. Yet it pleased her – it showed he was an intuitive man and one she could be honest with.

'I don't,' she agreed. 'To be honest, I haven't ever lost a moment's sleep over any client before. Yet even though I ought to be relieved, I can't seem to let go. I'm burning to know everything that's happened to her in the last thirty years since we drifted apart. I don't like to think of her being alone and friendless.'

She went on to tell him briefly of Susan's insistence that she was going to plead guilty and how she had said she was surrounded now by people who were just like her. 'But she can't know what prison is really like when you are on a life sentence,' Beth said passionately. 'My guess is that she's had a whole string of sadness and disappointment, even before Annabel's death. If this little girl was, as I suspect, the only good thing in Susan's life, it's no wonder she flipped. I really believe this is a true case of diminished responsibility, and if so she needs help, not to lose her freedom forever.'

'Maybe that doesn't bother her because she has no conception of what freedom means,' Roy said.

Beth looked at him curiously. There was an odd note to his voice which she couldn't quite read. 'What makes you say that?'

'Just a feeling. You said her teenage years were dominated by her senile grandmother, then her mother having a stroke. It's possible she spent her entire youth being a carer.'

'She did say both her parents died within six weeks of

one another, ten years ago,' Beth said, looking at Roy aghast. 'Bloody hell! Surely she wasn't looking after them since she was sixteen?'

'It's quite possible.' Roy nodded. 'That would kind of add up with what I learned when I went round to where she lived when Annabel was born. I spoke to her old next-door neighbour.'

'What was her reaction to what Susan had done?'

'It hadn't even crossed her mind that her former neighbour and the woman involved in the Dowry Square murders were one and the same. She was incredulous. That in itself is evidence that the woman we arrested was quite different from the one she used to be.'

'I can vouch for that,' Beth agreed wholeheartedly. 'I still can't equate the timid, gentle girl I knew with a gun-toting wino.'

'The neighbour didn't want to believe me. She said Susan was the old-fashioned kind, she baked her own bread, made jam and cakes and sat knitting and sewing in the evenings. It seems she moved there early on in her pregnancy, but no one really got to know her until after the baby was born.'

'How much does she know about Susan's past?'

'Nothing,' Roy said. 'But then this woman was only too keen to tell me Susan was the kind who was more interested in others than talking about herself. She made cakes for the old age pensioners, she got their shopping. That sounds to me like someone who has spent their life taking care of others.'

Beth nodded agreement. 'So what happened when Annabel died?'

'It seemed everyone in that street shared her grief. Annabel was by all accounts a little star who used to wave to people through the window, she had played with many of the other small children. The neighbours immediately offered help and consolation, they all went to Annabel's funeral, but Susan withdrew into herself. She stayed indoors with the curtains closed. But as the neighbour said, that was quite understandable, and they thought if they gave her time she'd come out of it. Then about six months later they found she'd moved out. No one saw her leave, she didn't say goodbye to anyone. The first they knew of it was when a van arrived to collect her furniture.'

Beth had already discovered from the landlord at Belle Vue that Susan had only lived there for two years.

'So where do you think she was for the eighteen-month period before she went to Belle Vue?' she asked Roy.

'That we don't know. She was claiming benefits when Annabel was alive, but cancelled them when she moved out of Ambra Vale in Clifton Wood. Maybe she was living with a man who was taking care of her, it could have been Annabel's father. There isn't even any record of her seeing any doctor in Bristol, and that's unusual after losing a child.'

'I don't suppose she had any faith in them any longer, not after the way Doctor Wetherall treated her,' Beth mused. 'It doesn't bear thinking about what she went through mentally, to end up hanging around that surgery, plotting to kill the people she blamed for her loss.'

'There isn't a lot of help about for anyone when a child dies,' Roy said tersely. 'Your friends don't know how to behave towards you. I don't think counselling does much good either. It's something you have to come to terms with all by yourself.'

Beth thought that perhaps she was stirring up painful memories for Roy, and felt she'd better try to steer the conversation in another direction.

'What would you do about Susan if you were me?' she asked.

'Give her case to someone you trust, then just write to her and offer your friendship,' he said simply.

Beth thought about that for a moment. Steven Smythe was every bit as able a solicitor as her, and he'd probably be quite happy to let her continue to go and see Susan once in a while. That could work out quite well.

Over a third drink, they began talking about property prices. Beth had noticed they'd begun to rise quite steeply again since she'd bought her flat. Roy said he was very glad he'd bought his cottage during the recession a few years earlier, because it would be well out of his price range now.

'You live in a cottage?' Beth said with some surprise. She'd imagined him living in a modern place.

'It's a far cry from the idyllic roses-round-the-door kind of cottage,' he said ruefully. 'I bought it very cheap in an auction because it was practically falling down. At the time I thought a big project was just what I needed. I'm not so sure now.'

Beth guessed he meant to take his mind off his son dying and his marriage breaking up.

'More work than you imagined?' she asked.

'Not half. Almost every job is dependent on something else. Like I couldn't just get the roof mended, some of the beams had to be replaced first. I got that done, then I thought I'd make a start on new window-frames, but the floor-boards were rotten and some of them caved in, that's when I found the small lake down in the foundations. The water pipes were leaking.'

'How old is it?' she asked, mentally picturing him up to his neck in muddy foundations.

'About a hundred and fifty years old,' he said. 'Built as a farm labourer's cottage, two up, two down, but no one had lived in it for some fifteen years. It was almost hidden with brambles and bushes. I must have been mad to buy it.'

'I bet it's got something good about it,' she said, amused by his sardonic attitude.

'The view is great,' he agreed. 'Fields all round, when I'm out clearing the ground on a warm sunny day, I think it's heaven. But when I get home on a cold wet evening, and I can't get the fire going, I'd gladly give up and get myself a flat in the city.'

'I'd love to see it,' she said impulsively and instantly wished she hadn't been so forward.

'Then we'll pick a nice day,' he said, his dark eyes

twinkling. 'And when I've had a few days off so I can tidy up a bit.'

They talked for a while about their ideas of an ideal home. Beth said she'd like a Georgian house with spacious rooms, large windows and a garden laid out to lawn and trees. 'With a housekeeper and a gardener, so I don't have to look after it myself,' she added laughingly.

Roy said his ideal was what he'd already got, only with everything finished. 'The kitchen all fitted out with a dishwasher and washing machine,' he said dreamily. 'No more bags of plaster, lengths of cable and pipes. A gleaming bathroom. Furniture and nice curtains.'

'What kind of home did you live in as a child?' she asked.

Roy grimaced. 'A council house in Southmead.'

Beth was surprised that he came from the same big, rough housing estate north of Bristol as many of her clients. She had thought by the way he spoke and acted that he came from a middle-class background.

'Joining the police was a way out,' he said, as if guessing what she was thinking. 'Some of my mates joined the Forces, a few emigrated to Australia, the ones who stayed mostly got into trouble. That's how it is there, you get out, or get sucked right in.'

'Are your parents still living there?' she asked.

'Dad died some years ago. Mum's got a little flat in Keynsham now, near my sisters. They are both married, with three children between them. I'm not far from them either, the cottage is in Queen Charlton. Do you know it?'

'Oh yes,' Beth exclaimed, remembering the tiny hamlet south of Bristol she'd come across once when she took a wrong turning on her way back from Bath. It was right in the country, but only about five miles from Bristol. 'It's so pretty. You were lucky to find anything affordable there.'

'That's what persuaded me,' Roy said. 'But what about your folks? Where are they?'

'Sussex, but my mother's dead now, my father's in a nursing home. My brother and sister are still in that area.'

'So what made you come to Bristol then?' He frowned as if he thought that was odd.

'To get away from them,' she said lightly.

'You surprise me.' He turned in his seat and looked right at her, making her blush. 'You've got the kind of confidence which usually comes from strong family ties.'

'I haven't lived at home since I was eighteen,' she said. 'The confidence comes from looking after myself.'

'Is that why you want the Georgian house with a housekeeper and gardener, rather than a partner?'

Beth bristled. 'Don't start psychoanalysing me, for God's sake.'

'I wasn't, I'm just interested,' he said. 'My father was a miserable old sod. He gave all of us a hell of a life. That gives me some understanding of families, and what they can do to one another.'

Beth never told anyone what her father was like, she hid it away as she did most things she felt bad about. But for once she was tempted to spill it all out.

'I don't like my father either,' was all she could bring

herself to say. 'He's an overbearing snob. I suppose it's because of him that I never wanted marriage.'

'My father had the reverse effect.' Roy grinned. 'I think I was determined to prove I had it in me to be the perfect husband. I was only twenty-one when I met Meg, and I couldn't wait to marry her.'

'And were you happy?'

Roy appeared to be considering that for a few moments. 'Happy in as much that we had a better life together than with our families,' he said eventually. 'Looking back, we had very little in common. I had my work, she kept house, but that was the way it was for most couples in those days. We'd been married for nine years when Mark was born, by then we'd just about given up hope of children. He became the pivot of our marriage, and so when he died it just collapsed.'

'I'm sorry,' she said, putting a hand on his arm. 'Do you still see Meg?'

He shook his head. 'She got married again. I hope she's happier now.'

'And you? Are you happier?' she asked. Even as she asked that question, Beth wondered at the departure from her usual chilliness. In her work she had to question people all the time, but she never normally felt curious about anyone in her private life. Roy was intriguing her, though, for he was an attractive mix of toughness and sensitivity. She guessed he was in the habit of hiding the latter – with his background and job he would consider it a liability. She didn't think he was in the habit of dropping his guard, any more than she was.

'Mostly.' He grinned boyishly. 'Marriage wasn't much fun, it was just a dreary kind of plod most of the time. I've had far more excitement since I was single. I find I like being on my own. Though I can't say I'll relish it when I'm old.'

'Nor me.' She grinned. 'But I'm blowed if I'll commit myself to someone just for the dubious pleasure of having company in the distant future.'

'Do you ever feel lonely now?' he asked curiously.

Beth thought about that for a moment. Loneliness was something she had always denied, after all she wasn't like some people she knew who couldn't bear to be alone for one night without phoning someone to break it up. But then she had trained herself to make sure she wasn't stuck with time hanging on her hands and nothing to do.

'Only on the occasional wet weekend,' she said. 'I suppose I keep myself too busy to succumb to it.'

'So I have to invite you out on a wet weekend then?' he said with a wide grin.

Beth felt herself recoil, just as she always did when someone tried to move in on her. She liked Roy, his intelligence, his sense of humour and his integrity, but she didn't want him getting any romantic ideas about her.

He must have sensed what she was thinking for when she didn't reply he laughed. 'I feel an amazingly dry spell coming on,' he said. 'It's okay, Beth, I was only thinking of going to the pictures, or a meal together, not forcing you to be my sex slave or getting you to do my washing.'

'Well, that's a relief,' she said, laughing as she tried to hide her confusion at having her mind read. 'Now, I'm starving, so how about going and getting something to eat? I'm paying.'

Later that evening, once she was in bed, Beth pondered on why she couldn't be like other single women and feel optimistic about every eligible man she met. Roy was extremely eligible, nice-looking, tall, amusing – he had a good job, and she had enjoyed his company. He'd even been too gentlemanly to let her pay for the pizza. Why did she always have to be so wary?

But she knew the answer to that only too well.

She was frightened of intimacy. It wasn't that she didn't ever fancy anyone enough. There had been dozens of times when she'd got all the right signals, felt an electric current flowing between her and the man, even an overpowering desire to make love. But once she was in bed with him she kind of froze up.

Up until a few years ago, every time she met a new man, she really believed that this time it was going to be different. When it failed, she blamed the man for not being a good enough lover. He was too rough, coarse, quick, he wasn't clean enough, or too clean. She was too drunk, or not drunk enough. She'd used any excuse rather than face the truth, which was that the fault had to lie within her. She couldn't admit any of this to the man, so she put on an act, pretended everything was wonderful, and hoped against hope that the next time it would be.

She couldn't bring herself to do that any more. It was better to remain celibate than go through the misery of pretence and the bitterness which came with it.

Self-help books, she'd read them all. They taught her what was to blame of course, but then she'd known that all along. Putting the blame in the right quarter didn't solve the problem, however.

Beth loved her brother and sister, but every time she saw them together with their partners and children, she felt wounded. She could sense the joy they got from sex, it kind of oozed out of them. With each one of her sister's and her sister-in-law's pregnancies she'd felt a mixture of envy and disgust. She squirmed with embarrassment when they breast-fed their babies, it was all too animal-like for her to take.

So she had kept her distance. Her visits were short and infrequent, and she avoided occasions like Christmas which she'd found to be emotional mine-fields. Expensive presents took the place of the involvement she would have liked to have had with her nieces and nephews. She had deprived herself of their love and affection.

A tear trickled down her cheek as she lay there, unable to sleep. She knew others saw her as a woman who had everything, an absorbing career, plenty of money, beautiful clothes and a nice home. They couldn't be blamed for assuming she had never wanted a husband and children.

And she would never admit to anyone that she would gladly give up everything she had for a man who could make her feel like a real woman.

Chapter six

Susan carried her food tray across the canteen, keeping her eyes down to avoid looking directly at any of the other prisoners. She had been here for only nine days, but it seemed more like nine months. Seeing two vacant seats at the end table, she made straight for it, but suddenly she tripped on something, and the tray fell from her hands as she tried to stop herself falling head-first on to the floor.

A roar of laughter burst out as the tray clattered to the floor, the dinner of cottage pie, cabbage and rhubarb tart and custard flung out in all directions. It looked like vomit against the green tiles.

Susan realized immediately that she had been tripped up purposely, and frightened by such malice, her first thought was to run and hide. But running wasn't an option, for Miss Haynes, one of the prison officers, was already advancing on her, grim-faced.

'Pick it up, Fellows,' she yelled, as if Susan was deaf as well as clumsy.

Susan knew by the sniggers around her that it would be folly to make any sort of complaint, and as she knelt down to try to scoop the mess back on to the tray she fought back the desire to cry. She wouldn't put it past Haynes to make her eat it. She had already discovered that humanity didn't exist in prison, not from the other prisoners or the officers.

'Scrape it into the slop bucket and get a pail of water to clear it up,' Haynes yelled again. She looked round at the women grinning at the nearest table. 'I suppose you think that was funny?' she said. 'Little things please little minds!'

Susan rushed to do as she was told, embarrassed by the way everyone was looking at her.

A blowsy woman in a pink sweatshirt was standing by the slop bucket, scraping the remains of her own food into it. 'Don't let it get to you, love,' she said. 'They do it to everyone new. They like to see how you'll react.'

'It's a bit childish,' Susan said with a sigh.

'We're all like kids when we're in here,' the woman said, and handed the bucket and cloth to her. 'Some cry all the time, some fight, but the best way to cope with it is to laugh.'

As Susan hurried back to clean the floor, she wondered what anyone could find to laugh at in here. She wished now she'd turned the gun on herself after she'd shot the doctor.

In her naivety she had imagined prison to be something like going into a religious retreat. No comforts of course, but a chance to be alone most of the time, and in utter silence. But the noise in here was deafening and relentless. It never let up, not even at night: women shouting, swearing, crying, even screaming, trying to pass messages

99

on to one another, others banging on the doors. She was in a cell with another woman called Julie who prattled on about nothing all the time and even the sound of her voice grated on Susan's nerves.

It was so hot and airless, she would lie there at night in the dark feeling as if she couldn't breathe. The cell was so small, just the bunks and a toilet and wash-basin, nowhere even to sit properly for there wasn't enough headroom on the bottom bunk. She hated having to wash and dress in front of Julie, and having to use the toilet made her squirm with embarrassment – she would hang on for hours in the hopes of getting a minute alone. But Julie didn't suffer from the same problem, she even laughed about it when she made terrible smells and noises.

Then there was the brutality.

On her second day Susan had seen one woman punched in the face by another prisoner while they were exercising outside. Since then she'd witnessed countless cat-fights and overheard all kinds of hideous threats to prisoners who weren't liked for some reason. But worse still than the open aggression was the semi-concealed kind. She would see women whispering to one another in association time, and could sense by their scowls and gestures that they were plotting something against someone. She lived in fear that it might be her.

Once she'd cleaned the floor and taken the bucket back to the kitchen, her appetite was gone. It was perhaps as well, for it was time to go back to the cells.

Once there, she lay down on her bunk and picked up her book. But she was only pretending to read, she couldn't see well enough and it occurred to her she needed glasses.

It seemed very strange to her that she kept becoming aware of things which hadn't affected her outside. Her eyesight was one of them. Of course, she hadn't tried to read anything for a very long time, so her vision may have been impaired for some while. She hadn't noticed smells outside either, yet here it was so airless she was aware all the time of odours of stale food, toilets, sweat and feet. There was her own appearance too. She had no sooner got here than she saw how awful she looked; her hair was a mess and her face was so red that it stunned her that she'd got like that without ever noticing.

But she realized now that she had been in a kind of stupor ever since she got the idea of avenging Annabel's death.

She had never given any thought to what would happen to her after she had achieved her objective. It hadn't mattered to her. But if she had considered it, she certainly wouldn't have expected that her mind would suddenly become sharper, or that she would find herself thinking about how she had once looked, the meals she used to cook, the pleasure she took in country walks or gardening. And now that her mind turned to these things, she missed them terribly.

The first weekend in here hadn't been so bad, for the other women on her wing were quite welcoming. They had already found out what she'd done and seemed in awe of her. Julie had been a hairdresser once, and she had insisted on washing and cutting Susan's hair for her.

Another woman, Sandra, had offered her some makeup, and Frankie, a real tough nut who looked like a man, had set to work to tell her which screws and other prisoners she should be careful with and advised her to ask for work so she got some money every week.

But sympathy and awe soon faded once they realized she wasn't tough or cunning. They began to snigger at the way she spoke, her shyness and her naivety, and by the end of her first week all the women on the wing were openly ridiculing her, calling her a 'muppet', their word for someone mad or simple-minded.

Susan couldn't fight back in any way. She had neither the physical strength nor the verbal skills to knock anyone down. So she did what had always served her best in the past, tried to be as inconspicuous as possible and voiced no opinions.

But as she lay there in her cell, looking at a book she couldn't actually read, she felt angry with herself. She had always allowed people to walk all over her, and if she hadn't, her life might have been very different. Her mind slipped back to the day when her mother came home from hospital, seeing it as clearly as if it were yesterday, not twenty-eight years ago.

It was in early December, and as Susan ran to open the front door when she heard her father's car pull into the drive, she wished it could have been better weather for her mother. A bitterly cold north wind was swirling the last of the fallen leaves into the air. Apart from the holly bush by the gate which was covered in berries, everything else looked as drab as the sullen grey sky.

Grabbing the wheelchair her father had just bought, she ran out eagerly, full of excitement because she had been dying to show Mother all the changes that had been made downstairs. Father's old study next to the dining room was now Mother's new bedroom, and the old downstairs cloakroom had been converted into a bathroom. Susan had worked like a slave to get things ready. It was she who humped pile after pile of books upstairs, cleaned up after the builders, painted, cleaned and arranged the furniture.

'It's so good to have you home again, Mummy,' she exclaimed as she opened the passenger door where her mother was sitting. 'You're going to be as right as ninepence once you get inside.' She folded down the side of the wheelchair and pushed it right up to the car seat the way a nurse had shown her. Her mother had lost a lot of weight and regained the use of her left arm, so it wasn't too difficult to get her into the wheelchair.

'Good girl,' Mother said. She could speak a little by then, only the words were slurred, almost as though she was drunk, so she didn't speak unless it was important. She brought up her left hand and caressed Susan's cheek. 'It's good to be home.'

'Not too much excitement all at once,' Father said warningly as Susan pushed the chair back indoors and he followed on with Mother's suitcase. 'You'll have to curb that desire to show her everything the first day, Suzie. She needs rest and quiet still.'

It was wonderful to see her mother's face light up at the converted study, to see the way her good hand reached out to touch the pretty quilt on the bed and precious little ornaments Susan had brought down from upstairs. The fire was blazing away, a couple of lamps were on to banish the cold grey weather outside, and when Susan carried in a tea tray laid with the best bone china and a plate of butterfly cakes she'd made, a tear of emotion rolled down Mother's cheek.

Susan sighed at the memory of that day. She had been so sure then that her mother would make a full recovery once she was settled in at home. She felt so important, dynamic, and so tender towards her. She had rosy visions of cosy chats by the fire in the winter, of sharing little chores, neighbours calling and the house ringing with laughter, and of taking her mother out visiting in the wheelchair when the weather was fine.

But it wasn't like that at all. A few people called at first, but they didn't come again when they saw how difficult it was for Mother to speak. There was no further recovery. Her speech didn't improve, she never managed to walk again, and as the months went by and she found her disabilities more frustrating, she became tetchy and demanding.

She developed an irritating habit of tapping her wedding ring on the spokes of the wheelchair whenever she wanted to draw Susan's attention to something. It could be anything, usually trivial, a cobweb in a corner, an unwashed glass, a smear on the window, and she wanted Susan to deal with it at once. Often a pot on the stove would boil over while she was called away, making even more work for her.

Susan felt guilty at being irritated with her mother, so she'd tried even harder to anticipate anything she might find to complain about. It left her in a state of exhaustion from which there was no respite.

The weeks, months and years became an arduous circle of washing, cooking, cleaning and waiting on both her parents. Father never helped out with anything, he took the view that as he was paying Susan a wage, that relinquished him from any responsibility. He didn't even keep his promise that she could have Saturdays off. More often than not he would pretend he was going into the office to catch up with some work, when in fact he was going shooting or playing golf.

A nurse came in twice a week to give Mother a bath, and a physiotherapist came for an exercise session for one afternoon. But everything else fell to Susan – getting her mother up and dressed in the mornings, taking her to the lavatory countless times during the day, cutting up her food, giving her medicine and helping her do the exercises the physiotherapist recommended.

As well as tapping on the wheelchair, Mother would also ring her little bell if Susan left her for more than half an hour on her own. She liked to be wheeled into the kitchen or sitting room or wherever Susan was working. It was painful to listen to her mother trying to ask questions, but even more annoying was the criticism, for although she knew she couldn't do anything much for herself, she was determined Susan should do everything her way.

If she could just have gone out on her bike now and

then lain on her bed to read a book, or sat in the sun in the garden, maybe she wouldn't have felt so weary. But she never got the chance. She hated herself for resenting the hard work and the responsibility, for having no friends and day-dreaming of going out to work in an office, or going off to a dance or the cinema in the evenings.

She hardly even had time to read the newspaper or a magazine, and when she did it made her lot in life seem even worse. England was in the grip of Flower Power, and it seemed to Susan that every other young person in the country was going to rock concerts, love-ins and wild parties, but the nearest she got to feeling like a hippy was buying an embroidered cheesecloth smock in Stratford and singing along with 'The Marrakech Express' on the radio.

She remembered the dejection she felt when Beth wrote in the summer of '69 and said she was going to university in London to study law in October. Somehow Susan just knew that would be the last letter. Beth even prepared her for it by saying she wouldn't have time to write so often and she didn't know where she'd be living in London. But then her suspicions that Beth had found new friends when she said she couldn't come to Stratford two years earlier had grown even stronger in the past few months when a sudden chill had come into her letters.

All the humour was gone and there were none of Beth's usual accounts of what went on in the shoe shop where she worked on Saturdays and in the holidays. She didn't bother to report on boys she fancied, the way she used to, or clothes she'd bought and films she'd seen. It was as though she'd long since grown out of her old friend, and now found writing at all a tedious chore.

It was particularly hurtful to Susan when she re-read letters Beth had sent less than a year before. In those she had been full of concern for Susan, advising her to stand up to her father and make him get a nurse or housekeeper for her mother, so she could be free to have a career. She had even suggested that they could still share a flat in London.

There was no further mention of sharing a flat in that last letter, no more pleading with her to tackle her father. Beth didn't actually say goodbye, yet it was there, invisibly, in every word. She was moving on.

At that time the newspapers and television made much of 'Free Love'. According to them, every single person under twenty-five was sleeping with anyone they fancied, the fear of pregnancy now removed by the contraceptive pill. Yet Susan's sexual experience was limited to kissing the boy who had walked her home from the dance in Stratford when she last saw Beth. She knew she wasn't going to gain any more experience either, she never had a chance to meet any boys.

It was just before Christmas of that same year that she realized that with or without Beth, she was trapped at home for good. That afternoon she had battled through the crowds of Christmas shoppers in Stratford just to get some new lights for the tree, as the old ones were broken.

Mother was distraught when she got back. She'd wanted to go to the lavatory, but the door handle which Father had promised to fix had jammed again, and she wet herself sitting in her wheelchair. She made it quite clear, even if her speech was laboured, that Susan was responsible, because she'd been gone for so long.

As Susan hadn't so much as stopped for a cup of coffee, let alone chat for a minute with anyone or even look in the shops, she was very hurt. She couldn't help thinking as she mopped up the urine and changed her mother, that before long this might be a regular thing, the way it had been with Granny.

Father didn't come home that night until after nine, yet again, and used the same old excuse that he'd been working. But as she put his warmed-up dinner in front of him on the kitchen table and smelled whisky on his breath, she knew he'd been in the pub.

After he'd left the kitchen, she began to cry at the unfairness of it all. Her day began at seven in the morning when she got her mother up and cooked breakfast. Every minute of the day was accounted for, and it was now after ten and she still had to help her mother into bed before she could sit down and put her feet up.

It wasn't right. Father might at least come home straight from work and share a meal with them, sit and talk to Mother in the evenings. He should have fixed that door handle and it should have been him that got the Christmas tree lights. It wasn't right that he left everything to her.

'What's the matter?' her father asked from the door-way. He must have come back to the kitchen to get something.

Susan looked up at him, but there was no concern in his once kindly eyes, only irritation.

'I'm fed up,' she sobbed. 'I don't have any life or friends. I can't go on like this, it isn't fair. I want to leave and get a job in London like Martin.'

'What sort of job could you get?' he said scornfully. 'GCEs in Domestic Science and Geography won't get you far.'

At the time when she got her disappointing results Father had only laughed and said it didn't matter about maths or science, and she would still make a first-class secretary anyway. Now it seemed he was taking Martin's view, that she was stupid. 'I could go to secretarial college like I always wanted to,' she sobbed out.

'And who do you imagine would pay for that?' he said curtly. 'I'm working every hour God sends just to keep a roof over our heads.'

'I could get any job then,' she said wildly. 'I could be a waitress or a filing clerk.'

'You'd see your mother put in a nursing home just to be a waitress?' he said, his bushy dark eyebrows rising in shock. 'I don't believe I'm hearing this.'

'Get someone else in here to look after her, then,' Susan cried. 'I can't do it any more.'

'I can't afford it, nursing care doesn't come cheap,' he said bluntly. 'I'll tell you how it is. If you insist on leaving your mother, then she'll have to go into a nursing home. Can you imagine what that would do to her? Not only stuck in a home filled with sick old ladies whose minds have gone, but knowing that her only daughter was so selfish she preferred waiting on tables to taking care of her.'

'You don't expect Martin to give up his life,' she bleated out plaintively.

Martin had always been a thorn in her side. The ten-year difference in their ages meant they had never been playmates. In fact by the time Susan was five or six she had learned to keep well away from him. He was cruel, delighting in hiding or breaking her favourite toys, slapping her for no reason, and hissing abuse at her out of their parents' hearing.

She had been overjoyed when he went off to university, and that was the same year Father began teaching her to shoot. She was too young to realize then that that made Martin even more jealous of her. She was receiving the attention and admiration from their father that he felt he should be getting. She couldn't ever forget that day in winter when Martin crept up behind her as she was standing looking at the river, and pushed her in. She almost died of shock and cold, and she knew that was what he intended, for he ran off back indoors. Unknown to him she could swim a few strokes, and she managed to get out, but she was smacked for telling lies and saying her brother pushed her. Her mother never believed anything bad of Martin.

From then on, he never let up. Each time he came home on a visit he was nastier, belittling her, suggesting she was too dim to get a real job. He said she was fat, ugly and a parasite. He joined Father in making her wait on him hand and foot. But her father never noticed.

'Martin has an important job in the city,' Father said now, and he gave her a steely look which meant that if she dared say anything detrimental about his son, she would be sorry. 'He's worked hard for his position. Now, stop being so stupid and get your mother ready for bed. If she was to hear what you are saying she might very well have another stroke.'

Looking back, Susan saw that she should have realized her father was trying to blackmail her and called his bluff. He did have the money for a nurse, but not only did he not want to spend it on his wife, he didn't like what a nurse meant. She'd insist on regular hours, she wouldn't do the cleaning, cooking and everything else. He'd have to do that, or pay another person too, and he wouldn't be able to go off to the pub, play golf and go shooting.

But at the time Susan was too naive and trusting to see all that.

It was 1973 before she lost any trust she'd had in her father when she discovered he had a mistress. She had seen lipstick marks on his shirt collars several times while she was washing them, but she refused to think it was anything more than him giving one of the women in his office a hug, until she found a note from Gerda in his jacket pocket.

Gerda was the typist Father had taken on when Mother first had her stroke. Susan had met her once when she called at her father's office to get a lift home. She was about forty, red-haired and quite attractive in a common, busty sort of way.

The note was brief but very telling, as it was an apology

for Gerda being grumpy with her father the previous evening. She said she couldn't help it because she was afraid the time would never come when they'd be together for always. But she did love him and she was prepared to wait.

'You bastard,' Susan said aloud, forgetting that Julie was up on the top bunk.

'Who's a bastard?' Julie asked. Susan looked up to see the other woman's face upside down, she was leaning over the edge of the top bunk looking at her.

Julie was thirty-five, a hard-faced bleached blonde who had been in prison dozens of times for both prostitution and theft. She had three children who were living with her mother while she awaited her trial for robbing one of her customers. While she didn't seem to be as nasty as some of the women on the wing, Susan still thought she'd better explain herself.

'I was thinking out loud,' she said. 'About my father. Sorry, I didn't mean to disturb you.'

'What did he do to you?' Julie asked.

'Nothing much to me, but he got himself a mistress after my mother had a stroke,' Susan explained. She wasn't going to go any further and admit her feelings for her father turned to hatred after that. Just the thought that he was carrying on with another woman, waiting for his wife to die so he could be with her, killed all the love she once had for him.

'All men are bastards,' Julie retorted, but her tone was friendly, and she climbed down from her bunk and sat down beside her, moving Susan's legs over on the bunk. 'Did you do him for it?'

Susan had the impression that Julie had been a victim of abuse from men for her entire life. 'No,' she said, and smiled at the woman. 'I didn't have any murderous instincts in those days.'

Julie grinned back, and Susan caught a glimpse of the very pretty girl she'd once been. 'Why did you shoot those people?' she asked.

Susan had said nothing to anyone about herself up till now, and she had intended to keep her silence for ever. But now, after the incident in the dining room, she desperately needed a friend.

'Because they were responsible for my daughter's death,' she said simply.

She knew Julie loved her children, even if she was absent from them for long periods, and seeing the shock and sympathy on her face, Susan suddenly wanted to tell her the entire story.

'But why didn't you get them for it right after your kid died?' Julie asked, when Susan had finished, wiping tears away from her eyes.

'I was too stunned at first,' Susan said. 'I just wanted to die myself. I moved out of Bristol, I didn't come back until two years later. Then one night I was walking to my cleaning job up on the Downs and I saw the doctor and that bitch of a receptionist. They were snogging in a car. That's what really got me, they were both married with kids, and there they were carrying on like that. It was just like my father and his woman.'

Julie smirked. 'Good for you. Where'd you get the gun though?'

'It was my father's service revolver,' Susan said, and told her how she'd been taught to shoot as a girl.

'So you just went down to that surgery and blasted them out?' Julie asked, her expression incredulous. 'Why didn't you track them down and do it somewhere secret? You'd never've been caught then.'

'I suppose I wanted to be caught,' Susan admitted. She suddenly saw the absurd side of that and began to laugh. 'I must be mad,' she said. 'Why would anyone want to end up here?'

'You going to plead insanity?' Julie asked, and grinned when she saw the look of horror on Susan's face. 'It don't mean you get locked away in a place full of loonies, not unless you're really out of it still. They call it Diminished Responsibility, you just make the shrink see you couldn't help what you done, like you was so upset that something pushed you into it. A mate of mine who killed her old man pleaded that. Didn't even have to be tried, the lawyers just decided it between them. She only got five years.'

'I don't think the doctor's wife and the husband of the woman I killed will be satisfied with me getting anything less than life,' Susan said. She'd had time to think about them and their children now, and although she wasn't exactly sorry for what she'd done, she did feel guilty about the children.

'Huh,' Julie snorted. 'When they get told their other halves were 'aving it off, they won't feel quite so bad about you.'

'I couldn't bring that up!' Susan exclaimed.

Julie laughed. 'You are a loony if you don't. Just think, you'll get your revenge every way up. You've done away with the people that let Annabel die, cut off all the sympathy for them, and what's more you'll be out of 'ere in a few years.'

Susan had been absolutely certain she wanted to be put away for life when she was first arrested, but just nine days in here had already eroded away that certainty. By dismissing Beth she hadn't had any further legal advice, and hearing Julie's opinion was like finding she had a parachute strapped to her back as a plane went down.

'Are you sure?' she asked.

'Yeah, of course I am,' Julie said. 'So no more arseing about, you tell your brief when he comes next that's what you want. Lay it on thick about what a bad time you've 'ad. All that stuff about yer dad, and anything else you can think of. Next thing you know you'll be outta here.'

Susan felt more cheerful then. 'Do you think I can get some glasses while I'm in here?' she asked tentatively. 'I can't see well enough to read any more.'

'Yeah, just ask to see the doctor,' Julie said. 'While you're there, you start tellin' him stuff about yourself. He's a nosy bastard, likes to think of himself as a shrink. Tell 'im you're depressed an' all while yer at it, and he'll give you some pills. It helps to have something to take the edge off the day.'

By lights out that same day, Susan felt just a little better. She guessed Julie must have passed on at least some of what she'd told her, for there had been sympathetic smiles from several women at tea-time, and she'd been saved a chair by the television during the evening's association time. While it was impossible to concentrate on the programme because of the noise all around her, it was preferable to being excluded.

Julie had asked her earlier about Annabel's father, and her question came back to Susan as she lay there hoping that tonight she'd be able to sleep. So much had happened to her since that she'd virtually shut Liam out of her mind.

She could see his face so clearly tonight, his dark eyes always creased up with laughter, snub nose, curly dark hair tumbling over bronzed shoulders as he worked in the garden. Her father called him a 'Didicoy', his word for someone lower even than a gypsy. But Liam wasn't a gypsy, he was well educated, he'd even been to college. He was just a free spirit who moved from town to town, sleeping in his old camper van, doing whatever gardening or odd jobs he could get.

He had knocked on the door one day in early March 1985. He said he'd been doing some tree-felling for one of their neighbours and he'd been told they had some dead trees that needed cutting down too.

Any new face at the door was a welcome distraction to Susan. She even welcomed canvassers when the local elections were on, for any company was better than her own. She'd been stuck in that house for nineteen years, seeing no one but the district nurse or the odd neighbour. The highlight of her week was going to the supermarket.

Sometimes she felt she would go mad with the sheer monotony of her life.

She would have invited Liam in even if there hadn't been three dead fruit trees in the back garden needing attention, just because she hoped he'd stay for a while and chat. But she was very glad she had a good excuse, because she certainly wouldn't have wanted him to realize how desperate she was for company.

He sat at the kitchen table drinking tea and chatted to her mother. Susan was touched by how patient he was with her poor speech, how he seemed instinctively to know that she still had a sharp mind and needed to communicate with new people.

She could remember standing with her back warm against the Aga, just watching him as he talked about gardening. She was thirty-four then, and she guessed he was around the same age. He was about five feet nine and slim, but judging by the way his thighs filled up his worn jeans he was very muscular. Yet although he was very attractive in a rugged sort of way, it was his passion for gardening that appealed to her most that day.

Gardens and nature were about the only subjects aside from household chores that Susan could really talk about with any confidence. She felt she was dull, she knew she looked old-fashioned because the clothes she bought had to be practical, and until that day she hadn't really cared.

'Take Liam to see trees,' Mother said with difficulty. 'Father never has time for anything.'

'Was that a note of bitterness I heard in your mother's

voice?' Liam asked as they walked down the garden together. 'Sorry if I'm being nosy.'

Susan thought he was very intuitive to pick up on something like that when her mother's speech was so impaired. She didn't find it nosy, just caring.

'Yes, I suppose it was,' she admitted. 'My father doesn't spend much time here with us, though to be fair to him he's getting a bit past cutting down trees.'

Susan had never thought of her father as old, for he had remained the way she remembered when she was small, straight-backed and slender, and even if his hair had turned white, it made him look more distinguished still. He didn't retire until he was seventy, and even now at seventy-six he was still out almost every day either shooting or playing golf. Not to mention seeing Gerda.

'So do you look after your mother full-time?' Liam asked, looking curiously at Susan.

'Yes,' she said. 'I was sixteen when she had her stroke and my father asked me to look after her.'

'That's no life for a young woman,' he exclaimed in horror. 'Your father must have a few bob to live in such a big house, can't he get a nurse for her?'

'He's got other things to spend his money on,' Susan said lightly. She didn't want to sound bitter too. 'I've only got myself to blame, I should have put my foot down a long time ago.'

She showed him the dead trees and they talked for a while about the work involved and what could be planted in their place.

'A magnolia would be nice in place of the one by the

house, and I think a willow down by the river,' he said. 'Or will your dad object to spending his money on trees too?'

There was a delightful note of impudence in his voice, and Susan had a feeling he'd already worked out a great deal more about her family than he'd been told.

'I shall make sure he coughs up,' she said, giggling a little. 'So just tell me how much it will cost, along with pruning and generally tidying up. I do my best to look after it, but it's too much for me alone.'

He perched on a stone bench and rolled up a cigarette, all the while looking around him thoughtfully. 'It's a lovely garden,' he said at length, his dark eyes sweeping over the swathes of daffodils just coming into flower. 'It will be a pleasure to work in it, so let's say fifteen quid a day. I could do two days a week until September. Your dad will get his money's worth.'

Father was apoplectic when Susan told him that she'd hired Liam. He was warming his backside at the fire in the sitting room, having arrived home at nine when the dinner Susan had saved for him was nearly dried up.

'How dare you agree to such a thing without asking me!' he raged. 'As though I care if there's a couple of dead trees in the garden. I've got better things to do with my money than waste it on a garden.'

Susan looked at him coldly. He might still be a handsome man, but over the years he'd lost what she had once loved about him, his sense of humour and his caring nature.

'Like spending it on keeping that woman I suppose?' she said, surprised at herself for being so brave. 'Don't deny it. I know it's Gerda.'

He took a step towards her, his hand raised.

'Don't you dare hit me or I'll leave right now,' she said quickly. 'You wouldn't want to have to look after Mother yourself, would you? Or pay for her to go in a nursing home?'

'How dare you speak to your father like that!' he roared at her.

'Because you've ruined my life by compelling me to stay here and take on your responsibilities,' she snapped back, so angry now she didn't care what she said. 'What kind of a father would ask a sixteen-year-old to nurse a stroke victim? If it wasn't for you and the moral blackmail you've kept me here with, I might have been married with a home of my own and children by now. Seeing as I have to be here, the least you can do is pay for Liam to do the garden. It's the one bit of pleasure Mother and I get.'

He stalked off then, stamping up the stairs to his room, not even going in to see Mother and say goodnight. After that he stayed out more than ever, sometimes not coming home at all. Susan often found Mother crying about it, and that hurt worse than anything, for she too was a blackmail victim – she knew where she'd end up if she made a fuss. All Susan could do to get back at her father was to stop saving him meals, but that didn't seem to bother him. He did leave money for Liam, though, and Liam came twice a week from then on to work in the garden.

All through that spring and summer Susan found herself living for the days Liam was there. While her mother took her naps in the afternoons, she would go out into the garden and work alongside him, and she told him things she'd never told anyone before. Like the two brief relationships she'd had with men. The first was when she was twenty-three, with a builder who'd come to retile the roof. The second, when she was thirty, was with someone from an organization that helped elderly housebound people.

'I thought I was in love with both of them,' she admitted shyly. 'But I suppose it was just the excitement of doing something I shouldn't be doing. It didn't amount to much anyway, just kissing and cuddling, but then I didn't get any opportunity for anything more.'

'Your father's a selfish old bugger keeping you tucked away like this,' he said with feeling. 'You're a pretty woman, Suzie, and it's terrible you've seen nothing of the world, and had no fun. You should make a break from it, tell him you can't do it any more.'

'How can I do that, Liam?' she shrugged. 'He'll put Mother in a home, probably move the other woman in here. I couldn't do that to Mother, I love her.'

'But she's selfish too,' he argued. 'She's got a keen mind, Suzie. She knows it isn't right to keep you here forever. Christ, she could live to be ninety and how old will you be then?'

'Over fifty,' she said glumly.

'Too old to have babies then,' he said, and he patted her cheek. 'And that sweet face will be lined with bitterness too. Get out now while you can change things for yourself.'

Liam's work finished in September and he kissed her tenderly on his last day. 'I'll be back to see how you are in December,' he said, holding her tightly as if aware she was quivering all over. 'If you feel brave enough to take a chance on a new life then, I'll help you to do it.'

He held her face between his two rough hands and just looked at her, his dark eyes smouldering. 'You're like a budding rose,' he said eventually. 'I'd like to see those petals open, to share your sweetness and beauty.'

She stood in front of her mirror that night and looked long and hard at herself and for the first time in her life she did see a pretty woman looking back at her. Maybe she was a bit plump, but her complexion glowed, her eyes sparkled and her hair shone. She wanted to run off with Liam, she wanted more of his kisses, to lie naked in his arms and discover all the mysteries of sex. She didn't care if he didn't want to marry her and settle down in one place, just to be with him would be enough.

Her mother died on the last day of September, just three weeks after Liam had left. She was sitting in her wheelchair by the Aga as Susan washed up the lunch things, and when Susan turned around her mother had fallen asleep.

About half an hour passed, and Susan noticed Mother's nose was running, and she went over to wipe it. It was then that she suspected she was dead, for she didn't move irritably, and when Susan felt for her pulse there was none.

Of course Susan cried, yet it didn't feel so very terrible – after all, she'd died in her sleep, her daughter right there with her. She couldn't have felt even the slightest pain or she would have made some sound.

It was odd that her father came back early that afternoon. The doctor had not long left, saying it was a heart attack, and there would be no need for a post mortem as he'd seen her several times in the past weeks. Susan had been mentally debating whether or not to call her father at the number she'd found some two or three years earlier in his diary. She was very glad that hadn't proved necessary.

He looked stunned when Susan told him, and disbelieving too when he saw his wife was still in the wheelchair, though Susan had wheeled her into her bedroom. Perhaps he felt guilty then for all the years he'd been so callous to her, for he stayed in the bedroom with her, right up until the undertaker called to take his wife away.

Susan began to wonder a week or two after her mother's funeral if the reason her father came home so early that day was because his relationship with Gerda had ended – he hadn't gone out again. At first she thought this was a mark of respect, but as the days passed, he still stayed in. The only time he left the house was to go to the bank or to drive Susan to the supermarket. He got up at his usual time, washed, shaved and dressed just as carefully as he always had, ate the food she put in front of him, but hardly spoke. Yet it didn't seem as if he was angry about something Susan had done or said, he was just withdrawn and nothing broke through it.

It turned cold in mid-October, and he took to lighting the fire in Mother's room, that had once been his study, and staying in there, sitting in the big leather armchair, staring at the fire.

In her own way Susan was every bit as confused about the future as her father appeared to be. She had gone from being constantly rushed off her feet to finding time hanging on her hands. She was free in one respect, to go off with Liam if he did come back for her, or to get a job, but each time she looked at her father she wondered how he would manage if she wasn't there, the way she always had been.

One evening she tried to make him talk to her. She planned to tell him she wanted to get a job, and if he didn't get alarmed about that, maybe she could suggest he sold the house and moved somewhere smaller. But as she felt unable to launch into that straightaway, she asked him what was wrong and if he was cross with her about something.

He looked up at her blankly. 'Why would I be cross with you?' he asked.

'I thought maybe about me getting Liam to do the garden,' she said. 'And the things we said to one another that day.'

He just sighed in a dismissive way. 'We had her mother here for all those years, spoiling our lives,' he said. 'Martin cleared off because of her, and then I thought everything was going to be good again once Granny died. But Margaret turned into her mother before we even had a chance. It wasn't fair.'

Susan just sat there, the only sound in the room the crackling of the fire. Her initial reaction to that strange explanation, if that was what it was supposed to be, was acute disappointment that her father couldn't have found it in him to thank her for all she'd done to ease his burden over the years. Yet despite her disappointment, she saw he was quite right – her mother had become like Granny. Maybe not really difficult or demented, but the presence and the problems were much the same.

He didn't speak again for some minutes, and when he finally did, it was to say that it was Martin he felt for.

'I should have been able to do more with my son,' he said, his voice crackling with emotion. 'He was like a stranger when he came home for the funeral.'

'He made himself a stranger,' Susan retorted, remembering how Martin had arrived just the night before the funeral, and gone to bed as soon as he'd eaten some supper, with barely a word to either of them. 'He hadn't been home once in five years. He hardly ever wrote or phoned. He didn't even remember Mother's birthday,' she added. She wanted to remind her father how mean Martin had always been to her, of the insults and constant sarcasm she'd had to put up with. But she didn't voice that, her father was in low enough spirits without her adding to it.

Martin had driven home just a couple of hours after the funeral. The last thing he'd said to her was, 'Get yourself a proper job now and stop sponging off Dad.'

'Poor Martin,' her father sighed.

That was too much for Susan. 'Poor Martin! He

didn't even care enough to ask if there was anything he could do for you, before he shot off,' Susan blurted out bitterly.

'I don't blame him for that. It was my own fault,' Father insisted, looking at Susan with mournful eyes. 'I let Granny drive him away. I should have thought of him first and put her into a home.'

'It wouldn't have made any difference,' Susan snapped, angry that he didn't remember it was she who bore the brunt of the bad times with Granny. 'He'd left for university long before Granny even got bad, as you very well know. The truth is, he always cared more about himself and his career than us.'

'I shall have to make it up to him,' Father said sadly, as if he hadn't heard what she said.

Her father had a massive heart attack on 6 November, while in Stratford, just six weeks after his wife's death. He was in a bookshop when he keeled over, and he died on the way to hospital in the ambulance.

Martin was quick to come home then, Susan telephoned him at his office in London soon after the policeman had called to tell her what had happened. It was half past four when she rang. Martin was at the house by eight-thirty, and if she imagined his haste to get there was out of concern for her, that was soon dashed.

Martin was very like their father, tall and slender with the same dark hair and thick eyebrows, but he'd always had a kind of sullen downturn to his mouth that stopped him from being handsome, and his eyes were cold. He had never married, and if there were women in his life he had never spoken of them. Susan knew less about him than she did of many of the men in the village.

He had only downed one scotch when he asked her if she knew where Father kept his will.

'I haven't even thought about that,' she said, shocked by such haste.

'Well, I suggest you think on it now,' he said sarcastically. 'He might have made some requests for his funeral in it.'

'It's not that at all,' she said, seeing right through him. 'You just want to know what he's left you.'

He caught hold of her arm and twisted it right up her back until she shrieked with pain. 'So what if I do? That's more honest than you staying here pretending to be Florence Nightingale when all you really are is a lazy, fat parasite.'

The following day Martin left, dropping in to see Father's solicitor on his way home. He rang Susan that evening and curtly told her to go ahead and arrange for the funeral at All Saints Church. As there had to be a post mortem because Father hadn't been examined by the doctor for several months before his death, the funeral was delayed for some two weeks, and in that time Martin didn't call her or come back once.

During that time Susan felt very strange – weak, weepy and completely disoriented. There had never been a time when she was alone in the house, or when she hadn't had to cook for someone else. There were strong winds that autumn, and they howled right round the house making her nervous at being alone. She jumped at every little noise, she had to leave a light on at night, and although a couple of the neighbours invited her to stay with them for the nights, she felt unable to leave the house.

One day she would feel exhilarated that she was free now to go off with Liam, the next she was looking for obstacles to prevent her. She knew so little about men, so how could she know whether she could trust Liam? Then there was the house. She expected it had been left jointly to her and Martin, so it would have to be sold, but until that happened someone had to stay here and look after it. She didn't want to have to see Martin again, she was terrified of him and she knew he'd be even nastier once there was no one else around to hear and see him.

What kind of job could she get? She wasn't qualified to do anything except housework. She felt so low in herself that she even found herself agreeing with Martin's opinion of her.

Martin came again for the funeral. It was scarcely over when he informed her of the contents of the will. He read it to her aloud, knowing full well how much it would upset her.

'To my daughter Susan I leave the sum of two thousand pounds and my service revolver,' he read first, looking up from the will and smirking at her.

'To my beloved son Martin,' he continued, his voice rising with malicious intent. 'I bequeath the rest of my estate. The Rookery, the family home, with all its contents. My savings, and my stocks and shares. I hope this will in some little way compensate for any estrangement Martin might have felt from both myself and his mother over the years. We both loved him dearly and were so very proud of his achievements.'

Susan felt a tightening of her gut as she remembered both the wording of that will and Martin's smug grin that accompanied the reading of it. She wouldn't have minded if her father had left everything to a charity, just as long as she and her brother had been treated equally. But why was there no 'beloved' in front of her name? Not one word of thanks for caring for her mother for all those years. She had in fact been treated like a servant, paid off when her services were no longer required, with not one shred of thought for her future.

It was, she knew now, the beginning of the end, for Martin unleashed something within her that day which was to change her for ever.

Susan pressed her face into her pillow. Even after all this time, and even more painful events, the memory of that day still roused such intense anger inside her. How different might it have been if she had managed to keep in contact with Beth? She wouldn't have let Martin take everything from her.

Just thinking of Beth made the tightness within her subside a little. Although it had been a monumental shock to meet up with her again, and distressing that Beth should see what she'd become, she couldn't help but be glad she'd come back into her life.

A smile seemed to creep up from within her as she remembered how even as a child, Beth always knew how to handle every situation. She was the one with the ideas, and the push to make them happen.

Beth had even solved the problem of how to get over Susan's embarrassment at buying her first bra. They were thirteen, and it was only when the weather grew hot that summer and Susan was wearing more flimsy clothes that her mother had noticed how big her breasts had grown. She kept on saying Susan must have a bra, and ordered her to go to the ladies' underwear shop in town to be fitted.

Susan attempted to go in there twice, but each time she saw the formidable women in the shop, she got so frightened and embarrassed that she backed off at the last moment, which made her mother very angry because she didn't have time to go with her. Then Beth arrived for the summer.

She noticed the new bosom immediately, but instead of making Susan feel more embarrassed, she was envious, for she was still flat-chested. Then Susan confided in her about her bra-buying problem.

'You don't have to put up with those old biddies prodding you around,' Beth said confidently. 'I'll measure you. I've seen my sister do it. Then we buy one from Marks and Spencer. You can try it on in the toilets, and if it doesn't fit right we take it back and change it again.'

Susan didn't mind Beth measuring her one bit, even if she was shocked to find she was already a 36. It was Beth who selected a pretty lacy bra from Marks, without batting an eyelid, and oversaw the fitting of it in the public toilets. Fortunately it was right first time, but it was Beth's praise once Susan had got her dress on back over it that made her feel wonderful.

'Gosh, you look really grown up,' she gasped. 'You just looked chubby before, now you look like a pin-up girl. You're so lucky.'

But then, with Beth beside her Susan got far bolder about all sorts of things that summer. Beth taught her to do handstands, to smoke a cigarette, and how to put on makeup and nail polish. She had a little bag of makeup her sister had given her, and though neither of them was old enough to wear it in public, Beth claimed they needed to practise for when they were. Out at the little camp they'd made in the woods the previous year, they'd pretend it was a beauty parlour, and take it in turns to beautify each other.

Susan could hear Julie snoring in the bunk above her. Usually it irritated her, but tonight it gave her the same comfort she'd felt when she and Beth used to lie side by side in a field reading.

She knew she was right in dismissing Beth as her solicitor. It wasn't fair to burden her with a case she couldn't win, nor did she want her trawling through the more shameful aspects of her past. But she was touched that Beth still cared enough to want to defend her. That was far more than she deserved.

Chapter seven

'So you want me to take over?' Steven Smythe looked at Beth questioningly. His deep blue eyes were almost popping out of his head with surprise. 'Are you quite sure?'

Belt felt irritated. It was Monday morning and she had thought of little else but Susan and her defence all weekend. It had been difficult enough for her to call Steven into her office and explain her predicament, for Steven wasn't one for being satisfied with just the bald facts. He'd already asked so many questions which she saw as irrelevant, and the fact that as usual he looked a mess didn't help. He had spilt something on his tie, his shirt was badly ironed, and his fair hair looked as if it hadn't seen a comb in weeks, let alone a pair of scissors. Could a lawyer who gave so little thought to his personal appearance handle something as serious as this?

'I've said I'm sure, haven't I?' Beth retorted irritably, itching to tell him to smarten himself up. 'I've already explained why. Susan's afraid our childhood connection might cause problems.'

'I understand that all right,' he said equally sharply.

'Why me though? Why not Brendan or Jack? They've had more experience in murder trials.'

Brendan and Jack were the two senior partners in the firm.

'Because neither of them would allow me to help,' she said, thinking the truth was more likely to influence him. 'Look, I care about Susan, even if our friendship was a very long time ago. I don't believe she could help what she did and I can't let her go down for life without attempting to prevent it.'

'What if I said I didn't want you poking your nose in either?' he said.

She was just about to snap at Steven again when she realized he was teasing. His blue eyes were twinkling with amusement. She thought then that perhaps this might work, maybe they did have something in common after all. 'You won't.' She smiled. 'You need my help, you haven't handled a murder before.'

'You should smile more often,' he said, looking hard at her. 'It makes you beautiful.'

'Don't start creeping,' she retorted. 'Now, I'd better fill you in with everything she's told me so far.'

'Well, that's it,' Beth said half an hour later. 'What do you think?'

'I'd say there's almost enough already to present a case for diminished responsibility,' he agreed. 'That is, if she can be persuaded to drop pleading guilty to murder. But we need to know who the father of her baby was, and where she went for the eighteen months when she didn't appear to have been in Bristol. Might she have been with him?'

Beth shrugged. 'Go and ask her.'

'I'll go tomorrow afternoon, I've got someone in court in the morning. Shall I tell her you want to visit her too?'

Beth nodded. 'Be very tactful about it though. Try and sound her out to see if she still wants me as a friend.'

Steven smiled. 'Tact is my speciality, I have been told I'm so tactful I'm ineffectual.'

'If you get more out of her than I did, then I'll scotch that rumour,' Beth said. 'I appreciate you being so understanding, Steven, I half expected you to tell me to sod off.'

Steven gave her a long, cool look. 'It's good to find you've got a heart tucked away under those designer clothes. I'd begun to doubt it.'

He left her office, and Beth sat down at her desk to look at the case files of clients she was currently dealing with. But she found as she opened the first one that she couldn't concentrate enough to take in what she was reading.

Leaning her elbows on her desk and supporting her head in her hands, she thought about Steven's last remark to her. She didn't mind that until today he'd thought her heartless. Even people who knew her far better than him had often offered that opinion about her. Perhaps it was only because of meeting up with Susan again, and all the emotions that had surfaced, that she herself knew it wasn't actually true.

But what had started people seeing her that way? Was it her manner? Or did she do something which created an image that never left her? Did she inherit it from her father? He was after all the best example of real heartlessness she knew.

'Probably,' she murmured to herself as she picked up the hastily written notes about Susan she'd jotted down over the weekend to remind herself of everything she had to tell Steven today. She checked through them to make sure she had covered everything.

One of Steven's irrelevant questions came back to her. 'Why did you go to Stratford-upon-Avon for a holiday? I'd have thought Sussex by the sea was a better place to be in August.'

Her brief answer to that was that she went with her mother, Alice, to visit her Aunt Rose. But as she thought back on the real reason they were there, she suddenly felt very shaky and remembered that was the first time she was accused of being heartless.

Beth gripped the arms of her chair, seeing herself in her mind's eye as a ten-year-old in a faded, outgrown pink dress, standing by her mother's bed as she flung clothes into a suitcase.

'You're as heartless as your father!' Alice sobbed. 'You didn't think of what this would do to me, all you care about is yourself.'

Through the bedroom window Beth could see plump, jolly Aunt Rose talking to Uncle Eddie as he leaned against the railings on the drive smoking a cigarette. Their car, a green Rover 90, was highly polished as always. It was Uncle Eddie's pride and joy, and he'd come down in it at Beth's request to take her and her mother away to safety in Stratford-upon-Avon.

'I didn't ring them for me,' Beth insisted, beginning to cry, for her mother could barely see out of one eye it was so swollen and black, and each time she moved she winced with the pain in her ribs. 'I did it so Daddy couldn't hurt you again.'

A week earlier, school had broken up for the summer holidays. Beth had been out playing with a friend, and when she arrived home about four-thirty in the afternoon she had found her mother lying on the kitchen floor.

Beth knew immediately by the blood on Alice's mouth that her father had hit her again. She also knew that this time her mother had to be far more seriously hurt because usually she went to great pains to hide these incidents from Beth.

She was frightened because of the blood. Robert, her fifteen-year-old brother, would have known what to do, but he wasn't home, he was working on a farm some miles away for the whole summer. So she knew she'd have to deal with it herself.

'Can you hear me, Mummy?' she asked, kneeling down beside her mother.

To Beth's relief Mother opened her eyes. 'Just help me up, Beth,' she said in a strange, croaky voice. 'I must have fallen over.'

She took a long time to get up, and she was holding her side and wincing with the pain. Beth helped her into the sitting room, got her to lie down on the couch and then brought a basin of water and a cloth to bathe her face for her.

'It's probably not as bad as it looks,' Mother said. 'I only stayed on the floor because I felt dizzy.'

Beth was used to her mother telling fibs about the injuries she always seemed to be getting. Serena, her older sister, had explained to her once that Mummy didn't want anyone to know Daddy did those things. Last time Serena came home from her college and saw their mother with another black eye, she'd got really cross with her and said she ought to leave him. Robert had joined in too and said he agreed, and that they could get a flat in Hastings.

Beth wasn't old enough to understand the complexities of grown-up relationships, but she knew she would run away from anyone who hurt her. Her mother's face was swelling up almost as Beth looked at it, and as she was alone in the house with her, with her father likely to come back very soon, she was afraid.

'Shall we run away, Mummy?' she whispered to her. 'I could pack us some things.'

'Don't be silly, Beth,' her mother said weakly, beginning to cry. 'I can hardly walk, let alone run. Besides, where would I go with you to take care of?'

'We could go to Aunt Rose's,' Beth said without any hesitation. Aunt Rose was her mother's sister and in Beth's opinion she was the kindest, jolliest person in the world. Rose and her husband Eddie didn't have any children, and they had a caravan. Two or three times a year they went touring with it, and they always came to Copper Beeches to see Alice and her children en route.

Dozens of times Beth had heard Rose suggest that she brought the children up to Stratford-upon-Avon for a holiday. But they had never been.

'I couldn't let Rose see me like this,' her mother said, dabbing her bruised face with the wet cloth and wincing with the pain. 'She'd blame your father.'

'Well, it was him, wasn't it?' Beth said. 'He's mean and cruel. I hate him.'

'You mustn't say such things,' her mother exclaimed in horror. 'He's your father.'

That made no sense to Beth. But she tucked a blanket round her mother and said she would make her a cup of tea.

After Beth had put the kettle on she went out into the stable yard and sat down on a bench to think about what she should do. Her father's old rusting Humber wasn't there, and that meant he'd probably gone into Hastings and wouldn't come back until late that night.

Everything about her parents and her home life was a puzzle to Beth. Seen from the end of the gravel drive, with pasture land railed off on either side, Copper Beeches looked very splendid, especially in summer when the rows of beech trees almost met and formed an archway. The house had wide steps up to a large studded front door, and with its long arched windows, tall chimneys and the stable block to one side and a conservatory on the other, it looked like the home of very rich people.

But once you were half-way up the drive it soon became apparent that this wasn't so. The stucco on the house was falling off, the window-frames were crumbling, and many panes of glass in the conservatory had fallen out years before. Weeds grew between the cobbles in the stable yard, and the roof was sagging. Her mother struggled to try to keep the lawn cut and the flower beds tidy, but as she so often said to her children, it was a house that had been built to be cared for by a team of servants, and it was as much as she could do to keep the inside clean and tidy.

None of Beth's friends at school lived in such a big house, but they all had better clothes and toys than her. Their houses might be tiny in comparison, but they were mostly much nicer. Copper Beeches was dingy, it smelled of damp and mould, and everything, from the furniture and carpets to the bedding, was worn out.

In every other family she knew, fathers went to work, but not hers. He didn't cut the grass or mend things, he just pottered about, tinkering with his car, or sat in the library reading. In the evenings he mostly went into nearby Battle to the pub. Beth was pretty certain too that no one else at her school had a father who hit their mother.

He was always saying, 'I have a position to maintain,' which sounded to Beth as if this was supposed to be a reason why he didn't work, but it made no sense to her. She had once asked Robert to explain, but he just laughed and said, 'His position is the joke of the village.' That didn't make any sense to her either.

Serena, however, had spoken more plainly when Beth asked her about it. She said, 'It means our father is a terrible snob, and a parasite. A parasite is something which lives off something else. Like a flea. Father lives off rent he gets from tenants. He's too lazy to do a hand's turn himself.'

Beth wished either Robert or Serena was here now to consult. But Robert only popped home now and then while he had this farm job, and Serena was working in a restaurant for the summer, so she wouldn't be home at all. Telephoning Aunt Rose seemed the most sensible thing to do.

So she went back into the house, made her mother some tea, and found some change and her aunt's telephone number. Then, once she felt she could leave her mother for a while, she rode her bike down to the phone box in the village.

After Beth had blurted out how she'd found her mother, Aunt Rose had said she and her husband would get there as soon as they could. 'Don't tell Mummy you've rung me,' she said warningly. 'I don't want to give her time to think up excuses, or your father an opportunity to prevent her leaving. Just go home and look after her till we get there.'

So that was exactly what Beth did. And now, two days later, Rose and Eddie were here, just as they'd promised, so Beth couldn't understand for the life of her why her mother called her 'heartless'. Surely if she'd done nothing, that would have been heartless?

Beth came out of her reverie, a little shocked that after all these years that incident still stung. It seemed to her that her mother should have praised her for being cool and level-headed. A more emotional child would have run screaming to a neighbour, and then everyone would have known what a brute Monty Powell was. But then, her mother wasn't blessed with much common sense, that was evident in the way she stuck by her husband, however badly he treated her and his children.

Beth didn't really believe that character was passed on genetically. She'd grown up with siblings who were considerably older than herself, so she'd learned from them rather than from her parents. Seeing her mother's weakness from an early age had shown her that stoic acceptance only brought grief. Likewise, her father's laziness had instilled the work ethic in her. They were perfect examples of how she didn't want to be.

Beth sighed, flicking through the files on her desk, not really reading them. If only her mother had listened to Aunt Rose that summer and filed for divorce. But she wouldn't, she was too worried at leaving Robert at home with his father, and perhaps too she believed that even a brutal, lazy snob of a father was better than no father at all.

It seemed strangely ironic to Beth that the same summer she realized how dysfunctional her own family was, she was introduced to the Wrights and decided they were the exact opposite. Indeed, she'd taken the images of their perfect, happy family with her right through to adulthood.

She could still picture the Wrights' house, The Rookery, as clearly now as if she'd seen it just a few days ago, a mysterious-looking place, almost invisible from the road because of the thick bushes and trees surrounding it. It had tall chimneys and latticed windows, and the garden ran down to the river, lock and weir. She remembered now that Susan had said there were no rooks in the trees any more, as her father always shot them because he couldn't stand the noise they made.

Susan had taken her in to get a picnic that first summer and she'd thought it was the most marvellous house she'd ever been in, not a bit creepy as she'd expected. Beautiful polished old furniture, a hall with wood panelling and carved newel posts, a kitchen kept warm by an Aga, and Susan's mother, plump and jolly, making fairy cakes which she let them eat still hot. Then there was the glorious huge garden. Parts of it were kept almost wild, with flowering shrubs and trees, there was a small pond tucked away, a summer-house, dozens of fruit trees and a lush green lawn that sloped down to the river Avon, flanked by beautiful flower beds.

Beth didn't see Susan's grandmother because she was taking a nap, but she saw her friend's pretty bedroom and her collection of dolls with exquisite clothes made by her mother. There were no dank, gloomy rooms in that house, no hideous old oil paintings or broken furniture. And Susan had a father who worked in an office. Beth never met him either, but she'd seen a photograph of him that day and remembered he was handsome, smiling, and she knew without a doubt that he never hit his wife or children.

During subsequent holidays Susan didn't ever take her into her house again, but there had never seemed anything odd or sinister about that as there was no real reason to. If it was fine weather they went out on their bikes, if it was wet they hung around the shops in Stratford, or went to the pictures. And as Beth had never had friends home to play with her, it didn't really occur to her that other children did that. Yet there were, looking back, oblique hints that all was not well. Susan did mention that her granny was a trial, that she made nasty smells and was always breaking things. She always seemed to be mentioning hanging out the washing for her mother too.

Beth could surmise from that now that the old lady was suffering from Alzheimer's disease, that she was incontinent, and that Mrs Wright was run ragged caring for her practically twenty-four hours a day. But she'd known nothing of such things back then, what young girl would unless they'd experienced it in their own family?

Beth wondered now whether Susan didn't tell her about it because she was ashamed. Or whether she felt she'd said quite enough for Beth to understand, and thought her hard-hearted too because she never commiserated with her.

Likewise, when Mrs Wright had her stroke, Beth didn't really know what that meant. Susan did relate in her letters that she was partially paralysed, with her speech impaired, but she gave no graphic descriptions as to what the implications in caring for her would be. Besides, Susan seemed only too happy to look after her mother, in one letter she'd joked about it being a good way of getting out of real work.

In Beth's imagination Mrs Wright was still the smiling,

plump woman she'd met, the only difference being that she now sat in a wheelchair and directed Susan to make the cakes and cook the dinner. As Beth's own home life was so awful, she even envied Susan. She visualized her sitting companionably by the fire with her mother on a cold afternoon, or Susan taking her for a walk in her wheelchair when it was fine.

Of course she knew now that she should have read between the lines of Susan's letters and realized that the reason she didn't seem to know anything about rock music or current books and films was because she had no time or opportunity for these things. When Susan apologized for her letters being very short and dull, Beth should have cottoned on that she was over-tired and got no stimulation to write anything jollier.

But at that time Beth was in the sixth form, struggling with her own problems. It was enough for her that in almost every letter Susan kept urging her not to give up her dream of being a lawyer, and reminded her that she was clever enough to sail through all the exams and shine at the end of it. If it hadn't been for that, Beth might very well have abandoned school where she felt like a pariah, left the home she hated and found some dead-end job.

'You owe her a lot,' she muttered to herself, and felt a stab of shame that she'd purposely let their friendship wither and die when she started at university.

Maybe her reasons were sound. Cutting herself off from everyone who knew the old Beth was the only way to create a new one. She remembered how she spent what seemed a huge chunk of her first grant cheque on new clothes — a red velvet maxi-coat, long black boots and a dramatic black hat. It was vital to look sensational, that way she could banish for ever the memory of shabby hand-me-downs, of ridicule from her peers and pity from neighbours. In that outfit she didn't need Susan to tell her she was clever, she knew she was. No one would dare humiliate a girl who looked that way.

'It wasn't the way you looked that did it,' Beth murmured to herself. She knew now it was the defences she'd built round herself that stopped them. And she would never know what good things she kept out, along with the bad.

Chapter eight

Steven Smythe was very surprised by Susan Fellows when he made his first visit to her the following day.

He knew of course that people in Dowry Square had thought she was a wino, therefore he expected her to look rough, with wild hair and perhaps some teeth missing. Yet the most outstanding thing about Susan Fellows was her very ordinariness: she was the kind of woman Steven would expect to work in a cake shop or a supermarket.

She was in fact an almost exact opposite of Beth in every way, small, dumpy and nervous, and Steven's first impression was that she was a little dull-witted too. It was hard for him to see how the implacable Beth Powell could have ever struck up a friendship with her.

But no sooner had he got over that surprise than Susan gave him another. She said she was worried she'd upset Beth by dismissing her as her solicitor. Steven was amazed, he wouldn't have expected someone charged with a double murder to give a jot about anyone else's feelings. He'd barely got into the interview room at the prison and introduced himself before she launched into an anxious explanation.

'Don't worry, you haven't upset her,' he replied. 'She understands your reasons completely, and that's why she sent me in her place. But she does hope you'll let her visit you now and again, as a friend.'

Susan clearly hadn't expected that, for her lower lip trembled and her eyes swam with tears. Steven had read in the police report that she'd showed no emotion on her arrest, so this was a break-through as far as he was concerned. Or else Beth meant far more to her than he'd been led to believe.

'Is that allowed?' she asked.

'Well, we're from the same law firm. The prison officers have no way of knowing whether or not we are both really working on your case,' he said with a smile. 'Beth's lost a lot of sleep over you. She needs to see you, to know how you are coping. We both hope you will finally come round to agreeing with us how you should plead at your trial.'

'I don't see how I can plead anything but guilty. I've admitted what I did, there were witnesses,' she said almost wistfully. 'Surely it's all cut and dried?'

Steven heard that note in her voice and was pleased. It was quite common for first offenders to believe they deserved harsh punishment, especially a woman who'd taken another's life. Yet after a couple of weeks in prison most changed their views, and their pleas.

Steven sensed she was basically a very honest woman. It was in her face, and the way she spoke. After hearing from Beth about the awful room she lived in, he was quite convinced that she'd been through hell since her daughter died. All he had to do was discover exactly what kind of hell.

'Few things in the legal profession are entirely cut and dried,' he said. 'There is always a loophole somewhere, but to look for that I have to know everything about you. Now, why don't we just talk generally today? I'd like to get to know you at least as well as Beth does.'

Susan's head jerked up. 'She doesn't know me at all. We were only fifteen when we last met in Stratford. We probably didn't exchange much more than twelve or fourteen letters after that.'

'Why did you stop writing?' Steven asked gently. 'Just grew out of each other? Or was it something else?'

'Beth went off to university, and I was stuck at home taking care of my mother,' Susan said with a shrug, as if that explained it enough. She paused, perhaps realizing it didn't. 'There were no hard feelings on my part. I must have been a very dull pen pal in the last couple of years. I expect I'd have thought there was something wrong with her if she persisted, with all those student parties, dances to go to, and boyfriends.'

Steven had always been good with female clients. He had been told by some of them that they never noticed they were being questioned, it had just seemed like conversation to them. He hoped he could make Susan feel that way.

'Because all you had to write about was the cooking and cleaning?' he asked.

She nodded, then began describing an average day. There was no bitterness in her tone as she explained how

148

her mother needed help with everything – dressing, going to the lavatory and being wheeled around to where she wanted to be. It sounded exhausting, for there wasn't just the nursing care, but the housekeeping too. 'I was lucky if I got into bed by twelve at night,' she finished up. 'Then Mother often rang for me during the night. I had a struggle to find time to write to Beth, let alone search around for something interesting to tell her.'

'And you were so young,' Steven said sympathetically. 'You must have felt bitter sometimes, everyone else your age doing the whole Sixties bit, whooping it up, the peace revolution, the wild clothes and music, while you were playing Mum to your own mother. How long did this go on for?'

'Eighteen years,' Susan said with a sigh. 'But I wouldn't say I was bitter, that's far too strong. I loved Mother and I wanted to take care of her. But there were moments when I questioned the fairness of it. I was standing down the garden watching the river one day,' she went on with a half-smile. 'I saw the river as my life going by, with me just stuck there watching. It made me feel so sad. One day, I shortened a skirt, just to look like everyone else then in their minis. Father told me to let it down again. He said it was incongruous for someone taking care of an invalid. I must have been the only girl in the Sixties wearing knee-length skirts.'

'Was he often like that?'

'Well yes, I suppose he was.' She sighed. 'I think he stopped seeing me as his daughter, or even a real person. I was just the one who looked after him and Mother.'

Gradually Steven got her going, and she began telling him how as the years went by her father began to come home later and later, how she never had Saturdays off as promised, how isolated she was from the real world. Steven was appalled, for he had no doubt that what she'd told him was the truth. He even suspected she was playing down the grimness of it out of loyalty to her mother. It was almost like one of those Victorian melodramas, a young girl locked away from the world for eighteen long years.

'I would never have wanted Mother to go into a home,' Susan explained. 'But I did start to blame Father because he wouldn't pay for more help. He said he couldn't afford it, but I knew that wasn't true, and it hurt to find he wasn't the generous man I'd always believed he was. He didn't seem to care either that I was so cut off. Television was my only real link with the outside world, but it was also torture as it showed me everything I was missing. Do you remember Pan's People who used to dance on *Top of the Pops*?'

'I loved them.' Steven beamed.

'So did I, they were so beautiful, so sexy and graceful. But I hated them too because they were everything I wasn't, they had the whole world at their feet. Whereas I wore slippers all day.'

Steven found that almost unbearably sad, for just the mention of Pan's People whizzed him back to his student days. He could remember lolling on the floor of the flat he shared, a bottle of beer in one hand, a joint in the other, arguing with his mates about which girl was the most gorgeous.

He tried to imagine what Susan had looked like as a young girl. The image which sprang to mind was of Judith Durham in the New Seekers, singing 'The Carnival is Over'. Plump, straight hair with a full fringe. Not a beauty perhaps, but wholesome and very warm. The kind of girl he recalled he and his flatmates always fell back on when they wanted a home-cooked meal, a shirt ironed, or someone to mother them a bit.

'What pop stars did you like?' he asked.

'The Beatles, of course.' She giggled a little and suddenly she looked far younger. 'I adored David Bowie too, and Marc Bolan. I think I liked them because Father said they were pansies.'

'I tried to look like Marc Bolan for a while,' Steven said, laughing at the memory. 'I had long hair then and I dyed it black. When my father discovered I sometimes put on makeup too, he had a fit.'

Susan laughed for the first time. She had a delightful laugh, like water running over stones.

'I can't imagine you dressed like him, you're too big,' she said.

'I don't think I succeeded in looking like him.' Steven grinned. 'I certainly didn't attract any girls with it either. But tell me, Susan, who did you admire? I don't mean pop stars, another woman perhaps that you looked up to.'

'Vanessa Redgrave,' she said without any hesitation. 'She was so lovely, and such a good actress, but she used to speak out about the Vietnam War in rallies and things. You wouldn't think anyone in her position would care.'

'What about Germaine Greer?' he asked. 'I seem to remember she was something of an icon to most young women then.'

'What she said was lost on me,' Susan admitted with a little giggle. 'I didn't have a clue about men, and I'd been brought up to believe that women must take the servile role. Even if things had been different, and I'd gone out to work, I don't think I'd have been the liberated type. I only ever wanted to be a wife and mother.'

'Just supposing you had been free to go out to work, what would you have liked to have done as a job?'

She laughed again. 'The possibilities were a bit limited, given that I had no qualifications. But I think I'd have liked to be a gardener.'

'Really?' This surprised Steven almost as much as hearing she admired Vanessa Redgrave.

'If it hadn't been for the garden back then, I think I would have given in to despair,' she said thoughtfully. 'There's something about tending plants, watching them grow, that's very healing. Maybe if I hadn't had to take that squalid room in Clifton Wood, found a place with a garden, I might not have ended up the way I did.'

Steven felt a surge of elation. Was he getting closer to discovering the reason behind Susan's actions? 'Why's that?' he asked, keeping his tone light.

'I would have had something else to focus on,' she said with a shrug. 'The room was so awful, I had to get out of it. I used to find myself making for that little square by the surgery, day after day. Instead of watching plants grow I was watching those two. It sort of took me over.'

Steven lost the idea that she was dim-witted then and there. It wasn't a vacant look in her greenish-blue eyes as he'd first thought, but rather that she preferred to live somewhere else in her mind than in the present.

'Where did you live before that, after you left Ambra Vale?' he asked.

She winced.

'Bad memories?' he said softly, and reached across her desk to take her hand. 'I've got two children, Susan, I can well imagine the hell of losing one.'

'Everyone says that,' she said sharply. 'But it's something you have to experience to understand. It's like you are dead too, shot through the heart, but still breathing and walking about. There's no sunshine any more, all the beauty of nature you used to see all around you, that's gone too.'

Steven was dismayed when he glanced at his watch to find their time was almost up. He had covered a great deal of ground about Susan's early home life, and he didn't want to leave now, just as she was talking about her feelings. But he knew he must because he had another appointment back at the office in half an hour.

'There's a great deal more we should talk about, but no time left today,' he said. 'I'll come again at the end of the week. Do you think you could tell me about Annabel's father then, and where you stayed before Belle Vue?'

'You want a lot,' she said, looking at him with cold eyes. 'I don't know I can tell you that.'

'My mother always used to say, "Better to tell it all than

let it fester inside." I didn't know what she meant by that when I was a boy,' Steven said. 'I do now.'

'My mother used to say, "Least said, soonest mended,"' Susan retorted. 'That makes a lot more sense to me.'

'I think that expression refers to things said in the heat of the moment,' he said reprovingly. 'What I meant is quite different. Think about it, Susan, maybe try writing some of it down. Then I'll see you again on Friday.'

'Is Beth a talker?' she said unexpectedly, just as he was getting up to leave.

'No, she isn't,' Steven admitted. 'We've worked in the same office for a year now, and I still know nothing about her. Was she a talker when you knew her?'

'Yes and no,' Susan said thoughtfully. 'She didn't talk about her family much, but she could chat non-stop about anything else.'

'Why did you ask me that?' Steven said.

Susan blushed. 'I don't know exactly. I suppose it's just the same as you wanting to know all about me, so you can understand why I killed. I always thought if I was ever to meet Beth again she'd be sort of larger than life, dynamic, full of bounce. But she isn't like that, she seems sad to me. I just wondered why. She's not married either, is she? Has she been?'

'I don't think so,' he said. 'But if I find out I'll tell you. Only it will have to remain a secret between us,' he added, tapping his nose and winking at her.

Susan laughed again, perhaps more at the silly face he was pulling than at what he'd said. 'You're all right,

Mr Smythe,' she said. 'Thank Beth for me for sending you.'

As Steven drove back into Bristol it was Susan's remark about Beth he was thinking about, as much as anything she'd said about herself. It was a little ridiculous to consider seriously a judgement on someone's character made by a person who had known her thirty years ago, but Susan struck him more and more as thoughtful and astute.

Beth had intrigued him right from the first day she had arrived in the office. His first sighting of her was as she bent over to unpack a box of books in her office, with her back to him. She was wearing a plum-coloured suit with a slim, long skirt which had a split at the back. He remembered curbing the desire to give her a wolf-whistle, for the combination of her curly black hair against the red of her suit, and her long, shapely legs in sheer black tights, was very sexy.

Instead he introduced himself and offered to help her with the books. She straightened up, looked him up and down and said something about how she needed to do it herself so she would know exactly where each book was. Dramatic was the only word that summed up how she looked. In high heels she was as tall as himself, and her face with her pale ivory skin, wide mouth and rather cold eyes appeared almost ghostly framed by the mane of black hair. She was not a beautiful woman by any means, but alluring in the manner of old silent-movie film stars.

Steven winced as he remembered how he'd put his foot

in it right then by questioning her as to where she came from, why she'd chosen to work in Bristol, and where she lived. With hindsight, it would have been far better merely to have introduced himself, offered to get her some coffee and disappeared. Friends often teased him about being like a large over-enthusiastic puppy, and he certainly was that day, trying too hard to be liked, almost to the point of slobbering over her.

Beth made herself quite clear from that first day. 'I appreciate your interest,' she had said in a chilling tone, 'but I'm a very private person. I'll be happy to confer with you about clients' cases or other legal matters, but nothing more personal.'

That, it transpired, was exactly how she operated. She was snooty and cold, never chatted to anyone in the office, appeared to have no sense of humour, and the only time he saw any animation in her was when they discussed a case. But her striking looks and elegant, often sexy clothes suggested there had to be another side to her, a side that was yearning to show itself.

It was only at the office Christmas party last year that he saw a glimpse of a warmer person beneath that tough shell. She had bought presents for each of the office girls, not the usual chocolates or a bottle, but carefully chosen personal gifts, all beautifully wrapped. She'd also brought in that morning a large tray of delicious canapés for the party. They were all home-made. For the first time in the three months she'd been with the firm, she unwound a little, and drank quite heavily. He thought he sensed in her a reluctance to go home too.

Four days later, when she came back to work with her arm in plaster, having fallen and broken it after leaving the party, Steven felt sure that she'd been alone for the whole of the holiday, and probably in pain too, with no one to call for help. His curiosity about her was heightened with sympathy then, and he began to study her more closely. She was an enigma, excellent at her job, totally committed, fair-minded and honest too. Whilst she gave nothing of herself away, she invited confidences from others. Steven often found himself telling her things he wouldn't normally have divulged to anyone.

Snooty she might be, but she was no snob. She didn't talk down to the people beneath her, in fact she seemed far more relaxed with the office cleaner and young thugs from housing estates than she was with her peers. She was also very patient and considerate with any new staff, taking the trouble to explain things carefully, which none of the other lawyers did.

It soon became clear to Steven that Beth's snootiness was a carefully constructed act, designed to keep people like him, who wanted to know more about her, at bay. That made her even more intriguing.

Steven began to smile at the absurdity of studying another lawyer, when it was his client he should be thinking about. But then he was guilty of the same kind of absurdity in his private life too.

He portrayed himself as a happily married family man, but there was nothing happy about his home life any more. His wife, Anna, was a drunk, and his girls, Polly and Sophie, were suffering because of it. Night after night he'd go home to find Anna out cold, the house in a mess and the girls tearful and hungry.

Again and again he had pleaded with Anna to get help to stop drinking. She would promise him she would, but the next day she'd start again. He'd lost count of the times she'd gone out and stayed out all night. On Sunday nights it would be he who was washing and ironing the school uniforms for the morning, just as it was he who did the shopping, the cooking and the cleaning.

There was only one real solution to prevent her messing up the children's lives any further. That was to give her an ultimatum, to stop drinking or he'd throw her out. But he hadn't done that because he knew she would almost welcome being thrown out, so she could do just as she liked. She'd said often enough that she drank because she was bored with him and her dull life. If he had believed she really could look after herself, he would have been glad to rid himself of the responsibility and the constant bad scenes. But he knew she couldn't, and he couldn't bear the thought of the woman he once loved ending up being arrested for drunkenness, or begging in the streets.

He felt like a juggler, trying to keep all the balls in the air at once, trying to be mother and father to his girls, running the home, hiding Anna's drinking from friends and family, and doing an exacting job too, all the while pretending he hadn't a care in the world. It was the pressure of pretending, the lack of anyone to confide in which made him despair sometimes. At times he had fantasized about Anna being killed, run over, or her kidneys finally giving up, just so it would end. He had even thought of killing her himself in really dark moments.

'That might make Beth sit up and take notice of you.' He grinned at the preposterous idea. But it was true, committing a serious crime was one way to get yourself noticed, and taken care of. Maybe that was the reason Susan did it.

'Well?' Beth leaned her hands on his desk, looking down at him. 'What did she say?'

Steven thought she looked stunning today. She was wearing a light grey trouser suit and a red polo-necked sweater with matching lipstick, her hair slicked back into a bun. He grinned impishly at her, amused that Susan had rattled Beth's chains enough to make her come haring into his office, something she'd never done before. He still didn't understand why this seemingly implacable woman could have retained such affection and concern for someone so different from herself.

'Lots,' he said, determined to wind her up a little more. 'I discovered she would like to be a gardening Vanessa Redgrave, married to Marc Bolan if she could have her life all over again.'

'Marc Bolan's dead,' Beth snapped.

'So he is,' Steven retorted. 'I've got to get home now. I'll tell you all about it tomorrow.'

'Come and have a drink with me first,' she suggested, a note of pleading in her voice.

He was so staggered by this U-turn from her usual

standoffish manner with him that he felt himself blush. 'That's a very tempting offer,' he said. 'But Anna's out and I've got to see to the kids.'

'Let me come home with you then,' she said. 'I could cook us all a meal.'

Steven hardly knew what to say. Aside from being unable to imagine her cooking a meal for anyone, he hadn't thought her capable of caring about anyone enough to be so desperate for news of them.

He'd have dearly liked to take her up on it, but Anna wasn't really out. Polly, his eight-year-old, had rung him only a few minutes after he got back from the prison, saying Mummy was sick and in bed. That of course meant she was drunk yet again, and the house would doubtless be in a shocking state.

'No, you c-c-can't do that,' he said, stammering because he hadn't time to think up a plausible excuse. 'I mean, I'm not prepared. Neither are the girls.'

Beth looked at him sharply. 'Is everything all right at home?' she asked. 'Anna's not ill or something?'

'Er, no. She's fine, just gone out for the day. The house will be a tip.'

'Well, why don't you go home, pick up the girls and bring them to my place?'

Steven felt that since she was offering the hand of friendship, to refuse it would look very odd.

'God, you're persistent.' He half smiled. 'Do you want to know about Susan that badly?'

'Yes, I do.' She put her hands on her hips and looked at him defiantly. 'But it would be nice to meet your girls too. So go and get them. I could have a meal ready by the time you get back.'

'Beth, they are six and eight.' He sighed. 'That isn't your scene.'

She gave him a challenging look. 'How do you know? Just because I haven't any kids of my own doesn't mean I'm a child-hater.'

The thought of having a meal cooked for him was greater than his fear that one of the girls might blab about Anna. 'Okay, I give in. But don't hold it against me if it turns out to be a disaster.'

'It won't be,' she said. 'I was a little girl once myself. I know what they like. Now, you know where my flat is in Park Row, don't you? It's number twelve.'

'Please behave, girls,' Steven said to his daughters as they drove down Whiteladies Road towards Beth's flat. He adjusted the driving mirror so he could see them both in the back seat, and wished he'd got them to change out of their school uniforms.

Polly, the eight-year-old, was like him, fair, with blue eyes, and tall for her age. Her newly arrived big teeth looked too large and slightly crooked in her mouth and like him she always seemed untidy. Sophie was more like Anna, with dark brown hair and eyes and plump, apple-like cheeks.

'Of course we'll behave, Daddy,' Polly assured him. 'But I hope she won't give us some weird food.'

'Whatever she cooks for you, eat it,' he said, getting anxious now, for Polly's idea of weird included most meats, salad, anything spicy or with herbs. 'And while Beth and I are talking you must leave us in peace.'

'Will we be able to watch telly?' Sophie asked.

'I expect so,' he said, wishing he'd had the foresight to bring one of their videos with him. 'And don't say anything about Mummy being sick. She's gone out with a friend if Beth asks about her.'

The girls were impressed by the way the front door of the flats opened automatically after Beth had spoken to them on the entryphone, but less so by their first view of Beth leaning over the banister as they went up the stairs.

'She looks like Cruella De Vil,' Polly whispered.

There was a delicious smell of garlic as they went into her flat, and the girls were struck dumb by the restrained elegance of the sitting room and the view of Bristol from the window.

After introductions, Beth smiled down at the girls. 'I should have asked your daddy what you like to eat. But I've played safe and made cheesy omelettes and tomato salad, and I've fried some potatoes. I hope that's going to be okay?'

Both girls looked relieved. Omelettes were one thing they'd eat anytime, anywhere.

Whatever Steven might have thought about Beth previously, she was surprisingly good with children. She chatted easily, showed them around her flat, and gave them a drink of apple juice while she dished up the meal. They ate in the cheerful red and white kitchen at a small round table by the window.

'This is great,' Polly said with real enthusiasm as she tucked in. 'I love the potatoes.'

'They are only boiled ones, fried up with some garlic,' Beth said, pouring some wine for Steven and herself. 'My sister does them for her girls and they liked them when they were your age.'

'Mummy drinks too much of that,' Sophie said, pointing to the wine.

Beth wouldn't have thought anything of the childish remark but for Steven's obvious embarrassment. He had blushed scarlet and his retort to Sophie, 'What a ridiculous thing to say', suggested the child was right. But Beth made no comment and told them she'd made chocolate Angel Delight for their pudding, because when she was little that had been her favourite.

'I got you a video to watch too, while Daddy and I talk,' she said as she put sundae glasses with the chocolate pudding in front of them. She'd squirted some cream on the top in a spiral and both girls grinned delightedly. 'You've probably seen it already, it's *Beauty and the Beast.*'

'They've only seen it once at the pictures,' Steven said. 'They loved it too, they've been on at me to get the video.'

Steven was touched by the way Beth was with his girls, cool as she always was, but interested and surprisingly caring. It was amazing she'd thought to get a video for them, and the pudding served in such posh glasses proved she really hadn't forgotten what it was like to be a small girl.

'Why haven't you got a husband?' Sophie asked as she spooned out the last of her pudding.

Steven wanted to snap at her again, but Beth just laughed.

'I kept looking for a prince,' she said. 'And none came along.'

'I wouldn't care about getting married if I could live somewhere nice like this,' Polly said. 'I'd have animals instead of children.'

'That sounds quite a good idea,' Beth agreed laughingly. 'I'd like a dog, but it's not fair to have one in a flat, especially when I'm out at work all day.'

'So you like dogs?' Steven said. 'I would have imagined you with cats.'

Beth shook her head and winced. 'No, they're too superior for me. If I got a pet it would have to reward me with lots of slavering love.'

'What's slavering?' Polly asked, scraping the last of the chocolate pudding from the glass.

'Like this!' Beth said, and leaned over towards her, licking her cheek and panting.

Polly giggled in delight. 'Down, doggie, down,' she said.

'Can we watch *Beauty and the Beast* now?' Sophie asked. 'Or should we help you wash up?'

Beth smiled. 'What a good girl,' she said, patting Sophie's hair. 'No, you watch the video and Daddy and I will stay here and talk. Just call out if you need us.'

Steven put the video on for the girls and felt relieved to see them curl up on the settee together to watch it. As he went back into the kitchen Beth was putting some cheese and biscuits on the table. She poured him another glass of wine.

'They're lovely girls, a credit to you and Anna,' she said. 'Now, come on, tell me about Susan.'

As Steven explained everything which had passed between them, and his own thoughts on Susan, time and again he was distracted by the incongruity of fate. He'd spent the best part of a year trying to find out more about this woman, and suddenly here he was in her flat, his children in the next room, and he was just so comfortable. It was so long since he'd been waited on, his glass filled, a plate of cheese placed before him, the dirty dishes disappearing like magic into a dishwasher, that it brought it home to him even more poignantly just how bad his home life had become.

'I can hardly credit she spent eighteen years looking after her mother.' He sighed. 'Talk about being buried alive! But time ran out all too quickly. Still, at least she wasn't hesitant at talking, I think next time I'll be able to get her to open up about Annabel's father.'

'Was she against the idea of me going to see her too?' Beth asked.

'No, she was touched you wanted to,' Steven replied. 'Tell me, did she look a bit like Judith Durham as a young girl?'

Beth thought for a moment. 'Yes, she did, come to think of it. Not so big, straight shiny hair, a fringe, lovely skin, clear eyes. A pretty face. Age and trouble haven't been too kind on her looks.'

'What were you like then?' he asked.

'A scrawny beanpole with a chalk-white face,' she said, but her laugh had a trace of sadness in it.

'And was your life at university as Susan imagines, wild parties every night?'

'No,' she said. 'I studied by day, waited on tables by night. I was always intending to write to Susan again, but like her I didn't get time, and I suppose I too thought I had nothing to say that would interest her. Then it got to the stage where I thought it was just too late to try and pick up the pieces.'

Steven picked up that she didn't like him turning things around to ask her questions. 'I'm sorry, if you think I'm prying,' he said. 'It's just that I want to get the picture of you two together. You see, I don't think she's had another friend since, so how she related to you is all-important.'

'We were both loners,' Beth said thoughtfully. 'Of course, you don't know that at ten, you think you haven't got many friends because you're plain or dumb or something. You don't find out what you really are till much later. I think our family circumstances were an influence. Susan couldn't take friends home because of her grandmother, with me it was my father.'

'What about your father?'

Beth shrugged. 'A man who liked to think he was Lord of the Manor, in reality he was living in the past, the house crumbling around him because he was so out of touch with reality.'

Steven raised an eyebrow.

'Don't ask any more,' she said wearily. 'My father is someone I prefer not to think about.'

'But he's still alive?'

'Yes. My brother put him in a nursing home a couple of years back after my mother died. I never see him, if that's going to be the next question.'

Steven thought he'd better give up on that tack. 'I think Susan's ready to change her plea,' he said. 'If we can prove that for the last four years she went through hell, I think we've got every chance of getting her off with a light sentence.'

'There was more from the receptionist's husband in the local paper this evening,' Beth said suddenly. 'Pictures of him and his children at home. It looks like he's on a crusade to get Susan hung, drawn and quartered. Understandable, of course, but there's something about his tone which doesn't ring true.'

'Can I see it?'

'Look at it in the office tomorrow,' she said. 'Polly and Sophie will want to know about it. I don't think little girls should know such things.'

'There's a lot more to you than meets the eye,' Steven said. 'I didn't expect you to be in tune with children, or to be so domestic.' He glanced around the kitchen, noting not only the way everything sparkled, but odd homely touches – a hand-knitted tea cosy like a thatched cottage and a gaily coloured wooden parrot on a perch by the window. 'Were you ever married?'

'No, Steven,' she said and her face tightened a little. 'I haven't been. I never met anyone I liked enough to settle down with. But now and again, when I meet nice kids like yours, I think I'd like to have been a mother.'

Steven sensed that was as far as she was prepared to go. He looked at his watch and saw it was nearly half past nine. 'I must take the girls home now,' he said. 'They are usually in bed by eight.'

Beth got up and looked into the sitting room, smiling when she saw the video had actually finished and the girls were asleep. She beckoned for Steven to come and look. Polly was sitting up, her head lolling over to one side, and her younger sister had her head on her lap, sucking her thumb.

Steven sighed. 'They won't like being disturbed,' he said.

'I'll carry Sophie down to your car, you carry Polly,' she said. 'Maybe they won't wake up.'

The girls woke as the cold air outside hit them, but said nothing more than a sleepy farewell to Beth. As Steven drove off he looked in his driving mirror and saw Beth still standing there on the pavement beneath a street light. He wondered what she was thinking.

Chapter nine

Susan had a black eye when Steven visited her at the prison on Friday.

'Good God!' he exclaimed in horror. 'Who did that to you?'

She could barely open the eye to look at him, but even so she half smiled. 'It's not as bad as it looks. I can live with it.'

Steven wondered how a woman who had led such a sheltered life could be so resigned about being hurt by another woman.

'I won't suggest you make a formal complaint,' he said, knowing that would make things worse for her. 'Just tell me, between ourselves, why she did it.'

'Because of what I did of course,' Susan said, looking at him as if his question was stupid. 'She'd seen the pictures of Roland Parks and his children in the paper and decided I needed a good hiding.'

Steven wished he'd had the foresight to ask the prison governor to remove anything about Susan and her crime from newspapers before they were brought on to the wing. That wouldn't stop information about her getting through of course, it could still be passed on during visits, but just the time that took, and getting the news second or third hand, usually had a diluting effect. He was a little puzzled though, for it was unusual for prisoners to react with aggression to a crime like Susan's. Violence was usually only meted out to child abusers.

'Have you thought about what I asked you last time?' he said, as time was too short to discuss bullying any further.

She nodded.

'Okay then,' Steven said. 'Suppose we start with Annabel's birth? You had her at St Michael's, I understand. Was her father there at the birth?'

Susan blushed and looked down at her hands. She didn't want to talk about her love affair with Liam. She guessed Mr Smythe would want to know if he was her first lover, where and how she met him, details she had never revealed to anyone.

'I split up with her father before I came to Bristol,' she said hurriedly. 'If you really need to know about him, I'd rather tell Beth.'

'That's fine,' Steven replied, he certainly didn't want her clamming up with embarrassment now. 'Just start with Annabel's birth then. Was it a difficult one?'

'No, it was very quick. I went into labour during the night and by nine in the morning I'd called the ambulance. She was born at two in the afternoon without any stitches or anything afterwards.'

'Well done,' he said admiringly. 'My wife had dozens when the oldest was born and it took a day and a half. How long did you stay in?'

'Four days,' she said. 'But it was too noisy there, I was glad to get home with her.'

'Any help at home?' he asked.

'I didn't need any,' she said with a touch of indignation. 'New babies sleep all the time.'

'Mine didn't,' he said, and she laughed.

'Well, maybe I was lucky, Annabel was just so easy from the start,' she said, a dreamy expression coming into her eyes. 'It was the loveliest time, just her and me. I slept when she did, just sat about cuddling her when she was awake. I wanted to hang on to every moment of it.'

'You loved being a mum then?'

'Oh yes.' She sighed. 'It was just the best thing ever, the first time I took her out in her pram I was so proud. People used to stop and speak to me in the road, to look at her, you know. I felt that at last I was a real person, sort of finished and complete.'

'But you must have been lonely on your own with her?'

She frowned. 'No, not at all. People spoke to me in the street, I'd pop in and have a coffee with some of the older people who were home during the day. Besides, there's so much to do with a small child, the days went past too quickly for me sometimes. When Annabel was in bed I had sewing and knitting to do. I did feel very lonely at home with my mother, but never with Annabel.'

'I used to like taking my girls to the park when they were very small,' Steven confided. 'Putting them on the swings and stuff. Where did you take Annabel?'

'Brandon Hill mostly,' she said. 'I loved it there in summer, it's so high you can see all over Bristol. When

Annabel got to the toddling stage she liked to look in the pond and see the waterfall running down through the rocks.'

'My girls liked that too,' Steven said. 'They used to bully me to take them up there to feed the squirrels.'

'The squirrels were Annabel's favourite,' Susan said. Her voice began to quaver and her eyes filled with tears. 'We used to take nuts for them, she had names for every one of them.'

She could see Brandon Hill as clearly as if she were standing there looking at it, the last autumn before Annabel died. The squirrels were mainly on the part closest to Berkeley Square where Beth and Steven's office was. The grassy banks rose steeply there, up to Cabot Tower on the top. In the summer the grass was shaded by the big trees but in November it was hidden under a carpet of fallen leaves.

In her mind she saw Annabel running excitedly ahead of her, in her red duffle coat and navy-blue woolly tights, her legs still plump with baby fat.

'Come on, Mummy, run!' She could hear her high little voice shouting out and see her turn, holding out her small hands as if she imagined she could pull her mother up the steep bank.

'I can't run as fast as you,' Susan would say breathlessly. 'The squirrels will wait till I get there.'

Annabel's eyes were dark like Liam's, melting pools of chocolate with long, thick lashes. Her hair curled like his too, always tangled, however much Susan brushed it. One of the neighbours in Ambra Vale called her Smilabel, because she was always smiling. Susan couldn't remember her ever being grumpy, not even when she first woke.

'She gave them all girls' names,' Susan said, aware that while thinking about her daughter she must have been silent for some time. 'There was Wendy, Lucy, Mary and Linda, I remember, I used to say that some of them had to be boys, but she wouldn't have it. She said they were too pretty to be boys.' She paused and looked at Steven. 'I suppose that was because there weren't any men in our life.'

Steven thought perhaps she felt a little guilty about that. 'My girls give all animals girls' names too,' he said. 'They've got a rabbit called Florence which is really a boy.'

There was a pause. Steven didn't know what to say next.

'Can you imagine how you'd feel if one of your girls was taken from you?' Susan asked him, her eyes brimming over.

Steven shook his head.

'You try to hold on to every single memory,' she said softly. 'The scent of her hair, the smoothness of her skin. I lie awake at night and try to hear her singing nursery rhymes. Sometimes I'd be in a shop and a child would call its mother, and I'd jump, thinking it was her. Yet you do know your own child's voice, no other child's is quite the same.'

'Where did you go to after she died?' Steven asked. He didn't feel able to ask her about her death, not now while she was already upset.

173

'To Wales,' she said, her voice suddenly taking on a harsher tone. Steven looked at her expectantly, but she seemed reluctant to go on. 'I joined a sort of commune,' she said eventually.

'A commune?' Steven exclaimed. That was the last thing he'd expected. 'I thought they all disappeared in the early Seventies?'

'It wasn't like those,' she said sharply. 'This one was a kind of religious group.'

'How did you come to join it?'

'I was out walking in Leigh Woods, about three months after Annabel died. A couple came along and they asked me what was wrong because I was crying. They were so kind, they walked home with me and suggested I went to their church. They said it would help me.'

Steven nodded. 'Go on,' he said as she seemed to be faltering.

'I was so desperate, I'd have tried anything,' she said, and she tried to smile as if she thought it was all a bit foolish now. 'It wasn't the kind of church I was used to, no proper vicar, an altar or organ. Just a hall and a piano, with lots of singing and people getting up and saying how finding Jesus had made them whole again. I can't really explain why, but I did feel better for being there.'

Steven knew the kind of group, life's rejects, the poor, the cranky, the socially inadequate, and troubled ones like Susan, all gathering together for mutual consolation. He had known clients who had joined such groups for a while, and remarkably, it sometimes made them turn away from crime.

'Was it someone in the group that suggested you moved into the commune?' he asked.

She nodded. 'A man called Reuben Moreland. A psychic healer.'

Steven raised an eyebrow questioningly. Susan blushed. 'He said he could make me well again. Each time I talked to him I felt stronger, so I believed in him. Anyway, he took me over to look at this place he had in Wales and I liked it. They grew their own vegetables, had a few chickens, and they did craft work which was sold in gift shops to help keep the place going. I thought it was just what I needed.'

There was a defensive note in her voice which suggested to Steven that things had turned sour later, but she wanted him to understand why she was attracted to the place initially.

'It was so lovely and peaceful,' she went on. 'It was late summer then and the scenery so beautiful. I had nothing and no one back in Bristol. I was good at gardening. I could sew, knit, cook and make jam. Reuben showed me these little plaster cottages they made and painted by hand, I thought I'd like to do that. He said I would be an asset to the commune.'

'Did you have any reservations?'

She sighed. 'Only about giving up everything I owned. That did seem a bit like burning all my bridges.'

'Why were you expected to do that?' Steven asked, alarm bells ringing in his head.

'Reuben said money and possessions were what held us back from being really free. One of the conditions of joining the commune was that you had to give everything to it. I didn't have much money, only about a hundred pounds in savings, but I had good pieces of furniture from my parents' home, bits of jewellery that were my mother's. I didn't like the idea of them all being sold. They meant a lot to me.'

Steven felt it was going to transpire that this Reuben was nothing more than a trickster who preyed on the lost and vulnerable. 'But you did agree to it?'

'Yes. You see, I wanted what Reuben promised, a happy, simple life. It seemed to make sense that while I still had all that stuff from the past, I couldn't move on.'

There was a shake in her voice, and her eyes were filling with tears again. Steven felt they were for more than losing all her possessions – Reuben had clearly duped her in other ways.

'Did he persuade you into doing it by saying he loved you?'

She nodded and hung her head.

Susan could remember the day Reuben said it so clearly. It was a lovely day, the afternoon sun coming in through the window of the little sitting room in Ambra Vale. As she polished the furniture she was thinking about whether or not she should let everything go and move to Wales.

When Annabel died, and for weeks afterwards, Susan's home and belongings meant absolutely nothing to her. She had wanted death herself. Many a night she'd been so consumed with grief that she could easily have walked up to the Clifton Suspension Bridge and hurled herself off. But gradually, after joining the church and meeting other people who had troubles like her, she had begun to see her home as a refuge again. Maybe she had experienced the worst that life could throw at her here, but there were so many good memories as well.

She was ecstatic with excitement when she first found her house in Ambra Vale. Maybe it was only a two-up, two-down Victorian terrace, the front door opening straight on to the street, but it had a good feel about it and she knew she could make it cosy.

She papered and painted it all herself. The pretty Laura Ashley wallpaper she chose suited both the period of the house and the furniture she'd brought with her from Luddington. She put the round walnut supper table and the four matching chairs from the old sitting room in front of the window, a couch against one wall, and the rocking-chair next to the gas fire. She re-upholstered the chair in pale blue Dralon, and made a loose cover in a blue print for the couch. With books and ornaments on the shelves in the fireside alcoves, and the traditional-style blue-patterned carpet from her parents' old bedroom on the floor, it was just perfect.

She found it odd she could think of everything as being perfect, without Liam. The day she left Luddington for Bristol she had been convinced that the pain inside her would never leave her. Maybe it helped that she went to a new place that held no memories of him, and that she had too much to do to dwell on the past. But it was the moment she first felt her baby move inside her that all the misgivings, the worries and the sorrow about her past seemed to fly away. Hundreds of women had a baby alone, there was no stigma to it any more, she was blessed with a trouble-free pregnancy. She was happy.

When Annabel was born, she was filled with such joy she even found it in her heart to forgive Martin, and wrote to him telling him he was an uncle and enclosing a photograph of Annabel. She wasn't really surprised he didn't reply and she felt too strong and happy to let it hurt her.

Other mothers she met when out walking with her baby often said they couldn't wait till they could go back to work, but Susan never felt that way. Money was tight as she only had income support to live on, but being at home with a small child was utterly fulfilling to her.

Every day she felt blessed. Whether she was out in the park with Annabel, reading to her, bathing her or feeding her, she felt a sense of purpose she'd never known before. Every stage of her development, crawling, then walking, the first words, mastering toilet training, was so totally engrossing. She had a little friend, not just a child, and every day was sheer enchantment.

But then Annabel died and Susan's whole world collapsed around her, leaving a huge, gaping void where the little girl had been. There was no point in cooking, gardening, sewing and cleaning when she had no one to do it for. Mostly she just stayed in bed with the curtains tightly closed. It was too painful to see Annabel's paintings on the kitchen wall, her little clothes still waiting to be ironed and put away.

Once she began going to church, the sympathy and

understanding from the people there had made her start to eat regularly again, to clean up and go out occasionally. But she still couldn't go into Annabel's room without crying. It was just as it was when she was alive. The Peter Rabbit duvet cover that matched the curtains and the frieze round the walls still smelled of her. Susan couldn't bear to go through the boxes of toys or the shelves of dolls and soft toys and pack them to give them away. She had tried to give the room a good clean once, but when she pulled out the bed and found an old baby's drinking cup beneath it, she became hysterical with grief.

She believed Reuben was right in saying that once she left this house, she would recover completely. He had said only the good memories would move with her, the bad ones would disappear. Yet however much she wanted to leave all the sorrow behind, it was so hard to face giving up everything.

A tap on the window startled her. It was Reuben, and she rushed to open the front door.

Reuben was a relic from the Flower Power days of the Sixties. Although he was in his early fifties, he wore his long grey hair tied back in a pony-tail, one earring, love beads round his neck, and the Christian symbol of two fishes tattooed on his forearm. He was tall and thin, with sharp features, but his eyes were mesmerizing. Right from their first meeting Susan had seen them as two blue laser beams that seemed to burn right down into her soul.

That day he was wearing faded jeans and a pale blue tee-shirt, and he was perspiring heavily, having walked up the steep hill from Hotwells.

'I was afraid you'd ignore the door-bell,' he said in his compellingly deep, husky voice. His blue eyes swept over her face as if searching for evidence she'd slid back into depression. 'I had to see you, Sue, I don't think I made it quite clear last time we met about my own motives for wanting you to come to Wales.'

She invited him in and took him into the kitchen to get him a cold drink. He wandered out into the garden.

Susan remembered suddenly feeling very nervous. He had only called at her house once before, they always met at the church or at the Rowan Tree café up in Clifton. Even when they went to Wales he picked her up at the bottom of the street. She wondered what he meant by his motives, she didn't think he had any, other than wanting her to become a whole person again.

Carrying the glass of orange juice, she joined him in the garden. It had been something of a challenge to turn what was a series of steep steps overgrown with weeds and ancient buddleia bushes into a garden. It was dangerous for a small child – the only flat part was down by the kitchen door – and Susan had put a gate up by the steps for fear of Annabel climbing up and falling back down. But it was pretty now as the many alpines and rockery plants she'd planted had covered the ugly breeze-block walls. Right at the top there was a good view of the Cumberland Basin and across to South Bristol.

Reuben drank the orange juice in one long gulp, then turned to her, took her hand and made her sit beside him on the bench. 'You know I want you to come to Wales because I believe I can heal you completely there, don't you?' he said, turning on the bench to look at her.

She nodded.

'You see, here in a city there are so many negative and destructive forces at work which countermand my powers. Once you are in a serene and beautiful environment, away from pollution and noise, surrounded by love, you will be far more receptive. You will become like a child again, learn to trust, to laugh, to let the holy spirit enter you. I want to do this for you, because I know what you are capable of.'

He paused for a moment or two, putting his hand on her cheek and caressing it. 'You are so full of anxiety and suspicion. That is those negative and destructive forces at work. So I came here today to explain why I chose you, over dozens of others who would like to join us.'

'Why?' she asked.

'Because you are a sweet and gentle person, a peace-maker. And because I love you.'

Susan didn't think he meant 'I love you' in a romantic way. At the church they used the word 'love' all the time.

'That's a nice thing to say,' she replied a little awkwardly. All her new friends from the church talked about their emotions, and were prone to analysing others too. She still found it a little embarrassing.

'I meant I love you as in, I want you to be my woman,' he said.

Susan was startled by this, it was the last thing she'd expected. She stiffened.

'Don't recoil from me, Sue,' he entreated, putting both his arms around her and holding her tightly. 'The first time I saw you, so lost and full of pain, my heart went out to you. Let me show you what joy there can be in loving intimacy.'

All at once he was kissing her.

It wasn't thrilling the way it had been with Liam, but then she had been wanting him for a long time before it finally happened. But it was pleasant, and it was good to feel desired again.

Had Reuben asked her if she wanted to go to bed with him, she would have said no. But he didn't ask, or try to persuade, he just got up, took her hand and led her upstairs. There was a moment or two in the bedroom, as he stripped off his clothes, when she almost turned and ran. He smelled of sweat, he had no underpants beneath his jeans or socks under his trainers, all of which repelled her, and his body was very white and bony. But she'd left it too late, for suddenly he was kissing her again and pulling off her clothes so fast there was no going back.

Yet whatever her reservations were, within minutes of being naked in the bed with him she lost them all. She didn't know whether or not it was because she'd been starved of love for so long, or just that he was an accomplished lover, but she moved into a blissful state where nothing mattered but here and now.

He said at one point that he was giving her 'sexual healing', and she almost broke into laughter, reminded of the song. But he wasn't joking, he meant what he said, and it did seem to heal her.

He stayed there with her for several days, and he wooed

her with all the things they would do together in Wales. Long walks exploring the beautiful countryside, gardening together, listening to music and sharing a life which would be complete. He said he wanted her to have his baby.

'I really thought it was going to be for ever,' she said to Steven, a lone tear trickling down her cheek. 'I really wanted what I'd seen in Wales, good friends sitting down to dinner every night together, all the work shared for the common good, all the sadness of the past banished by a new kind of life. Reuben didn't have to promise undying love for me and say we'd have a baby together to get me there. I probably would have gone anyway.'

Steven felt a rush of sympathy for her, and disgust that any man would prey on someone so vulnerable.

'Tell me, Susan, did you see your stuff sold before you left for Wales?'

She shook her head. 'Reuben told me to pack one bag of clothes to take with me, that's all. He said I could take a couple of personal things if I wanted, and he would handle everything else. He said he wanted to protect me from the pain of it all.'

'Was your father's gun one of those personal items?'

'Yes.' She looked embarrassed. 'I don't really know why I wanted to hang on to it. I suppose it was just the good memories of going shooting with him. Then there was the photo album of Annabel and a couple of rings which were my mother's.'

'Tell me about the commune,' Steven asked.

'It was an old, rambling place, quaint and a bit dilapidated, half-way up a hill, miles from anywhere. There were outhouses where we did the craft work, and a couple of rooms above the old stable.'

'How many people?'

'Including Reuben and me, we were twelve in all, two couples, four single men and six women. The youngest was Megan, she was only twenty-two, Reuben was the oldest, the others mostly younger than me, in their early thirties. We had a rota for chores, everything from laundry and cooking to looking after the vegetable garden. Mostly it worked very well, because if you were busy in the craft workroom, someone else was cleaning or cooking the meals. You could opt out of certain chores if you were better at something else. Megan, for example, was a brilliant artist, but she was hopeless at cooking or cleaning so she painted all day, every day. One of the men, Justin, was much better at handyman stuff, so he did that.'

'What about you?'

She pulled a face. 'Well, that became one of my bones of contention. I wanted to work outside in the garden, and in the craft room, but because I was good at cooking and housekeeping, I kept being expected to do that. It became very tedious, the food budget was tight, we didn't get much variety.'

'And what about you and Reuben? Did you love him?'

A look of pain crossed her face. 'I'm not sure that I did at first, I think it was more gratitude for being flung a life raft. But it kind of grew from there, for it was just how he said it would be. I was his woman, I felt safe and

184

happy, and we spent a lot of time together, alone. I couldn't forget about Annabel, of course, that was still there like a dull ache inside me.'

'And what about the others? Did you get on with them?'

'At first I thought they were all fantastic characters.' She smiled. 'They all, including young Megan, seemed to know so much more than me about everything. In the evenings I would just sit and listen to them talk about the places they'd been, the things they'd done. But after a while it all became very repetitive, sometimes I felt they were telling lies too, and they all had so many hang-ups. Shannon, one of the women just a bit younger than me, was always talking about her father raping her as a child. Anyway, it transpired she was living in a fantasy world. She'd been brought up by her grandmother and an aunt. No father at all.'

'A bunch of crackpots then?' Steven raised an eyebrow.

Susan half smiled. 'Crackpots, losers, dreamers. A couple of the men had been in prison, the only real common denominator was that we'd all been rounded up by Reuben, our so called Psychic Healer, when we were needy.'

'So when did you wise up to that?' Steven asked.

'When he brought a new woman into the house,' she said sadly. 'He'd told me in the past that we were both free to have sexual relationships with other people, and that petty jealousy was what caused breakdowns in "families" like ours. But I'd never wanted one, and I didn't think he did either. It was an awful shock to me.'

'I'm sure it was,' Steven said. 'But what about everyone else? Did they think he was right to do what he did? Or were they sympathetic to you?'

'They thought everything he did was right,' she said with a touch of bitterness. 'I can understand why, of course. He had this way of making you believe in him totally. He brought the money in, made all the decisions. He was a very calm man, you see, he had this way of looking at you when you made some kind of protest, as if you were just a child who needed loving out of it. He would talk at our evening meals, hold us all spellbound, and we all wanted to please him. I think if he'd told us all to take poison we would have done. You see, we all bought into the idea he did everything because he loved us all. We were all people who couldn't really hold our own lives together, for one reason or another. He held us together.'

'So you felt rejected when he brought this new woman in?' Steven asked. 'Is that what made you turn against him?'

'I didn't turn against him,' she said firmly. 'I just got disenchanted with the whole set-up. I began to look at some of the things we made there and work out what he could sell them for. I soon realized he was making far more out of it than was coming back into the house. He wasn't the altruist I'd thought he was.'

'Did you say anything to him or anyone else?'

'No, I couldn't prove it. He didn't keep accounts books, he sold the stuff for cash from his van, no tax or anything like that.'

'So when and why did you finally leave?'

'Early April of '93. Reuben went away, and I left while he was gone because I didn't want to cause a scene.'

Steven felt deeply for her, her whole life seemed to have been spent avoiding causing a scene, when perhaps it would have been far more beneficial to scream and stamp her feet, rather than let more injustices be piled on to her.

'How did you manage to live? Did you have any money left at all?'

She shrugged. 'No, but I sold Mother's rings. They weren't worth much, but it was enough to pay the train fare back to Bristol and get that room in Belle Vue.'

Steven thought about it all for a moment or two. He wondered why, if she was together enough in Wales to realize what Reuben was, and get out, she fell apart when she got back to Bristol.

'Can I ask when you started drinking?' he said.

'I was never an alcoholic,' she said indignantly. 'I liked a drink now and again. That's all. I began to drink more once I was back in Bristol, just because it was a way of numbing the edges.'

'So would you say you were depressed then?'

'In despair describes it better,' she said thoughtfully. 'I had nothing and no one. Nothing to look forward to, just pain behind me. I felt like someone thrown on the scrap-heap. I phoned my brother once, I was feeling so bad. It was a stupid thing to do really, I might have known he'd only be nasty. When he was, I felt even worse.'

Steven felt a twinge of anger that there was no organization which could help people in Susan's position. They had to commit a crime before anyone took any notice.

'How did you pay your rent?' he asked. 'There's no record of your signing on.'

'I did office cleaning in the evenings.' She told him that it was for a firm in Bristol. She had a key and let herself in and out to do the work.

'Why did it take you two years to shoot Doctor Wetherall and Pamela Parks, Susan?'

She looked at him for a few minutes with her one good eye, the other remaining disconcertingly shut.

'Reuben said wickedness never goes unpunished. Well, they were having an affair, on top of letting Annabel die from negligence. So I watched and waited for something bad to happen to them. When it didn't, I decided I had to punish them myself.'

Steven felt suddenly chilled by that explanation. Everything she'd said prior to that was understandable and reasonable, but the cold, calm way she'd decided to mete out her own punishment had a ring of true madness about it.

He knew he ought to dive straight in and get some detail about this alleged affair between Wetherall and Parks, as it could be valuable in discrediting the couple. Yet for some strange reason he didn't feel able to question her further about it. The small, stuffy room seemed to be closing in on him, he needed time to think about what he'd heard, and he wanted to consult Beth.

'I think we'll end it there for today,' he said, looking at his watch. 'I do hope your eye will be better by the next time I come.'

Chapter ten

Susan woke to the sound of her own screaming.

'Shut up, you stupid bitch,' the woman in the bunk above her growled, bringing Susan back to where she really was. In prison.

She was afraid to shut her eyes again, she didn't want to slip back into the nightmare. She had been trying to run, weighed down by the weight of Annabel in her arms. But her legs wouldn't seem to move, and though she was shouting to people to help her, they just stared at her.

That wasn't what happened that day in May four years ago. Her legs did move, faster than she would've believed possible. She didn't shout at anyone. But the terror in the dream was exactly as she felt that day.

She could picture everything that happened that morning so clearly. It was Annabel's rasping breathing that woke her.

The previous day Susan had taken the child to the doctor and been told her temperature was nothing more than a virus, but she was so anxious about her that she took her into her bed that night to keep a close eye on her. In the early hours of the morning Annabel had woken and Susan had given her more Calpol and a drink.

But as Susan woke again, this time to the sound of harsh breathing, she instinctively put her hand on her daughter's forehead and found she was burning up. In horror Susan jumped out of bed, pulled back the curtains and examined her.

She knew right away this was no harmless little virus but something really serious. Annabel's dark hair was sticking to her head and face with sweat, her plump cheeks were fiery with fever, and her lips dry. Susan lifted her nightdress and found the rash was still there, worse than the previous night, bright red against her white skin. But even more frightening, Annabel didn't seem to know her.

Running down the stairs to the phone, Susan noticed it was just after half past eight, which meant the surgery would be open. When she got through, to her dismay the same hard-nosed receptionist who'd been so difficult yesterday, said once again that a home visit wasn't necessary, but that Susan could bring Annabel into the surgery now and she'd try to fit her in.

With hindsight, especially after the casual way Dr Wetherall had treated Susan's concern the previous day, she should have disregarded that and phoned for an ambulance immediately. But frantic with worry and desperate for the doctor to see Annabel, she rushed back upstairs and flung on the first things which came to hand. She didn't even stop to comb her hair or dress Annabel. She just wrapped her in a blanket and ran to the surgery with her in her arms.

It wasn't that far, just down the hill and along Hotwells

Road to Dowry Square, a ten-minute walk normally. But the child was heavy to carry, and Susan's fright at hearing her laboured breathing made it seem much further. The rush-hour traffic into Bristol roared past her, and the exhaust fumes seemed to be filling her lungs and making Annabel's breathing even worse.

'The doctor will soon make you better, my darling,' she whispered to Annabel, trying to lift her more comfortably on to her hip.

The snooty blonde receptionist was no more comforting or sympathetic than she'd been the day before, not even when she saw Susan staggering under the weight of the four-year-old, who was barely conscious in her arms. She still curtly ordered her to go into the waiting room and wait her turn.

'He must see her now,' Susan pleaded. 'I think she's got meningitis.'

'Mums always think the worst,' the receptionist said crisply and turned away as if Susan's fears were ridiculous.

The minutes seemed like hours as she sat there waiting, cradling Annabel in her arms. Other patients tried to speak to her and one woman said, 'She don't look at all well,' but Susan was far too anxiously straining her ears for her name to be called to reply.

Then at last her name was called and she rushed into Dr Wetherall's consulting room. He was sitting behind his desk, going through some papers, and barely looked up as she came in.

Although prior to the events of the day before, she hadn't had much reason to see Dr Wetherall, Susan had always thought he was a good doctor, purely because he was good-humoured and patient. He was a big man, perhaps six feet, and a little stout, with thick grey hair and an all-year tan. He told her once he got it out on the golf-course. She knew he had four children of his own, their photographs were on his desk, and once when Annabel was a young baby he'd been sympathetic that Susan was bringing her up alone.

But there was no sign of good humour that day, or patience. He lifted Annabel's nightdress quite roughly, listened to her chest briefly, tucked a thermometer under her arm and checked her ears. It was Susan who pointed out the rash. She explained how it didn't disappear if she pressed a glass on it, and her fears that it was meningitis.

'Nonsense,' Dr Wetherall said, giving her a withering glance. 'I wish I had a pound for every hysterical mother who diagnosed that! She's just got a bit of a fever,' he said, consulting the thermometer. 'Give her Calpol every four hours and plenty of fluids.'

'But I've already been giving her that,' Susan pleaded with him. 'Look at her, she doesn't even know where she is! Please let her go to hospital!'

'She doesn't need hospital,' he insisted, looking cross with Susan for even daring to suggest it. 'She could be coming down with rubella or maybe flu. Home is where she needs to be, tucked into bed. Now, do you want a new prescription for Calpol?'

Livid with rage and frustration, Susan stalked out carrying Annabel and went back to the reception desk. 'Could you phone for an ambulance, please?' she asked the blonde woman. 'Annabel's really ill, I must get some help for her.'

'Did Doctor Wetherall say she needed to go to the hospital?' the receptionist asked, looking down her thin nose.

'No, but he's wrong to think it's only something minor. I know it's serious,' Susan replied, her voice growing high with agitation.

'In that case I certainly can't phone for an ambulance,' the woman said tartly. 'Now, take her home and put her to bed. That's where she belongs.'

Susan couldn't even ask her to ring a taxi, she had no money on her, and she didn't have enough at home anyway. All she could do was rush out, angry tears running down her face.

Fear gave her new strength and speed for she actually ran up Ambra Vale. She knocked at Mr Potter's, three doors away from her, because since he retired he was usually at home, and he was fond of Annabel.

Mr Potter took one look at her and got his car keys. 'You should have come to me first thing,' he said, running a hand over the child's hot forehead. 'I'd have taken you straight away.'

At the Children's Hospital on St Michael's Hill, they did take Susan seriously. The sister in charge in the casualty department took just one look at Annabel before whisking her away into a cubicle. Within minutes a doctor came to her and examined her, and said she was to be admitted immediately.

Susan knew within an hour that Annabel wasn't going to pull round. The doctors and nurses were working hard on her, but it was obvious from the anxiety in their faces that it was to no avail. No one said she should have been brought in earlier, they made no comment that the Dowry Square practice had refused both a home visit and an ambulance. But Susan sensed their anger at such negligence.

Two hours later Annabel slipped away without ever regaining consciousness. Susan had to hope she'd sensed her holding her hand, and felt her kisses on her chubby little face.

The nurses were very kind and sympathetic: they held Susan and did their best to comfort her. But there was no way of comforting her, the only light in her life had been snuffed out. Her baby, her whole reason for living, was dead.

She remembered how as she sat there beside the bed, just looking at Annabel, she tried to convince herself that it was all just a terrible nightmare and any minute she'd wake up at home and find Annabel in bed beside her, strong and healthy. But there was no movement in her chest, no breath when Susan moved closer to kiss her.

The red flush on her face was gone, her dark eyelashes lay on her cheeks like two little fans. She looked as if she was sleeping peacefully. But those fat little fingers would never curl round her mother's again. Susan would never hear her laugh or call her Mummy again. Her dark eyes were closed for ever.

There was a picture of some squirrels on the wall of the little isolation ward. Annabel would have squealed with delight if she'd been conscious when she'd been brought in here. She would have almost certainly given them all names too. But she hadn't even been aware of it, and Susan was never going to see her feeding her pet ones on Brandon Hill again.

Everything that happened after that was a blur now. She supposed someone took her home, maybe they even stayed with her for a while, but she couldn't remember it, or the days that followed. She thought perhaps she got into bed and stayed there.

Only two things stood out, stark and hideous, in her memory. The first was her last view of the little coffin with a teddy bear of pink carnations on top of it, as it slid away at the end of the service in the crematorium. She was aware that almost everyone from her street had turned out for the funeral. She heard their voices expressing their sympathy. Yet she couldn't recall any of their faces, however kind their words were.

The second vivid event was the morning after the funeral when she woke to find herself alone in the house and realized that it *was* all real and Annabel was gone for good.

'What're you bawling for now?' Frankie's voice broke through her reverie, and Susan realized she was indeed crying.

She had been to court again a couple of days before. It was prison procedure for the women to pack up all their belongings when they were going back to court, in case they were granted bail or were moved to another prison. If they were remanded in custody again, as Susan was, on their return to the prison they were often put in a different cell. So now she was with Frankie, the fourteen-stone woman who practically ran the wing. She looked like a man with her short, spiky black hair and barbed wire tattoos round her arms. Susan was very afraid of her.

'I'm sorry,' she said, drying her eyes on the sheet. 'I was thinking about my daughter.' She hadn't actually told Frankie about Annabel herself, but as Julie, her old cellmate, was as much of a gossip as anyone else in here, Susan knew everything she'd told her would be common knowledge.

There was a rustling sound in the dark cell, then a thud as Frankie jumped down from the top bunk. 'It don't do to think about the past in here,' she whispered, her tone unusually gentle. Normally she would thump anyone who disturbed her. It was said she was on remand for taking a Stanley knife to someone's face, and everyone kept out of her way if they could. But now she laid a hand against Susan's cheek and smoothed it. 'I'm yer mate now, and I'll look after yer, darlin'.'

The following Monday Beth visited Susan. She had expected to find her looking forlorn, but instead Susan gave her a wide and welcoming smile, very reminiscent of the ones so long ago.

'You look nice,' she said, looking admiringly at Beth's navy and white pin-striped trouser suit. 'But you always did wear your clothes well.'

'Did I?' Beth said with some surprise as she sat down.

'I thought I looked like a walking rag-bag. Everything I had was just hand-me-downs from Serena.'

'Few of us see ourselves as we really are.' Susan shrugged. 'It usually takes someone else to show us.'

As Susan sounded and looked so perky, even with her recently blacked eye still a vivid purple, Beth assumed she must have found a new friend in the prison, someone who was being kind to her.

'Did someone do that for you?' Beth said.

'There was you,' Susan said, and blushed. 'You made me believe that it was okay to be timid and gentle. But that seems a silly thing to say now I'm stuck in prison for a violent crime.'

Beth half smiled. It was rather unbelievable. Had anyone been asked to guess which girl, at fourteen or fifteen, would end up in trouble, she knew they'd have picked her, never Susan. 'Aside from me?' she asked. 'Someone you met as an adult?'

'I don't think there's actually much difference between the real me and the way others see me,' Susan said with a little grin. 'But there was someone who showed me a glimpse of the woman I'd always wanted to be.'

Beth leaned her arms on the table. Susan's overall appearance was improving. Her hair had some shine in it now, and the ruddy colouring in her face she'd had on her arrest was fading. Beth thought that proved it must have been caused by being outside in all winds and weathers, not by drink as they'd all supposed. The ghastly maroon jogging suit didn't do a lot for her, though. Beth supposed it was just something that had been dished out to her.

'So who was this man who gave you a glimpse of heaven?' she said lightly.

'Liam Johnstone, Annabel's father,' Susan said.

'Tell me about him,' Beth suggested. 'Where did you meet him?'

Susan explained he'd come to do the garden at Luddington, and described what he was like both in looks and character. As she spoke of how close they became, her voice was tender with affection. There was gratitude, too, for he had clearly brightened that period of her life.

'He had finished the job in September, and he had to move on,' she said. 'He kissed me on his last day, and he was as sad as me that we had to part. But he promised he would be back later in the year and said if I was ready to leave by then, he would take me with him.'

'Did you intend to go with him?' Beth asked.

'I thought about nothing else,' Susan said dreamily. 'But I couldn't see how I could just walk out and leave Mother. As it happened, though, I never did find out whether I was brave enough to do it, because first Mother died, then Father six weeks later.'

Beth thought that was a lucky twist of fate, but she couldn't say so. She just grimaced in sympathy and let Susan carry on.

'So there I was left all alone in the house,' she said almost flippantly. 'It was really weird having nothing to do and no one to look after, but I couldn't really be happy that I was free at last. I was too angry with Father for leaving me nothing but his bloody gun.'

'Just a minute.' Beth interrupted her. 'All he left you was his gun?'

'Well, there was two thousand pounds too,' Susan admitted. 'But that was hardly compensation for giving up my life for him and Mother, was it? He left everything else to Martin, who never did a hand's turn to help any of us.'

'But the house, that must have been worth a fortune,' Beth gasped, seeing in her mind's eye the lovely old house of mellow red brick, the beautiful garden and the river flowing by it.

'I hadn't ever considered that, but Martin was all too quick to see it. He didn't give a toss about making me homeless.' Susan sighed. 'He said I could stay on till he'd sold it, but that Christmas he didn't even send me a card. He always was a self-centred, cruel bastard. I don't think he has ever had any feelings for anyone but himself.'

Susan's words brought back a sharp memory for Beth. It was during their second or maybe third holiday together, and they were sitting down by the lock behind Suzie's house, their feet dangling over the edge as they waited for boats to come into the lock. Suzie had mentioned almost in passing that her older brother had come home the previous evening, and she seemed a bit scared of him.

Beth knew he was the same age as Serena, therefore she'd always assumed he treated his little sister the way Serena treated her – little presents, making a fuss of her, and asking her about her schoolwork.

'What's wrong?' she asked. Suzie was biting her lip and she looked a bit pale.

'I hate him coming home,' she admitted in a small voice, turning her head as if to check he wasn't in the garden watching her. 'He's always nasty to me. He says cruel things.'

'Like what?' Beth relied on both Robert and Serena for the comfort and affection she never got from her parents, so she found it hard to imagine anyone's brother or sister could be nasty.

'That I'm fat and stupid,' Suzie said, and a tear trickled down her plump cheek.

'You aren't fat or stupid,' Beth said stoutly. 'You're sweet and pretty. He's the stupid one if he can't see that.'

Beth couldn't remember anything more, perhaps a boat came into the lock and distracted them. She didn't think Suzie ever said anything about her brother again either. But obviously Martin had always been a nasty piece of work. Yet another thing she'd failed to pick up on about her friend.

'Why didn't you contest the will?' Beth asked, her indignation rising. 'The courts are very understanding when someone has spent their life being a carer, then doesn't get left enough to support themselves.'

Susan smiled placidly. 'Maybe I would have if Liam hadn't come back,' she said. 'I had been working myself up into a frenzy of rage. But then, lo and behold, at the beginning of December Liam came knocking on the door, just as he said he would. By then I'd begun to doubt him too, so I'm sure you can imagine how thrilled I was. Suddenly the house and Martin didn't matter a bit.'

Beth noted that Susan's voice took on a husky, sensual quality as she spoke of Liam. This was the adult woman she didn't know, so very different from her childhood friend.

It struck Beth then that she was at a real disadvantage. Susan's character had changed and been remoulded by circumstance, events and the influence of others, and the image she had of it in her head was hopelessly out of date.

She thought it incongruous that a shy, middle-class, somewhat frumpy woman would fall for a man who looked and lived like a gypsy. She wouldn't have expected her old friend to have a baby outside of marriage, or to get involved with the long-haired leader of a commune. And as for killing anyone . . .

Steven was equally baffled, but he didn't have his opinions clouded in the way Beth did. His first view was that Susan was as soft as butter, and a willing victim of her parents, her brother and Reuben. But if that was so, how did she leap out of that docile stance to become an avenger of her child's death?

The answer to this had to be something they hadn't tapped into yet. Beth guessed she and Steven would just have to keep digging until they unearthed it.

'Liam must have been very shocked that both your parents had died?' Beth asked, wanting to be convinced that this man was not another fortune-seeker like Reuben later on.

'He was astounded,' Susan agreed, and smiled as if the memory of that still pleased her. 'Oh, Beth, he was so lovely, I'd never had anyone concerned about me before. He felt bad that I'd handled two funerals without any help, he was furious that Martin was being so evil. But what really made me feel none of that mattered any more was just his presence. He understood how I felt, he wanted to make things better for me.'

Beth wanted to believe that. But she knew that Susan had ended up in Bristol without him. It was a bit like reading the last page of a novel first. 'And so there was nothing any longer to prevent you having a love affair?' she said, raising an eyebrow.

Susan giggled. 'No, nothing and no one,' she said. 'I was very wicked. I opened a bottle of Father's best wine, and we slept in Mother and Father's bed that night. It was so lovely.'

'You deserved something good to happen after all you'd been through,' Beth said. She had a picture in her mind of Susan in a winceyette nightdress under her parents' rose-pink satin eiderdown. Gypsy Liam didn't fit well into that picture at all. 'Was he your first lover?' she asked.

'Yes.' Susan grinned, a little shamefaced. 'I never met anyone stuck at home. I'd given up hope that I ever would. So I had to grab it, didn't I? To hell with the consequences.'

'Did you even stop to think about contraception?' Beth asked.

As she said that, she remembered how she and Suzie

had discussed what they'd do if they got pregnant. They were only fourteen at the time, and neither of them had even kissed a boy, so it was purely hypothetical. Suzie had claimed she would kill herself!

'I don't remember.' Susan giggled. 'But even if I had, I wouldn't have known what to say to Liam about it. Besides, at my age it hardly mattered anyway.'

It would have mattered very much to Beth. But then she had every reason to be suspicious of men.

'So you just leapt into it then?' she prompted.

'Yes. Without a second thought. It's odd how you can remember every detail about some things, but nothing about others,' Susan said pensively. 'There was a full moon that night and it was frosty. As I was drawing the bedroom curtains, Liam came up behind me and we looked out at the garden together. The moon was shining down on the river, it was like there was a silver bridge across the darkness of it, and the frost on the grass was glistening.'

'It sounds very romantic,' Beth said awkwardly.

Susan barely heard what she said. She wasn't listening, she was remembering. Liam had slipped his arms around her and kissed the back of her neck. 'There's magic in the air tonight,' he whispered. 'Everything is just right for us, so don't be scared.'

He slid his hands up under her sweater as they stood there and unfastened her bra. As his hands cupped round her breasts she gasped with pleasure. She entered into a brand-new world that night, one she had never imagined in her wildest dreams. The thrill of his bare chest against hers, the soft wetness of his mouth, the hardness of his body pressing into her soft flesh. There, in her parents' big soft bed, the same one she'd been conceived in thirty-four years before, she discovered what rapture really meant. All her inhibitions left her as he explored her with his fingers and his lips, she heard herself begging for more, and she didn't care if she was behaving like a slut.

'A thirty-four-year-old virgin,' Susan said with a giggle. 'I thought I was too old to fall in love. But it was like being a young girl all over again, Beth. I never guessed it would be like that. I thought I'd be scared, that it would turn out to be smutty and I'd feel bad. I didn't, though, it was wonderful, the best thing that's ever happened to me.'

'And after that night?' Beth was unnerved by the rapturous glow on Susan's face.

'He stayed with me from that night, right through Christmas and on till half-way through January, and we never seemed to sleep.'

'What were your plans?' Beth asked. She knew now why Susan hadn't felt able to tell Steven all this. 'Did your brother know you had a man there?'

'I didn't know or care if Martin knew,' Susan laughed, showing those small, even teeth Beth had so often envied her for as a child. Surprisingly, they were still as white now as they had been then. 'I felt so strong, so happy, he hardly even crossed my mind. I didn't have any plans. I was living right in the present, the past and the future weren't important any more.'

'But you said Liam only stayed until mid-January. How did you manage when he went away?'

'It was tough to be alone again, but he had to work,' Susan said carefully, as if this was something she'd told herself a hundred times before. 'You see, he looked after gardens all over the place, some he'd been doing for years. He couldn't let his customers down just because of me. Sometimes he was gone as long as four weeks, but mostly it was only one or two. I tried hard not to get upset by it.'

'So how long did this go on for?' Beth asked. If Annabel was born in April of 1986, she had to have been conceived the previous July, around eight months after Susan's parents died.

'Right up till Martin finally sold the house in August,' Susan said. 'The fun we had that summer! We used to go skinny-dipping in the river at night, we'd get drunk and dance out on the lawn, we often made love out there too. I've never had so much fun. He made me feel so sexy and naughty. That's what I meant about the glimpse of the woman I'd always wanted to be.'

Beth began to feel irrationally irritated. She didn't want to hear above love-making on dewy grass, or dips in the river. She wanted to know whether Liam was on the make, how Susan came to live in Bristol alone, and all the relevant details. 'Oh, come on, Sue,' she said impatiently. 'You must have been in the early stages of pregnancy by August. You weren't children, for goodness' sake tell me what happened to Liam.'

A cloud passed over Susan's face. 'Martin turned up

unexpectedly one day. Liam wasn't there at the time, but Martin had found out about us, and he was furious with me. He said I was a half-witted slut and asked how I dared have some gypsy living in his house. He said I'd got to get out.'

'Are you saying Liam skipped off before you left there then?'

'No, he didn't.' Susan riled up in indignation. 'We were in love, everything was wonderful between us. He was only working away for a few days. When he returned I told him what Martin had said, and we talked about what we should do. He wanted me to find a place in Stratford, but I knew it was hard to find flats or houses to rent. I also thought I'd be happier making a new start somewhere else, where no one knew me. I didn't want people gossiping about me.'

Beth nodded. 'But why Bristol?'

'We used to go there sometimes when I was little,' Susan explained. 'We stayed with some relation of Mother's in Clifton. It had always seemed a wonderful, exciting place to me, what with the zoo up on the Downs, the parks, the big shops and the docks. It wasn't too far for Liam to travel to his customers, and we thought he'd soon find new ones there too.'

'So Liam came with you then?'

'Well, no.' Susan faltered momentarily. 'You see, I didn't realize I was pregnant then, and as he had a big job he had to finish, I said I'd come here to find a place for us.'

Beth wondered how a woman who had hardly been

out of her home town before could possibly trek off alone to a big city. And if Liam was so caring, why did he let her?

'Right! You came to Bristol and found the house in Ambra Vale. Now, what about Liam?' she asked bluntly.

'I couldn't contact him when he was working, he always phoned me. I found the house, got back to the house in Luddington to pack, but he still didn't phone. I was getting panicky then, but I figured if the worst came to the worst and he hadn't phoned by the time I had to leave, I would leave the Bristol address with the neighbours and they'd pass it on to him. But I never saw him again.'

'So the last contact you had with him was before you went off to Bristol?' Beth felt she had to get that straight.

Susan nodded glumly. 'I should have left my address with other people too, left a letter for him at The Bell in Shottery where he used to drink. I reckon Martin told the neighbours not to tell him where I was.'

Given what Susan had already said about Martin, Beth thought it was quite likely he did put his oar in, but it didn't say much for Liam's love for her that he was so easily deterred. She thought the most likely explanation was that he was already feeling trapped before the Luddington house was sold. Maybe he even encouraged her to go to Bristol so that he would never run into her again by accident.

But she wasn't going to air that view. It was kinder to let Susan think he really couldn't find her.

'It must have been awful for you,' she said instead. 'Especially when you discovered you were pregnant too.'

'Oddly enough, finding I was pregnant helped me get over him,' Susan said pensively. 'I know he did really love me, but he was a free spirit, he'd lived like a gypsy for most of his life. Even if he had managed to find me, I don't think he would have fitted into an ordinary sort of life.'

'I'm glad you can be so generous towards him,' Beth said with a touch of sarcasm. 'I don't think I'd have been if I'd had to bring his daughter up alone.'

'If it wasn't for him coming along when he did, I would never have known love,' Susan said, almost as a reprimand. 'You must know what I mean, Beth? Falling in love, making love, that's what turns you into a real woman, isn't it?'

Beth felt inexplicably angry as she drove back to the office later. She couldn't understand why Susan was so accepting of Liam's desertion. All that twaddle about how falling in love made her into a real woman was just so much hogwash. She was pathetic! She'd let her brother take that beautiful house without so much as a protest. She should have taken legal action against Dr Wetherall when Annabel died, but instead she lay down and waited for some hippie guru to fleece her!

Then, when she was left with absolutely nothing, she finally decided to take some action and shot two people!

She had to be mad!

Beth's mood wasn't helped during the afternoon by a series of clients who were either blatantly lying to her or so cocky about what they'd done that she felt like slapping them. By the time she left the office at five, she was tense with anger and frustration.

When she arrived home and opened the front door to find two inches of water in the hall, that was the last straw.

It was clear the washing machine she'd left running that morning was the culprit. The water had run out into the hall, and now it was seeping on to the living-room carpet too. She let out a bellow of pure rage, punched the wall with her fist and burst into hysterical tears.

'Beth!'

She turned on hearing her name being called to see Steven running up the stairs. 'What on earth's the matter?' he called out.

'Look!' she snarled, pointing a shaking finger at the hall floor. 'The bloody washing machine!'

He leapt up the last few steps, peered into the hall, then put one hand on her arm. 'Calm down. It probably looks worse than it is.'

'Calm down!' she yelled at him. 'This has just about put the hat on the day I've had. Any minute now I'll get the people downstairs complaining their ceiling's coming down.'

'No you won't, I expect the floor is concrete,' he said calmly, and without any hesitation he slipped off his shoes and socks and waded into the flat.

Beth slumped against the wall, still sobbing. Steven reappeared a couple of minutes later with a bucket and cloth and a couple of towels. He put the towels down by the living-room doorway to prevent any more water running in there, and began mopping up.

'It's not that bad,' he said from his bent-over position. 'It's mostly run out here, the kitchen floor has a slight slope. Lucky it's all tiled. The carpet will soon dry, and as it's clean water, it won't leave a mark.'

His optimistic view did nothing to help Beth. She knew she was showing herself up, but she couldn't stop crying, or even help. She stood there helplessly, tears streaming down her face as he mopped and wrung out the cloth again and again.

'Right. Come on in now,' he said as he finally stood up. He held out his hand to her. 'Go and sit down. I'll just finish off in the kitchen and make you a cup of tea.'

A few minutes later Beth had a mug of tea in her hands and her sobs had turned to mere occasional sniffs and gasps. 'I'm sorry you had to see me like this,' she said, feeling very embarrassed. 'I don't know what came over me.'

She had never imagined Steven to be so practical, he had always struck her as one of those men who couldn't change a car wheel or even put in a new light bulb. She supposed that was purely because he was always so untidy. But he had been so quick and thorough, and his blue eyes didn't hold a trace of mockery.

'We all have days like that sometimes,' he said sympathetically, perching on the edge of the couch as he sipped his tea. 'Want to tell me about it?'

She looked at him and felt ashamed. His feet were still

bare, his trousers rolled up to show very white, bony ankles. He'd taken his jacket off, and the shirt beneath it hadn't been ironed on either the sleeves or the back. His hair needed cutting. He looked like the one who needed looking after.

He had such a nice face, she thought, kind eyes, full lips that suggested a generous nature. She really couldn't understand why she'd been such a bitch to him in the past.

'There's no sensible explanation,' she admitted. 'Susan irritated me this morning, then I just got more and more wound up this afternoon. When I opened the door and saw the water, I just flipped. What brought you round here anyway?'

'I tried to catch up with you as you left the office, just to ask how you got on with Susan today, but you were going like the clappers.' He grinned. 'My car was in the multi-storey near here, and as you'd left the front door open, I just came in on the impulse. I heard you yell out, and I thought you'd been burgled or something.'

'I feel stupid now,' she said sheepishly, dabbing at her eyes with a tissue and finding to her further shame that her mascara had smeared all over her face. 'But thank you for mopping it up.'

'It was nothing,' he said. 'I'll pull the machine out in a minute and see if I can see what went wrong with it. I'd better push off then and let you have a lie-down or whatever.'

'No, don't go yet,' she said, aware she owed him at least a bit of news about Susan in return for what he'd done. 'I'll just go and wash my face. I must look awful.'

In the bathroom Beth stared at herself in horror. It wasn't just her white face streaked with black, but the realization she'd completely lost control of herself. And in front of Steven of all people!

She could hear him pulling the washing machine out in the kitchen, and she was reminded of how often she'd been sharp with him in the past. She really didn't deserve his kindness now. She fervently hoped he would keep this incident to himself. She could imagine how gleeful some of the other office staff would be to hear she was capable of hysterics.

As she went back into the kitchen, Steven had pushed the machine back under the work surface. He had the hose in his hand.

'It's split,' he said, showing her a small hole. 'I'll take it away with me and get a replacement, it's an easy job to refit it.'

'You've been so very kind,' she said. 'I really appreciate it.'

'Maidens in distress have always been my thing,' he said with a smile. 'Do you feel like telling me about Susan, or has that got to wait?'

'Liam, Annabel's father, deserted her,' Beth said tartly. 'She's so pathetic she thinks he did her a favour just by making her pregnant.'

'I wouldn't say that's pathetic,' he said indignantly. 'Most women want a baby, maybe she wanted one far more than she wanted a permanent relationship.'

'It was irresponsible,' she retorted.

Steven smiled. 'We're all guilty of that sometimes,' he said. 'So are you saying Susan wasn't cut up about him vanishing?'

'She didn't appear to be, she was too full of little homilies like "Love turns us into real women". I found it all really annoying.'

'Ah, so that's what set you off.' He laughed. 'Shall I make us more tea? You might as well get it all off your chest in one go.'

Over a second cup of tea, Beth told him everything Susan had told her, including what Liam was like, and how Martin inherited the house and threw her out. 'She should have stuck up for herself,' she said angrily. 'Why do people let others walk all over them?'

'Some of us aren't tough enough to fight back,' he said.

Beth heard a note of wistfulness in his voice and she looked hard at him.

'Why? Who's walking all over you?' she asked.

He opened his mouth to say something, but closed it again. She knew she had struck a chord.

'Come on, tell me,' she said gently. 'Better out than in.'

He scratched his head and looked away from her. 'I can't,' he said eventually.

'Why? Because you're afraid I'll pass it on? Do I strike you as a gossip?'

'No, of course not,' he said quickly. He was blushing now, he looked like a guilty schoolboy.

'I don't think you'd tell everyone in the office about this incident,' she said. 'So please trust me.'

He sighed. 'Okay. It's Anna,' he blurted out. 'I know I

should get tough but I can't. She's got a problem with drink, you see.'

Beth was astounded. She had never met Anna, but she'd seen a photograph of her in Steven's office, a pretty woman with dark hair and a wide, vivacious smile. Right from her first meeting with Steven, Beth had always had an image of him leading the 'ideal' life.

She knew roughly where he lived, a desirable neighbourhood of semi-detached houses with neat gardens. Since she'd met Sophie and Polly and seen how well behaved they were, she had imagined Anna as the prop of the PTA, a woman who could make a prize-winning sponge cake at the same time as she ran up a fancy-dress costume.

Yet suddenly Sophie's remark about her mother liking wine too much came back to her, and she remembered Steven's reaction.

'Have you gone anywhere for help? How is it affecting the girls?' she asked.

'It's making the girls very anxious.' Steven's voice shook and his eyes were bleak. 'They never know what to expect when they get back from school. They can't rely on their mother for anything. It's me who keeps everything together, or tries to. As for getting help, Anna won't admit there is a problem.'

'I'm so sorry, Steven,' Beth said. 'I never guessed there was anything wrong, you always seem so cheerful.'

He shrugged. 'That's one of Anna's many complaints about me, I'm too cheerful, too boring, too everything for her.'

'Where are the girls now?' Beth asked.

'At a friend's house, they are staying over tonight,' he said. 'Otherwise I'd be rushing back to make their tea. But I didn't mean to spill this out. I'd better go, you've had quite enough drama for one day.'

'No, stay and have supper with me,' she said impulsively. He'd been kind to her and she was going to reciprocate.

'I'd like that,' he said, and half smiled. 'But I don't want to talk about my problem with Anna any more. Just admitting there is one is enough for today.'

As Beth cooked some pasta and made a Bolognese sauce, Steven sat on a kitchen chair and listened as she told him more about the visit with Susan.

They talked in general about Susan as they ate the meal. Her life taking care of her mother, and how unfair it was that her father left everything to Martin.

'I ought to talk to him,' Steven said. 'I mean, we do need to confirm that it is all true.'

'Do you doubt it then?'

'No, I don't,' he said. 'She strikes me as someone that was born to lose. Too accepting, too anxious to please. I suppose that's why she rushed full tilt into a love affair with the first man that came along,' he added sympathetically. 'She must have been so lonely. I expect it was much the same with Reuben too. No wonder she went right off the rails when the second romance failed.'

Beth put their empty plates into the dishwasher, made some coffee and suggested they went into the sitting room.

'I'm puzzled why she went for two such similar men, though,' Beth said thoughtfully as she sat down opposite Steven. 'If she got her fingers burned by Liam with his free spirit ideal, surely alarm bells would have rung when Reuben came on the scene?'

'I think most of us go for the same types again and again,' Steven said. 'Even when we know what the outcome will be.'

'Is that personal experience or merely observation?' Beth asked wryly.

'Both. I've always been attracted to complicated women, mostly with disastrous results. Anna once said it's because I'm so boring I have to pep my life up,' he said with a humourless laugh.

For some reason that riled Beth on his behalf. Maybe it had taken her a year to see there was more to Steven than an overgrown boy scout, but Anna was the one who'd married him and had his children. It wasn't fair that she should ridicule him now and destroy his self-esteem.

'I often think those who label others as boring are the real bores,' she said pointedly. 'They're too wrapped up in themselves to see or hear anything else.'

'Maybe that's so, but I suppose I am dull company compared with men who go womanizing, boozing or gambling. I have always played it safe, tried to maintain the standards I was brought up with. I seem to be a target for women who like that about me at first, but then once they've got me, ridicule me for it.'

Beth sensed his pain, and her heart went out to him for it reminded her of the way her father treated her mother. 'Did Anna have a problem with drink when you met her?' she asked.

'Not a problem. She was very much a party animal. Vivacious, fun-loving. Drinking tends to go with that, of course. All her previous boyfriends had been very possessive, she said they didn't like her to shine, tried to keep her under lock and key. She made it very clear to me that if I became like that she'd drop me. I've never been the jealous kind, I enjoyed seeing her being the life and soul of the party. She was beautiful, witty, and I loved the wildness about her.'

'I expect she secretly wanted you to be possessive too,' Beth said. 'Maybe she didn't feel valued without it.'

'Well, why say she hated it?' he said, frowning with puzzlement.

Beth smiled. 'Women can be very contrary. Anyway, when did the problem start?'

'After Sophie was born. She was fine with just Polly, we still went out quite a lot, had friends round too. But then when Sophie came along two years later, she had postnatal depression for a while. When she came out of that, she seemed to resent being tied down by motherhood. She kept talking about going back to work – she had been a graphic artist before she had the children – but she never actually attempted to find a job.'

Beth nodded. 'How did the drinking start?'

'At first, when the girls were tiny, it was purely social. I tried to make things better for her by babysitting so she could go out with her old friends. She often came home legless. Then she would have girlfriends in during the day, and that usually involved a bottle or two of wine. Before long I was regularly arriving home to find it in a terrible mess, and Anna half cut. It just progressed from there. Now she's rarely sober.'

'Poor you,' Beth said, remembering how sweet his children were and understanding now why he hadn't wanted her to go home with him that evening. 'Do you ever take a tough line with her?'

'I try,' he said, his voice faltering. 'But I know if I get too heavy she'll use that as an excuse to leave me.'

'Would that be such a bad thing?' she asked gently, feeling deeply sorry for him.

'I couldn't bear the girls to lose their mother,' he said. 'She might not be much of one, but she's all they've got.'

'I think they'd be happier without her,' she said. 'I know because of how it was with my father.'

Beth never told people about her childhood and the only reason she felt compelled to tell Steven about it now was because it seemed relevant to how it was for Polly and Sophie. She explained how isolated and distressed she felt as a child because of her father's unreasonable behaviour, and how her mother had stuck by him for exactly the same reasons Steven had just brought up about Anna.

'He wasn't a drunk,' she said. 'But he was a waster and a mean-minded bully. I suppose his problem was that he felt inadequate, his father, grandfather and great-grandfather had all been real go-getters. I imagine too he was spoiled rotten as a child.

'Anna has every right to drink herself to death if she thinks that is great fun, and sober people are boring,' she said forcefully. 'But she has no right to bring you and the children down with her. The worst thing about people like Anna, and my father, is that they have such huge egos. By pandering to them, letting them do what they want to do, you are stroking that ego and making them feel even more powerful.'

'She isn't egotistical,' he insisted. 'She can't help it.'

'Rot,' Beth said heatedly. 'That's just a cop-out from dealing with it on her part. "Poor little me, I can't help swigging away at a bottle and then crashing out and forgetting to feed my kids!" If you start to believe that, Steven, she'll never sober up! If my mother had left home with us kids when we were small, we'd have been no worse off financially than we were at home. We wouldn't have had to witness the ugliness. We could have had a home where there was peace and laughter.'

She paused for a moment, not sure whether or not she was wise to continue. But she decided to do so anyway. 'I grew to hate my father, Steven. Hate him so much I'd have cheerfully killed him given the right opportunity. Polly and Sophie will grow to hate Anna if you let it go on. And worse still, they might very well become alcoholics themselves, or find themselves another one to marry or live with. That's what children of alcoholics do.'

Suddenly Steven began to cry. Beth looked at him in horror from across the coffee table. His face crumpled as the tears ran down his cheeks. It was a pitiful sight. She was aware she'd been very blunt, but she hadn't thought for one moment she'd said anything awful enough to make him break down.

'I'm so sorry, Steven,' she said in alarm and went round the coffee table to sit next to him. 'I should have kept my opinions to myself.'

In her need to comfort him, she put her arms around him and drew his face down on to her shoulder, smoothing his hair, the way she used to with her mother when her father went for her. She had never repeated it with anyone else since, and she was surprised she could.

'Look, don't take my word for it,' she said. 'Go to an expert, talk to them and get them to tell you what to do.'

'It isn't what you said,' he sniffed. 'I think it's only the release of talking about it. I hide it every day, I even tell the girls Mummy's ill. I never guessed you'd had a blighted childhood either. It was so brave of you to share it with me.'

'We're a fine pair,' she said, and tried to laugh, but her eyes were prickling with tears too. 'I've never told anyone that stuff before.'

She let go of Steven and went out into the kitchen to get some brandy for them both. 'I think we need something for the shock,' she said as she brought two glasses back in.

He had dried his eyes now and seemed almost composed again. 'You are a curious, fascinating woman,' he said, swirling the brandy round in its glass. 'I would have laid bets that a flood wouldn't faze you, and I certainly didn't expect you'd be the sort to give a shoulder to cry on.'

'Both were abnormal behaviour for me,' she agreed. 'But it's been a funny sort of day all round.'

She went on to tell him what Susan had said that annoyed her that morning. 'All that stuff about skinny-dipping in the river,' she said. 'She seemed so girlish and giggly about it. I think she wanted to prove to me that she had been desirable.' She stopped short, aware she wasn't making much sense. 'I didn't think it was appropriate to go on about that kind of thing,' she added lamely.

'She is a little odd at times,' Steven agreed. 'Take the gun! If that was all my father left me, I think I'd have thrown it in the river, I certainly wouldn't have kept it all that time with a small child in the house. And why take it to Wales? It wouldn't be my idea of a keepsake.'

'She never told me that she could shoot, I mean when we were kids,' Beth said. 'Most children would, don't you think? It would be something to boast about.'

'Maybe her father told her to keep it a secret,' Steven suggested. 'It is a bit of a strange thing to teach a girl.'

'I think we could do with talking to all the men in her life,' Beth said. 'It might throw a different light on her. She can be very elusive at times.'

They had a second brandy, and then a third, and all at once Beth realized that she was talking to Steven as she'd never been able to talk to a man before. They discussed cases they'd been involved with before, told each other funny stories from the courts, and discussed the guilt they both felt when someone they were positive was guilty, went free. Steven was as fascinated as she was as to why one person from a family could become a criminal, while the rest, with an identical upbringing, were sober and upright citizens. Or why, in a whole family of villains, one would go straight.

'Look at my family,' Beth said. 'All three of us have turned out to be successful and well adjusted, despite our father.' She paused to grin at Steven. 'Well, Robert and Serena are well adjusted anyway, with much nicer natures than me.'

'But you were the youngest, and you probably saw the worst of your father,' he suggested. 'You realized very early on how weak your mother was, and were determined to be different.'

'Different was what I always felt,' she said grimly. 'I asked Serena once if she felt that way too, but she said she didn't. At school I was always on the outside looking in. Not bullied or laughed at exactly, just apart. I just didn't seem to have whatever quality is needed to make one acceptable.'

'I wasn't really one of the in crowd either,' he said with a smile. 'I was labelled a swot, and as I was no great shakes at sport, I just kind of stuck with what I knew best. But I was happy at university, were you?'

'Well, I didn't feel quite so weird.' Beth smiled. 'Mostly because there were plenty of girls much odder than me around.'

She poured them both another drink. 'I kind of re-invented myself for university anyway,' she went on. 'I dressed in a mysterious manner, big black hats, long coats, long scarves trailing behind me. Once I'd struck that pose it was easy to act out the part. One of my flatmates used to call me Greta Garbo.' She giggled.

'That's kind of how I saw you when you first joined the firm,' Steven admitted. 'Aloof, beautiful, but with a heart like a glacier. How did you see me?'

Beth was touched that he'd thought her beautiful, so she couldn't be entirely honest and admit she thought he was a nonentity.

'Kind of like a boy scout, I think,' she said thoughtfully. 'A bit too helpful, too earnest. You improved on closer inspection.'

'Anna says I am ingratiating,' he said dolefully. 'I'm not, am I?'

'No, you aren't,' she said firmly, despite having thought that about him in the past. 'It sounds to me as if Anna is just nasty to justify her own behaviour.'

'Most of the women I've known have been a bit nasty,' he said with a cheeky grin.

'You know why?' she asked. 'It's because you are too nice. Some women, including me I expect, see that as something to crush.'

'So what sort of men do you go for?' he asked.

'None,' she replied. 'Not any more. It's too bloody hurtful.' As the words came out of her mouth, Beth realized she was getting drunk. Sober, she would never make statements like that which gave away so much about herself.

He took her hand in his and squeezed it. Just that, no platitudes or asking for an explanation. 'So we're both walking wounded,' he said after a few moments' silence.

'And we spend our days defending more people like us.'

Beth had never thought of herself as being anything like the people she defended, but all at once she saw it was so, and for no reason she could explain she began to cry again.

'What is it, Beth?' Steven asked, and his arms went round her. 'Try and tell me.'

'I wouldn't know where to begin.' She sobbed against his shoulder.

He put one hand under her chin and lifted her face up to his, looking down at her with tenderness. 'I've seen a change in you since Susan turned up in your life again. So why don't you start by telling me how it was between you two?'

Chapter eleven

'We met on the bank of the river at Stratford-upon-Avon,' Beth said. 'Both ten, both alone, and I suppose, with hindsight, she was as desperate for company as I was. But at that time I thought I was unique in being lonely and anxious. To me, Suzie looked as if she hadn't a care in the world.'

She went back then, explaining how she was in Stratford staying with her aunt because her father had beaten her mother up. But as she went on to describe her first meeting with Susan, she found herself slipping back, recalling things she thought she'd forgotten.

It was very hot, and she was roasting even though she was only wearing the shorts and blouse Aunt Rose had bought her that morning. It had been embarrassing because she had said neither of her two dresses was fit to be seen out in, yet it was wonderful to be given clothes which weren't passed down, and that really fitted her.

Overall, Beth was glad she had called Aunt Rose and told her that Father had hurt Mother. Mother was still cross with her about it, but Beth felt she was secretly glad to be having a holiday with her sister.

Her aunt and uncle's house was only a small terraced

one, but it was a dream house to Beth, bright, clean and very comfortable. Mother had been put in the guest room, which was very pink, frilly and flouncy, similar to the way Aunt Rose dressed. Beth was in the cosy box-room. Yet the best thing about the house was that it was so close to the town centre. You only had to walk a few yards down the street, turn the corner and there you were right by the shops. Beth hardly ever went beyond Battle at home, and there wasn't much in the way of shops there. Stratford-upon-Avon had all kinds. Amazing toy and gift shops, smart coffee bars, you could buy anything from a quarter of sweets to a fur coat. Most of the people visiting here, however – and there were so many of them – seemed more interested in taking photographs of everything, from the old Tudor buildings to the flower displays, than buying stuff. But then Aunt Rose had said all these hundreds of people only came to see William Shakespeare's birthplace. Beth had only ever heard that name, she had no idea what the man had done that made him so fascinating. She hadn't liked to ask either, for fear of looking stupid.

They had arrived on Saturday evening after a very long and boring drive. On Sunday they'd stayed in all day because all the grown-ups were tired. Beth had been really worried they'd remain the way they were yesterday, with Mother crying and Aunt Rose flapping around making cups of tea and muttering things like 'I saw this coming years ago, but you wouldn't listen to me.'

But today Uncle Eddie had gone back to work. He fitted out caravans, and Aunt Rose said he was a craftsman, in a tone that sounded as if she meant Mother should have found someone like him. As soon as they'd got back from the morning's shopping trip, Aunt Rose had said Beth could go out and explore and leave the grown-ups to have a real chat. As her aunt gave her half a crown and told her to buy herself a bun or something for lunch, Beth got the idea she was expected to stay out till tea-time.

It was thrilling at first, so many shops to look in, so many people to watch. A great many of them were foreigners and she made a game of guessing where they came from. But it got a bit lonely after a while, and it was too hot for walking around, so she'd come down by the river to watch the pleasure boats, and that's when she saw the girl sitting under a tree.

She was wearing one of those smocked-front dresses, with puffed sleeves and a sash tied at the back, that Beth had always longed for. It was pink with mauve flowers and the smocking was mauve too. Highly polished blue sandals, snowy-white ankle socks and shiny bobbed hair completed Beth's idea of a kid who had everything, and she thought she was probably waiting for her mother to finish her shopping.

Girls at home who looked the way this one did always ignored Beth, so it took all her courage to get up the nerve to speak to her. But to her astonishment, the girl seemed to want to make a new friend as much as she did. She said her name was Suzie Wright, that she lived in Luddington, a nearby village, and she was waiting for her father to finish work to go home with him.

Beth had never found anyone before so easy to talk to.

Suzie didn't put on any airs and graces, not about her clothes, or anything. She said she was pretty dumb compared with the other girls in her class, but she didn't seem dumb to Beth because they'd read all the same books. In fact, she even knew that Battle was where the Battle of Hastings took place, and explained that William Shakespeare was England's greatest playwright.

Yet the thing which Beth liked most of all about Suzie was that she didn't seem to see Beth as some kind of freak because she was so tall and thin. The thrill of being told she looked lovely in shorts, that her curly hair was beautiful and that she had colouring like Snow White carried her home that afternoon on a cloud. She prayed that Aunt Rose would let her borrow her bike the following day and that she'd be allowed to go off and meet Suzie. She thought she'd just curl up and die if they refused.

Beth picked up a lot about her mother that holiday that she hadn't realized before. She was as much of a snob as Father. Aunt Rose said when they were arguing that Alice had only married Montague because she thought he had pots of money and lived in a grand house. Rose said she suffered from something called 'delusions of grandeur' and all she was getting now was her come-uppance for marrying a man she didn't love just so she could have position. Rose said that if she had any guts at all, Alice would take Beth and leave him, but she added that she knew she wouldn't do that because she was just as bad as Montague and wouldn't work for a living.

Mother had insisted that none of it was true, yet the

first thing she asked Beth about Suzie was what school she went to. Of course Beth didn't know, but Aunt Rose seemed to, and she was really sarcastic. She said, 'You needn't worry that your daughter's mixing with riff-raff here, I know of that family. The girl goes to The Croft, a private school. Mr Wright is the manager of a big insurance company and his house is one of the biggest in Luddington.'

After that information had been digested, Beth was free to meet Suzie every afternoon. Maybe Mother thought she always played in the Wrights' garden, but then she never actually asked. She was only too happy to be free to read or go out with her sister.

In fact, Beth only went inside Suzie's house twice in the whole month. Mostly Suzie was already waiting at the gate with her bike when Beth came along, and she seemed eager to get right away. Likewise, Beth only took Suzie to Aunt Rose's a few times, and always whisked her out again quickly, using the excuse that the shops or the park were more interesting.

'Looking back, from an adult standpoint,' Beth said to Steven, after she'd told him about how she met Susan and the impact she'd had on her, 'we were both hiding our family secrets. I didn't want Susan to know we were really poor, or that my father was a pompous wife-beater. She didn't want me to see that her granny was barmy. There was something more, too. We both felt inadequate in different ways. Suzie saw me as fearless, clever, always with a new idea up my sleeve for something exciting we could do. She wanted to be like that too. I wanted to be like her, sweet, feminine and genuinely classy, with the happiest family and the loveliest house in the world.'

'When did you start to wise up about each other?' Steven asked.

'I don't think we ever did, or perhaps our simplistic views of each other were actually very close to how we really were then,' Beth sighed and looked at Steven helplessly. 'But when you only see someone for a month in the summer, it's a bit like a holiday romance, isn't it? You don't get to see the ugly or boring bits. We did learn some things about each other, we both admitted we hadn't got any other real friends. She told me her granny was a trial, I told her my father was a bully. But as these things were never witnessed, neither of us could know how bad it was. I suppose, too, when we were together we wanted to forget that for eleven months of the year our lives were pretty miserable.'

'But you kept in touch with letters for those other eleven months?'

'Oh yes, a letter about every two or three weeks. But you must know how kids write to each other? Just sort of statements about what you've done, what books you've read. I expect when Susan wrote to Copper Beeches she imagined it was quite grand. You see, I used to mention the stables or the long drive in conversation. She didn't know about the broken windows, the holes in the roof or the mice all over the kitchen.

'Likewise, I only ever imagined her granny sitting knitting in her rocking-chair, with Susan's mother in a clean apron, making cakes. I certainly didn't visualize shitty sheets, or the old girl wandering around the house yelling her head off.'

'So you went up to Stratford for how many summers?' Steven asked.

'Five. After the first one I was put on the train alone. Mother stayed home with Father. But the summer we were going to be sixteen, Father wouldn't let me go.'

'Why?'

'Because he was mean-spirited. He didn't want me to have any fun,' Beth said vehemently. 'You see, Susan wrote after her granny died early that year, and invited me to stay at her house. We hoped that we might get to go dancing again – we'd been once the previous year – and chat up some boys.' She paused and half smiled.

'The year before, we'd spent most of the holiday looking for boys, we'd hang around in coffee bars, pretending to be French, you know, all that silly stuff teenage girls do. We reckoned that as we'd both be sixteen by August, with our exams over, we'd be adults.'

Beth could see herself reading that letter of invitation from Suzie. It was April, and she was sitting up in her bedroom, reading and re-reading it, her heart thumping with excitement.

The rain was so heavy she could hear water pinging in the tin bath left out on the landing under the leak in the roof. It was freezing in her bedroom, and she'd got the eiderdown around her. But just thinking about Stratford and Suzie made her feel warmer. She got herself a pencil and paper and huddling back under the eiderdown, worked out how much money she would have by August if she saved every penny of her paper-round money.

She only got £1 5s a week, and for that she had to cycle over ten miles every day, starting at half past six in the morning, regardless of whether it was raining or snowing. But she had to do it. When she was fourteen her father had told her he had no intention of paying out for anything for her any more, not even clothes or pocket money. He said it was time she earned her own money.

That was rich coming from him, as the most pocket money she ever got from him was the odd shilling on the rare occasions he was in a good mood. As for clothes, they were Serena's hand-me-downs, and mostly so old-fashioned she'd die rather than be seen wearing them in public. It was Serena who gave her mother money for her school uniform and shoes too.

Beth didn't mind doing the paper round in the spring and summer. Having some money of her own to buy a few new clothes and not feel ashamed if she bumped into anyone from school at the weekend made up for getting up at half past six. But in the winter it was awful. She had to set out while it was still dark, and some of the lanes she had to ride up were thick with mud. She got chapped cheeks, hands and legs from the cold and wet, and there was no such thing in their house as a hot bath before she went off to school. She had to try to wash the mud off her legs with cold water, then change into her uniform, wolf down her breakfast and cycle off to Battle again, still stiff with the cold.

Yet with spring on its way, and the promise of August in Stratford, it would soon be all right again, and maybe in September she could get a Saturday job in a shop instead. Turning back to her sums, she thought she could save at least £15 by August, enough to buy a really trendy dress and some shoes to go dancing.

The cold in her bedroom made her go downstairs again a little later for she had some homework to do. There was no sign of her mother, and Beth assumed she'd gone into the village, so she spread her books out on the kitchen table, as near to the stove as she could get, and began working.

Ever since she'd seen the Wrights' kitchen in Ludding-ton, the one at home made her feel terribly ashamed. It was clean – her mother scrubbed at it constantly – but it was so old and scruffy that cleaning didn't make it look any better. Many of the quarry tiles on the floor were broken, some missing altogether, the paint on the cupboards was dingy and chipped. Nothing shone the way she remembered it did in the Wrights' kitchen, everything looked as worn out as her mother. The gloom didn't help either. Two of the window-panes were broken and covered over with cardboard. The only thing that made it bearable was that it was warm from the stove.

Her father came in a few minutes later. 'Where's your mother?' he asked brusquely. 'I haven't had my morning coffee.'

'I'll get it for you,' she said, getting up from the table, but wishing she dared ask why he couldn't get it himself. She had been told by her mother that as a young man her father had looked just like Robert did now, tall and very handsome, with wide shoulders and thick black hair. But there was nothing admirable about Monty's appearance any more. He was very overweight, with flesh hanging around his jowls like a bloodhound's and a huge stomach. His hair was thin, grey and lank, he had food stains down the front of his cardigan, and the collar of his shirt was none too clean either. But the thing Beth hated most of all about him was his eyes. They were brown, speckled with green, and very cold. For all his inactivity, they darted round every room, studied every face, searching for something to complain about. If he had ever had any good qualities, Beth thought that he had lost them all now, and it showed.

Beth had asked Serena if she knew why he was such a pig. Serena said she thought it was all tied up with him failing to match up to his ancestors, and being over-indulged as a child. She claimed that like most bullies he was really a coward, afraid to go out and get a proper job in case he failed, and as long as he was still getting just enough rent from the remaining few tenants he had, he could still pretend he was Lord of the Manor.

But that explanation did nothing to make Beth like him any better.

She put the kettle on, and while it was boiling went to the pantry to get the coffee. The jar was empty.

'There's no coffee left,' she said, immediately feeling tense. 'I expect Mother's gone to get some.'

'No coffee?' he roared out. 'She knows I always have it at eleven.'

'I'll make you some tea instead,' Beth said hurriedly.

'One drinks tea at breakfast. Only labourers drink tea at eleven in the morning,' Father retorted scathingly.

He was almost as fond of pointing out labourers' habits as he was of saying he had 'a position to maintain'. He said labourers kept coal in their baths, wiped their noses on their sleeves and had a great many other disgusting habits. He was one to talk – Beth had seen him piss out of his study window because he was too lazy to walk upstairs, and he rarely even shaved in the winter, let alone had a bath.

Beth tried to appease him by saying her mother wouldn't be long, and even suggested she rode into the village to get some coffee herself.

'Do that,' he snapped at her.

Beth glanced out of the kitchen window at the heavy rain and shuddered. She'd already got wet once that morning on her paper round and her coat and outdoor shoes were still soaked. But she knew that if she complained he would clout her.

'May I have some money then?' she asked.

'Money?' he roared out. 'Your mother has the house-keeping money.'

'But she isn't here,' she pointed out.

'Then use your own,' he said.

Later, Beth was to wonder whatever possessed her to say she was saving her money for her holiday in Stratford. But it just came out.

'You won't be going there again, my girl,' he said, his eyes narrowing with malice. 'You'll work all through the summer. If you think I'm paying for trips for you to see that shrew of an aunt of yours, you are much mistaken.'

'But Daddy, Suzie has invited me to stay at her house, please let me go,' she pleaded.

He moved so quickly she didn't have time to dodge him. He caught hold of her shoulder and punched her so hard in the face that she fell back against the stove, burning her hand.

'You'll go nowhere again,' he yelled. 'From now on you'll find a job during every holiday, and you'll give your mother half of what you earn for your keep. Got that?'

Recalling that ugly scene made tears spring up in Beth's eyes. She was left with a black eye and a split lip, the same injuries he'd inflicted on her mother so often. She remembered lying there on the cold floor cursing him to hell and back, and swearing to herself she'd make him pay for it.

'What is it?' Steven said gently, seeing her tears, and with that Beth found herself blurting out what had happened that day.

'He sounds like an absolute monster,' Steven said, slipping his arms round her as he'd done earlier and holding her tight. 'No wonder you hate him.'

'I couldn't bring myself to admit to Suzie why I really couldn't go,' she said, drying her eyes, comforted by his arm. 'I think I made out in the end that I had been offered a good job. But it hardly mattered anyway, because as it happened her mother had the stroke and I don't suppose she would have been able to spend any time with me, let alone have me to stay with her.'

'So did you work all the holidays from then on?' he asked.

Beth nodded. 'Saturdays too, in a shoe shop in Hastings. Father used to make me bring my pay packet home unopened. He'd pocket half, it never even went to Mother.'

Steven smoothed her hair and sighed. 'You had to stay, I suppose, if you wanted to go to university?'

'Yes. But I think I would have left, found a job and a room, if it hadn't been for Suzie,' she said. 'You see, I often told her in my letters that I wanted to leave home, even if I didn't spell out why. Each time she wrote back she urged me not to do that, she made me believe I was too clever for a dead-end job, and that was all I'd get without qualifications. Her opinion was the only one I really trusted, even Serena and Robert weren't wholly reliable. I suppose our father made out to them I was dumb, as they didn't seem to have much faith that I'd make it to university. They often suggested it might be better for me if I got a job as a nanny for a couple of years.'

'But they presumably knew how it was for you at home? Susan didn't, did she?' Steven pointed out.

'That was all part of it. You see, everyone, my brother and sister, teachers, neighbours, pitied me. I used to see it in their faces. That saps your ambition, Steven, it weakens your resolve, and it makes you feel worthless. Suzie didn't pity me, she admired me. I told her at thirteen

I wanted to be a lawyer after we'd seen a film together about one. I suppose I presented her with a pretty good case as to why I'd be good at it, and she never let me drift away from it. I always felt indebted to her for that, I can remember thinking of her on the day I graduated, and wishing she was there.'

'It was a great shame all round you didn't stay in touch. If you'd still been friends when her parents died, you could have made that swine of a brother of hers share the inheritance.'

'I know,' she said dolefully. 'And maybe if we'd remained friends I could have influenced her to break away from her parents years before and make a life for herself. I've thought about that over and over since I met her again.'

'We've all got our own "if onlys",' he said with a sigh. 'But I suppose you got caught up with all the social life at university, made more exciting friends.'

'I didn't,' she said. 'I remained a loner. I was never the girl I'd been when I was with Suzie, ever again.'

There was something so plaintive about that statement that Steven turned on the settee to look at her face. Her lower lip was trembling, a deep and terrible sadness in her green eyes. He remembered how Susan had remarked on Beth's sadness, and clearly it hadn't been there while they were still friends. He had no doubt that talking about the past had opened up an old wound. That wound must have been inflicted somewhere between her last visit to Stratford and when she went to university, for she'd already stated that she re-invented herself there.

'What happened to you, Beth?' he said softly. 'I know something did. Tell me.'

Her eyes met his, then darted away. A guilty look he'd seen so often in clients' faces. 'It's late,' she said tersely, her whole body stiffening beside him. 'It's time you went home.'

She was right, of course, it was after twelve, but the way she was frantically trying to pull down the shutters was just confirmation he was right too.

'I told you about Anna because I trust you,' he said. 'I think I knew, too, that you would help me to face up to it and deal with it. So please trust me, and let me help you.'

Her wide mouth twisted scornfully. 'What's this, some kind of plea bargaining?'

Steven took his courage in both hands. 'People's minds and bodies aren't like your washing machine,' he said carefully. 'When something is damaged you can't just go out and get a new spare part. It has to heal. I think . . .' He paused. 'No. I know,' he said more forcefully, 'that you've got a wound which hasn't healed. I won't claim I can heal it, but at least let me look at it.'

'What are you, some frustrated shrink?' Beth said scathingly. 'I'm a grown woman, I don't need a man who can't even press his own suit to suggest I'm troubled.'

Steven blushed. 'I don't get enough time to iron the girls' clothes as well as I'd like to, let alone ponce myself up,' he said. 'Don't try to hurt me to cover up your own pain.'

'You've got a bloody cheek,' she said, getting up and

flouncing across the room. 'You came here uninvited, I cooked you supper and gave you drinks as a way of showing my appreciation for your dealing with my flood. Okay, maybe because I told you about my childhood, you think you've got the right to pry into everything about me. Well, you don't. Everything I told you tonight was background to Susan, nothing more.'

Steven stood up. He was afraid to persist in case he smashed up the groundwork they'd already laid down this evening. Yet he could sense he was close to getting the truth. She hadn't actually opened the door to fling him out, and there was a certain note in her voice which suggested that subliminally at least, she wanted to spill it all out.

'It happened somewhere between sixteen and eighteen,' he said gently but firmly. 'Something so shattering you couldn't even tell your friend. That's why you dropped her, isn't it? You could have gone to see her in Stratford once you were at university, but you didn't dare, in case you let it slip. I'm right, aren't I?'

Beth just stared at him, eyes wide, face chalky-white, and her wide mouth slack. It was the expression of a child who had been caught doing something wrong. She was terribly afraid. He moved towards her and caught her up in his arms. 'Don't be frightened,' he whispered, holding her tightly. 'I'll never use it against you, I only want to make you better.'

She went limp in his arms, and suddenly she was crying, leaning on his shoulder and sobbing like a small child. 'It's okay,' he said, stroking her curly hair with one hand, holding her tight with the other. 'You are safe with me, Beth. Just tell me.'

'They raped me,' she croaked out. 'Three of them, in an alley, one after the other.'

Steven was struck dumb with horror. He certainly hadn't expected anything like this, he'd been thinking more along the lines of her getting pregnant, or being jilted by a boyfriend. In his profession he'd met many women who were rape victims, and he knew how it blighted their lives.

His instinct was purely paternal. He picked her up bodily, carried her to the couch, then cradled her as he would have done his own girls if they were hurt.

'You've said the worst bit now,' he said soothingly, stroking her hair back from her face. 'Now tell me exactly how it happened.'

'It was in the Christmas holidays, early January 1968, in Hastings. We had the January sale on at the shoe shop and instead of going straight home I went to the Rococo coffee bar,' she blurted out, as if wanting to get it over with as quickly as possible. 'Everyone at school went there all the time, it was "the" place to hang out. But I'd only ever been there during the day, because I wasn't allowed out in the evenings. It was about six when I got there, and I thought I'd hang about and catch the half past seven bus home. If Father said anything about being late, I'd make out I'd been stocktaking.'

Beth's face was taut with tension and she gripped Steven's arm tightly as she told him exactly what happened that night.

The reason she wanted to stay in Hastings, despite it being bitterly cold, was because she'd met a boy called Mike on the bus whom she really liked, and she knew he went to the Rococo. She didn't think she looked too bad in her work clothes, black mini-skirt and skinny-rib sweater, and she could take off her school coat as soon as she got in there.

The Rococo was above a shop, two rooms fitted out with lots of low seating and dim lights, a steamy place with loud music from the juke-box. To her disappointment Mike wasn't there. She drank several cups of espresso, chatted to a couple of girls she knew from the shop, put a few records on the juke-box, and finally at around twenty past seven she left a little disconsolately to catch the bus home to Battle.

Frost was glistening on the pavements, and the wind coming in straight off the sea was so cold it seemed to cut right through her. The streets were completely deserted now, and it seemed strange to see all the lighted shop windows without anyone looking in them.

She heard someone whistle at her, and looking over the street towards the clock tower, she saw two boys waving to her. It was too dark to see clearly but she thought one of them was Mike and ran over to him.

It wasn't until she was just a few yards away, that she realized it wasn't Mike. She didn't know either boy. The one she'd thought was Mike, was several inches shorter, and older by at least three years. Close up, he looked rough and dirty, the only similarity was that he had blond hair cut in a Beatle style like Mike's.

'I thought you were someone else,' Beth said, stopping short, terribly embarrassed by her mistake.

The boy she had thought was Mike said something about what did it matter if she didn't know him and made some crack about her being so tall.

She was well used to jokes about her height, but they always stung her, and she always retaliated with an insult. 'Maybe you think that because you are rather stunted,' she said in her best snooty voice and turned to walk away.

'Wha'cha mean?' he called out, then came after her, looking up at her scornfully. She was scared then, wishing she hadn't made the remark – she could smell drink on his breath and his leather jacket and grubby jeans suggested he was one of the town's hard cases.

'I'm sorry, I shouldn't have said that. It's just that it's not very nice having people making jokes about how tall I am,' she said, moving away from him.

'They should put a lamp on yer 'ead and turn you into a lamp-post,' his friend chimed in, and roared with laughter at his own joke. ''Ere, Bob, look 'ow skinny 'er legs are an 'all,' he added gleefully.

'The nearer the bone, the sweeter the meat,' Bob with the blond hair laughed sneeringly.

Beth began walking away from them fast. But they followed her, making remarks about her hair, her school coat, and the fact that her feet were big. She was frightened even then. The streets were deserted, and she was scared they might follow her on to the bus.

'Please leave me alone,' she said, stopping and turning towards them.

'Please leave me alone,' Bob repeated in a parody of her voice. 'You ain't 'alf posh. I always wanted to shag a posh bird.'

Beth ignored that and walked on, and when she saw a man come out of a side turning and call out to them, she thought they'd be distracted enough to leave her.

A quick glance was enough to see he was much older than the other two. He was tall and well built, wearing a black Crombie overcoat, and he had a droopy moustache and an almost shaved head. As the two younger ones stopped to speak to him, she hurried on, but their voices carried on the wind and she could hear they were talking about her.

Suddenly all three of them were trying to catch her up. The one called Bob shouted out to her and asked if she'd wanted to meet 'Bonio'. 'We call 'im that 'cos 'e's 'ard,' he added, and gave a raucous laugh.

She had only about twenty-five yards to go to the bus stop now, she could see it up ahead. But there was no one else waiting, not a person in sight anywhere, and the three men were whispering together.

Her heart was hammering with fear and she willed the bus to come now so she could sprint to it and be gone. Then suddenly the two younger men were on either side of her and they clamped their hands on to her arms.

'Bonio's got something 'ard 'e wants to show yer,' Bob said.

She let out a scream but it was stifled immediately by a hand from behind her. She was pulled and pushed into a passageway between two shops, at the end of which was a narrow, dark alleyway.

Beth tried to get away, but they were too strong. When she kicked out at the one called Bonio, he only laughed.

'Spirited, ain't yer,' he said. 'I like that. There's not many birds wot put up a fight with me.'

Until the moment Beth saw Bonio unbutton his coat and pull down the zipper on his trousers, she'd imagined they were going to beat her up. That was frightening enough, but now she saw rape was their intent, she was absolutely terrified. She screamed again and tried to shake off the hands holding her, but they had her in such strong grips she couldn't. They forced her down on to the ground in the alley and the one whose name she hadn't heard stuck something, a scarf or a handkerchief, in her mouth to silence her.

She was seventeen, and her only experience with boys until then had been a few kisses. But now she was on the hard, cold ground, and the man was yanking up her skirt, ripping her tights and then her knickers apart at the crutch, and he was leering down at her, urging the other two to hold her tight while he had what he called 'his go'.

Beth could smell cat's pee and rotting rubbish, but it was so dark she could see nothing more than the walls of the shop yards looming either side of her. Then even that was obliterated by the man lying down on top of her and forcing himself into her.

'I bet she's a bleedin' virgin,' the blond one chortled close to her ear as he held her tightly. 'Is it tight, Bonio?'

She tried to scream despite the gag and even managed

246

to make some noise, but Bonio put the side of his hand hard against her throat to choke her, and she could hardly breathe, let alone continue to try to make herself heard.

The pain was excruciating, she felt as if she was being split in two. Then suddenly he stopped and the next one took over, pushing her even harder down on to the rough ground, muttering filthy things about her being wet and hot.

When it was the third one's turn she was too stunned and broken even to attempt to fight any more. She saw Bonio turn towards the wall, only a couple of feet from her head, to relieve himself, and somehow that act of contempt for her and her feelings was every bit as bad as the rape.

'She's like a bill poster's bucket now,' the man whose name she hadn't heard remarked as he got to his feet, then kicked her in the side as she lay there, too ravaged even to cry, let alone move. 'Filthy slag. You liked it, didn't you?'

They were gone with the speed of rats in the dark, leaving her lying there in the filth like a piece of sodden rubbish.

'Oh, Beth.' Steven's sigh brought her back to the present, and she saw he had tears trickling down his cheeks. 'I thought I had the right words to say for any occasion, but for once I can't say anything except how sorry I am.'

She was shocked at herself for telling it all so graphically, but she felt a huge sense of release that she'd been able to. In the weeks that followed that night she'd done her best to erase most of it from her memory, and what she was left with was just her shame. Yet reliving it again, it wasn't shame she felt, only sorrow that her life had been permanently tainted by it.

'What can anyone say?' she sighed. 'I know now that only a very small percentage of men can do that kind of thing, but for a very long time I was terrified of all men.'

'What happened, did you report it?' Steven asked. He was shocked to the core. It made him feel ashamed of his gender. He had hoped that by getting her to tell him it might heal her, but he couldn't see how anyone could ever get over something as monstrous as that.

Beth didn't answer for a moment. Even now, at forty-four, with vast experience under her belt, she was shivering again just the way she had that night as she struggled to get up, with that disgusting mess running down her legs.

They savaged her youth and innocence, stole from her something she could never regain. At that point she was already a little wary of men because of her father, but she'd still been like any other young girl awaiting her first romance. She would sigh over romantic songs and poems, ponder on the meaning of the little yearning feelings in her body she didn't understand. Then suddenly after that vicious attack everything was ugly, they took everything from her.

Wriggling away from Steven, Beth got up and went over to the window, pulling the curtains back to look out.

The view in the dark was like black velvet in a jeweller's shop window, strewn with millions of diamonds. Yet out there in the seemingly sleeping city she knew from statistics that there would be other women either remembering the horror of rape, or even submitting to it as she stood there.

Steven came over to her and stood by her side looking out, his shoulder just touching hers.

'I staggered out into the street screaming,' she continued, knowing she must complete the story, but the aftermath was almost as bad as the rape. 'I ran right into a bunch of women on a night out together. They saw the state of me and took me straight to the police station.'

'What was that like?' Steven said. He wanted to know everything, but he could see her trembling, and he was afraid of pushing too hard.

'Precious little compassion, sympathy or tact,' she said sharply, glancing sideways at him. 'Thank God it's not like that now for rape victims. They asked me a lot of questions, some so personal I felt as if I was being raped again. Then they left me to wait alone in a room while they went to get my parents. We didn't have a phone at the house, you see.'

Beth could still picture that interview room. She'd been in hundreds, maybe even thousands just like it since, but she'd know that one again even if she were led to it blindfold.

It was about eight by eight, painted pea green, with no window, and it stank of cigarette smoke from the last occupant. A table and two chairs were the only furniture.

She remembered a message scrawled on the wall: 'Jesus lives, it's me who is dead'. It seemed to be a profound message that night. She could smell those men on her, she wanted to scratch at herself because she felt so dirty. Someone brought her a mug of tea but she couldn't drink it because she was trembling so hard.

'Monty, my father, came in. Mother had stayed home, I think at his insistence,' she went on. 'He was purple with anger, and for a minute or two I thought it was because of what had happened to me. But it wasn't. He was furious at being dragged away from the TV on a cold night. Guess what his first words to me were?'

'If it were one of my daughters who had been raped I think mine would have been, "I'll get them and kill them,"' Steven said. 'But I guess that wasn't what he said?'

'No, nothing that would make me think he cared about me,' Beth said, her lips quivering. 'He said, "This is just like you, always the trouble-maker. I suppose you led them on."'

Steven shook his head in bewilderment. It never ceased to astound him how cruel some parents could be.

'I think even the police sergeant with him was shocked,' Beth said. 'He tried to say what a terrible ordeal I'd had and this was no time for recriminations. But he might as well have talked to the wall, Father was too wrapped up in himself to listen. He had a spotted cravat around his neck, I remember, he kept pulling at it as if it were choking him. The sergeant said I must be examined by the police surgeon, then they'd take my statement, but Father wouldn't have any of that. He just kept saying I was a stupid fool and he was taking me home.'

'He didn't want the police to catch those men and charge them?' Steven gasped in disbelief.

Beth shook her head. 'Know what he said to the sergeant? "Come now, my good man, look at the length of that skirt. She was asking for it."'

'I wanted to die then,' Beth said, her voice rasping with hurt. 'He was saying it was all right for those men to rape his daughter. But it didn't end there, Steven. He got the police to drive us home, and when we got in he hit me with his slipper and told me I stank like a polecat. He punished me, even after what I'd been through.'

Steven took her in his arms and rocked her. Once again he found himself robbed of any words of comfort. He wondered how Beth had managed to hold on to her sanity.

'What about your mother?' he asked eventually. 'Surely she didn't take the same line?'

'She did what she always did, wouldn't go against Father openly,' Beth sniffed. 'She came to me later that night when he was asleep and tried to comfort me. I know she was distraught, but somehow that sneaking into my room only brought home how feeble she was.'

'And later? Did you go back to school? Was anything said?' Steven asked.

'Mother was crying most of the next few days. I suppose I just withdrew into myself, I can't really remember much about that time now. But Father must have felt some remorse because he did say a while afterwards that it was his way of protecting me. He told me that if the men were caught and charged, it would be me who would suffer most in the court case, and whether the men were convicted of rape or not, I'd be pointed at, and the stigma would remain for all time.'

'I'm sure that didn't make you feel any better,' Steven said, still holding her tightly.

'No, it didn't. Had he apologized for his harshness that night, it might have been different. It wasn't until years later, when I saw the process of law in rape cases and what the victim has to go through, that I agreed he had a point.'

'Did you tell anyone else at the time?' Steven asked.

'No, never,' she said into his jacket. 'Not even Serena or Robert. Apart from my parents, you are the only person who knows.'

'That was a huge, terrible secret to be carrying inside you,' he said. 'How did you bear it?'

'By planning my escape,' she said simply, moving back from his arms. 'I worked like crazy for my A-levels that spring. University was the way out, and I had to get there at all costs. I told myself that if I failed I'd end up as worthless as my father.'

She laughed suddenly, and Steven looked at her in consternation.

'Don't worry,' she said, seeing his expression. 'I'm not cracking up, only thinking of the revenge I took on Monty. You see, I didn't let him off scot-free,' she went on. 'After I'd got to university, I made it quite clear on rare visits home that it was only to see Mother. I never said a kind word to him. As he got older and frailer, I'd be as callous with him as he'd been to me. I'd grin at his aches and pains, belittle him in any way I could. I made out that I talked about him in the village, and before long he wouldn't go there any more. I would whisk my mother away on holiday and leave him to fend for himself. Then, when she died, I told him he was going to agree to go into a home otherwise I'd tell Robert about the rape. That shook him up, he didn't ever want his son to know. Serena and Robert were astounded that he agreed so readily, and that he told them to sell the house to pay for it.'

Steven felt uneasy then. The man may have been a monster, but bearing a grudge for all those years, then blackmailing an old man, did seem to be extreme. 'You must let it go now, Beth,' he said, his mind turning to Susan and what the need for revenge had brought her to. 'Try and forgive him.'

She turned to him and to his surprise kissed his cheek. 'I wish I could,' she said, putting one hand on each of his shoulders and looking right into his eyes. 'You are the first man I've ever been able to open up to, Steven. Don't you find that sad?'

Steven guessed that she meant far more than that.

'Yes, it's sad,' he agreed. 'But you are over the first hurdle now by talking about it to me.'

She smiled at him, and for the first time since he'd known her he saw real warmth in her eyes.

'You are such a nice man,' she sighed. 'And you've got to get over your hurdle and do something about Anna. Promise me you will?'

'I will,' he said, and meant it. He could see now why Susan had admired Beth so much. She was courageous, and he suspected now she'd gone in for criminal law because of a real need to help others. She had managed to turn something bad into something good and noble.

'And we'll get Susan off together,' she said, patting his cheek. 'And we'll stay friends?'

'All for one and one for all,' he said. 'And now I must go home.'

Chapter twelve

In the weeks that followed her revelations to Steven, Beth sensed a slight change in herself. Nothing dramatic, but she did seem to be less detached from other people, less guarded, and certainly less pessimistic. She had panicked for a moment or two the morning after her conversation with Steven, terrified he would pass on what he had told her, but as soon as she saw him that day, she detected something in his face which told her he would never betray her trust.

Maybe it was just that which made everything better – she couldn't remember ever trusting anyone implicitly before. Even as Christmas loomed closer, she didn't feel her usual dejection. In the lunch hour she shopped for presents for her nieces and nephews and found herself enjoying it. When Serena rang and asked if she'd like to spend Christmas with them, she agreed immediately, without asking first if Monty was coming out of the home for the day.

Fortunately, as she laughingly told Steven later, Serena had gone on to say that he was staying in the home anyway. Beth said her new-found Christmas spirit didn't quite stretch to welcoming the sight of her father.

As for Steven, he had finally given Anna an ultimatum. To his utmost surprise she didn't seize the opportunity to leave as he'd expected, but went straight to her doctor for advice. He recommended she should spend a week in a private clinic for drink and drug dependency, and she booked herself into one almost immediately. Now she was back home again, and trying very hard with the help of the AA and Steven to kick drink for good.

Steven was cautiously optimistic. His joy that Anna had chosen to stay with him and the girls gave him hope for both her recovery and their marriage, but at the same time he was aware she was likely to backslide on some occasion. This was the hardest part for him, for although he knew trust was crucial, he found it very difficult not to keep phoning Anna during the day to check on what she was doing.

Beth often found herself moved by Steven's understanding of human frailties. One day over lunch, which they quite often had together now, she told him that having him as a friend was like switching on another light in a gloomy room. Although they'd both laughed at the analogy at the time, and Steven asked how many watts he was, that was how she saw it. He'd thrown light into the dark corners of her mind.

It was in fact love she felt for Steven, though of course she couldn't voice that for fear of being misunderstood. It was after all the platonic kind, not romantic. She loved his compassion, the little kindnesses that he bestowed on almost everyone he came into contact with. She had never had a confidant before, never thought she wanted or needed one either. Yet she found it so warming to know she could tell Steven anything, without fear he would repeat it. He confided in her too, and it made her feel valued in a very special way.

She could laugh at herself with Steven, something she'd never done with anyone before either. But above all, discovering she could care deeply for another human being was solace for her soul. She hadn't believed she was capable of that.

Susan appeared to have settled down in the prison regime. Steven reported that she even seemed to have found a kind of contentment there. Freedom, as Roy Longhurst had pointed out, didn't appear to mean much to someone who had never really experienced it.

Beth had so many pressing cases of her own that she had only been able to visit Susan once, but Steven kept her abreast of everything anyway. He was awaiting Susan's psychiatric reports and a reply from his letter to Martin Wright requesting an interview.

As for Roy, Beth hadn't forgotten about him, but with so much else going on around her, he hadn't been uppermost in her mind. So when he phoned, just a few days before Christmas, and asked her out to dinner that evening, she was pleased. Just the sound of his deep voice gave her a quiver of unexpected excitement and she agreed without a second thought.

'I'm really glad you fancy it,' he said, sounding very relieved. 'Because I was a bit premature. I booked a table on the Glass Boat just after I last saw you. I knew it would be hell trying to find anywhere half decent in the run-up to Christmas.'

'So who would you be taking tonight if I was busy?' she asked, amused that he'd had the foresight to book a table but had omitted to tell her.

'No one,' he said. 'I'd make out I was ill. You see, after I'd booked it, I got the colly wobbles that you didn't like me and I was afraid to ring you in case you told me to get lost. I'm an insecure person you see. Afraid of rejection.'

Beth laughed and said she'd meet him at eight. After she'd put the phone down she realized that just a few weeks ago such a statement, true or false, would only have irritated her. She was definitely unwinding.

Beth had heard that the Glass Boat was excellent, but she'd never been there before, and as the taxi dropped her by Bristol Bridge and she saw the floating restaurant, with all its lighted windows reflected in the dark water, she suddenly felt ridiculously girlish and thrilled.

She felt she looked good in the new red dress she'd bought for the party on Boxing Day at Serena's. It was slinky, mid-calf length, with short sleeves, quite plain but for a trimming of red feathers around the scoop neck. As there had been no time for the hairdresser's she'd washed her hair herself and scrunch-dried it. Though she normally felt wearing her hair loose like a wild black storm made her look like an ageing groupie, tonight it seemed appropriate. She wondered if Roy would even recognize her, having only seen her before with her hair scraped back and wearing business-like suits.

Roy was already nursing a drink in the small bar when she walked in. He glanced up, looked away, and then looked back, his face breaking into a wide smile as he realized it was actually her.

'Beth!' he said, jumping up. 'You look sensational! Utterly gorgeous.'

'You don't look so bad yourself.' She smiled. He was wearing a beautifully tailored dark suit and a dazzling white shirt. 'How are you?'

'Overworked, but feeling very festive and jolly.' He grinned. 'How about you?'

'About the same,' she said, looking around her, and smiled because the Christmas decorations were very pretty and the restaurant beyond the bar looked so stylish yet cosy with its candles and flowers.

It was a memorable night. Most of the other diners were in big parties, but although they were noisy with their party-poppers, crackers and great screams of raucous laughter, it didn't seem intrusive, only atmospheric. The meal was absolutely delicious, and the service attentive but discreet. Each time Beth glanced out of the window at the river, she was charmed by the illuminated bridge, the many Christmas trees and coloured lights in the offices opposite, and the swans cruising regally by in the inky water.

Roy was such good company too, making her laugh with tales of police blunders, and disaster stories about the building work in his cottage.

'So I take it the cottage is turning into a real home at last?' she said eventually, smiling at him.

He nodded. 'I've done a lot recently. But you'll have to come and see it soon, I've even laid a path to the front door so your elegant shoes won't get plastered in mud.'

By the time they had coffee and a brandy, Beth felt she didn't want the night to end. Roy was such good company – funny, interesting, intelligent and sexy.

As she watched him walk a little unsteadily to the men's room, she thought that it was odd she should consider sexiness as an attribute. She was usually very uncomfortable with men with that quality.

As he came back up the stairs she could see he was hiding something behind his back and smirking like a schoolboy.

'What?' she said as he stood beside the table looking down at her.

'You look good enough to eat,' he said.

Beth giggled. 'Haven't you eaten enough for one night?'

'Da-dum!' he said, pulling a sprig of rather weary-looking mistletoe from behind his back. 'Just a titbit will do. One kiss.'

Beth thought he looked adorable as he said this. He had such a soft, smiley mouth, and such lovely dark eyes. She didn't care if other people in the restaurant were watching, she wanted him to kiss her.

It was the most perfect kiss. Soft, warm lips, lingering just long enough to make her wish she was standing, with his arms around her. One of his hands caressed her cheek, presumably the other was still holding the mistletoe.

A cheer went up from the next table. Beth blushed as she realized it was aimed at them.

'Umm,' Roy said thoughtfully as he sat down opposite her again. 'That titbit was scrumptious.'

All at once the old familiar anxiety came back. He would want to go back to her flat with her, and he wouldn't want to leave either. This seemed confirmed when later she heard him ask the waiter to order him a taxi. Yet to her surprise when he came back to their table, he bent down and kissed her neck and said, 'I've ordered a taxi. I'll get him to take me on to Queen Charlton after dropping you off. To get one taxi so close to Christmas is rare, two is an impossibility.'

They had to walk along the cobbled quayside to Bristol Bridge as cars couldn't get down there, and it was very cold after the warmth on the Glass Boat. Beth had only a fluffy shawl around her shoulders, and she was unsteady on her feet too, but Roy put his arm around her and cuddled her close to him.

The trees on the quayside were strewn with coloured lights, and Roy stopped beneath one to kiss her. Beth seemed to melt against him, losing all her inhibitions, and it was Roy who broke away first, looking down at her upturned face.

'You are beautiful, Ms Powell,' he said softly. 'The Christmas lights are making jewels in your hair, and your mouth is the most kissable one I've ever seen. Happy Christmas!'

That Christmas was the best one Beth could remember. But then, perhaps that was partially because of the after-glow from the evening with Roy. They had kissed passionately all the way to her flat, but he hadn't pushed things by abandoning the taxi and asking to come in. The next day he sent her a lovely Christmas flower arrangement, with a note thanking her for a wonderful evening. He wished her a happy Christmas and said he would phone when she got back.

He had struck the perfect balance. Keen, but not so pushy it made her nervous. She left Bristol at midday on Christmas Eve, and despite her conviction there would be traffic jams right around the M25, the roads were quiet and she reached Brightling, the village near Battle where Serena and her family lived, by half past five.

When Beth had worked in London, she'd seen Serena at least four times a year, usually staying overnight. But since moving to Bristol she'd only visited her once, and she sensed that her sister felt hurt by this, even though she knew what a long drive it was. So Beth half expected Serena to be cool with her, at least for a while. But it hadn't been that way.

She got a joyous welcome from Serena and her husband, Tony. Beth's two nieces, Becky and Louise, aged eighteen and sixteen respectively, acted as if she were visiting royalty, escorting her to the little guest-room, helping her unpack, and admiring her clothes and shoes with wild enthusiasm.

Serena was well named, for she was serene. She was beautiful too, and had been from childhood. Her hair was dark and curly just like Beth's, but she had always worn hers cut short, and it emphasized her big, dark, smouldering eyes which were said to be inherited from their grandmother. She was fortunate too that her skin was olive-toned, not pale like Beth's.

Even at fifty-four, with quite a few grey hairs, wrinkles round her eyes, and her once slender shape becoming matronly, Serena was still a head-turner. She wore loose flowing clothes in vivid colours and ethnic chunky jewellery, which gave her the appearance of an exotic flower. But on top of her looks, Serena was a very social person, and a great organizer. Not only had she decorated the cottage so it looked like Santa's grotto, she'd laid on enough food for the Third Army and planned a full itinerary for the next three days.

It started as soon as they'd eaten supper, when they went out for drinks at a neighbour's, then on to the midnight service at Brightling church. Christmas Day began with Buck's Fizz while they opened their presents, and at midday when Robert, his wife Penny and their two young sons Simon and Edward arrived, several neighbours came in for pre-lunch drinks.

So it went on, people coming and going, visits out to other neighbours, right through till Boxing Day evening when Serena threw her customary big party. As always, Beth was amazed by Serena's ability to serve food and drinks to scores of people, including a small army of children watching videos upstairs, and still remain unflustered and looking beautiful.

Yet it was the third day of the holiday that meant the most to Beth. Tony took Becky and Louise to Brighton in the morning, so Serena could spend a few hours alone with her sister. They sat in the sitting room by the fire with their feet up and relaxed.

'You seem very much happier,' Serena said at one point. 'Relaxed and cheerful. Is it the job or a man?'

As Serena was ten years older than Beth, their relationship had often seemed more like aunt and niece than sisters. Serena had left home at eighteen for much the same reasons as Beth, but she was always very anxious about leaving her younger sister to bear the brunt of their father's bad moods. She did her best to make up for her absence by giving Beth clothes and other little gifts, and she had always stood up for her. Yet even now, at fifty-four, and her younger sister a successful solicitor, Serena still carried a burden of guilt. To her the fact that Beth hadn't married and had children of her own was a reflection on her inability to do more for her as a child.

Beth knew this and it added to her own inner sadness sometimes. Serena was an earth mother, she poured out love unstintingly, not only on her husband and children, but on friends, neighbours and just about anyone else who crossed her path. She did everything with love – work, decorating and furnishing her cottage, arranging the flowers in the church, even visiting their father, who didn't deserve a moment of her time. Beth thought she would give her sister what would be her idea of the most perfect Christmas present – to hear her younger sister was happy and fulfilled.

'The job *and* a man,' Beth said with a big grin. 'I love it in Bristol, I'm really happy there, and there's a romance blooming.'

Beth didn't think this was a lie exactly. After that dinner with Roy, any normal woman would expect it to turn into a full-blown romance. It was obvious he wanted her, he was unattached, she had felt the kind of flutters which meant it was special.

'Oh Beth, I'm so glad,' Serena said excitedly. 'Tell me all about him.'

Beth found it surprisingly easy to make Roy sound like Mr Right. His job, his cottage, his sense of humour, even his looks were all so attractive. She didn't have to exaggerate, and just talking about him gave her a warm glow.

'I hope he's good in bed too?' Serena giggled.

'I haven't tried that yet,' Beth said, wishing her sister didn't always have to be so earthy.

'Why ever not?' Serena exclaimed.

'I haven't known him that long,' Beth replied, and that led to explaining how and why she and Roy became friends.

Serena was enthralled to discover that the woman she'd heard about in the news was her sister's old friend and that Beth was very much involved with the case. Beth explained how Susan had come to shoot the two people, and how she'd met Roy because of this.

'It was fate that brought you and Suzie together again,' said Serena thoughtfully. 'And Roy too. Flow with it, there's got to be a reason behind it. I'm sure Roy is the one for you.'

It was so typical of Serena to suggest some sort of spiritual connection was at work. She lived her whole life that way, believing nothing was down to chance and destiny was preordained.

But for once, Beth wanted to believe that too.

Beth left Brightling in the early evening to drive back to Bristol. As she drove through dark, deserted roads she found herself thinking about Robert and Serena. Beth had always considered herself to be the odd one out in the family. Serena and Robert were gentle, kind beings. They were loving and giving, slow to take offence, quick to praise. They seemed so uncomplicated, so forgiving. Yet Serena had said today that both she and Robert had carried a great deal of resentment about their childhood into adult life, and that they'd both had several disastrous relationships before finding real happiness with their present partners.

'I was becoming just like Mother,' Serena said at one point. 'I let men push me about, do what they wanted to me. I suppose I thought that was all I was worth. Robert told me once that he used to be cruel to women, and he saw in himself more than a passing resemblance to Father. I went to see a psychiatrist, thanks to a girlfriend who wouldn't let me fall apart. Robert got taken in hand by an older woman he had an affair with. We both learned to put aside the terrible examples we'd been shown at home, and we found our real selves.'

This was something of a shock to Beth, who had always imagined both Robert and Serena had sailed through life without any angst. 'What about me then?' she asked. 'I don't let men push me around, and I'm not a bully either. But I still dwell on stuff that went on at home.'

She wished then that she could tell Serena about the rape. She wanted her sister to know the real reason she

266

wasn't whole. But she couldn't bring herself to. Aside from upsetting Serena, Mother had made her promise she wouldn't ever tell her brother and sister, and a promise was a promise.

'You are the opposite to me,' Serena said thoughtfully. 'I dealt with it all by going out of my way to try and make people love me. You never give anyone the chance. I'm really glad you weren't promiscuous like I was as a young girl, that can be very damaging too. But being so chilly isn't right either. You have robbed yourself of a lot of joy. Try harder this time, Beth, for me. Give this policeman at least half a chance.'

It was very late when Beth got home, and her flat seemed stark and bare after the colour and glitter at Serena's. But the red light was flashing on her telephone and when she listened to the message she felt better. It was Roy. 'Just checking to see if you got home safely,' he said. 'Ring me, however late it is. There's frost on the roads and I won't sleep till I know you are there.'

She rang him back at the number he'd given her during their date. He answered on the first ring.

'I'm home,' she said. 'You can go to sleep now.'

'Was it a good Christmas?' he asked.

'Really great,' she said. 'And yours?'

'Better than I expected,' he said. 'But then I've been on duty most of the time. Can I ring you tomorrow and arrange to meet?'

'By all means,' she said. 'I'll look forward to it. Now sleep tight.'

*

Steven came into Beth's office soon after she'd arrived at work the next day. It was great to see him again, and after exchanging the usual questions about Christmas, Steven admitted he'd had a tough time with Anna.

'I was warned Christmas is a bad time for recovering alcoholics,' he said glumly, 'booze being so much a part of it all. She was very edgy and sarcastic, everything I said seemed to annoy her. But she didn't relapse, I'm really proud of her for that. All the same, I was glad to come back to work.'

Beth said she thought Anna was very lucky to have such an understanding husband. Steven grinned.

'I don't know that I could be called understanding exactly,' he admitted. 'I kind of escaped into my own head, thinking about Susan's case and how we must push ahead and talk to the men in her life.'

Beth nodded, she'd thought the same thing. 'Any reply from Martin Wright yet?'

'Yes, it came this morning,' Steven said. 'He sounds as egotistical as we imagined. Refused point-blank to come to Bristol to talk to me. But he has deigned to say he can see me on January 6th at his home. We'll have to track Reuben and Liam down too.'

Beth thought about it for a moment. 'There's not much we can do till after New Year,' she said. 'But I could go up to Stratford-upon-Avon on the Saturday after,' she suggested. 'I could call on Susan's old neighbours and ask them if they know where Liam is.'

'I'd offer to come with you, but I can't leave Anna,' Steven said. 'She's still very shaky, easily upset, and going off somewhere with you might just tip her over the edge.'

'That's okay,' Beth replied. Steven looked drawn and tired and she guessed he had understated how bad things had been over Christmas. 'I might be able to get my pet policeman to come with me. Not as a policeman of course, but as a friend.'

Steven grinned. He knew about their date and had noted the glow about her the following day.

'What's that silly grin for?' she said, but her tone was affectionate.

'Just the hope it might work out for you two,' he said. 'Meanwhile, what about Reuben?'

'Let's think about that after we've found Liam,' she said. 'We've got enough on our plates for now.'

Roy was working right through New Year, but he said he'd be delighted to go to Stratford-upon-Avon with Beth on the following Saturday, and suggested they made a weekend of it and stayed in a hotel overnight. 'Separate rooms,' he said, almost too quickly, before Beth had even had a chance to think how she felt about sharing one. 'I know of a really nice place, with a great restaurant, so I'll book it if you'll let me.'

Beth agreed, but as soon as she put the phone down, she went straight into Steven's office to tell him.

'Should I?' she asked, leaning on the window-sill and looking down at the square below. 'Am I asking for more hurt?'

Although she hadn't actually told him that she had a problem with sex, Steven was a hundred per cent certain she did, and this was her way of confirming it.

'How much do you like him?' Steven asked. 'On a scale of one to ten?'

'I think ten,' she said, still not turning to look at him. 'But I'm scared.'

'You! The indomitable Ms Powell scared?' he teased her. 'I bet poor Roy is quaking in his boots too.'

'Don't be silly,' she said, turning round to face him. 'Why should he be scared?'

'Because he's been hurt too, and you are a great prize,' Steven said. 'Men aren't as confident about these things as they like to make out. Just go, Beth, have a good time and see what happens. I don't think Roy is the kind to turn snotty if you don't invite him into your bed.'

She was silent for a moment, gazing out of the window again.

'What is it, Beth?' Steven asked.

'Do you think I should tell him?'

'Yes, I do, if you think he's that special,' Steven said, getting up from his desk and putting his hand on her shoulder. 'It will help him to understand you.'

'You are a love,' she said, turning to him and patting his cheek. 'You've helped me more than you know.'

'Just go off and have a great time with Roy.' He smiled. 'But don't get so involved you forget to try and track Liam down.'

Beth spent New Year's Eve alone. She had been invited to a party in Bath but she declined, preferring to stay in rather than face trying to get a taxi on the busiest night of the year. At midnight she put on her coat and went out on to her balcony with a drink to watch fireworks going off all over the city.

The previous year she had been in a very low state, what with her broken arm and having spent the whole of Christmas alone and in pain. She recalled that she'd been full of bitter thoughts at the sound of church bells ringing out and all the revelry, for it seemed to her that her whole life had passed without her ever experiencing even a fraction of the joy and happiness everyone else seemed to feel that night.

Yet she didn't feel the same this year. The church bells seemed to be ringing out a message that the past was over and done with, the future new and exciting. When Roy telephoned a few minutes after twelve to wish her a happy New Year, and said he couldn't wait until Saturday, she realized it was just the same for her.

He called for her at eight-thirty on the Saturday morning. They wanted to get an early start as it would be dark by four. As Roy drove, Beth brought him up to date with everything she and Steven had found out about Susan.

'Tell me,' he said when she'd finished, 'do you still like her? I mean, if circumstances were different, would you be able to pick up your old friendship?'

Beth thought for a moment. 'I don't know,' she said. 'It's an imponderable, isn't it? She's in prison, I'm a lawyer. There's too much water under the bridge.'

'Yes, but do you still like her, despite that? You see, I once had to arrest an old friend of mine. We hadn't seen one another for maybe fifteen years, and he'd been involved in an armed attack on a building society, so I didn't exactly have any hesitation about it. But I found I still liked him, I couldn't help it. He still liked me too, even though I'd nicked him.'

'It's difficult to say. For one thing, the whole prison visiting bit prevents us both from being ourselves,' Beth said thoughtfully. 'There are flashes of the old Suzie, but mostly she's a different person to the one I knew.'

'In what way?'

Beth thought for a moment. 'She's coarser, she used to be so ladylike, she wouldn't sit on a toilet seat for fear of catching something. I can remember us discussing kissing once when we were about twelve. She thought the idea of tongues was absolutely disgusting,' she said with a giggle.

'Well, we all get over that hurdle.' Roy laughed. 'She wouldn't be so prissy after a year or so in some hippy commune, would she?'

'That's partly what I find so hard to get my head round,' Beth said thoughtfully. 'I can relate to her having the affair with the gardener. It was kind of romantic, and almost any woman as lonely and uncertain about her future as she must have been would have done the same. When I heard about how she lived in Ambra Vale with Annabel, that too seemed in character. She adored Annabel, that child made up for all the previous sadness and disappointments in her life. Had she shot the two people just after Annabel died, I would understand everything completely.'

'I take it you mean you can't get your head round the Reuben bit?' Roy asked.

'No, I can't. It all seems peculiar to me. From what

272

Steven said Susan got herself together again while she was with Reuben. Yet if she really did, why did she lose it again when she came back to Bristol? It just doesn't fit in with the character of the girl I remember.'

'It would fit in if she did lose her mind,' he said, turning his head to look at her. 'Don't you believe that's what happened?'

'I might if I knew there had been another trauma in Wales. But according to Steven she just got disillusioned about it, nothing more. Is it possible for someone to slip in and out of rationality?'

Roy shrugged. 'That's one for the psychiatrist.'

They reached Stratford-upon-Avon at ten-thirty, and after a late breakfast and some coffee, they drove out to Luddington. Beth found she knew the way and recognized many of the houses, despite a great many of them sporting new porches and garages, but it looked very different from the way she remembered it.

'I suppose it's just because it's winter,' she remarked. It was a cold, grey day, the fields were brown bare soil, and the leafy greenness which was imprinted on her memory was missing. 'It's sort of familiar, but strange.'

But the little village green, the pretty half-timbered and thatched cottages and All Saints church were just as she remembered. The Rookery, however, was almost invisible behind trees and shrubs; they drove straight past it at first and had to turn back when Beth realized they'd missed it.

Roy pulled up opposite the drive. 'That's it?' he asked in surprise. 'It looks spooky.'

He was right, it did. The sort of place where you'd think twice before walking up the drive in the dark. Beth had always thought of it as mysterious, but that was only because of all the trees around it. They had all grown a great deal since then and almost enveloped the house now, concealing many of the windows.

The five-barred gate Suzie was often swinging on when Beth called for her was gone – perhaps the new owners couldn't be bothered with opening and closing it when they drove in. But it wasn't possible to see what other changes had been made because of the trees.

'I wonder if the ghost of mad old Granny keeps them awake?' Beth said.

Roy chuckled. 'Even if it doesn't, they'll have reporters hounding them when Susan's case comes to trial. I don't think we'd better try them for any information, do you?'

Beth looked at the two small cottages right by where they were parked. They were probably once council housing, but had been gentrified with porches and new windows. Beth seemed to recall that one of them was a shop back in the Sixties. The other looked as if it had elderly owners, judging by the old-fashioned net curtains and small holder for milk bottles, and as the cottage windows looked directly on to The Rookery, the people living there were more likely than anyone to know what went on over the road.

'Let's try here,' Beth said.

The door-bell was answered after what seemed an eternity by a small, elderly, grey-haired woman, almost drowning in a thick Arran sweater which came down to her knees.

'I'm sorry to trouble you on a Saturday morning,' Beth said. 'But I'm trying to find my friend who used to live across the road. Suzie Wright. We kind of lost touch when I went abroad.'

Beth braced herself for outrage, but clearly this woman hadn't connected her old neighbour with the murderess in Bristol, for her expression was one of kindly interest.

'She went off when the house was sold,' she said, looking Roy and Beth up and down. Presumably they passed muster for she asked them in, commenting that it was too cold to stand chatting with the door open.

She took them through to a warm, cosy living room at the back of the house, with a small couch and an armchair by the fire.

Once they were inside, Roy turned to the woman. 'This is very good of you, Mrs . . .' he said, holding out his hand to shake hers.

'Mrs Unsworthy,' she said, and shook his hand.

'My fiancée Beth has been trying so hard to find Suzie,' he said, astounding Beth with his charm. 'You see, we want her to come to our wedding.'

Beth shot him a glance, but he didn't bat an eyelid. 'So we thought if we took a drive up here today and asked around, we might be able to find her,' he went on. 'You said the house was sold. When was that?'

'I can't remember exactly,' she said, sitting down on the chair and beckoning them to take the couch. 'Eight, nine years I should think. Terribly sad for Suzie, she'd nursed her poor mother right from a girl, then she died, and her father just a few weeks later. That scoundrel of a brother of hers sold the house, right under her.'

'My goodness!' Beth exclaimed. 'Martin did that? How awful for her! You must tell me everything.'

Mrs Unsworthy's face took on new animation. She made them tea and offered them some rather stale fruit cake, and proceeded to tell them all about the Wrights.

Mr and Mrs Unsworthy had bought their house just a couple of years before Susan's grandmother died. Their contact with the Wrights then was little more than saying good morning, but they were told by other people in the village that the old lady who lived with them was senile.

'I used to feel so sorry for Margaret Wright,' she said. 'I had a dog in those days, so I often walked down by the river with him, and I'd see Margaret hanging out washing in her garden. Rows of sheets, so I guessed her mother was incontinent. I talked to young Suzie more. Sometimes I'd be out doing the front garden as she came home from school and we'd chat a bit. She was a nice girl, very helpful to her mother, and kind of old-fashioned. I didn't really get to know Margaret until the old lady died. I think that was the first time I went in their house. I went to see if there was anything I could do. Margaret said she'd be glad if I could stay and have a cup of tea with her, she said she hadn't had much sensible company for years. But the poor woman had a stroke herself just a few months later, and then it was Suzie who had to stay home and look after her.'

Beth thought that Mrs Unsworthy would make a good

witness for the defence for she spoke quite forcefully about how unfair it was that Susan spent her entire youth as a carer. 'The poor dear came in here sobbing like a little girl the day she heard her father had left the house to Martin,' she said indignantly. 'She couldn't believe her father could do that to her. And neither could we.'

Beth decided to push things along a touch.

'Another old friend told me Suzie had an affair with the gardener,' she said, making herself giggle as if she didn't believe it. 'Could it be true, Mrs Unsworthy?'

At that the old lady pursed her lips in disapproval. 'Yes, she was carrying on with him,' she said. 'We used to hear them larking about in the garden late at night. His old van was always parked outside until my John asked him to put it somewhere else. Terrible old thing it was, all rusty.'

'Why didn't he put it on the drive?' Roy asked.

'I expect Suzie thought that would make it obvious he was staying the night with her,' Mrs Unsworthy said. 'Or maybe she was afraid Martin would see it.'

'Were you shocked when she took up with him?' Roy asked. 'We heard he was like a gypsy.'

'I'm not one to gossip,' the old lady said, folding her arms across her chest. 'That poor girl was owed a bit of fun after what she'd been through. But she could have done better for herself. Don't get me wrong, I'm not a snob. But he had nothing but the old van, and of course until we heard about Martin getting the house, we thought Susan would inherit everything. We were worried in case that man was a fortune-hunter.'

'So did she run off with him?' Beth asked. 'I mean, when the house was sold.'

'No, she must have come to her senses,' Mrs Unsworthy replied. 'Or maybe that brother of hers shook some sense into her. She went off in a van alone with all her furniture. Do you know, she didn't even bother to come and say goodbye to us!'

'Really!' Beth exclaimed. She knew Susan had told both her and Steven that she'd left messages for Liam with her neighbour, and this had to be the one she meant. 'Are you saying she didn't even leave a forwarding address or anything?'

'Not a word.' Mrs Unsworthy pursed her lips. 'She didn't even tell me the date she was going. One day she was there, everything was normal. The next I saw a furniture van outside and a man carrying stuff out to it. If I'd known it was her leaving, I'd have gone over. But I thought it was Martin taking his ill-gotten gains.'

It was very clear the old lady had been very fond of Suzie and had known her pretty well. She portrayed her as a very capable, calm, stoic and kind person.

'How could she have gone off without a word to me?' Mrs Unsworthy's eyes suddenly filled with tears. 'I was so hurt, I couldn't understand why, especially as she'd run to me when her brother was so nasty to her. My John said she'd write in a week or two, but she never did. I didn't even get a Christmas card from her.'

Beth found that completely mystifying too. She had always thought of Susan as being the kind to be sentimental about people. And someone who had always cared for old people wasn't likely to hurt the feelings of someone who had been kind to her.

'Did she write to anyone or leave her address with someone else?' Beth asked.

'No one I know.' The old lady sniffed. 'Lots of other people from the village came and asked me the same thing. She was liked by everyone, you see. Everyone felt bad about what that brother of hers had done to her.'

'Would she have left her new address with the people who bought The Rookery?' Roy asked.

Mrs Unsworthy shook her head. 'They came and asked me if I had it some months after they moved in. There were a few letters for Suzie, you see. They knew there was some bad feeling between her and her brother, so they thought if they sent them on to him, he might not give them to her.'

Beth looked at Roy questioningly.

'Did the gardener come looking for her?' Roy asked.

'Not here he didn't.'

'Have you seen him since?' Roy asked. 'I believe he used to do lots of gardens in this area.'

'Never clapped eyes on him again,' she said quite firmly.

'Can you think of anyone else in the village that might know where he is?' Roy asked.

'They might know at The Bell in Shottery,' she said. 'He drank down there a lot.'

'Well, that was strange,' Beth said as they got back in the car. 'Why would Susan tell me she left her address for Liam when she didn't?'

'Because the affair was already over?' Roy suggested. 'Maybe she made up all that lovey-dovey stuff to make herself feel better about it?'

'She convinced me,' Beth said. 'The only thing I found odd was that she seemed to get over him so quickly.'

'Maybe she didn't say goodbye to Mrs Unsworthy or keep in touch because of her pregnancy?' Roy suggested. 'You said she was the old-fashioned kind, perhaps she was ashamed, and didn't want people talking about it?'

Beth nodded in agreement. As she herself was the kind who never told anyone anything personal, she could perfectly well understand that. 'Let's give the pub a try, if that fails we can always go and look at Anne Hathaway's cottage, it's just by it.'

The inside of The Bell at Shottery was disappointing. Beth had imagined that an old pub, so close to the tourist attraction of Anne Hathaway's cottage, would have its old-world charm still intact. But it had gone the way of so many other pubs – fruit machines, piped music and wall-to-wall carpet. Not even a real log fire.

Yet it was welcoming, with a Christmas tree and decorations still up, and as it was the wrong time of year for tourists, most of the customers appeared to be local.

Roy bought a pint for himself and a glass of wine for Beth and they stayed at the bar while they considered who might be a likely person to ask about Liam.

There was a small group of older men sitting by the pool table, their tweed jackets and sturdy boots suggesting they were farmers. 'Shall we give them a whirl?' he asked.

'Go and ask them on your own,' she suggested. 'I'll wander over if it looks as if you are on to something.'

'I thought you were all for female emancipation.' He grinned.

'I am,' she agreed. 'But men of that age talk to other men more readily. Besides, you're the super-sleuth, not me.'

Taking his beer with him, Roy went over to the men. 'I wonder if any of you could help me?' he said. 'I'm trying to track down a gardener by the name of Liam Johnstone. I'm told he drinks in here. Would any of you know him?'

The men exchanged glances.

'Was that the name of the long-haired gypo?' one of the group asked a big man wearing a maroon waistcoat under his jacket.

'Aye, his name were Liam,' the big man replied in a rich Warwickshire burr. 'I used to drink with him. Dunno where he is now though, haven't seen him fer years.'

'That's a shame,' Roy said. 'He used to do a friend's garden. I thought his work was good. Any idea where I might find him?'

The big man shook his head. 'Plenty of folk have asked me that, and I'll say the same to you as I said to all of them, he must have took off down South.'

'Did you know him well?' Roy asked. He liked the look of this old man who was at least seventy-five but fit and strong, with a weatherbeaten face.

'I'd say so, we used to drink together. I liked him even if he did look like a gypo.'

'Can I buy you all a drink?' Roy suggested to the group. He thought it might oil the wheels of their memories.

After four pints had been brought over, Roy turned to the big man, who had introduced himself as Stan Fogetty. 'I was told Liam had a girlfriend in Luddington,' he said. 'Would you know who she is? I might be able to trace him through her.'

'Only girl I know about was young Suzie Wright. But she ain't around here any longer either,' Stan replied, then launched into the tale of how this same girl was robbed of her home by her brother. The indignation in his voice and the animation on the faces of the other men showed that this had been hot gossip around here at the time, and something they all felt strongly about.

Beth sidled over at that point and she and Roy listened carefully, as if fascinated by a bit of local history. Stan's version was much the same as Mrs Unsworthy's, the only difference being that Stan was born and bred in Luddington and knew Charles and Margaret Wright much better than Mrs Unsworthy.

'Reckon young Liam felt sorry for little Suzie,' Stan said. 'There was plenty that thought badly of him, like he was after what was coming to her. But I knew that weren't true.'

'What was he like then?' Roy asked.

'He were an odd bloke,' Stan said thoughtfully. 'Clever, well-educated, but a real nature boy, kept away from cities and didn't give a toss about money and possessions. He were a kind man, he'd got friendly with Suzie when he was doing the Wrights' garden, he liked her and thought she deserved better than being stuck in that house looking after her mum and dad. He used to say that to us all, didn't he?' Stan looked round at his friends and they all nodded in agreement.

'So the parents died, and then what?' Roy asked.

'He just stuck by her,' Stan shrugged. 'He told me more than once she were very capable, but he didn't think she could cope on her own.'

'So where did she go when the house was sold?' Roy asked.

'Dunno,' Stan said. 'Went off without a word to anyone.'

'Liam was still here then, I take it?' Roy said.

'No, he shot off about the same time.'

'So he could have gone off with her then?'

'No, not Liam.' Stan grinned broadly. 'He weren't the settling kind. We had a drink one night just before the house was sold and I asked him if he'd be going with her. He said something to the effect that she needed a more normal bloke than him, and he was already getting a bit tired of her trying to straighten him out.'

'What do you think he meant by that?'

'Meals on time, fussing over him. You know what women are like!'

Roy turned to smile at Beth. 'Sounds like that poor girl got a raw deal all round,' she said. Then, looking at Stan, she asked, 'Why do you think her father left the place to his son? Had she done something which upset him?'

'Well, my dear,' Stan looked at her appraisingly, 'it's the way blokes like Charley think. Sons inherit, that's the way it's always been. Give it to the girls and they'll just get married and the property goes out the family.'

'A bit old-fashioned, and cruel in this case as Suzie had lived there for so long,' Beth retorted.

'A fool I'd call him.' Stan grinned at Beth. 'I used to go shooting with him at one time, nice enough bloke but he always got things all arse up. His boy was born during the war and by the time Charley got home he'd been spoilt by his mum and gran. He were the soft, bookish kind, a real disappointment to Charley. Don't reckon they ever got on. Then Suzie came along and she were the apple of Charley's eye. He taught her to shoot, y'know! She were good at it too, for a girl. Many's the time I went out rabbiting with Charley and she came tagging along too.'

'Really!' Beth exclaimed. 'But how strange, if he idolized her, that he wasn't kinder to her later on.'

'Well, like I said, he always got things arse upwards,' Stan retorted. 'When his wife had the stroke he seemed to change towards Suzie right away. Never said a word about what a little brick she were, just kept going on about how smart his son was, how well he'd done fer himself in the city. It made some of us mad, we all knew Martin was a snotty little bastard, who didn't give a toss about his folks.'

'So are you saying he left everything to Martin to kind of make up for not having much time for him when he was little?' Beth said, trying to clarify what the man meant.

Stan shrugged. 'Sommat like that, I guess. Some said he did it to spite Susan because she got shirty with him

284

when she suspected him of knocking off another woman. Some said it were Martin forced his hand. But whichever, it were a right shame. Suzie would have stayed here I reckon, married a local bloke, maybe had a couple of kids. She were a dyed-in-the-wool country girl.'

'What a sad story.' Beth sighed. She wondered what would happen in this pub when Susan's trial began and they all discovered what else had befallen her. 'To think we only wanted to find Liam to do our garden! Do any of you know other friends of his we could try? Or people he worked for?'

Stan looked thoughtful. 'I could give you a dozen names of people he worked for, but like I said when we first got chatting, there's lots of people wanted his help when he moved on, and they couldn't find him. Don't know where 'is folks are, or if he had any, he never said. Only place you might find out is down the police station.'

'Police!' Roy exclaimed, his eyes widening in surprise.

'Well, it's a long shot, but they towed his van away. It had stuff of his in it.'

'When was this?' Beth asked.

Stan scratched his head. 'Years ago now. He left it parked up the lane from the Wrights' house. Rusty old Volkswagen camper it were, he used to live in it. It were there for months, then someone nicked the wheels. No one had seen Liam for a while, so someone called the police to take it away.'

Chapter thirteen

'It's very strange that Liam didn't return to this area,' Roy mused over dinner that night. 'I could understand him scooting off for a while if he thought he was going to get a lot of flak about abandoning Susan in her moment of need. But you'd think he'd miss all those people he worked for.'

They were in the restaurant of the Welcombe Hotel, a gracious country house hotel with its own golf-course, about a mile outside Stratford-upon-Avon, which Roy had booked them into. Beth had expected something small and quite ordinary, but it was very grand; it had a vast drawing room with a huge log fire, comfortable couches and armchairs, and sumptuous bedrooms. Beyond the windows of the restaurant were floodlit formal gardens and a splendid view of the golf-course and surrounding countryside. It was the sort of place which would be fully booked most of the year with golfers and tourists, but so soon after the New Year there were only a handful of guests and the other people in the restaurant that night were mainly locals.

Stan had directed Roy and Beth to two other people in nearby villages who had employed Liam, so they had called on both of them after leaving the pub. Fortunately these people knew nothing about Susan Wright, so they didn't have to listen to repeats of the saga about her dastardly brother.

They had a far better picture of Liam now: reliable, hardworking, honest, well-educated and considered a real gentleman, despite his unorthodox appearance and life-style. He sounded a remarkable man, judging by the affectionate manner in which people spoke of him, even after several years' absence.

The first house they called at had several acres of garden and a swimming pool. Mrs Jackson, the wife of the surgeon who owned it, said Liam used to come to her every spring, and again in October for two weeks. He did the pruning, heavy digging and any tree or shrub planting. She said her husband had asked him dozens of times if he would be their full-time gardener, but he always refused. Apparently he found ordinary garden maintenance, mowing lawns and weeding too dull and he didn't like to be stuck in one place for too long. Mrs Jackson said they were disappointed when he didn't turn up as usual in the autumn of 1986. She thought he might have gone to Scotland as she knew he often spent the winter working for the Forestry Commission there.

The second house they called at was just a cottage, but it had an equally large garden, most of which was woodland. The couple who owned it were in their eighties, both a little deaf and wandering slightly in their minds, so they couldn't say with any accuracy what year it was when they last saw Liam. But they did say he'd come to them every November for more than twelve years. They had always put him up too, as the weather was usually bad and he got so dirty cutting back the brambles and burning them. They were both touchingly wistful about him. They said they had always looked forward to him coming because he would also do little jobs around the house they could no longer manage, and they liked his company.

'Why would he leave his van behind?' Roy said as he poured Beth another glass of wine.

'Maybe it had broken down?' she suggested. 'He might have known it wasn't going to be worth having it mended. Could you check with the police here?'

'I doubt they even have a record of it now. It would have been scrapped soon after it was towed away,' he said. 'Besides, I'll get myself in hot water if it gets out I've been going around asking questions when I'm not on official police business.'

'But you only stumbled on something curious while you were a civilian,' she said. 'You haven't been a policeman today, just my friend.'

'I don't think it would be seen in that light.' He grinned. 'For one thing, we got Mrs Unsworthy to talk about Susan without revealing the true nature of our interest. I was her arresting officer, for goodness' sake! Then in a nearby village we pretended we were looking for a gardener. If Stan and Mrs Unsworthy put their heads together, they might very well be ringing the local police themselves to complain about us.'

Beth could see what he meant. 'I wonder if I should tell Susan that I've been up here?'

'I wouldn't, not yet anyway. Let's just see what unfolds.'

Beth woke early the next morning, and for a brief moment was confused about where she was. But she reached out for the bedside light, and as soon as she saw the quaintly old-fashioned room with its chintz curtains, her confusion vanished.

She got out of bed to make a cup of tea, but it was cold because the heating hadn't come on yet. As she waited for the small kettle to boil, she pulled back the curtains and looked out.

Her room overlooked the front drive and the fields and woodland beyond. It was just on dawn, and a thick frost covered everything so thickly it looked like snow. She thought that almost anyone would put such a view on top of their wish list, yet Susan, who had lived with an even more outstanding one than this for most of her life, hadn't once remarked on missing it since she was arrested.

The sound of the kettle boiling stopped Beth's reverie, and she hastily made a cup of tea and went back to her warm bed. She wondered if Roy was awake yet, and if he was, was he thinking that she must be frigid?

After the meal last night they had moved into the drawing room and had several more drinks by the fire. Had they been alone, Beth felt she might have been able to really talk to him, hold his hand, and that a few kisses might have encouraged her to invite him into her room later. But another couple on a golfing weekend had come and joined them by the fire, and kept talking to them, so by the time the bar closed Beth was too sleepy even to consider anything more. Roy had kissed her at the door of her room, and she'd come in alone.

This could-she, couldn't-she stuff was almost worse than jumping in with both feet and finding things were as awful as ever. At least that way she always lost her romantic ideas about the man immediately. She knew now she didn't want to lose Roy, yesterday had been so lovely. He was such a good companion, relaxed, amusing, thoughtful and stimulating. He didn't try too hard either, the way most men did. None of that trying to impress her that she always found so tedious.

Yet he did impress her. He had a natural charm that made everyone open up to him, a clever way of wording questions to get at the truth. Part of this of course was influenced by his job, just as it was with her, but he had a real interest in people. By the time they'd left the old couple in the late afternoon, he really knew them well. As they were driving back to the hotel he'd made some remark about them being yet another old couple whose children didn't bother with them. She asked him how he knew this.

'The photographs of their grandchildren were all baby ones. But they are obviously all grown up now,' he said, looking surprised she hadn't picked up on this. 'The old girl said, "There isn't much for young people right out here in the country," that's her excuse for no one coming to visit.'

Beth thought he was probably right. That was probably the reason why they had befriended Liam too. But she wouldn't have thought of it herself.

She wondered though how many more times Roy would ask her out before he lost his patience with her. Most of her previous promising relationships had fizzled out that way. Over the years she had been called everything from a prick-tease to a cold-hearted bitch, and though she hadn't lost any sleep over that most of the time, thinking about Roy reminded her of how she'd felt about James Macutcheon.

James was a solicitor too, in a firm in Chancery Lane. Like Roy, he was strong, charming, affectionate and good fun.

She was thirty-four then. James was a year younger, tall, blond, with the kind of poise that came from a loving, comfortable, upper-middle-class family. She had fallen in love with him by their third date, and by the fifth she was afraid he would lose interest if she didn't go to bed with him. When he invited her over to supper one evening at his place, a smart flat in Chelsea, she was ready to take the plunge.

Everything seemed so perfect – soft music, candle-light, and the Chinese meal he'd got delivered was one of the best she'd ever eaten. They lay on a couch cuddling later, and she wanted him, really wanted him in a way she'd never known with a man before.

But all at once his kisses became too forced, he was sticking his tongue half-way down her throat, and his hand was going up her skirt. She wanted him to arouse her gently, but he thrust his fingers inside her so hard it hurt, and all her desire vanished. She tried to make a joke of it, asked if he could just slow down a bit, but he muttered something about how he knew she was the kind to want it rough, and yanked her knickers down.

Just remembering it brought tears to her eyes. She didn't let him force her, she wriggled away.

'I don't like it rough,' she said, crying by then as she pulled her knickers back up. 'I wanted to be loved, not raped.'

If he'd looked shocked or apologetic, or got up to embrace her, it might have ended differently. But he just lay there on the couch, his trousers unzipped, his hair all tousled, and looked at her with cold disdain.

'Grow up, Beth,' he said in a cold voice. 'What did you come here for, if not for a fuck?'

She was out of the door before he could even get up, running down King's Road with her shoes in her hands, looking frantically for a taxi.

In the months that followed, she went over and over that evening again in her mind, asking herself what gave him the idea she liked it rough. It seemed logical to her that any man would guess when a woman didn't leap into bed on the first date that she was the kind who wanted to be seduced with tenderness.

The worst thing about it was she had fallen for James, believed he felt the same, and that he sensed there was a good reason for her hesitancy. Clearly she was wrong on both counts as he hadn't run after her to apologize. He never contacted her again. All he did for her was to take her right back to being seventeen again, feeling dirty and humiliated.

After that experience she'd lost trust in all men. She only accepted a date now and again, and got a taxi home alone. She never went out with anyone more than twice. She felt she was safer leading a celibate life, she couldn't be hurt that way.

As she snuggled back under the covers, she decided that Roy was very different to James in his outlook. He'd known deep sorrow, he was sensitive and kind, and she knew she must try to talk to him about her problems.

After a huge breakfast they put their bags back in Roy's car and went for a walk. Beth put on a woolly red hat, gloves and matching scarf, and Roy laughingly said her nose was turning red to match them, and kissed it.

'I love walking on frost,' she said gleefully as they took a footpath from the hotel up over the fields to Stratford. 'There's nothing quite like that scrunch.'

'Cracking ice is even better,' he said, thumping his heel into a frozen puddle and grinning like a schoolboy.

All at once Beth felt the need to say something. She slid her arms around his middle in a hug, and rubbed her cold nose against his.

'You're doing a good job on cracking this ice maiden,' she said. 'I can feel myself thawing. Don't lose patience with me yet, Roy, there are reasons why I'm like I am.'

She held her breath, expecting either questions she couldn't answer, or silence because he was mystified. But instead he put a hand on either side of her face and looked right into her eyes with understanding. 'I guessed as much,' he said. 'But patience is something I have by the cartload, and I'm a good listener too. When you want to tell me about it, just say.'

'How did you guess?' she said a little later as they walked on hand-in-hand through the fields. Their breath was like smoke in the cold air, and the sky was leaden as if snow was on the way.

'You are extraordinarily defensive,' he said. 'When I first met you in the courts I noticed then how everything was tight about you, the way you moved, the way you talked. Even though we had a very stimulating chat, you gave absolutely nothing away about yourself.'

Beth frowned. 'Well, surely no one does on a first meeting?'

'Most of us do,' he said, and grinned. 'Whether we mean to or not. Anyway, that evening when we went for a drink after Susan's arrest, you had a go at me for asking if you had a man. That isn't a normal reaction for a woman as lovely as you, Beth! Most women, when asked such a thing, laugh and then give you the whole nine yards as to why they haven't.'

'Do they?' she said with some surprise.

He nodded. 'Perhaps they wouldn't if they thought the man was an arsehole, or on the make. They might not always tell the truth either. But moving conversation on to a slightly more personal note is the way we make friends.'

'So that's why I don't have many friends,' she said, and smiled ruefully. 'So why did you bother with me then?'

'Because I was intrigued, especially when it turned out

Susan was a childhood friend, and I saw how it affected you,' he said, his eyes twinkling with amusement. 'I saw a glimmer of the girl you once were, the woman you could be if you stepped out from behind your professionalism. I wondered what made you so defensive, and afraid.'

Beth took a deep breath. 'I will tell you soon,' she said. 'But not today, I don't want to spoil things.'

Steven drove along Acacia Avenue slowly, looking for number 27. It was a miserable grey day, very cold with intermittent showers of sleet, but fortunately the M4 had been surprisingly traffic-free, and he'd enjoyed the drive up from Bristol.

He had of course expected that Martin Wright would live in a smart house. Windsor was a good area, and he knew the man had got a great deal of money from the sale of The Rookery. But he hadn't really expected anything quite as grand as this road. It was tree-lined, with neat grass verges and wide drives leading up to detached houses that had to be worth half a million at least. They were the sort of homes that came with swimming pools in the back garden, domestic help and children at private schools.

He stopped the car when he saw Wright's house, a Thirties mini-mansion with a green tiled roof and Art Deco stained glass on a central round staircase window. It was painted white, with a portico over the front door and three lots of windows on either side. The drive itself was the expensive kind Steven had seen advertised in glossy magazines, laid with shiny cobbles which were sealed so that no weed could ever lift its ugly head. It was a far cry from Steven's semi-detached with its scrubby lawn and the children's artwork stuck up in the windows.

'Even further from the place his sister ended up in,' Steven muttered to himself as he parked his car out in the road. The large wrought-iron gates were shut, preventing him from driving on to the drive, and Steven saw this as further evidence that Wright was intending to be difficult.

Steven was nervous. Everything he knew about this man suggested he was a nasty piece of work. Anyone so ruthless, so uncaring about his sister, wasn't likely to be easy to talk to. He was glad now that Beth had bullied him into getting his suit cleaned and his hair cut. She'd said he was to drop her name into the conversation too, as she didn't want Martin to think Susan hadn't got a friend in the world.

The door-bell was answered by a middle-aged woman wearing a white overall. She had gold-rimmed spectacles and a superior expression.

'Mrs Wright?' Steven asked, even though to Susan's knowledge Martin had never married.

'No, I'm his housekeeper,' she said.

'Smythe, from Tarbuck, Stone and Aldridge. I have an appointment with Mr Wright,' Steven said.

She allowed him in and left him waiting in the hall while she went towards the back of the house.

'Mr Wright will see you now,' the housekeeper called out a few moments later. She was standing by the door she'd disappeared through earlier, indicating he was to go in.

Martin Wright was standing by the fireplace in a room which was an attempt at a Victorian gentleman's library, with leather chairs, walls lined with books and an antique rosewood desk inlaid with mother-of-pearl. But it didn't really work – the proportions of the room were all wrong and the dark red carpet and curtains made it oppressive rather than opulent.

'Plenty of money but no imagination,' Steven thought maliciously. He decided he would ask to use the lavatory later on so he could check out a little more of the house.

'Steven Smythe,' Steven said, holding out his hand. 'Thank you for agreeing to see me.'

He was surprised by Wright. In his imagination he'd been a short, portly man. In fact Martin Wright was as tall as Steven himself, slender and straight-backed, his dark hair flecked with grey, a handsome man with strong, even features and few facial lines, even though Steven knew he was fifty-four. His eyes were the only thing he had in common with Susan, they were the same pale greenish-blue.

'First let me say I see absolutely no point in talking to you,' Wright said crisply, sitting down at his desk. 'The police have already interviewed me, and I am certainly not prepared to be a witness in my sister's defence.'

Steven was tempted to say that if he was called to be a witness he'd have no choice but to attend, but resisted the temptation.

'It's only background information I'm after,' he said, smiling pleasantly. 'May I sit down?'

The man waved his hand at the seat furthest from him. Steven ignored it and took the one closest.

'When you were told of your sister's arrest and the charges laid against her, what was your reaction?' he began.

'Reaction?' Wright raised his eyebrows. 'Horror, of course.'

'Not disbelief?'

'Of course not. Suzie always was an irrational, highly emotional woman,' he said, crossing his legs and moving in his chair so he wasn't looking directly at Steven.

'No sympathy? You do know that she holds the man and woman she shot responsible for her child's death?'

'There are ways of dealing with such things without resorting to murder,' Wright retorted crisply. 'No, I have no sympathy with her whatsoever.'

'Did you ever see Annabel?'

'Who's Annabel?'

It crossed Steven's mind that Wright was trying to wind him up, and he was succeeding.

'Her daughter, Mr Wright. Your niece, who died of meningitis,' Stephen said sharply.

'No, I didn't.'

'But you did know of her existence?'

'Yes. Suzie sent me a photograph once, and a foolish gushing letter reminding me the child was my niece. I don't know what she expected of me.'

'I don't believe she expected anything at all of you,' Steven said. 'It was her way of offering the olive branch.'

Wright got up from his seat and stalked over to the

window, a distance of only a few feet. He was wearing a very well-cut dark grey suit. 'I take it you've been given the full Cinderella story then?' he said, leaning one hand on the window frame and staring out into the garden. 'Suzie always had a tendency for drama. The truth of the matter is that my father was an old-fashioned man who believed the eldest son should inherit. As that was his wish, I was bound to honour it.'

Steven felt like pointing out that an honourable man would have made some provision for the younger unmarried sister who had devoted her entire youth to taking care of their parents. But the whole point of coming here today was to get to know the man better, not to antagonize him.

'I'm sure you are aware Susan could very well have contested the will,' Steven said evenly. 'She would almost certainly have won too, given the length of time she'd cared for your parents. But she didn't, and that meant she had to live in drastically reduced circumstances. I believe that when she wrote to tell you about Annabel, it was her way of showing she felt no bitterness to you.'

'How long have you known her?' Wright asked with a disparaging sniff.

'About three months,' Steven said.

'Well, I've known her since she was born and I know perfectly well why she wrote that letter. She wanted a handout.'

Steven bristled. He understood exactly how euphoric new parents felt, and that they wanted to share their joy with friends and relatives. 'I don't believe that was her motive at all,' he said calmly. 'You are her brother. If she hoped for anything at all from you, it was only that you take an interest in your niece.'

'That to Suzie would mean money. She was always a parasite.'

'That's not what I've heard from Beth Powell, one of the partners in my law firm,' Steven said.

As Steven mentioned Beth's name, a flicker of surprise crossed Martin Wright's face. Clearly he had known of the friendship.

'Beth has known your sister since they were both ten,' Steven continued. 'According to her, Susan didn't choose to stay home and take care of your mother, the role of carer was foisted upon her at an age when she couldn't know the long-term implications of it. By the time she had realized what it meant, despite the fact that she would rather have got a job and become independent, she was trapped. It seems your father always claimed he couldn't afford a nurse. Furthermore, he said if Susan wasn't prepared to do the job, he would put your mother in a home.'

'Suzie's favourite role was always that of martyr,' Wright said dismissively. 'There was absolutely no question of my father putting Mother into a home, he was devoted to her. Suzie stayed because she had it so easy there.'

'I'd hardly call caring for an invalid and housekeeping in such a big house, working seven days a week for mere pocket money, easy.' Steven retorted. 'She had no fun, no friends, no life of her own. I'd be more inclined to call it slavery.'

He could understand now why Susan was intimidated by this man. He was so cold he was almost reptilian. And a liar too.

'Suzie would imply slavery.' Wright shrugged. 'It sounds just like her. The truth of the matter was she was too lazy to make a life of her own. There were no locks on the doors. If she felt so strongly she could have upped and left at any time.'

'Emotional ties are every bit as strong as locks,' Steven said. 'But even if you don't agree that she was compelled to stay and care for your parents, surely you must feel she deserves sympathy and understanding for what she went through losing her only child?'

'I agree, that was sad,' Wright said, but his cold eyes suggested he had no conception of what losing a child would do to anyone.

'She was devastated,' Steven said more forcefully. 'But what made it so much worse for her was that Annabel needn't have died. The doctor was negligent, he turned her away from his surgery, dismissing her symptoms as a viral infection. Susan was alone, with no one to turn to for support or comfort. Absolutely nothing left in her life. I don't condone what she did, but I can understand why she did it. Can't you?'

'What did you come here for?' Wright interrupted. 'If it was in the hope you could get me to make an impassioned appeal for lenience, you're barking up the wrong tree.'

'Not at all, Mr Wright,' Steven said through clenched teeth. He couldn't believe anyone could be that unfeeling. 'I have other people who will come forward to tell the court how unfairly life treated Susan. I just wanted to see for myself what her brother was like, and how you lived.' He wished he could add that he thought Wright was merely adding to Susan's credibility, but he didn't dare go that far.

'What is that supposed to mean?' Wright asked, a touch of menace in his voice.

'Did you know that at the time your sister shot those people, she was broken down with grief, living in a damp, cold attic room, cleaning offices to pay the rent?' Steven said. 'A gesture from you might have made all the difference.'

'I had no idea where she was,' Wright said, for the first time sounding a little nervous.

'I think you did, Mr Wright,' Steven replied, more calmly than he felt. 'Susan telephoned you at your office in May of 1993, not long after she arrived back in Bristol. She asked you for help, didn't she? That's when she told you Annabel had died.'

'She caught me at a bad moment,' Wright said quickly. 'And anyway, she didn't make herself very clear.'

'I think if my sister was to ring me and tell me her child was dead, that would be clear enough for me,' Steven said archly.

'It would have been hypocritical for me to make a fuss about it when I'd had nothing to do with the child when she was alive,' Wright blustered. 'Besides, I don't like being contacted at the office.'

Steven knew he had in fact been abusive and had refused to lend Susan money to tide her over until she got a job. But there was little point in bringing that up now.

'Susan had no other way of contacting you, except at your office,' he said calmly. 'You didn't let her know when you moved here, did you?'

'Why should I?' Wright said, his voice rising slightly. 'She was nothing to me. The moment she was born I was pushed out –' he broke off suddenly, his faint blush showing he was dismayed that he'd let slip the real reason for his animosity to his sister.

Steven would have very much liked to probe further about this, but he doubted Wright was capable of opening up about anything, so he just made a mental note of his reaction to pass on to the barrister at Susan's trial.

'The war made a lot of fathers strangers to their children,' he said, softening his voice. 'Susan couldn't help that. But anyway, your father was far kinder to you than he was to your sister. He let you pursue the career of your choice, made no demands on your freedom. And he left you everything. As I see it, the only things he did for Susan was to burden her with responsibility he should have shouldered himself, teach her to shoot and give her his gun. I'd say you were the one that had it easy.'

As he said this, Steven got up – he wasn't going to wait to be thrown out. The man was odious and any further questioning was unnecessary.

'Thank you for seeing me,' he continued. 'You may very well be called as a witness, that will depend on Susan's plea. And a Happy New Year to you. I'll let myself out.'

*

At the start of February Beth drove over to Wales on Friday evening after work. She was alone because she felt unable to ask Roy to accompany her again when the trip necessitated staying overnight in a hotel.

They had been out together several times since New Year, to the cinema, for a drink, and she'd cooked him Sunday lunch one day at her place. They had kissed and cuddled, but Roy hadn't attempted to take things any further, and Beth still didn't know if she was ready to tell him about her past.

The more she saw him, the more confused she became. One moment she was burning to see him, the next she was dreading it. She wasn't dreading actually being with him, it was only the burden of knowing that sooner or later she would have to bring things to a head and tell him about the rape. Sometimes she even imagined it would be easier never to see him again than to live with the perpetual anxiety about it.

She hoped that by going away alone for this weekend, she might be able to clarify her feelings. She had never been farther into Wales than Cardiff before, and although it was very cold, no rain or snow was expected, so she hoped she might be able to do some walking.

Since the start of the year, she had visited Susan three times. They were not fact-finding visits, she left those to Steven. Her role was that of old friend, and as such she and Susan mostly just reminisced and filled in the years since they'd last seen each other. She had found she liked Susan as much as she had as a girl. Maybe the innocence had gone, for in many ways she was more worldly than Beth now, but her warmth, and the way she cared far more about others than herself, were still the same.

Time and again Beth thought what a good social worker Susan would have made. She had a knack of drawing out confidences and she had a deep understanding of people, both her fellow prisoners and the officers.

They were talking about drug-related crime on one visit, and Susan said she believed addicts should be registered, the way they used to be years ago.

'It would put the bloody drug barons out of business,' she said with surprising passion. 'They'd give up bringing drugs into the country, and the addicts would be seen by qualified people, in clinics, get drugs that are pure, and be encouraged to kick the habit.'

Beth didn't agree and said so.

'If you spent just a couple of days in here you'd soon see it my way,' Susan said fiercely. 'The women here have to steal and sell themselves to support their habit, there is no other way. But remove the need to do that and you'd halve the drug-related crime overnight. Without pushers on the streets, there would be far fewer new addicts.'

'I didn't know you were the oracle on drugs and addiction,' Beth said with just a touch of sarcasm.

Susan gave her a scathing look. 'You haven't changed,' she said, and then half smiled. 'You always were a bit judgmental. You don't necessarily have to shoot up heroin to understand why some people succumb to it. Any more than you don't have to murder someone to understand that either. It's all about putting yourself in someone else's shoes for a minute or two.'

'So having murdered someone helps you understand a drug addict, does it?' Beth said.

'Yes, it does. I think we share a similar basic flaw in our characters,' Susan said, and folded her arms defiantly. 'It's all about doing something regardless of the fact that it will lead to destruction. With drugs it's your own destruction, with murder it's someone else's. But I'd say the original compulsion is quite similar in both cases, basically a lack of self-esteem.'

'So that was your problem, was it?' Beth asked.

Susan didn't answer.

'Well, speak up then,' Beth taunted her.

Susan gave her a cold look. 'Don't mock me, Beth. Of course I haven't got much self-esteem. Why else would I let people walk all over me? I could never articulate what I really felt, I kept it all inside. A great many addicts start out the same. They found drugs made them feel good about themselves. Of course, the feel-good factor doesn't last, so they do it again, and again. Before long they are hooked.'

'Are you trying to say you felt better once you killed Wetherall and Parks?'

'Yes, I did.'

Beth looked hard at Susan and saw that she really meant what she said. It made her feel just a little nervous, though she didn't quite know why.

'Does that mean if you hadn't been arrested you might have killed again?'

Susan laughed mirthlessly. 'I made sure I was arrested! It was the equivalent of taking a really big overdose. That way you know you won't be around to do it again.'

Beth had left the prison that day with plenty of food for thought. Ever since Steven had met Martin Wright and found him to be even more callous and obnoxious than Susan had led him to believe, he'd had a slightly different view on her case. He had put forward the suggestion to Beth that Susan had started to crack at the time of her parents' death, not, as they had previously supposed, when Annabel died. She'd been under a great deal of strain for years – the two deaths in such a short space of time, the contents of her father's will, and of course her brother's nastiness had all added to it. This, Steven felt, would explain why she got involved with Liam, and why she acted in such an uncharacteristic manner by moving away without telling her old friends and neighbours where she was going.

Steven had showed Beth a medical report about how pregnancy often dispelled depression and anxiety, even in patients who had suffered severely from it for years. There was evidence, too, that many women didn't have a relapse after the birth of their baby, the joy they felt in being a mother kept it at bay.

Steven felt, and he'd consulted a psychiatrist for confirmation of this view, that when Annabel died, Susan was utterly broken, for along with natural grief, all her old wounds opened up again. He felt sure Beth would discover that her time in Wales had merely been a kind of remission, and that when she finally returned to Bristol with nothing, and no one to turn to, she fell apart mentally.

Beth was inclined to agree with him. If she could just get some proof that Reuben had been another hard-hearted swine who had used Susan for his own ends, then pushed her out, she was sure they could present a watertight case of diminished responsibility.

Beth reached The Crown in Cardigan at half past nine. Brendan, Beth's colleague at the practice, had recommended the small inn, as he and his wife often stayed there, and Emlyn Carlisle, the town nearest to Hill House, Reuben's place, was only about twenty miles further inland, Susan had told them.

The inn was everything Brendan had said it was, beautifully furnished and decorated, and very warm and comfortable. Simon, the landlord, was attentive and friendly. When Beth said she thought she was too tired for a proper meal in the restaurant, he offered to bring up a tray to her room.

It was very cold but bright the next morning and Beth set out for Emlyn Carlisle straight after breakfast. Simon had informed her it was something of a ghetto of what he laughingly called 'Save the Whalers', a generic term for old hippies, animal rights activists, vegetarians and other non-conformists. He suggested she should stop at the pub in the High Street in Emlyn Carlisle and have a chat with the landlord first, as he apparently knew everyone for miles around and would be able to give her directions to Hill House.

Beth was wearing walking boots, jeans and a thick padded coat. She hoped that after she'd talked to Reuben, she'd have some time left for exploring the countryside.

A health shop, several small crafts shops and others selling crystals, candles and Tarot cards suggested that Simon was right about Emlyn Carlisle having a large proportion of 'alternatives' amongst its population. The pub Beth had been directed to wasn't officially open when she got there, but as the door was open and she could see a man behind the bar restocking the shelves, she went in anyway. She apologized for doing so and explained that Simon at The Crown in Cardigan had suggested she got directions for Hill House here.

The man looked typically Welsh, as short and sturdy as a pit pony, dark-haired with a ruddy face. 'Hill House?' he repeated, frowning as if puzzled by the request. 'You know someone up there?'

'No,' she said. 'I just want to have a talk with the owner. Do you know him, Reuben Moreland? I understand it's a sort of commune. Is that right?'

'They like to call it that, but a coven of witches, crooks and drug addicts is how I see it,' he said. He seemed agitated and sort of shuffled down the bar away from her, as if even saying that much was dangerous.

Beth thought it would be better to lay her cards on the table. 'I'm a solicitor,' she said, and put her card on the bar in front of him. 'I am representing someone who once lived there. That's why I need to talk to Moreland.'

The man picked up her card, read it and looked at her

again, this time with a smile. 'You'll be lucky,' he said. 'He hasn't been seen around here for ages.'

'So who is living there now?' Beth asked, pleased to see he was unbending. 'I'd be grateful for any information before I go there.'

'You don't want to go up there alone,' he said, looking horrified. 'Too many dogs and queer people. Anything could happen to you.'

Beth hadn't for one moment expected to be warned off. 'Really!' she exclaimed in surprise.

He leaned on the bar. 'Yes. Look, it's dangerous, see,' he said conspiratorially. 'They're like animals, living in filth, out of their minds on drugs. All of us down here give them a wide berth.'

Beth thought that the man was probably exaggerating, prejudiced because the residents of Hill House weren't conventional. But on the other hand she would be foolish to go up there unprepared.

'I have been told Moreland cons vulnerable people to come and live there,' she admitted. The man nodded in agreement.

'I've seen some of the wrecks that run away from there,' he said. 'I've made complaints to the police, but it seems they can't do anything because Moreland owns that place. They said they need evidence of a crime before they can act. But he isn't there now anyway, he hasn't been seen around for a long while.'

'If it's his place and there's people living there, they must know where he is,' Beth said.

'They probably do, but I can't see any of them telling you.'

The man launched into a vitriolic account of vanloads of grungy dead-beats arriving during the summer for wild parties. He said that the locals were frightened to go away on holiday for fear their houses would be broken into. Cars had been stolen; the fields and woodlands were left littered with rubbish, needles and syringes found by children on the sides of the lanes.

Beth felt it couldn't have been like that while Susan was there, for she would have said so. Nor did it sound as if anyone made or sold craft work any more. She thought it was likely that the present situation had come about since Reuben went away.

Then, just as she was beginning to think she would have to go to the local police for advice, the landlord told her that there was a girl living down here in the village who had lived at Hill House.

'She's not much better than the rest of them,' he said, wrinkling his nose with distaste. 'But she does work, paints pottery, and she doesn't have anything to do with that bunch up at the house any more. You could talk to her. She lives in the last cottage along the road.'

Beth thanked him for his help, then, leaving her car in the pub car park, she walked to the cottage he'd directed her to.

It was a tiny cottage and very shabby, the once white walls stained green with mould and paint peeling off the front door. Beth knocked once, and the door was opened by a pregnant woman wearing a paint-daubed smock over jeans, her straggly blonde hair badly in need of a wash.

Beth told her briefly that she was trying to find Reuben Moreland.

'I don't know where he is,' the girl said defensively. 'I don't have nothing to do with that lot up at his house any more.'

She had a London accent, softened by a faint Welsh lilt. Beth thought she was probably only in her middle to late twenties, but her weary look and grey skin tone made her seem older. Beth introduced herself, handed the girl her card to confirm it, and said she was making enquiries on behalf of Susan Fellows who had lived at Hill House.

The girl gave a little gasp. 'She shot two people in Bristol, didn't she?' she said. 'I saw it on the news. I couldn't believe it, she was a real lady.'

'So you knew her?' Beth asked. 'Your name wouldn't be Megan, would it?'

'Yeah,' the girl said, but her eyes narrowed in suspicion. 'How d'you know that?'

'Just a guess. Susan mentioned you,' Beth said. 'She said you were an artist. May I come in and talk to you for a moment?'

Megan immediately looked wary. 'I don't want any trouble,' she said.

'I'm not here to make trouble for anyone,' Beth said. 'Just a little background information, that's all I want.'

Megan reluctantly opened the door wider. 'The place is a bit of a mess,' she said. 'I've been rushing to finish a job, so you'll have to take me as you find me.'

'A bit of a mess' was something of an understatement.

It wasn't a home at all but a dusty, cluttered workroom. A large table in the centre of the one room was covered in vases and lamp bases, which Megan was in the process of hand-painting. Boxes of plain white pottery were stacked on one side of the table, on the other side were more boxes containing the finished articles.

'I do the hand-painting, then they collect them to glaze and fire them again,' Megan said by way of an explanation.

'Susan said you were very talented,' Beth said, looking at a lamp base decorated with pink flowers which wouldn't have looked out of place in Liberty's. 'She was right, you are very good.'

Megan shrugged. 'It's all I can do,' she said. 'I wish I had a real studio and a kiln, but the pottery in Cardigan pays me well, so I can't complain. I don't know how I'm going to manage when the baby comes, though.'

Beth glanced around her. It really was a hovel. Rough plaster walls hadn't seen a coat of paint in decades, the meagre fire burning in the grate barely took the chill off the room. The staircase was bare boards, and even the kitchen area at the far end of the room was littered with more boxes, and a film of china dust covered everything. Beth couldn't imagine how Megan could think of having a baby there, for she doubted it was any better upstairs.

Megan sat down on a stool by the table, and indicated to Beth to sit on the one easy-chair by the fire. That had chipped arms and torn upholstery.

'Don't mind if I carry on while we talk, do you?' Megan said, picking up a paint brush. 'Like I said, I've got a rush job.'

'Is this the kind of work you did at Hill House?' Beth asked, looking at a bowl decorated with tiny violets. It was exquisite work, the finished article would probably sell for £30 or more.

'Nah.' Megan grimaced. 'We used to mainly make little plaster cottages and paint them up, crap stuff for the tourists. Reuben wouldn't go for anything that needed a kiln or nothin'.'

Beth gathered that meant Reuben went for quantity rather than quality.

'You were already at Hill House when Susan arrived, weren't you?' she asked next. 'Can you tell me how she was then?'

'Loopy,' Megan said bluntly. 'Going on about how God had punished her by taking her baby.'

'Punished her!' Beth exclaimed. 'What for?'

'I dunno.' Megan shrugged. 'She never said. But she weren't the kind to do anything bad, so I put it down to her being crazy with grief. Anyway, most of the people who came there were on some sort of weird trip. I didn't used to take much notice. I got to like Sue, though, she got the place clean, cooked nice things for us. She was very,' she paused again, presumably searching for the right word, 'mumsy, that's it. Liked to look after people. Once she settled down, she was nice.'

'So she didn't stay loopy?'

'No, she was as sane as you or me in a few weeks. She got to love the place, she was happy. She liked walking, being outside, flowers and all that.'

Beth sensed by the warmth in Megan's voice that she had become fond of Susan, perhaps Susan had even been a good influence on her.

'So what went wrong? Why did she leave?' Beth asked.

'Same reason everyone always left, they wised up that Reuben was a shit.'

'But Susan was having a relationship with him, wasn't she?' Beth asked.

Megan gave a humourless laugh. 'He had one of those with all the women, including me,' she said. 'He called it "sexual healing". He was a real bastard, conned us all into thinking we were special. Then he'd move on to the next one.'

'All the women had been "his women"?' Beth said in surprise.

'Sure, what else would make a woman live there and work so hard for him?'

'But did Susan know this? I mean, when she first got there?'

'No, it were a kind of rule we didn't bandy that around,' Megan said, and giggled as if she found it embarrassing. 'The last two had left by the time Sue got there anyway. I didn't give a shit about Reuben any more, and the two others he'd been with had someone else, so we didn't say nothing. Besides, I thought Sue was good for him. He was nicer with her there. Guess he liked the way she looked after him and the house. It kept him off my back too, so I wanted it to work out for them.'

'But Susan did find out about the others?'

'She got slapped in the face with it,' Megan said. 'He

came in one night with this tart Zoë and Sue had to like it or lump it.'

'Who was this girl and where did she come from?' Beth asked.

Megan shrugged as if she didn't know.

'Well, how did Susan take it?' Beth continued.

'Not as bad as I expected. I caught her crying a few times, but that was all. She used to say she'd fix Reuben one day, and she did really, the place fell apart after she left. I think that's why he lost interest and cleared off.'

'So who is up at the house now?'

'A load of freaks,' Megan said with a grimace of distaste. 'They come and go, they've turned the place into a right tip. If Reuben doesn't come back soon and turn them out, the house won't be worth a light.'

'So how long has he been gone?'

Megan shrugged. 'Two years maybe. I can't remember exactly and he's probably been back since I left. I went soon after Sue, couldn't stand it no more without her. I wanted to move right away but I didn't have the money.'

She went on to explain that this cottage had belonged to an old man called Evan, he'd taken her in and let her sleep in his spare room.

'I'd only been here a few weeks when he had a heart attack and died,' she went on. 'Evan's solicitor said I could stay on as a tenant until they found out who'd inherit the cottage.'

'So you might have to leave at any time then?' Beth said.

Megan shrugged. 'I guess so, haven't heard anything for ages.'

Beth was getting a much clearer picture of this girl, for she was like a great many of her clients. She guessed Megan had run away from home too young, lived in squats, experimented with drugs, been abused by many men before she even met Reuben. Yet despite the squalor of her living conditions and her unkempt appearance, there was something very decent about her. She wasn't living off the state, and there was no sign of drug use.

'Is the baby's father staying here with you?' she asked.

'No, he skipped off as soon as he knew,' Megan said with a tight little laugh. 'But then all men are bastards, aren't they? Sue used to say that. She was right. She were the one that made me try doing other kinds of painting.'

'Really?' Beth exclaimed, though not really surprised, Susan had always been good at noting talent in other people.

'Yeah.' Megan smirked. 'She saw me copying a picture of some flowers out of a book one day. She got me to try doing it on other things. I did a frieze round the kitchen window, painted on fabric and stuff. She told me I was talented.'

Beth heard the pride in her voice and the gratitude to the woman who had encouraged her. It took her right back to when Susan had made her feel that way.

'Have you got any idea how much other people gave Reuben to live there?' Beth asked.

'Whatever they had.' Megan shrugged. 'Roger had a nice car, he had to sell that. Heather told me she gave him two thousand pounds. But I reckon he got the most out of Sue.'

'Really?' Beth said. 'I didn't think she had much.'

'Neither did she till she found the note from the auctioneers in Bristol.' Megan gave a tight little laugh. 'She'd been hunting around in his things while he was out, trying to find proof of how much he made from the craft stuff. She never did find anything about that, only the note. He got over seven thousand for her gear. She was savage. She hadn't known it was worth that much.'

Beth was puzzled now. She couldn't understand why Susan hadn't told Steven that. 'Are you sure?'

'Yeah, she showed me the note herself. You could check up if you don't believe me. It was a proper auction firm in Bristol. They keep records, don't they?'

Beth mentally made a note to contact all auctioneers in Bristol. Such evidence would be very useful. 'Would you come up to Hill House with me?' she asked.

Megan stopped painting and looked at her in horror. 'You're joking, aren't you? They'd set the dogs on us.'

'How many people are living there?'

'About eight, last time I heard,' she said. 'But it changes all the time. They probably won't know where Reuben is anyway, don't think any of the ones there now have ever met him.'

'But it's his house, isn't it?'

'Yeah. What difference does that make? They're just squatters. They took it over.'

'Look, I must go up to look at the house,' Beth said firmly. 'Will you just come part of the way with me? You can stay in my car, and if anything happens to me you can use my car phone to call the police.'

'I'll lose painting time.' Megan gave Beth a shifty look, which suggested she wanted to be bribed.

'I'll give you twenty pounds,' Beth offered.

'Okay.' Megan promptly put her brush down. 'But I stay in the car, right?'

The road out of Emlyn Carlisle led to a narrow lane going upwards into open countryside with no further houses, then Megan directed Beth off this lane on to a mere track between fields. Beth could appreciate that in spring and summer it would be very beautiful, but it was too wild and remote for her.

Megan sat hunched up in an old sheepskin coat, and with the car heater on, Beth soon became very aware of the girl's unwashed body. But morose as she looked, she did chatter, about how lovely she thought Hill House was at first, and how different it was to London where she grew up.

'We lived in a council flat in Rotherhithe,' she said. 'Five kids and me mum, all in three rooms. I used to dream of fields and the seaside, like other girls dream of film stars. I met this Welsh bloke one night in a pub, and when he said he'd take me to Wales I didn't stop to think whether I could trust him, or even how far away it was. He dumped me in Swansea. I s'pose he was married all along.'

'How old were you then, Megan?' Beth asked.

'Sixteen,' she said. 'And I've been in Wales ever since. I had a couple of years in Swansea, doing all sorts, then I met Reuben and came here. It was like the sun came out at last.'

Beth nodded. She could guess what 'allsorts' meant. She supposed Reuben must have seemed like her saviour.

'Susan come from a good home, didn't she?' Megan said. 'She was very particular, always cleaning and polishing. I used to tease her and call her S.S. for spick and span. She ought to have been married to some normal bloke. But I s'pose her little girl dying really did her head in.'

'Did she ever talk about her?' Beth asked.

'Not really, it was like it hurt her too much. I used to catch her crying sometimes though and I knew she was thinking about her. Was that doctor she shot the one that let her little girl die?'

'Yes,' Beth said. 'Did she ever say anything about him?'

'Only that if he'd been a real doctor he would have known how ill her little girl was. I couldn't believe it was really her when I heard her name on the news. She might have been a crack shot, but I didn't think she'd ever turn a gun on a human being.'

Beth's head jerked round at that. 'You knew she could shoot?'

'Well, yeah. She used to shoot rabbits and wood pigeons with a shotgun. Didn't she tell you that? Without her we'd have hardly ever eaten meat. She used to make really yummy casseroles.'

'Was it her shotgun?'

'No, Reuben's. He couldn't shoot straight though. I think it pissed him off she was so good at it.' Megan stopped abruptly as they had arrived at Hill House.

They could see the farmhouse through a few trees, nestling against the side of a hill. It looked very much as Beth had imagined, grey stone, small windows, only more dilapidated, with weeds growing out of the roof. Smoke was coming out of the chimney, but there was no sign of anyone, not even the dogs she'd been warned about.

'Be careful,' Megan said, looking at Beth anxiously. 'Leave straight away if they get heavy.'

'Don't worry about me, I'm big enough to take care of myself,' Beth said, and pointed to the car phone. 'Use that in an emergency.'

Chapter fourteen

Beth stopped in her tracks as a wild-eyed, skinny lurcher came hurtling out of the farmhouse towards her, barking frantically. He looked capable of tearing her to pieces.

'Good boy,' she said, hoping he wasn't that way inclined. She liked dogs, and they usually liked her, but there was always an exception to the rule.

The dog stopped short in front of her, looking at her curiously, but his tail began to wag. She held out her hand for him to smell it, then stroked him. 'That's better,' she said, patting his head. 'Are you going to let me knock on the door?'

There was a pall of dirt and decay all around her, empty beer cans, bottles and other debris strewn around on the muddy ground. The house was sagging with age and neglect. In one corner of the yard rotting refuse was piled high, nearby was an old ambulance which had been painted red. It had 'The Devil's Disciples' emblazoned in yellow along the side, and one tyre was completely flat – it was the kind of vehicle often used by travellers. She couldn't see any other kind of transport. A door to what she thought might have been the workshop in Susan's time here was hanging off its hinges and inside she could see what looked like piles of spare parts from motors.

Looking at the house again, Beth shuddered, for the many broken window-panes covered over with tin and cardboard gave her a fair idea of the occupants. Even the front door looked as if it had been on the receiving end of many a boot. She could no more imagine Susan living in such a place than in an igloo.

She was just about to rap on the door when it was wrenched open by a man of about twenty-five, with long black hair, one hooped earring and a thick sweater nearly reaching his knees.

'Wha'cha want?' he said in a strong Birmingham accent.

'I'm trying to find Reuben, the owner of this house,' Beth said, smiling pleasantly and petting the dog to show she wasn't hostile.

'He ain't here, so fuck off,' the man replied.

Beth drew herself up to her full height and looked him in the eye. 'Please don't take that aggressive tone with me,' she said firmly. 'You see, I'm a solicitor, and if you won't answer my questions then I shall just have to go to the police and ask them. Now, will you please tell me where Reuben is?'

'I dunno,' he said, backing away with fear in his eyes. 'Never met him.'

'Is there anyone here who has?' she asked. She thought the man was very likely a heroin addict. He was very pale and thin, with dark circles beneath his eyes. He looked twitchy.

'Not now, his mate left a while back.'

'So who do you pay your rent to?' she asked.

'Don't pay no rent,' he said, his eyes dropping from hers. 'We're just staying here.'

'Minding the place for him, are you?' she asked, turning slightly to look at the view. Even on a cold February day it was beautiful, for the house overlooked a valley, with woods on the far side. 'To check no squatters move in?'

He looked furtively towards her car, perhaps noticing there was someone sitting in it. 'Yeah, some'at like that,' he said. 'But it ain't no business of yours, so piss off.'

'Who pays the rates and electricity?' she asked.

Before he could reply, a woman appeared behind him. She was older, perhaps in her late thirties, with a rose tattooed on her forehead and a scarf tied turban-style round her head.

'Who is she, Tom?' she asked, looking curiously at Beth.

Beth explained. There was a slightly cultured tone to the woman's voice, and although her clothes, a long flowing green jacket and trousers beneath, were dirty, she had a kind of elegance. 'So I want to know who pays the rates and electricity,' she finished up. 'Someone must, otherwise the council would have evicted you by now.'

'I don't know,' the woman said, looking uneasily at the man she had called Tom. 'We never thought to ask.'

'Perhaps you'd explain to me how you came to move in here then,' Beth said. 'You see, if you pay no rent and you have no proof Reuben gave you permission to live here, technically you are squatters.'

'Look, we're not doing any harm,' the woman said, her voice rising as if she suddenly realized Beth really could be trouble. 'We keep ourselves to ourselves. We were told by Reuben's friend it was cool to stay here.'

'How long have you lived here then?'

'About fourteen, fifteen months,' she said.

'And Reuben hasn't come back in all that time?'

'No,' she said. 'I wouldn't even know him if he did.'

'Do letters come for him?' Beth asked.

'Yeah, from time to time,' Tom answered.

'And what do you do with them?'

Tom suddenly rushed at Beth, pushing her away with one hand. 'Fuck off, you nosy bitch,' he yelled. 'It's nothing to do with you. Get out now before I call the dogs.'

'Set any dogs on me and you'll end up in court,' she said coldly. 'Then you'll have to answer a great many more questions.'

His punch came so suddenly and unexpectedly she didn't have time to move away. It landed on the side of her jaw and knocked her over backwards. As she lay there on the filthy ground she saw his leg move to kick her and she got a brief flashback of the men in the alley all those years ago. But this time she had no intention of taking anything lying down. She rolled over and leapt up. 'That's it,' she said, moving back out of his range. 'I'm going to the police. I'll make sure they come with a search warrant.'

As she fled to her car, she heard Tom shouting out abuse, but he didn't follow her. Jumping in the car, she saw Megan had the car phone in her hand. 'I'm calling the police,' she said. 'I saw him hit you.'

'Tell them I'm just driving away now,' Beth managed to get out, for she was winded, not just from the run to the car, but from the blow on her jaw. 'Give them the number and they can phone me back in a minute.'

Hastily she started up the car, drove up nearer to the farm and quickly turned it round in the open space in front. A black Dobermann had been let out and he ran full tilt towards the car, jumping up at her door and snarling. Tom and the woman had been joined by two other men and even through the closed windows Beth could hear them shouting further abuse.

It was only as they got back on to the track that Beth became aware Megan had her face covered with her scarf. 'It's all right now,' she said to the girl. 'They wouldn't have been able to see you from that distance.'

'They'll soon find out it was me,' Megan said in a weary voice. 'I shouldn't have agreed to come. You don't know what nasty bastards they can be.'

Beth rubbed her chin ruefully. 'I can imagine,' she said. 'But the police will sort them out, don't you worry, and I'll make sure they take care of you too.'

It was after eight when Beth finally got back to her hotel in Cardigan. She had a nasty bruise coming up on her chin and she still felt a little shaky. It had been a very strange and unsettling day all round.

The local police in two cars had met her at the bottom of the track. One constable stayed with her and Megan in her car to take their statements, while the other three policemen went up to Hill House. Around half an hour later they came back down the track, with Tom in the back of one car, under arrest.

Beth dropped Megan home, then drove on to the police station alone. She was there for almost three hours, talking to the station sergeant for part of the time. He said that however strange the police and locals had found Reuben and the residents in his 'commune', they had never been any trouble until about eighteen months ago. They kept themselves to themselves, and were no threat to the community.

Since then, coinciding with Reuben's absence, the police had been inundated with complaints. But there was little they could do as it was private property. A few months earlier, after finding themselves unable to contact Reuben to make him take responsibility for his rowdy guests, they had checked with the local council and the electricity board. They hoped that if the bills weren't being paid, they might have some lever to work with. But the bills were being met monthly by direct debit through Reuben's bank, so their hands were tied.

When Beth explained her interest in Reuben, the sergeant became more interested. He knew about the shooting in Bristol, but he hadn't known that Susan Fellows was a former resident at Hill House.

Beth told him that she believed Reuben warranted an investigation into extortion, but the sergeant seemed doubtful. He said he had called at Hill House himself on a couple of occasions in the past and it had always struck him as a happy hive of industry, not a hideaway for lost souls. Along with the craft work sold at fairs and in shops all over Wales, the residents had grown their own vegetables, and Reuben had allowed local farmers to cut the hay in his two fields for their animals. He said that didn't point to Reuben being a man with much to hide. As far as the sergeant was concerned, he just wanted Reuben to come back and evict his troublesome squatters. His only real concession was to say that now the man Tom had been arrested and charged with assault, he thought he could get a search warrant to check out the house and everyone living there.

Yet Beth got the distinct impression that all the policeman really hoped to gain by this was to see the squatters flee. He didn't seem very anxious to pull anyone else in for questioning, much less help her.

Disheartened on leaving the police station, Beth went back to see Megan. She found her worried that the arrest up at Hill House might bring repercussions for her. She seemed aghast when Beth asked if she would be a witness for the defence, to put her side of how it was for Susan when she lived at Hill House.

'It's bad enough for me as it is,' Megan said defensively. 'Everyone round here thinks I'm a slapper, I haven't got one real friend. I'd like to help Susan, but I've got the baby to think of.'

Beth talked to her for some time, pointing out that being a witness wasn't going to reflect badly on her, and it would help Susan enormously. She also suggested Megan should go to the local council offices and see if she could get rehoused before the baby was born in April. Megan seemed unaware she could get help with rent, even grants for baby equipment. In fact, Beth felt she was a little simple and desperately in need of some guidance.

Then, just as Beth was about to leave, Megan suddenly began talking about the girl Zoë Reuben had brought into the house.

'I never liked her,' she said, becoming animated for the first time that day. 'She was one of those posh girls from a rich family. I wondered what she wanted with Reuben, she weren't his usual sort.'

'How old was she and where did she come from?' Beth asked.

'I think she was about twenty-three. She came from Bath, her dad was a dentist. She looked down her nose at all of us, and she never did a hand's turn about the place.'

Beth perked up. A dentist in Bath would be easy to trace. 'Do you know her surname?' she asked.

'It was Fremantle,' Megan said. 'She showed me her passport once and it was in there. She was always boasting about how she'd been half-way round the world, and how she could always find a bloke to pay for her. I think that's why she latched on to Reuben.'

'So did she leave with him?'

Megan nodded and went on to say that this was after Susan left Hill House. 'I guess Sue had had enough by then, pushed out of her bedroom, that tart always rubbing it in that she had Reuben now.'

'Was she nasty enough to make Susan go what you called "loopy" again?' Beth asked.

Megan looked thoughtful. 'I didn't see that, but then

Sue weren't one for scenes and shouting and bawling. She went really quiet, not saying a word, so she must have been really upset. It had come out of the blue, hadn't it? Suddenly she was pushed out and someone young, prettier and all that took her place. I'd have been savage if I'd been her. But she was quite laid back about it. She just told us all one night while Reuben and Zoë were away somewhere that she was going. She left the next day.'

'What did Reuben say when he found she'd gone?'

'The bastard just laughed. He didn't give a fuck. It wasn't long after that he went off with Zoë and everything started to fall apart.'

'Where did they say they were going?' Beth asked.

'They didn't. Never said a word about going to anyone. Just upped and left. I never saw them again.'

Beth thought about that for a minute. 'How did you all live after he'd gone then? Reuben brought in the money, didn't he?'

'We went and signed on at the Job Centre,' Megan said. 'We like explained to them that we had no money for food. So they gave us Giros. But then some of the others wanted more, and they claimed rent allowance too. That was when I got scared and left.'

'What do you mean, you got scared?'

'Well, it's fraud innit?' Megan replied, looking nervously at Beth. 'Saying someone charges you rent when they don't?'

There was an awful lot more Beth wanted to know. Details of where Reuben found Zoë, what Susan's reaction had been at the first sighting of her, and how Susan was as she left the house. But she could see Megan had run out of steam, and it was so cold in her house that Beth felt as if she was turning into a block of ice. So after persuading the girl to go to the council, and the local welfare department, Beth left, leaving her card so that Megan could phone her if she thought of any more to tell her.

But as Beth lay soaking in a hot bath later, she felt dejected. She had a bigger picture now of how it was for Susan at Hill House, yet without meeting and talking to Reuben, what had she got? Only what she'd set out with yesterday, a grief-stricken woman joining a bunch of cranks and losers. Even if Megan did agree to be a witness, she wasn't really sure the girl's input would help that much. While she had said Susan was 'loopy' when she first arrived, she had recovered, become 'mumsy' and kept the place together. A woman who could stand for being replaced by a younger woman without causing a big scene, and leave quietly, looked sane enough. But then Susan had always been very good at hiding her true feelings about things.

Beth remembered how on one of their holidays, probably the third one because they'd been at senior school for a year, Susan had stiffened at the sight of a slightly older girl. They were in Stratford that afternoon, just hanging about by the river because they hadn't got any money to spend.

'Let's go for a ride on our bikes,' Susan said, grabbing Beth's arm and pulling her along.

As it was normally Beth who made all the suggestions about what to do and where to go, she immediately guessed that this sudden need to rush off had to have something to do with the red-haired girl in checked Capri pants and a tight sweater.

Beth was no stranger to bullies herself, so after they'd got right away she asked Susan about the girl. 'What's she done to you?' she asked point-blank.

Predictably, Susan pretended she didn't know what Beth was talking about. It wasn't until they'd reached their little camp in the woods where presumably she felt safe that she admitted she was frightened of the girl.

'She calls me "Wrights", she said with a sigh. 'She got that from the register I suppose, it says Wright, S. Anyway, she's always yelling out things like "Human Wrights" and "Animal Wrights", stupid stuff really, but it's embarrassing. She's in the year above me, her older sister used to work in Daddy's office and he sacked her for something.'

'Is that why she picks on you?' Beth asked. She too got taunted about her father, and she knew how hurtful it could be.

'I think so.' Susan hung her head and Beth saw a tear rolling down her face.

'Why don't you confront her and ask why she takes it out on you?' Beth asked. That was how she always tackled bullies, and mostly they backed off.

'Daddy's always sacking people,' Susan whispered. 'Mummy said most clever men aren't very patient. I don't suppose her sister did much wrong and I feel bad about it.'

'Well, tell her that then,' Beth said, thinking that was quite simple.

'I can't say anything about Daddy!' Susan exclaimed, looking horrified.

'Then just go up to her and ask why she's mean to you, and point out you've done nothing to her.'

'She'd hit me if I even walked up to her,' Susan replied.

Beth couldn't remember what happened beyond that. Maybe it was resolved, maybe the girl got bored with taunting Susan, because she never mentioned it again. But what stayed with Beth was a kind of wonder that even girls from ideal families could be picked on too.

Of course she knew now that the Wrights were far from 'ideal'. Mr Wright was a bumptious, self-centred man, and his son took after him. They'd had such bad luck too. Susan wouldn't have had anyone at home to confide in, if her mother was preoccupied with the grand-mother. Keeping her thoughts, anxieties and feelings to herself must have become a way of life to her.

Beth reflected on this for a little while. However bad her own home life was, she had always had Serena and Robert to confide in. Also, she had a more volatile nature, mostly able to give as good as she got when angry or hurt. Gentle Suzie just didn't have that safety valve.

After a late supper, Beth rang Roy, suddenly desperate to hear the sound of his voice. He was horrified she'd been struck by the man at Hill House, and she had the feeling he would have driven straight over to Wales to be with her right then if she'd needed him.

'I'm fine, I really am,' she said and went through everything she'd discovered during the day. 'But could you do something for me? Could you possibly run a check on Zoë Fremantle? I know it's a long shot, but we might be able to find Reuben through her.'

'I'll do it tomorrow,' he agreed.

Roy arrived at the police station at six on Sunday morning, and the first thing he did was to run a check on Zoë. He discovered she had one conviction for possession of cannabis, back in 1986 when she was eighteen and at art college, and a further conviction for shop-lifting the following year. In both cases she received a fine, and she gave her parents' address as 19 Widcombe Hill, Bath.

If it hadn't been so early in the morning, he would have telephoned Mr and Mrs Fremantle straight away to ask where their daughter was living now. But with time on his hands, and nothing more pressing to do, he thought he would just check the missing persons' list.

She was there. Reported missing by her parents in May 1993.

When he opened the file on the girl he found very little police action had been taken, and that appeared to be understandable. Zoë had moved away from home on innumerable occasions – by her parents' own admission she was wild, bad at keeping in touch, and she only stayed in any job long enough to get money to go travelling. The year before she was reported missing, she'd been in Thailand. Enquiries had been made among her old friends in Bath, but no leads had been found. In the light of reports from some of these old friends that Zoë didn't get on too well with her parents, her lack of communication with them didn't seem in any way suspicious.

Roy studied the photograph of Zoë on file. It was taken on a beach, with her wearing a bikini top and a sarong. She was a very pretty girl, with long blonde hair and blue eyes, around five feet eight and slender. He wondered what a girl like her, from a wealthy background and with a good education, would have in common with an ageing hippy. Drugs were the one thing which sprang to mind.

Roy then ran a check on Reuben Moreland, and found nothing. But he had a hunch that wasn't the man's real name anyway.

He thought about it for a while. While there was no evidence that this man had committed any crimes, Susan had on her own admission handed over all her property willingly, just as the others had done. But Moreland was certainly a dubious character, and Roy's long police service had taught him that such men usually warranted investigation. The 'commune' in Wales could very well be a cover for drug-dealing. Maybe Zoë, with her looks and good background, had encouraged him to expand this further. As she was now missing, Roy had a first-class excuse for poking around a little more.

Later on that morning, after ringing Mrs Fremantle and discovering Zoë was still missing, Roy had a consultation with his governor, who gave him permission to visit her parents in Bath.

*

Driving back from Bath to Bristol later that day, Roy felt saddened by the Fremantles' lack of real concern for their missing daughter. Their attitude appeared to be that Zoë owed them for having been born into an elegant Georgian home and educated at the best private schools. They had reported her missing in May 1993 only because she hadn't contacted them around the time of her birthday at the end of April. This, they said peevishly, was out of character.

Roy had heard a litany of Zoë's failings, her 'rough' friends, her endless travelling and her failure to get a 'proper' job. The last time her parents had spoken to her was New Year's Day 1993, when she'd phoned them from a pub. They didn't know where it was, or who she was with. They said they'd never heard of Reuben Moreland, and then they didn't know any of her friends' names. Roy had heard similar stories from other parents with missing children, but all of them had made some effort privately to find their children, if only to reassure themselves they were alive and well, and to send a message that they were concerned.

The Fremantles could easily afford to hire a private investigator, but they hadn't done so. Their excuse was 'We assume she is leading a life-style we wouldn't approve of.' Roy could hardly blame Zoë for staying away, if all she ever got when she came home were recriminations. He fervently hoped she was having a good time somewhere like Thailand, preferably having dumped Reuben for someone younger and less manipulative.

He thought it would be divine justice if the man arrived

back in England with his tail between his legs to find his house in ruins. He thought Beth would like that too. She hadn't sounded like herself last night on the phone, but then he supposed it wasn't reasonable for anyone to sound bouncy when they'd been punched in the face earlier in the day.

Although he had never had the opportunity to observe Beth working with any other client but Susan, he sensed she had never gone right out on a limb as she was doing with this one. It seemed to be more than just the childhood friendship thing too, almost as if she was working through her own past and problems as she raked through Susan's.

Roy considered himself to be a simple man. Even as a young man he hadn't yearned for fast cars, foreign travel or wealth, all he'd wanted was to be a good policeman, husband and father. The death of Peter, his son, and the subsequent break-up of his marriage a couple of years later, had come close to breaking him. For quite some time he'd constantly asked himself, *Why me?* He had met so many men who were almost oblivious to their children and unfaithful to their wives, but such things didn't happen to them. He still had no answer to why it had to be *his* son who had died, and he still mourned him. But in time he had come to see that it was only Peter who held Meg and him together, that their relationship was one of habit, rather than like minds, passion or even real friendship.

But with Beth he felt all that and more. She was on his mind constantly, just a day without a phone call or seeing

337

her seemed too long. He admired her keen brain, her often wry sense of humour – even her coolness excited him.

He wanted her passionately. He dreamed nightly of those long, slender legs, her narrow hips and her glorious black hair, but he knew too that he must wait for her to make the first move. But it was so hard waiting, knowing she was afraid because some man out there had hurt her badly. The need to know was tearing him apart, yet he was also scared that once she did tell him, he might not be able to make it better for her.

Beth opened the downstairs door at Roy's ring right on seven o'clock and went out on to the landing to look down the stairwell.

He was carrying a bunch of white lilies and a bottle of wine, but it was the weariness in his step that touched her most. She had got home from Wales just after twelve that lunch-time, and had a little snooze, and apart from her sore jaw she was feeling fine. Roy on the other hand had worked a twelve-hour shift.

'Hullo, Mr Detective Inspector,' she called out.

'Hullo, Miss Defence,' he called back, and managed to bound up the last few steps. 'Oh shit, what a nasty bruise!' he exclaimed, reaching out and touching it tenderly. 'I hope the Welsh police put him in leg irons and beat him with their truncheons.'

Beth laughed. 'It looks worse than it is, as my mother always said when Father clobbered her. But every cloud has a silver lining. If I hadn't had to call the police there,

I wouldn't have got them interested in checking out Reuben's house.'

'I've got a bit of news on that score,' Roy said, giving her a hug. 'But let me have a drink first.'

Beth made him sit down on the couch and poured him a glass of wine. 'We've got fillet steak, salad and baked potatoes,' she said. 'Everything's ready but the steak, that only takes a couple of minutes. So just say when you want it, you look very tired.'

'It's been a bit of a gruelling day,' he said, then went on to tell her about his interview with Mary Fremantle. Then he showed her the picture of Zoë.

'Wow!' Beth exclaimed. 'I think any woman would feel dejected being replaced by her.'

'I personally can't see what a girl like that would see in Reuben and a commune for weirdos,' Roy said. 'The only thing that springs to mind is that she thought he had money. Anyway, later on I spoke to the minister of the church where Susan met Reuben, his name is Peter Langdon. A good man, I'd say, caring and committed. He remembered Susan well, but he hadn't connected her with the shooting and was very shocked. He said he found it totally out of character as she was such a gentle, shy woman. But his views on Reuben were much harsher, he said he'd had his suspicions that the man was some kind of confidence trickster, but he'd never managed to get any proof. He also wasn't aware Susan had gone off with him.'

'Would he be prepared to act as a character witness for Susan, do you think?' Beth asked.

'Without a doubt,' Roy nodded. 'He even offered to go and visit her. He's a very sincere and genuine man. But the good news is that he had a photo of Reuben. It was taken at one of the church's little parties.'

Roy pulled it out of his pocket and handed it to Beth.

She laughed, for he looked even worse than she'd imagined, with his long, gaunt face, his greying hair tied back in a pony-tail, and a rather ostentatious embroidered sleeveless jacket over a Nehru-style shirt.

'He looks like a creep,' she said. 'I've always had an aversion to middle-aged men who try to look trendy. But I suppose he fits the bill as a "psychic healer".'

Roy smiled. 'Peter Langdon was appalled that he called himself that. He didn't recognize Zoë from her photograph, so it looks as if Reuben met her elsewhere. Maybe Susan will know where, and when.'

'She didn't even tell me or Steven about Zoë,' Beth said with a frown. 'She said there was a new woman, but nothing more. Why do you think that was?'

'The same reason she didn't tell you Liam dumped her,' Roy said. 'Pride maybe, not wanting to admit, even to herself, that she'd been had.'

'Poor Susan.' Beth sighed. 'So much bad luck and unhappiness. Let's hope it breaks for her soon, and we can at least find Reuben to stand as witness.'

'We'll be applying for permission to access to his bank account tomorrow,' Roy said. 'That should give us a lead as to where he is.'

Beth looked sharply at him. 'Do I hear the "We" as in police investigation?'

Roy looked a bit sheepish. 'Yes. We need to pull him in and ask him a few questions.'

On Wednesday evening Roy called round at Beth's place on his way home from work. 'Sorry to barge in uninvited,' he said as she let him in. 'But I thought you'd like to know we checked Reuben's bank account today.'

'And?' she said.

'Curiouser and curiouser,' he said. 'He hasn't touched it since April '93.'

Beth made him a cup of coffee as she listened.

'He had a credit balance of some two thousand pounds then. We looked back over the previous year and found he'd paid sums of two or three hundred into it about every four or five weeks. I assume that was money from the craft workshop. He had monthly direct debits set up for the council tax, electricity and a credit card. Those have been met every month. But there have been no other withdrawals at all, and no credits. At present there is a credit balance of around two hundred and fifty pounds.'

Beth handed Roy his coffee. 'I don't see what you're getting at,' she said, puzzled by the way he'd rapped it out. 'What's wrong with that? He couldn't pay money in if he wasn't getting any from selling his goods.'

'Or maybe he can't because he's dead,' Roy said darkly.

'Don't be silly.' She laughed lightly. 'The bank wouldn't be meeting his bills.'

'They would unless they were informed of his death. Direct debits just go on and on until someone cancels them, or there's no money left in the account to cover them.'

'He might have another account. Lots of people have one they use for regular stuff, and another just for spending.'

'That's true. But up until he paid in the last sum, he seemed to use that account for everything. There was a record of food in supermarkets paid for by cheque. Petrol, clothes, all sorts. They even checked back and found the record of the cheque from the auctioneers in Clifton from the sale of Susan's effects.'

'Of course he's alive,' Beth said sharply. 'I bet he shot off abroad. It shows he was a pretty responsible person to leave money behind for regular payments.'

'Absolutely everything about that bank account showed a responsible person,' Roy agreed. 'So you tell me why a careful and canny man, who we already know wasn't altruistic at all, would allow people to stay on in his house, rent free, using his electricity, unconcerned if they let the place fall into rack and ruin.'

'Maybe the people he left there were supposed to be paying rent?' she said.

'You said that the people living there now don't even know him!'

There was a harsh note to Roy's voice that implied even more than he was saying. All at once Beth realized he wasn't just sounding off a few ideas on her, he had thought this through and had drawn his own conclusions.

'You really do think he's dead. Don't you?' she gasped.

Roy frowned. 'I can't see any other explanation, Beth.

Reuben bought that house over twelve years ago. Aside from shooting off for a while every now and again, he's lived in it, got repairs done, built up a business of sorts from there. Who but a complete fool would go off for over two years and leave it at the not so tender mercies of a bunch of travellers?'

'He might have met his Waterloo with Zoë,' Beth suggested. 'She's young, wild, from a good background, probably as sexy as hell. That's enough to make any middle-aged man lose his grip.'

'I really hope that's what it is and they're holed up in Thailand or somewhere, doing drug deals or something that's made the place in Wales look like chicken-feed,' he said with a faint grin. 'But somehow I just don't think so.'

'Why?'

Roy shrugged. 'Well, if he was doing well wherever he was and didn't want to come back, he would have rung an estate agent and put that place on the market. You said yourself it's in a beautiful spot – even if the house is crumbling, the land is worth a lot.

'If things weren't going well he'd have come back by now surely? As for Zoë, the same thing applies. She'd have rung her parents if all was well, and asked for help if it wasn't.'

'Not necessarily,' Beth argued. 'Her father might be as big a pig as mine. She might have left Reuben ages ago and taken up with someone else. Young girls aren't predictable.'

'All females are unpredictable,' he said, and sighed.

'Especially you. I had expected you'd see the significance in all this immediately.'

'What?' she asked, frowning at him. 'What am I supposed to have seen?'

'Murder?'

'You think those travellers staying in the house could have bumped Reuben off?' she exclaimed.

'That's one possibility,' Roy said. 'Reuben could have come back, got stroppy with that lot for being in his house, a fight broke out and Bob's your uncle. Tom Whelon, the man who hit you, has a string of convictions behind him, everything from drugs to assault. Heaven only knows what we'll uncover when we check through the rest.'

An unpleasant cold and creepy feeling ran down Beth's spine. 'You're including Susan as a suspect too, aren't you?' she exclaimed. 'No, Roy! She couldn't have done that.'

'Why not?' he replied quietly, his dark eyes looking right into hers. 'You know the old saying, "Hell hath no fury like a woman scorned."'

Angry tears welled up in Beth's eyes. 'I thought you believed in her!' she retorted, raising her voice. 'You sympathized because of Annabel. How could you think this now?'

'Because I'm a policeman,' he said gently. 'I'm not saying it was Susan, I haven't even got any proof yet that Reuben and Zoë are dead. All I've got is a hunch. But most investigations start with just that.'

He reached out for her, pulling her into his arms. 'You

must have had almost as many clients who have fooled you as I've had people I've interviewed and believed innocent. I don't know about you, but it always makes me feel disappointed, and a little stupid. But this is different, Beth, you can't be detached about this because Susan is all tied up with your childhood, you feel she is part of you, like a sister.'

Beth sobbed against his shoulder.

Roy hugged her tighter. 'This probably isn't the right moment to tell you, but I love you,' he whispered, his lips against her neck. 'I think I'd even turn away from an investigation if you asked me to.'

Beth was astounded by what he'd said. She lifted her head to look at him. She could see by the resolute set of his mouth that he meant both things.

'I wouldn't ever ask you to do that, and you know it,' she said, her voice shaking. 'You'd better go now, Roy.'

'Why?'

'You know why,' she said firmly. 'Susan might not be my client any more, but I'm still very involved in the case and with her. I can't run with the hare and the hounds. And neither can you. So don't contact me again until you've done whatever you've got to do.'

He looked stricken, every line on his face sagging. 'No, Beth, please don't say that,' he pleaded.

'I have to, Roy,' she said, her voice trembling. 'Surely I don't need to spell it out to you, a policeman? I've already told you things about Susan that I shouldn't have done. I've unwittingly led you to another possible crime. I won't betray my old friend any further than I already have done.'

345

'But I thought we had something special,' he said, his voice cracking with emotion.

'I thought so too,' she said sadly. 'I didn't think it would be our jobs that came between us.'

Chapter fifteen

Beth walked wearily into the office the following morning, having hardly slept a wink all night. Roy was a good policeman, intuitive and shrewd, she knew that he wouldn't even think of embarking on an investigation into Reuben and Zoë's disappearance unless he was pretty certain a serious crime had been committed.

By now he would be discussing it with his governor, and before long Susan would be questioned again. This time every aspect of her time in Wales would come under scrutiny.

'You look a bit rough today! Are you all right?'

Beth looked up at Steven's voice to see him coming down the stairs. He had his overcoat on and his briefcase in his hand and was obviously going off to court.

'I've got something very important to tell you,' she said in a low voice. The door to the typing pool was open and she didn't want them to hear anything. 'But it looks like you're off to court?'

'I can spare five or ten minutes,' he said, looking at her anxiously. 'Is that long enough?'

'Enough for the bare bones,' she said. 'And that's quite apt under the circumstances.'

They went back up to his office, and the moment the door was closed, Beth blurted it all out.

Steven's face blanched. 'Oh, shit!' he exclaimed. 'God almighty, Beth, do you think he could be right?'

'I think he might be right in that Reuben's dead, but I can't believe Susan had anything to do with it,' she said, her lips trembling. 'I wish I'd never gone poking around over in Wales now, I wish I hadn't enlisted Roy's help in checking out that girl. I feel as if I've sold my old friend down the river to my new friend the policeman.'

Steven put his hand on her shoulder comfortingly. 'You can't look at it that way, Beth. Maybe you speeded things up by telling Roy what you'd heard. But the chances are the Welsh police would have gone down the same route eventually.'

'Susan's not going to see it like that,' she said, looking into Steven's eyes. 'She's going to think I'm responsible for renewed police interest in her.'

'She'll have nothing to fear if she knows nothing about Reuben's disappearance,' Steven said. He glanced at his watch. 'Look, I must go now. Keep your chin up. I'll see you at lunch-time.'

Beth had a free half-hour with no clients later that morning. Although she had a great deal of correspondence to catch up on, she ignored it and stood at the window, staring out at the garden in the square below. It looked as bleak as she felt, refuse blowing around, getting caught on the bare branches of the trees, even the grass was all worn and muddy.

Roy had told her he loved her last night. She ought to be happy about that, because she had no doubt she was in love with him too, but how could she be happy with something like this standing between them?

Her whole life seemed to have been like this, moments that should have been joyful spoilt by something from the past. Graduation day was one. Because she didn't want her father coming, she didn't tell anyone when it was, not even Robert and Serena. She had received a first-class honours degree, but she was the only student there with no one to see her accept it. She'd slunk away while everyone was taking photographs of family groups and gone back to her bedsitter, to cry instead of to celebrate.

When Robert's first son was born, she rushed to the hospital to see her new nephew, full of excitement. She walked into the ward, only to see her father sitting by the cot, and she had to back out without a word for fear of spoiling the moment for Robert and his wife.

But it wasn't always her father who ruined things, mostly she just brought it on herself. She didn't have friends, male or female, to share special occasions with, because she hadn't known how to let people into her life and keep them there. So many times in the past she'd been scornful of Serena because it seemed she wasted so much valuable time phoning friends for a chat, squeezing meeting someone for coffee or lunch into an already packed diary. Serena hated to miss anyone's birthday, she was there for them if they were sick or lonely. Her Christmas card list ran into four pages, and she spent a fortune on presents and throwing parties.

Beth could see now, thanks to Steven pushing his way into her life, that she had in fact been punishing rather than protecting herself, by holding everyone at arm's length. She'd give anything right now to have a girlfriend she could call up. Not to pour her heart out to necessarily, but to arrange a shopping trip, someone to have a laugh and a chat with. Just light-hearted silliness, the way it used to be with Susan.

She could see them that last summer they spent together, at the dance in the church hall. Suzie was in the tight red dress she'd bought that afternoon, which she knew her parents wouldn't approve of, Beth was in the emerald-green one that Aunt Rose had run up for her. They had danced together constantly rather than taking the risk of sitting down and looking as if they hoped boys would ask them to dance. Suzie was really good at The Shake – she managed to look sexy while Beth feared she looked more like an electronic scarecrow with a twitch.

'The wallflowers,' she murmured to herself. Neither of them had really believed that's what they'd be, it was just bravado to cover up their nervousness. Tall, skinny Beth and short, plump Suzie, two fifteen-year-old misfits who really believed it was only a matter of time before they woke up one day to find themselves beautiful women who would take the world by storm.

Yet fate had made them wallflowers. They put their roots down in the confines of the rocky places they both knew best, and stayed there. For Suzie that was entrapment within her family, for Beth it was learning. And like flowers that depend on the quality of the soil and the right weather conditions, how could either of them grow into something of beauty? Suzie had no out-side stimulus, she led a barren life of servitude. Beth had her roots poisoned by the rape, robbing her of any joy that would make her grow.

Beth sighed deeply, leaning her forehead against the cold glass of the window and thinking of the wallflowers which had clung to crevices in the wall around the old kitchen garden at Copper Beeches. Each year they grew more scrawny and weed-like, the once vibrant colours gradually fading to a sickly yellow, the perfume gone.

She should never have discussed Susan and her case with Roy, it was totally unprofessional. She felt ashamed she'd gone to Luddington to look for Liam with him, and even more angry with herself for asking him to check on Zoë Fremantle. Why couldn't she have anticipated that it might cause a conflict of interests?

She couldn't blame Roy, he wouldn't have been much of a policeman if he hadn't followed up suspicious-looking leads. The only thing she could do was to tell him she couldn't see him again until his investigation was over. But doing the right and honourable thing wasn't any comfort. She felt heart-sick and so alone.

It was another two weeks before Beth drove out to Eastwood Park to see Susan again. Roy and another police officer had interviewed her a couple of days earlier, with Steven present. Steven had said it wasn't a heavy kind of interview, Roy made his questions about Susan's time in Wales sound as if it was just part of the original investigation. But Steven had said that although Susan was very convincing when she told them that she left Wales while Reuben and Zoë were away from Hill House and that she had never gone back there or seen either of them again, the dates she gave didn't tally with her taking the room in Belle Vue.

Roy had contacted her old landlord, and he claimed she had taken the room almost a fortnight after she was supposed to have left Wales. When questioned about this, Susan insisted the man was mistaken.

When Roy asked her about Liam, she did finally admit that she had known he wasn't going to join her in Bristol, which was why she didn't leave her address with the neighbours, but as she pointed out, that was nobody's business but her own.

As Roy had honoured Beth's request that he stay away from her until the investigation was complete, she had no idea whether the police were any further forward. Steven felt they were still actively following up all kinds of leads, but he had no idea what direction they were taking. Being so much in the dark was playing havoc with Beth's nerves; she couldn't sleep at night, she had no appetite, and there had been many times when she'd been tempted to call Roy to find out what was going on.

But above all, her disquiet was caused by the feeling that she had betrayed her friend. She felt she must explain to Susan why there was a renewed police interest in her, and her own role in it, or have it on her conscience for all time.

She had an angry red spot on her chin, gripes in her stomach and she felt shaky with nerves. What she wanted more than anything was for Susan to convince her finally that she had no hand in, or knowledge of, the disappearance of those people from her past.

'What have you come for?' Susan said as she came into the interview room and saw Beth waiting for her. Her round face was tight with hostility. 'To try and get some more stuff to pass on to your boyfriend?'

It was a few weeks since Beth had last visited Susan, and it was something of a shock to see how much weight she had lost. On her arrest she'd probably been a size sixteen, now she was closer to a twelve. Her navy-blue track suit was hanging on her. Women usually put on weight in prison because of the stodgy food and lack of exercise. Was she starving herself?

'Don't be silly, Susan,' Beth said, trying to keep calm. 'I don't pass on anything to anyone that we talk about. Now, why have you lost so much weight?'

Susan shrugged and sat down, crossing her legs and folding her arms with a touch of insolence. 'What's it to you?' she said. 'Afraid I'll get skinnier than you?'

That was the kind of sarcastic remark women prisoners often made to her, and it made Beth feel even lower to see that her old friend was picking up all the bad habits.

'Don't be ridiculous,' she snapped. 'I'm concerned, that's all.'

'Oh, right!' Susan said. 'Like you were so concerned about me you went sniffing around looking for other crimes I might have done?'

Beth's heart sank, for clearly Susan had worked out for herself that Roy's line of questioning had been precipitated by her. 'I didn't go sniffing around for other crimes,' she said. 'I only went looking for Liam and Reuben to get them to be witnesses on your behalf.'

'So they've gone missing!' Susan retorted. 'I told you they were both wanderers, didn't I? As for that slag Zoë, she's probably tucked up with some sugar daddy. That's what she's into. I can't be held responsible for all the untraceable itinerants in England. What sort of a friend are you if you immediately think I must have bumped them off?'

'I don't think that,' Beth said truthfully. 'I would have to hear it from you before I'd ever believe it.'

'But you were quick enough to grass me up, weren't you?'

Beth sighed. 'Grassing up is telling tales, Susan. I didn't have any tales to tell. I still don't. As you know, Detective Inspector Longhurst has been working on your case right from the start. He came with me to Luddington to try and find Liam because he's become a friend. How could I not tell him about what happened in Wales? I only asked him to check out Zoë Fremantle in the hope that she might lead us to Reuben. When he found her on the missing persons' list, of course he had to start an investigation.'

'You haven't changed, have you?' Susan said with a sneer. 'You dropped me all those years ago because some man came into your life, and now you're doing it again. Don't try to deny it either, the reason you didn't want me coming up to London to share a flat with you was because of a man.'

'That's just not true,' Beth exclaimed. 'There was no man in my life, not ever.'

Susan grinned maliciously. 'Okay, so it was a woman, and you're a lesbian – you should come in here, the place is crawling with them.'

'I'm not a lesbian either.' Beth sighed. 'I've just never really got it together with men.'

'You were boy-mad at fifteen,' Susan snapped back, jumping to her feet. 'After that last holiday in Stratford that was all you used to write to me about. So if it wasn't a man or a woman you got tied up with, what was it that made you dump me?'

'I never saw it as dumping you,' Beth said hotly. 'Sometimes you just avoid contact with certain people because –' She stopped dead, not knowing what excuse to give.

'Because of what? They are boring? Too old-fashioned when you're Miss Smarty Pants at university? Not clever enough any more?'

Beth's stomach churned over. She got to her feet, wanting to leave immediately. But she knew she couldn't leave Susan thinking that she'd abandoned her for any of those reasons.

'No, Susan, it was because I was afraid I'd end up telling you what happened to me, and I didn't want to do that.'

Susan made a kind of derisive snort and put her hands on her hips. 'What sort of excuse is that? You pathetic bitch! You used to tell me everything, or so you said in those days. But you took me for a ride, didn't you? I was just someone to hang around with when you were stuck up in Stratford for the summer. I never meant anything to you.'

'That's not true, Susan.' Beth pleaded with her, backing away because the other woman's expression was so frightening. She'd never seen her angry before. 'You meant more to me than anything else. But what happened to me changed me, I couldn't tell anyone, especially you. It was too bad.'

'I'm in here for double murder. How much worse can "bad" be than that?' Susan sprang towards her as if she was going to hit her.

'I was gang-raped by three men,' Beth blurted out. 'Don't attack me, Susan. I swear to God that is what happened.'

Susan stopped short as if turned to rock. Her mouth fell open in surprise.

'Gang-raped?' she whispered.

'Yes, Susan. It was in January when we were seventeen,' Beth said in a low voice and sank down on to the chair. She would tell her, get it off her chest, once and for all.

Surprisingly, after all the years of refusing to say the words aloud even to herself, and the struggle Steven had to drag it out of her, telling the story of what happened came much easier this time. But her eyes still filled with tears as she spoke and her voice was shaking. She was aware of Susan standing to her right staring down at her, but she couldn't turn to look at her. 'Would you have expected me to go on writing jolly letters full of trivia after that?' she finished off.

There was utter silence for a moment or two. Then she heard Susan exhale. 'You poor bitch,' she murmured. 'I never imagined anything like that.'

Suddenly she was clasping Beth tightly, her face buried in her hair, and Beth could feel the wetness of her tears. 'I'm so sorry, Beth,' she whispered. 'But you should have told me.'

They stayed locked together for some moments, Susan rocking Beth in her arms, neither of them caring that if the officer outside the door should look in it would seem very odd. It was the way Serena had held Beth sometimes when she was just a little girl and it felt so safe and comforting.

'I couldn't, it was too awful,' Beth said eventually and disengaged herself to blow her nose. She was embarrassed now, not so much by her revelations, but by being so unprofessional in a place that demanded she should be cool and collected.

Susan kissed her forehead and went to sit down again. She looked winded, all the fight which had been in her such a short time ago, gone.

Beth told her then how it was for her afterwards, without even her brother and sister knowing. 'I was jealous of you,' she blurted out. 'I imagined you safe at home with your lovely parents, everything so clean, so bright and nice. My home was a tip, my father a pompous bully, my mother pathetic. I'd hidden all that from you, and it seemed best to move on so you'd never know about it, or about the rape.'

'You know, I was jealous of you too,' Susan admitted.

357

'You might have seen my home as bright and shining, but I wasn't like that, and that is exactly how I saw you. You were what I wanted to be – brave, clever, tall and elegant. What was I? A short, fat girl with a moon face and no personality. Even if mother hadn't had the stroke, I would never have set the world alight. I'd have stayed at home, got some dull little office job, and married the first man that asked me.'

'No, you wouldn't,' Beth said stoutly, even though she knew it was probably true.

Susan grimaced at her. 'Oh Beth, don't feel you've got to bolster me up. It took me a long time to come to terms with what I really was. I didn't truly find out until Annabel was born. I was born to be a mother, nothing more. But in those four years with her I saw that as the greatest of roles, true fulfilment. I used to think about you, imagine you in a wig and gown, and all the envy was gone. Everything, hanging her nappies out on the line, playing with toys on the floor, cutting little sandwiches into animal shapes for her, was all so lovely. Motherhood is a true vocation, Beth. But I had to be punished and she was taken from me.'

Beth had watched her face as she spoke, saw the tender light in her eyes, her mouth curling into a smile, and felt a lump come up in her throat at the injustice of Susan being robbed of her one joy.

'Why did you think you had to be punished?' she asked curiously.

Susan shrugged and looked away.

'Why, Susan?' Beth repeated when her friend didn't

answer. Beth felt she'd made that remark in an unguarded moment for Susan suddenly looked shifty.

'For being glad when my parents died. For not waiting for the right man to come along,' Susan said hastily. 'I lied to you about Liam being so wonderful, he was just a waster, and I was lonely. I knew it wouldn't really work.'

Beth knew their time was up, and she felt they had gone as far as they could for one day. 'I have to go now,' she said, standing up, and she held out her arms instinctively.

Susan rushed into them and held her tightly, leaning into Beth's shoulder as a child would. 'That policeman is a good man, even if he does seem to hope I'm a serial killer,' she murmured. 'I hope he's going to make things right for you.'

'I'm not seeing him for a while,' Beth said.

'Why?' Susan asked. 'Because of me?'

Beth suddenly realized she couldn't bring herself to admit that. It would frighten Susan into thinking Roy really did imagine she was a serial killer. 'No, of course not. I've got to work on myself for a while. I can't expect any man to free me from my past, only I can do that.'

'I'm sorry I was rough on you,' Susan said with tears in her eyes. 'I don't want you to come here again, Beth. Not until all this is over.'

'If that's what you really want,' Beth said. She thought Susan meant prison was tougher still when you kept being reminded of what might have been. 'Just tell Steven if you change your mind.'

As Susan walked back to her wing, waiting at each door

for it to be unlocked by an officer, all her thoughts were with Beth. In a way it was like having a previously locked door opened and seeing another room for the first time. Everything made sense now – the change in Beth's letters, the absence of real news, all the old humour gone. Maybe if Susan hadn't been so wrapped up in her own family problems she would have realized something terrible must have happened to her friend.

A vivid picture came into her mind of Beth swimming in the river that last summer they spent together. Susan had watched from the bank as Beth did a faultless dive into the water; she was wearing a red swimming costume, her slender body so lithe and graceful.

Susan couldn't dive, she was afraid to go in head first, she didn't even like jumping in, but lowered herself from the bank inch by inch. That seemed now to sum up the differences in their characters. Beth plunged into everything with gusto, she liked challenge and even danger. Susan couldn't leap into anything, she approached anything new with caution, and usually backed away, overcome by fear.

Yet she had learned after her parents died that she was capable of recklessness, that she could banish fear when circumstances demanded it. But poor Beth had that wonderful, inspiring spark in her, snuffed out by those evil men. It had clearly tainted her whole life, and as Susan walked back to her cell, she wept for her friend.

Chapter sixteen

Frankie was lying on the top bunk smoking a cigarette when Susan got back to their cell. Susan's heart sank at the sight of the other woman, for she had hoped she'd be working. It meant she would get an interrogation, just when she was least able to cope with it.

'More agro wif yer brief?' Frankie asked, her small dark eyes scanning Susan's face for tear stains or anything that might suggest some kind of drama.

'No, not at all,' Susan replied, struggling to compose herself. She had learned to her cost not to tell anyone in here anything that was important to her. She had believed when she told Julie about Annabel that she would keep it to herself, but by the next day it was right round the prison. At first everyone was kinder to her, but it didn't last. She knew now that information about fellow prisoners was like a drug to most of these women, and they came back for more and more, getting nastier and nastier if they couldn't get it.

Susan also knew now that because she was middle-class, naive and with no previous convictions, she was seen as an oddity. Everyone wanted to break her down, take her apart to see what she was made of. 'Don't make out you're simple' was something she had said to her almost every day. But she supposed she *was* simple. She had always believed what people told her, whether it was her father stating he'd put her mother in a home if she left; Liam telling her he loved her; or Dr Wetherall insisting Annabel only had a virus.

She supposed that being loyal was perceived as being simple too. She had never told tales on anyone in her entire life, and even though everyone in Eastwood Park passed on everyone else's secrets, she wasn't going to join them.

She had known right away when the police came back with more questions that it was Beth's doing, and she just couldn't understand how her friend could do such a thing. But simple she must be, because now after Beth's visit she was convinced her friend had no choice. She also felt completely gutted by her revelations, and heart-sick that she hadn't been given any opportunity to try to help her.

Maybe she was cut off from the real world by being at home with her mother, but she would still have understood the horror and devastation of rape. She would have asked her parents if Beth could come and live with them, and she knew they would have agreed once she told them how awful Mr Powell had been about it.

It was no wonder that Beth had lost that sparkle she used to have. To have to keep such a monstrous secret locked inside her was enough to send anyone mad. Susan knew the agony of hiding things herself, forcing herself to act as if she was untroubled by anything, when in fact her mind was a seething whirlpool of past mistakes and hideous memories. She lived in fear that one day they would all be discovered, slapped down in front of her and she would be compelled to explain them all.

It would be such a relief to let it all out to someone who cared enough about her just to listen and maybe hold her. There were plenty of people in here who would like her to think they were that person. They lay in wait like jackals for prisoners coming back from a visit with their solicitor or family member, hoping to be the recipients of some juicy morsel. How those women would love it if she was to reveal that the police were trying to pin more murders on her! Such succulent information would get a place saved for her at meal-times, they'd be offering her shampoo, hand cream, and drugs too. It would stop her being the butt of all the jokes for a couple of days.

Prison was a living nightmare, never knowing when the next nasty trick would be played on her, or when someone would attack her, physically or verbally. She couldn't eat – after a couple of mouthfuls she just felt sick – and she was constantly having to keep herself in check so that she didn't show how repelled she was by the personal habits of her fellow prisoners. The ignorance, the swearing, the wickedness some of them were capable of was very hard to bear. She ached to be able to walk outside, to feel the wind in her hair, the rain on her face, to have silence.

'What did he want then?' Frankie's voice called her back to the present. She had sat up now and in her black sleeveless tee-shirt and jeans, with her inch-long spiky hair, she looked just like a man. Her huge muscular biceps with the barbed-wire tattoos around them stretched ominously as she moved.

'Oh, just verifying something my brother told him,' Susan said airily. She wasn't so simple that she hadn't learned to lie since she'd been in here. Telling the truth just got you into worse situations. She had believed living in Hill House had prepared her for most things, but not this place. Sometimes it felt as if she'd accidentally fallen down through a man-hole cover and discovered a whole new stratum of life. It wasn't just the crimes they'd committed, drug-dealing, fraud, thieving or prostitution, they were a different class of animal altogether, and all so explosive and violent.

Frankie was typical of the women who dominated the place – ugly to look at, foul-mouthed, evil-minded, vicious and unpredictable. She got her kicks out of first be-friending and protecting new prisoners, then bending their will to hers. Susan was already passing over her tobacco and her phone card to her. That was because Frankie stopped the woman who gave her the black eyes from hurting her again. Susan didn't care about either as she didn't smoke and had no one to phone, so she might have given them to Frankie anyway. But she did resent the constant grilling that 'a minder' subjected her to. She couldn't have a conversation with anyone without the woman expecting her to pass on every last detail.

'Verify what?' Frankie asked.

'The value of my parents' house,' Susan lied. 'It was sold for two hundred thousand, I suppose you want to know that too?'

The sarcasm in her voice didn't go unnoticed. Frankie was down off her bunk like a flash. Standing in front of Susan, her arms folded belligerently across her big chest, she said, 'Don't get funny wif me. I look after you's and you'd better remember it.'

'I'm just tired,' Susan said, lying down on her bunk and hoping that by feigning sleep she would be left alone.

'Move over, I'll just lay down wif you's,' Frankie said, and prodded her. 'You're gettin' real skinny. I like that.'

Susan shuddered inwardly. She knew Frankie was a lesbian, she made no secret of that, but until now all her romantic interests had lain with MacAllister, a prison officer. Other women on the wing had said this was the reason Frankie often got out of working, because left alone in the cell, she and this officer could make love.

That had seemed ridiculous to Susan when she first came to the prison. She had believed prison officers had too much integrity for such things. She certainly couldn't imagine that MacAllister, a softly spoken Scotswoman with a kindly manner, would have anything to do with anyone as ugly or rough as Frankie.

But Susan knew now that taboos in place on the outside vanished in here. Married women with several children who had been heterosexual all their lives would suddenly embark on an affair, sometimes even refusing to go down for a visit with their husbands. Young girls who when they first got here sobbed their hearts out for their boyfriends were almost immediately lured into relationships

365

with older women. In association time she saw women openly kissing and fondling one another.

The lesbian prison officers were in a way the most despicable, for they had purposely chosen a job where they could dominate other women. Countless times Susan had seen one of them keep a girl behind in the showers, or in a cell, and punishments were meted out if their wishes were not complied with. Susan didn't think all the prisoners who went that way were real lesbians, she was sure they were only coerced into it because they were hungry for affection. But she wasn't that hungry herself, and until now she hadn't ever been the object of anyone's desire.

'Please leave me to have a nap,' she pleaded. 'I'm not feeling well.'

'Don't come all that Lady of the Manor bit wif me,' Frankie snarled at her. 'If I want to touch you up I will.'

Susan closed her eyes dismissively. 'You'll do no such thing,' she said sharply. 'Go and find one of your own kind to touch up.'

The slap across her face took her by surprise, but when her eyes shot open and she saw Frankie grinning maliciously and unzipping her jeans, the rage she'd been struggling to control for weeks, the anger she felt about Beth's rape, all suddenly erupted and she knew she must fight back.

Without saying a word in warning, she leapt off the bed and caught Frankie by the throat, pushing her back towards the wall by the lavatory. It was the speed of her attack which gave her the advantage, Frankie was several inches taller than her and very much stronger, but she'd been caught unawares.

'I'm sick of you,' Susan hissed at her, knowing she had to use brute force to hold the woman. 'Sick of your endless questions, your filthy language, the stink of your body and your bullying. Now you suggest you have the right to touch me up! You are odious. If we were the only two people left on this bloody planet, I'd top myself rather than be stuck with you.'

She tightened her fingers on Frankie's throat, using all the strength in her body to push the woman back against the wall and prevent her kicking out at her. 'I want to kill you,' she roared at her, banging her head back hard against it. She couldn't control her rage any longer for in her mind Frankie was just like the men who had raped Beth, and a representation of all the people who had contributed to her present predicament.

As she tightened her fingers around the woman's throat and saw Frankie's small dark eyes almost pop out of her head, she felt powerful. Close up she could see blackheads on her face, smell the onions from the shepherd's pie they'd had for dinner on her breath, and that nauseated her still more. 'I'll kill you,' she said, banging her head back again and again.

She had no idea how many times she banged Frankie's head against the wall, it felt as if she were just a big doll she wanted to smash. She didn't hear the door open or the two officers come charging in, she only knew they were there when they grabbed her arms. 'Let her go, Fellows,' one shouted. 'Let her go.'

As Susan was dragged out of the cell to the punishment block, at least she had the satisfaction of seeing Frankie slumped on the floor, unconscious.

Susan didn't come out of her own shock for some time. She remembered one of the officers admonishing her and saying she was shocked and appalled at her behaviour, then asking what Frankie had done to her. Susan hadn't bothered to answer, she was pretty certain they knew enough about the woman to guess. All she felt then was relief that she could be alone for at least twenty-four hours without anyone speaking to her.

It didn't matter to her that the punishment cell was bare of everything but a rubber-covered mattress and a blanket. By closing her eyes she could try to drift away somewhere beautiful.

She tried her old trick of imagining the sea, but that only made her aware of gurgling noises in the water pipes. She tried to turn the clonking sound of one of the prison officers' heavy shoes out in the corridor into the sound of horses' hooves on cobbles, but try as she might she couldn't visualize a sun-filled stable yard with fields beyond.

But then her mind flitted to Luddington, and she pictured herself on her bike, picking up speed as she went down the slight incline from the green opposite the church. Mentally she turned into the path down to the lock behind her old home, bumping over the pot-holes, and suddenly she could see Beth riding beside her, whooping as she splashed through a puddle.

Of all the places she and Beth liked to go in their first

couple of summers together, the lock was their particular favourite. All at once she was right there again, it was a warm summer's day and they were sitting side by side at the lock waiting for a boat to come along.

They loved the sound of the rushing water when the lock gates were opened, seeing the swans and ducks heaving themselves up on to the river banks to take a rest, the sunshine on the water and looking down at themselves reflected in it, distorted images like crazy mirrors at the fun-fair.

If they helped people with the lock gates, sweets or fruit were often thrown up to them. But the real fascination for them was the glimpse into family holidays. Neither of them had ever been away on real holidays with both their parents. Beth would talk of days out in Hastings with her mother or brother and sister; Susan had only ever been to relatives in Bristol. It was a curious concept to them both that some families hired a boat, taking all the children and even the dog, and slept and cooked on it for as long as two weeks.

'We could do it too, when we're grown up,' Beth said once, as she saw two teenage girls in bikinis sunbathing side by side on the bows of a cabin cruiser. 'We could just keep going and going until the end of the river. Maybe we'd find some wonderful place where we could get jobs in a shop or something, and we'd stay there for ever.'

The noise of wailing from another cell dragged Susan back to reality. She wanted to imagine lying on the deck of one of those boats, the sun burning into her skin, slowly chugging down the river. But someone was pounding on their cell door with their feet or fists. It was only then that she remembered with a jolt what she had done to Frankie.

It seemed incredible to her that she'd lashed out like that, with nothing but her bare hands. She'd never hit anyone in her life before, not even at school. It was amazing to her that she'd managed to inflict pain on Frankie, who was bigger and far stronger than herself.

The thought made her smile. At last she'd stood up for herself. Perhaps the other women would treat her with caution from now on.

The following morning Beth took a cup of coffee into Steven's office after she'd heard him saying goodbye to his client.

'Refreshments,' she said, putting the mug down on his cluttered desk. 'And I just wondered when you are going in to see Susan again.'

'I had arranged to go in today, but now it's tomorrow,' he said, shuffling a pile of papers together and putting them into a folder. He looked up at Beth with a worried expression.

'Something on your mind?' she asked, perching on the edge of his desk.

'Yes,' he replied. 'Firstly, the police rang earlier and said they've got some new evidence and want to interview her again tomorrow. So I rang the prison to inform them. What do I hear but Susan's been put on the punishment block.'

'Really! What on earth for?' Beth asked. 'Everything was fine when I saw her yesterday.'

'She attacked another prisoner.' Steven pursed his lips in disapproval. 'A serious attack too, the other woman had to be taken to the hospital.'

Beth was astounded. 'I can't believe that. She's so passive!'

'Is she? I'm beginning to wonder if we know her at all,' Steven said, with more than a touch of despair in his voice. 'Apparently it happened just after you left her. Her cellmate was in there alone, and the fight broke out. Apparently the other woman is a real hard case, so the prison officers were very surprised by it, especially as Susan's never shown any signs of aggression before. They think that if they hadn't intervened when they did, she might well have killed the woman.'

'Oh, shit,' Beth exclaimed, and slumped down on a seat by Steven's desk. 'I hope it wasn't my visit that wound her up?'

'I expect it had something to do with it,' Steven said wearily. 'What did you talk to her about?'

Beth didn't want to tell him, she knew he would think it was inappropriate and possibly foolhardy. 'Nothing much,' she lied. 'She was a bit hostile at first about me grassing her up as she called it. I remarked on how much weight she'd lost, and she took the opportunity to snipe at me a bit.'

'Sounds like she was pretty fired up already then?' Steven said.

Beth felt awkward then, and she didn't know what to say.

'Come on,' he said impatiently. 'I need to know. I don't want her coming out with something tomorrow in front of the police that I know nothing about.'

'She was goading me about dropping her when I went to university,' Beth admitted reluctantly. 'It ended up with me telling her about the rape.' She blushed furiously. 'Heaven only knows what made me blurt that out. Don't say it, Steven!' she added warningly.

'Don't say what?'

'That I shouldn't have.'

'She's your friend.' He shrugged. 'It's not for me to tell you what you can talk to her about. Anyway, what sort of effect did it have on her?'

'She reverted right back to how she was when we were girls,' Beth said. 'It was emotional and very comforting for both of us, I think.'

'Maybe that was the trigger,' Steven said thoughtfully.

Beth frowned, she couldn't see what he meant.

Steven got up from his desk and walked over to the window, then turned and looked back at Beth. He looked very worried, and weary too.

'Maybe she went back to her cell feeling angry at what had happened to you. So angry that when this other prisoner said something she didn't like, she lashed out.'

'It would have made her sad, not angry,' Beth said. 'I can't believe she would lash out at someone else because of it. She's a peacemaker, not a fighter.'

'Maybe we're mistaken about that,' Steven said glumly. He put his hands in his trouser pockets, and rocked on his heels. 'She has led us to believe that the only time she'd ever been violent was the day she went into the surgery and shot two people. We swallowed that, hook line and sinker, because of the tragic circumstances, and because of your knowledge of her. That's also why we can't believe she had any hand in these other people's disappearance.'

'Surely you haven't changed your mind just because she's attacked another prisoner?' Beth snapped at him. 'We both know what it's like in there!'

'Look, the police have got something or they wouldn't be wanting to talk to her again,' Steven said heatedly. 'They've been up in Wales and out in Luddington. Now she has shown us she *is* capable of sudden and irrational violence.'

'Aren't we all?' Beth retorted. 'Even the gentlest, calmest person can lash out with the right provocation. I would imagine being cooped up in a cell with someone who gets on your nerves is enough to blow anyone's lid off.'

'I know all that,' he said, making a despairing gesture with his hands. 'But there is something about her, Beth, something she's holding back. I've sensed it several times. Liam, Reuben and Zoë. What happened to them, Beth?'

She looked at him in horror. She had come to trust his sound judgement and his keen perception, but she couldn't bear to hear him doubt Susan. 'Don't, Steven,' she pleaded, putting her hands over her face. 'I don't care how many coincidences there are of people disappearing around her, I can't and won't believe she had anything to do with it.'

'She certainly has a way of making you believe in her,' Steven said wryly. 'She makes me feel that every time I'm with her. It's only afterwards I begin to get doubts.'

'Your job isn't to look for guilt,' Beth reminded him sharply. 'You're defending her, for goodness' sake. It's the police and the prosecution who have to do the ferreting.'

'Interview with Susan Fellows commenced at 9.15 a.m. at Eastwood Park,' Roy said into the tape-recorder. 'Those present are Detective Inspector Longhurst, Sergeant Bloom, and Steven Smythe, solicitor representing Susan Fellows.'

Roy began the interview by asking Susan to think back to August 1986. 'We know you went to Bristol on the 8th, we have confirmation from your old landlord in Ambra Vale that you looked at his house that day and paid a deposit. Is that correct?'

'Yes,' Susan replied.

'Did you go straight home to Stratford-upon-Avon afterwards?'

'No, I stayed the night in Bristol in a bed and breakfast,' she said. 'I went home the following day.'

'The 9th?' he said. 'Was Liam there when you got home?'

'No,' she said. 'He was working away.'

'By working away you mean he was sleeping at his work?'

'Yes, well, in his camper van,' she said.

'Where was this work?'

'I don't remember,' she said. 'He didn't always say.'

'So when did you see him again?'

'I didn't, he never came back again.'

'Why do you think this was?'

'I've already told you that, several times. He didn't want to be tied down.'

'But you were expecting his child,' Roy said. 'I'm sure you must have thought he had to take at least some of the responsibility for that?'

'That never came into it because I didn't know I was having a baby until after I'd moved,' she said, frowning with irritation because she'd told him that before too.

'So when was the last time you saw Liam?' Roy asked.

'The day before I went to Bristol,' she said.

'So that would have been the 7th of August?'

'I suppose so.'

'And he left the village in his camper?'

'Yes.'

'You didn't see him or his camper again?'

'No,' she said, and sighed deeply.

'But you must have seen his camper, it was still parked up in a lane in the village for some weeks after you moved away,' Roy said, looking at Susan intently.

'Was it?' she said, eyes wide with surprise. 'I didn't know.'

'I suppose you didn't know either, that on August 9th, the day you were in Bristol, he was working for a Mr Andrews, less than three miles from Luddington?'

'I can't remember after all this time where he said he was working,' she said.

'Then it's just as well Mr Andrews can,' Roy said

375

sharply. 'Apparently Liam completed the job during the afternoon, and left after arranging to return the next morning for his money. He didn't return. Can you explain that?'

Susan shrugged. 'Maybe he went on to another job, I don't know, I was in Bristol.'

'Not at that time, you arrived home in Luddington by bus, at around one-thirty that same afternoon.'

'If you say so,' Susan said, folding her arms and looking up at the ceiling.

'We have a statement from Mrs Vera Salmon, who lived across the road to you, that you sat next to her on the bus that day. She said you told her about the house you'd just found and seemed very excited about it.'

'I was,' Susan agreed. 'I was really happy.'

'Of course you were, you believed Liam loved you, and that moving to Bristol was a new start for you both. I expect you hoped he'd drop by or phone you later?'

Susan looked confused then. 'Well, yes, but he was working away.'

'No, he wasn't, Susan,' Roy said. 'He was seen by this same neighbour going into your house later that afternoon.'

'Well, maybe he did,' she said, colouring up. 'I can't be expected to remember what happened on what day, not after all this time.'

'I don't believe you can have forgotten anything about that day,' Roy said sternly. 'Not the journey back from Bristol full of excitement, talking to Mrs Salmon, or what Liam said to you when he called round. I believe that was the day he told you he had no intention of going to Bristol with you. I believe it ended in a fight in which you killed him.'

'Don't be ridiculous,' she retorted, then, jumping from her chair, she implored Steven to help her. 'Tell him, Mr Smythe! I couldn't have hurt him, I loved him.'

A little later Susan did admit tearfully that Liam had called round and they had an argument. But she said he had left the house by five-thirty and that was the last time she saw him.

She said it was quite possible his camper was still parked up in the village, but even if she had seen it, which she hadn't, it wouldn't have meant much to her either way, as it was always breaking down. As for him not returning to get the money owed to him for a job, she said he had always been a bit vague about money.

'Right, let's move on, to two years ago, 1993,' Roy said crisply. 'The disappearance of Reuben Moreland and Zoë Fremantle, from the house in Wales.'

'How can I help it if they've disappeared?' Susan asked incredulously. 'I was only one of twelve people living there.'

'Do the names Roger Watkins and Heather Blythe mean anything to you?' he asked.

'Yes,' Susan said. 'They both lived at the house while I was there.'

'Neither of them lives at Hill House now, but they've both made statements concerning Reuben and Zoë,' Roy said. 'They said that the couple left to sell goods at a craft fair in North Wales in early April. While they were gone you left.'

'That's right, I did,' she said.

'But Watkins claims he saw you over a week later in Emlyn Carlisle.'

'He's mistaken. I was in Bristol by then.'

'Was he mistaken in saying that Reuben had treated you very badly, bringing Zoë home with him and sharing what was once your bed with her?'

'No, that's true. That's why I left, I didn't like it.'

'You didn't take the room in Belle Vue, Clifton until April 28th, some two weeks after you left Hill House. I have seen a dated copy of the tenancy agreement you signed. So where were you for the two weeks before that?'

'In Bristol,' she insisted.

'Where in Bristol?'

She hesitated. 'I can't remember the address, a bed and breakfast place. I was looking for a flat during that time.'

'You weren't, Susan,' he said, leaning towards her. 'You were camping up in the woods near Hill House. Weren't you?'

Steven hadn't been perturbed by any of the questions and suggestions put to his client up till then. In fact he couldn't really understand why the police wanted to question her again, for they didn't appear to have any new evidence which would positively link her with the disappearance of these people. But the suggestion that she was camping near the house jolted him.

'That's completely ridiculous,' Susan said indignantly.

'You don't have to answer any further questions,' Steven reminded her.

'It's okay. I've got nothing to hide,' she replied, and she half smiled at him as if the line of questioning wasn't worrying her in any way. 'What on earth would I want to camp out in the woods for?'

'Revenge?' Roy suggested, raising an eyebrow. 'We have been up to those woods, the camping equipment is still there, a little the worse for wear after two years.'

'I have never had any camping equipment,' she scoffed. 'If you found stuff there it's nothing to do with me.'

'I didn't say it was your camping equipment, but it came from Hill House, it has been identified.'

'Why blame me?' she asked, wide-eyed, looking around at Steven as if for support. 'Anyone in that house could have taken it there. Reuben could have taken it there himself. He was always vanishing, he liked camping, anyone who ever lived in that house would tell you that.'

'The last time Reuben and Zoë were seen by anyone in Hill House was as they made their way towards that wood for a picnic,' Roy said. 'But they left the house with nothing but a small basket and a rug.'

'Well, there you go,' she said triumphantly. 'He'd taken the stuff up there before. He probably stayed up there for a while, then they went off abroad or something.'

'He couldn't leave the country without his passport,' Roy said with a faint smirk. 'We found that at Hill House. He left his van there too, and he hasn't touched his bank account either since then.'

'Then ask the others where he is,' she snapped. 'If they saw him walking off with just a rug, and he didn't come back, why didn't they report him missing?'

'They had their reasons,' Roy replied. 'Benefit fraud, for one. You see, when he didn't come back they had nothing to live on. So they signed on and claimed housing benefit. They could hardly report their landlord missing when they were supposed to be handing over thirty quid a week each to him. Could they?'

Susan laughed, surprising Steven. 'I think that's all a bit cock-eyed. You've just given a perfect reason for any one of them, or all of them, to want him out of the way. But not me. I didn't claim benefits I wasn't entitled to. When I left that house I left for good. I couldn't care less about what went on there.'

Steven agreed with her. He wondered what on earth Roy was playing at, and what he knew but wasn't saying. For he had to have something better than this.

'The glen in the woods was Reuben's "special place", wasn't it?' Roy continued. 'He took you there for love-making, didn't he?'

Susan looked blank as if she didn't know what he was talking about.

'I know he did,' Roy continued. 'He took all his women there. Heather, Megan and many others. But he told you all you were the only one, and at the time you believed it.'

Steven looked at Susan. For the first time in the interview she did look a little rattled. But she folded her arms across her chest and didn't reply.

'You might as well tell the truth now and get it over with,' Roy said, not unkindly, but with a faint trace of fatigue. 'You took that camping equipment up to the wood, piece by piece. You left Hill House when Reuben and Zoë were away, but you didn't come to Bristol. You camped out, knowing that Reuben would turn up with Zoë before long. You were seething with anger at being replaced by a younger woman and the humiliation he'd put you through. You intended to exact your revenge.'

'That's not true,' Susan said, angry red spots appearing on her cheeks. 'I *was* hurt that he'd treated me badly, but I was tired of all those dead-beats anyway and wanted a new start.'

'But your new start didn't work out, did it?' he said. 'Living in one room, working as an office cleaner! Hardly a step up.'

'Coming back to Bristol with all its reminders of Annabel was a mistake,' she snapped at him. 'As it turned out, I should have gone somewhere else. I floundered because I was depressed.'

Roy used his favourite tactic, silence. He just looked at her and didn't say another word.

He didn't think she had killed Liam. The man was sensitive, he probably felt bad about being unable to commit to Susan and he'd moved away because he didn't want people constantly reminding him of her.

But Roy was convinced she'd killed Reuben and Zoë. While he was interviewing Megan over in Wales, she'd told him how Reuben always took his new women to the glen, and she led him and two other police officers up to it. That was where they found the missing camping equipment which both Roger and Heather had independently mentioned previously.

While it was quite true that anyone could have taken the camping stuff there, even Reuben himself, the fact that it was left there was extremely suspicious. Everything about the glen made it an ideal spot for a murder – its remoteness, the way it overlooked Hill House. The sound of gunshot wouldn't be noticed, and a body could lie undisturbed for years, falling leaves and creeping undergrowth hiding it ever more securely.

It might have been a freezing-cold winter's day when Roy saw the glen, but he could imagine how beautiful it was in spring and summer, and how sacred it would be to anyone who had been taken there for love-making. He could well imagine, too, Susan's fury and jealousy when she was replaced by the young and beautiful Zoë. He thought it was well within her capabilities to plan their murder in advance. Only one unusual talent was required for this kind of murder, and that was patience.

Susan couldn't have known exactly when Reuben would return, or how long it would take him afterwards to bring Zoë there. She might have had to wait weeks. But patience *was* Susan's most notable virtue. It had been evident in everything he'd learned about her, right from when she was a young girl. She was someone who could wait for the right moment to get her revenge. Just as she had waited before shooting the people at the surgery. That was what made her so chilling.

He looked at her now, and noted how her pale greenish-blue eyes held that same distant look he'd observed when he arrested her for the shooting, and later when he questioned her at the police station. Roy thought that she had been able to remove herself mentally then from the reality of what she'd done, and she was doing it again now.

Yet there were faint signs of agitation at his silence. She was clenching and unclenching her fingers, from time to time she pushed her hair back behind her ears, and her lips looked dry. Lying didn't come easily to her, but she did have the patience to sit it out.

He decided it was time to break his silence. 'I believe it was guilt that made you depressed,' he said, leaning nearer to her across the table. 'I would say that you imagined by killing Reuben and Zoë you could wipe the slate clean and start all over again. But it wasn't that simple. Was it?'

He paused again, leaning back in his chair for a moment or two but fixing her with his eyes.

'It couldn't be, Susan. Could it?' he insisted. 'You were back where it all started. Reuben had persuaded you to leave your nice home, he'd sold all your belongings. The wonderful new life he said he'd take you to had turned sour. He'd rejected you in favour of a much younger woman. You were reminded of all that every single day you lived in the grim room in Belle Vue. Isn't it true that you were so full of anger you had to turn it on someone? And who better than Doctor Wetherall and his receptionist who you felt were responsible for Annabel's death?'

'They deserved to die,' she shouted at him, her eyes flashing. 'They let my baby die, it serves them right.'

'And Liam, did he deserve to die for not wanting to

settle down with you? Did Reuben deserve it for conning you. Zoë for humiliating you?'

'What do you know about anything?' She suddenly shot out of her chair on to her feet, her face flushed with anger. 'You can't begin to understand what it was like for me when Annabel died. She was my whole life, everything in the world to me. And but for those two arrogant, stupid people who wouldn't even get an ambulance for her, she might be alive today.'

'Sit down, Susan,' he said firmly, looking right at her. 'I do know what losing a child is like. It's the worst thing that can happen to anyone. But killing someone else doesn't put it right.'

Roy's remark wasn't intended to be an admission he'd lost a child too, but he thought maybe she felt he was just being patronizing, for she took a step backwards and glowered at him.

'Sit down, Susan,' he repeated, a little concerned by the fury in her eyes. All her earlier calm was gone, she looked poised to spring at him.

'I don't want to sit down,' she hissed at him. 'Are you so stupid that you think you can soften me up with something as cheap as that? You must be, you're trying to blame me for killing three people who just happen to have disappeared, without one shred of evidence. You're so stupid you can't even work out for yourself why Beth won't go to bed with you. Can you? Well, I'll put you out of your misery on that score. It's because she was gang-raped.'

Steven leapt from his chair. 'That's enough, Susan,' he

said, catching hold of her arm. 'This interview is about you, not about Beth.'

'You make me sick too,' she said, turning to him, throwing off his hand and grabbing hold of the lapels of his jacket. 'You pretend you're so bloody sympathetic but you don't give a toss about me. I expect you've got the hots for Beth too.'

Roy got up to intervene. For a small woman Susan was surprisingly strong and it took some effort to get her back on to her seat. 'That's enough,' he said firmly. 'We'll terminate this interview now and continue when you are calmer.'

Roy made the report into the tape-recorder that the interview was suspended at twelve-thirty, and Susan was led out of the room by Sergeant Bloom, leaving Steven and Roy alone.

'Whew!' Roy said, wiping the back of his hand across his forehead.

Steven could see he was very shaken, all the colour had gone from his face. 'I'm sorry,' he said simply. 'You shouldn't have had to hear that.'

Roy passed one hand over his face wearily. 'Is it true?'

'I haven't got the hots for Beth, we're just friends,' Steven said, feeling suddenly queasy because he felt he ought to have seen Susan's outburst coming and deflected it. 'As for the other matter, well, I'm sick that she came out with it. Beth's been trying to pluck up courage to tell you herself. She'll be horrified that you had to hear it that way.'

'How come you know?' Roy said, his eyes narrowing.

'That's not easy to explain, and I don't know that I ought to say anything more,' Steven said.

'Spoken just like a bloody lawyer,' Roy said sarcastically.

Steven sighed. 'It's nothing like you might imagine. Beth and I hardly knew one another until Susan was arrested. When Beth discovered it was her old friend, it kind of cracked her armour. I just happened to be the person who was there, and in talking over the case, long-buried things came to light. I can't discuss it with you, Beth wouldn't want me to. She'd want to tell you about it herself.'

'Why did she tell Susan about her and me?' Roy asked, a look of pain in his eyes.

It was only then that Steven saw for himself the depths of the policeman's feelings for Beth. Up till then he'd only seen the man in his professional role, fair-minded, but shrewd and hard-headed. It had crossed his mind more than once that Detective Inspector Longhurst wanted Beth more for her position than herself. This had worried him a great deal, as from what he knew of Beth now, he didn't think she could handle any further heartache. But only a man in love could look so wounded that other people had been privy to Beth's past, while he knew nothing.

'She wouldn't have said anything more than that you were a friend,' Steven said gently. 'Remember, she's been visiting Susan as her friend, not as her lawyer. Susan was just making a vicious stab in the dark. She hoped to throw you.'

'She succeeded,' Roy said dolefully. He rested his

elbows on the table and covered his face with his hands.

'Don't let her rattle you,' Steven said firmly. 'Get her back and carry on with the interview.'

Roy looked at his watch and frowned. 'It's lunch-time,' he said. 'We'll leave her to calm down and go on up to the pub for a sandwich.'

The pub on the corner of the main road was very quiet, the only customers were a few workmen having a drink and a handful of old men from the village. Steven felt a little inhibited by Sergeant Bloom's presence, for he guessed the man must be pondering over Susan's outburst. But it wasn't Steven's place to remind the man he must forget what he'd heard.

Once they were seated with sandwiches and coffee, Roy appeared to be entirely composed, and talked in general about the investigation in Wales, and about the statements he'd taken from Megan, Heather and Roger. This was all information which would come to Steven in due course anyway, but it was heartening to him that Roy wasn't withholding it out of spite.

He told Steven that both Heather Blythe and Roger Watkins said much the same things in their statements, and there was no collusion because they'd had no contact with each other since leaving Hill House.

They and everyone else at Hill House had assumed Reuben and Zoë had gone camping when the equipment was found to be missing. When Reuben didn't return within a few days for his van, they decided the couple must have gone abroad. But without leadership the house soon became a shambles. Heather was the next to leave after Megan, and Roger reported that her place, and those of the other original residents, were gradually taken by travellers who turned up and stayed. Roger Watkins hung on for about a year, and it was during that time he found Reuben's passport and realized that without it he couldn't have gone abroad.

Roger had expressed some concern for Reuben in his statement, thinking the man might have got into trouble through drug-dealing. But with the benefit fraud hanging over him, he didn't feel able to report him missing.

Roger's insistence that he saw Susan in Emlyn Carlisle appeared to be valid, in as much as he gave a description of a floral dress she was wearing, and it matched one the police had found in Susan's suitcase. There wasn't any forensic evidence as yet that Susan took the camping equipment to the woods, and Roy doubted there would be after all this time.

Steven felt he ought to feel triumphant that there was absolutely no real evidence that Susan had killed the couple, or indeed even any proof that the pair of them were dead. Yet faced with Roy's conviction that their bodies were up in the wood beyond Hill House, Steven found himself disturbed rather than pleased.

'I needed a word with you before the police come back,' Steven said as Susan was brought into the interview room. Her eyes were red and swollen from crying.

'I'm sorry I told Longhurst that about Beth,' she blurted out. 'I could have cut my tongue out afterwards. I was just angry with him and wanted to hurt him. But it's only Beth who will be hurt, isn't it?'

Steven was very surprised she could only think of Beth when she was in such a tight spot herself.

'Well, it's done now, you can't take it back,' he replied.

'She'll be very angry with me,' Susan said, her eyes cast down. 'If only I hadn't come back to Bristol. We'd never have met again and I wouldn't be messing up her life.'

Steven shrugged. 'Beth doesn't feel you've done that.'

He wished he could tell her that appearing in Beth's life again had perhaps been the very best thing that could have happened to her. Daily, Beth was opening up more and more. She was an entirely different person now to the stern, defensive woman who arrived at Tarbuck, Stone and Aldridge some eighteen months ago.

In fact, Susan's arrest had proved to be a catalyst in many more ways than one. Without all the emotions she'd brought out in Beth, where would he be? It was Beth who encouraged him to deal with Anna's drinking, and because of that support his marriage had a future at last. Anna was recovering, life at home was good again, and his friendship with Beth was a warm and deeply satisfying one.

'She will be angry when Longhurst tells her what I said,' Susan said despairingly. 'She loves him, Mr Smythe, I've ruined it for her.'

'I doubt that, Susan.' Steven put a comforting hand on her shoulder. 'Policemen are used to having unpleasant things thrown at them. Besides, but for you they might never have got to know each other.'

'But Beth won't see him while all this is going on, will she?' Susan said, looking at Steven with brimming eyes. 'It must be awful for her, like being piggy-in-the-middle.'

'You mustn't worry about that,' Steven said firmly. 'We lawyers don't let our work interfere with our social life. I've been in court fighting tooth and nail against a prosecution lawyer, then we go out for a drink together afterwards. I've got friends in the police force too, they might have arrested one of my clients, but it doesn't make us enemies.'

'But Beth needs to be with Longhurst now,' Susan insisted. 'She'll creep back into her shell if this goes on and on. I couldn't bear to think I robbed her of the happiness she deserves.'

Steven didn't know what to say to that. He knew Susan was right in believing Beth wouldn't see Roy until all this was squared away, she would see it as a point of honour. Maybe that time apart, and the things that the case might throw up, would be damaging to any future relationship with Roy, but he didn't think Susan should take that burden on her shoulders, she had a big enough one there already.

'Beth is a grown woman,' he said gently. 'You don't have to worry about her.'

'But I have to do the right thing by her,' Susan said, looking at him with bleak eyes. 'So I'm going to tell him the whole story this afternoon.'

Steven thought she meant about the rape and how she knew about it. 'That isn't necessary, the less said about that the better,' he said in alarm. 'You just answer the questions Longhurst asks you, nothing more.'

'I didn't mean about Beth,' she said, frowning at him. 'I meant the full story about the murders. A confession.'

Steven was so taken aback that he could only gape at her.

'Confession? Are you trying to tell me you did kill Reuben and Zoë after all?' he gasped out.

'Yes,' she whispered. 'I know they haven't got enough to charge me, yet. But Longhurst is a clever man and he knows I did it. He'll only keep on till he's got the proof. I can't take any more, I might as well own up now and be done with it.'

'I don't believe you killed them,' Steven heard himself say. His head seemed to be foggy, all that was coming through was that Susan was insane and she wanted to confess so that the questions would stop.

'I did, Mr Smythe,' she said and put one hand on his arm. 'It's nice that you don't believe it of me, but it's true. I don't suppose Beth will believe it either, but you must explain to her. She should forget me, and take her chance of happiness with Longhurst. I want that for her. I can help her.'

Steven didn't think he'd ever heard anything so implausible. Yet Susan had sincerity written all over her face. But that was what Susan was, a paradox. Admirable in so many ways, for her kindness, stoicism and timidity. He liked her. Really liked her, far more than he did most of his clients. Yet she had flown in the face of all those admirable qualities by killing: kindness becoming cruelty, stoicism lost in the need for revenge, and timidity in courage.

But even knowing she had killed two more people hadn't diminished his view of her. He still liked her.

'Beth wouldn't want you confessing to try and make things right for her,' he said hastily. 'I have to advise you against this, Susan. If it's because you feel pressured by all the questions, I can insist you've had enough for one day.'

'Beth always believed I told the truth.' Susan's head came up defiantly. 'She said once that was one of the nicest things about me. I haven't got much left that's nice about me any more. I've even learned to lie since I've been in here. I need to tell the whole truth now, if only to feel better in myself. You see, Mr Smythe, I am an evil killer. I need to be put away where I can't do any harm to anyone ever again.'

Chapter seventeen

Steven had to go out of the interview room for a few minutes to compose himself, leaving Susan with a prison officer. He would have liked to go outside in the fresh air, but that was asking the impossible due to prison rules and staff shortages. So he had to stand in the corridor, breathing in the fusty, hot air, and for the first time in many years he wished he had a cigarette, and a stiff drink to go with it.

He was completely stunned by Susan saying she wanted to confess to murdering Reuben and Zoë. He wondered now why he hadn't thought to ask her how she'd killed them, and what she'd done with the bodies. That at least might have indicated whether she was making it up, and if it was some sort of bid for attention or perhaps even a kind of glory.

Yet Steven knew in his heart it wasn't that. Susan might be many conflicting things, but she wasn't an attention-seeker.

Should he try and talk her out of it? Make her wait twenty-four hours until she'd had time to consider the full implications? He was certain that's what most defence lawyers would do, given that there was no real evidence against her, not even the most vital kind – the bodies.

Over the years Steven had had many clients who had been arrested for one crime, then for some reason or other, while in custody, they'd decided to own up to other things. Sometimes it was because they guessed the other crimes might be uncovered anyway, or that they thought the judge would look more kindly upon them. Now and again it was a need to unburden their guilt.

The judge certainly wouldn't look on Susan more kindly. She would spend the rest of her natural life in prison. And she knew that. Steven preferred to think it was her guilt that made her want to confess, and that way he would feel justified in letting her go ahead.

But this crazy stuff about helping Beth! If Steven had been told such a thing by another solicitor he would have laughed and said the person was certifiable. Yet Susan didn't appear to be mad, not at their first meeting, or any other one. Often she was about the most rational person he knew.

'I'm an evil killer.' He muttered her words to himself and then took deep breaths to try to quell the butterflies in his stomach. He saw 'evil killers' as men like Fred West, Peter Sutcliffe or Dennis Nielson. Cold, twisted men who got some sort of perverted thrill out of murder. Rose West and Myra Hindley had probably been equally evil, but right now as he stood here in a stuffy prison corridor, their part in the murders only seemed to him to be as assistants. He knew women's prisons held many murderers, but for the life of him he couldn't name one who had killed more than once.

394

He wished now he'd had some previous experience in a murder case. Perhaps then he could be more objective. He had always imagined that if he had to defend a murderer, he would do it to the very best of his ability but be very glad when he lost the case. He'd never heard of any lawyer believing their client innocent when they themselves admitted their guilt.

But that was how he felt. While knowing perfectly well that Susan did do the shooting at the surgery, he couldn't help but feel she was justified in doing it. When he looked back on her life and saw all the shit which had been dumped on her, he didn't think he would blame her if she'd opened fire on a hundred people.

But that was his real quandary, of course. He had so much wanted to steam into court and fight the prosecution by bringing up all the sad, miserable and tragic things which had happened to Susan. He wanted others to feel as he did, that she was pushed over the edge, couldn't help herself, so they'd be glad when she only got a short sentence.

Yet with another two murders thrown in, the picture was entirely different. There wouldn't be many tears for Reuben. But Zoë was young and beautiful, no one would think she deserved to die. Susan would become a hate figure. That bothered him more than anything, for like Beth he'd seen the goodness and honesty in her. To him she was a victim, too, of cruel circumstances that compelled her to step outside the law.

He looked at his watch and saw it was almost two. He had to go back in.

Steven had only a couple of minutes in the interview room alone with Susan before Longhurst and Bloom came back in. She seemed composed, even anxious to get started.

'Are you absolutely sure you want to do this?' he asked.

'Absolutely sure,' she said, looking right into his eyes.

'You do understand what this will lead to?'

'Yes, there will be no diminished responsibility. I'll get life,' she said, with great determination in both her voice and her eyes. 'And no, I don't want time to think about it. I have thought. My mind is made up.'

Steven thought Roy looked drawn and tired as he came back into the room. 'My client has instructed me that she wishes to make a full confession,' he said.

Roy's expression was almost laughable. His dark brown eyes widened, he looked in disbelief first at Susan and then at Steven and his mouth gaped.

But he recovered very quickly. He took off his jacket and hung it on the back of the chair, sat down and put a new tape into the recorder, tested it, then did the usual date, time and those present.

'Where would you like to begin, Susan?' he asked.

'On August 9th, 1986,' she said, looking toward the tape-recorder self-consciously. 'That was the day I killed Liam Johnstone.'

Steven looked at her in complete astonishment. A cold shudder ran down his spine. He opened his mouth to speak but nothing came out. Surely she hadn't really killed Liam too?

'I didn't mean to kill him,' she said, looking straight at Steven as if willing him not to interrupt. 'I was angry because he wouldn't come to Bristol with me. We argued, he began to walk out of the kitchen to leave the house, and I picked up a knife and stabbed him in the back.'

'What kind of knife was it?' Roy asked.

Steven noticed his voice shook just a little, even though he had managed to suppress his surprise.

'A French cook's knife,' she said, quite calmly. 'It was about ten or twelve inches long, a triangular blade. I'd left it out on the side after cutting up some meat earlier.'

Only that morning Susan had lied to Detective Inspector Longhurst when she said she couldn't remember anything much about that day. She could recall it all in fine detail, every word that was spoken, however much she wished she could forget.

It was hot and sultry, and the river at the bottom of the garden reflected the blue of the sky. She had got off the bus just before two, changed into a pink sundress, put her hair up in bunches, and after hastily preparing a chicken casserole for the evening meal, went outside to sit on the sun lounger under one of the apple trees. She was so full of excitement about the house she'd found in Bristol that she could barely wait for Liam to get home so she could tell him about it. Unable even to read because of her excitement, she closed her eyes and planned the colour scheme for the living room in her new home.

She must have dropped off to sleep for she woke suddenly at the sound of running water. Looking round, she saw Liam standing in the doorway. He was drinking a glass of water, wearing only a pair of jeans which had been cut off into shorts, his chest bare. His dark curls stuck to his head with sweat, or maybe he'd just put his head under the tap.

Calling out to him, she asked him to bring her some water and to come and hear her exciting news. When he didn't come out, she got up and went to the kitchen, and found him sitting at the table studying a map.

'Didn't you hear me?' she asked.

'Yes, but I was just checking something,' he said, still looking at the map.

'I've found us a wonderful little house,' she said, and gabbled on for a while about the size of the rooms, the garden and how lovely Clifton in Bristol was. In her excitement she didn't notice he wasn't responding, not until he got up from the table and caught hold of her arm.

'Suzie, I'm really glad you've found somewhere nice to live,' he said, his face stern and cold. 'But it's no good you talking about it as if I'm going to be there too. I told you I wasn't going to Bristol with you. I'm not going to change my mind.'

'But you must come with me,' she said. 'It's just perfect for us. You'll get lots of work around there too.'

'I have my work here,' he insisted. 'I told you I couldn't live in a city.'

'But it isn't like a city, it's really pretty,' she said.

He *had* said she was to find a place for herself, and that he was going to carry on the way he'd always done, living in his van, moving from job to job. He had even been quite fierce about it. But she hadn't really believed he meant it. After all, he'd told her he didn't like living in this house either, and he'd been here since last December.

He made her sit down, and repeated everything he'd said before. How he wasn't the settling-down kind, and he'd only stayed here because of the circumstances of her parents dying and her brother being so vicious. 'I really like you, Suzie,' he said, reaching out and stroking her cheek. 'We had some good times together. But you need a straight guy, someone steady who will look after you. I'm sorry if you began to think of it as a permanent thing, but every time I've tried to go before you got upset. I'll help you with the packing, do anything I can to make it easier for you. But that's all, Suzie. I need my freedom back.'

She argued with him, insisting he did really love her and that she couldn't live without him.

'That's not true,' he said. 'You've found your wings now, Suzie, it's time you made a life of your own, for yourself.'

'I don't want to,' she burst out, frightened by his harsh tone. 'I want to be with you, to care for you.'

'I don't want to be cared for the way you cared for your father,' he snapped back at her. 'It's not my scene to have dinner on the table when I get in, my clothes washed and ironed. Someone waiting on me. It shouldn't be your scene either. You've had a lifetime of looking after your mother and father, cooking, cleaning and chasing after them. It's time to stop that.'

'I won't do that if you don't like it,' she said wildly. 'I'll be whatever you want me to be.'

'I don't need a woman who just wants to mould herself around me,' he said impatiently.

She didn't understand what he meant by that. Surely that's what all men wanted, women who made everything nice and comfortable for them? She began arguing wildly with him, contradicting everything he'd said, and things she'd said herself, and she could feel herself growing angrier and angrier because she couldn't find the right words to convince him she was what he needed. She kept repeating that she loved him, and she needed him with her, but that seemed to make him even more determined.

Then quite suddenly his calm left him. 'You're suffocating me, for fuck's sake!' he shouted at her. 'Christ almighty, Suzie! How many times do I have to tell you I don't like living in houses, with meals on the table and a bath run for me? I hate it. I'm beginning to hate you too, Suzie because you are squeezing the lifeblood out of me.'

He turned away towards the door, and she knew he was going for good. She had to stop him, she couldn't live without him.

A French cook's knife was still lying on the kitchen unit where she'd cut up chicken for a casserole earlier, and in the heat of the moment she picked it up and she ran at his back with it.

In the split second before she thrust it into him, a voice inside her head was telling her this wasn't the way. But she was too angry, too desperate to stop, and with all her force she plunged the blade right into him, right up to the hilt.

'What have you done?' he said in a strange, strained

voice, half turning towards her. He tottered and fell sideways to the floor.

For a moment she couldn't believe what she saw – the knife embedded in his bare back, blood, thick and dark red, oozing out around it, dripping on to the tiles. She stood there looking down at him, her hands over her mouth in shock.

She came to sufficiently to pull the knife out a few seconds later. She pressed a clean towel over the wound. But he only made a little gurgling sound, then nothing more.

Nothing was ever so bad as that moment. She couldn't believe that in just a couple of seconds someone could go from arguing to death. Or that she could get angry enough to attack anyone. Part of her wanted to run to the phone and tell someone, anyone, what she'd done. But the longer she knelt beside Liam, knowing by then he was truly dead, the more afraid she got.

It was murder! The sort of thing she'd seen on the television and wondered at. The police would come, she'd be taken off to prison and her face would be in all the papers.

As she knelt there beside him, it was as though she was being sucked into a vortex. Time, place, even what they'd argued about had no meaning. She was sobbing, leaning over him, kissing his face, smoothing back his hair and telling him she didn't mean to do it.

It was at least an hour until the thought came to her that she could bury him in the garden. It was big, surrounded by trees and thick bushes, not overlooked from any other house. Even if someone was walking down by the river, there were too many bushes to see anything clearly. No one would know what she'd done, she would leave just as planned, and everyone around here would think Liam had just moved on. Maybe they'd even think he'd gone to Bristol with her.

The more she thought about it, the better the idea seemed. The people who were buying the house had fallen in love with the garden, they weren't likely to start digging it up. She even knew a place where the ground was soft.

The previous autumn, Liam had cut down some trees. One stump had been left, intended to be turned into a bird table, but it had sprouted from the base again during the spring. Only a few weeks earlier, Liam had insisted on digging it out, he said it was diseased and an eyesore. She didn't see why that mattered, seeing as she would be leaving, but he insisted.

He made a real mess of the lawn by digging such a deep and wide hole to get the roots out, and she got cross with him because she thought the new owners would be upset. Liam had promised to get some new turf for it, and a new shrub to plant. He had done it too, just yesterday while she was still in Bristol – she'd noticed it the moment she got home.

Distressed as she was, she got a little comfort from thinking of Liam tucked away under a new shrub. He'd loved the garden, and therefore he'd be happy to be buried in it.

Peeling back the turf and digging out the shrub was so

easy. It took no more than a few minutes. Digging the hole again, though, took a very long time, for she knew it had to be deep or foxes or cats might dig it up. But sheer panic and desperation kept her at it, and the plastic sheet she'd laid on the lawn to protect it was soon covered and the heap of earth grew steadily. She remembered thinking how lucky it was that her nearest neighbours were so used to hearing her moving around in the garden as she watered and weeded, even very late in the evening. If they could hear her tonight they wouldn't find it unusual.

She didn't know what time it was when Liam came home, perhaps half past four, but by the time she'd finished the hole it was well after nine, and dark. She'd had to make it a little longer than the original one, which was the hardest part, but she'd peeled back the grass there to lay it again later.

Pulling Liam's body out of the kitchen and across the lawn by his feet, in the dark, was awful. His head thumped down as she pulled him over the doorstep, and the thick trail of blood left across the kitchen floor made her feel sick. Once he was on the grass it was even harder to pull him, and she kept crying and having to stop. But she finally rolled him into the hole and began refilling it, glad that it was too dark to see the earth on his face and body.

Once the hole was refilled, she got a plank from the shed and laid it across the mound, then walked heavily all over it to flatten it, just as she'd seen Liam do after he'd dug the roots out. That was the very worst part, it seemed so cruel and so final.

It was much too dark by then to see anything, so she watered the pile of turf so it wouldn't start to die before morning, and went back inside.

Scrubbing the kitchen floor came next, bucket after bucket of water, turning bright red with the blood, before it came clean. She could remember lying down on the floor while it was still wet and sobbing her heart out. If she slept at all that night, she didn't remember, and first thing in the morning she was out in the garden again, pressing the soil down once more, replanting the shrub and laying the turf around it again.

Once she'd taken the plastic sheet away and brushed the last traces of soil from the lawn, then watered it with the hose, it looked much the same as it had the previous day. It wasn't quite so flat as Liam had made it, but she knew it would flatten out with time. Finally, she carefully hosed away all the blood on the grass.

'Are you sure you only stabbed Liam once?' Roy asked her.

Susan was quite startled by his question. While she was aware of telling the story as she relived it, she'd gone so far back into herself and that day that it was almost as if she were alone in the room.

'Yes, of course,' she said.

He asked Sergeant Bloom to get up and turn his back towards Susan, so she could show them where the knife went in.

Susan couldn't be exact about it. Liam's back had been brown and shiny with perspiration, nothing like the sergeant's dark uniform. But she told them she knew it was just below where his right shoulder blade stuck out.

'And he died instantly?' Roy asked.

'Not instantly. He sort of half turned and spoke before he fell down. I don't know how long after it was that he died. I was crying, pulling the knife out and trying to stop the blood. I wanted to ring for an ambulance, but I was too scared, then I realized he was dead.'

'What did you do with the knife?'

She looked up at him in surprise. 'I washed it and put it back in the drawer.'

'And his belongings?'

'He didn't have much,' she said with a shrug. 'Only a jacket, some underclothes, a couple of shirts and some waterproofs. I kept those for a while. Well, you would, wouldn't you, if someone had just walked out on you?'

Roy nodded gravely, chilled by her calm logic.

'And no one came looking for him?' he asked.

'No,' she said, looking him straight in the eye. 'But then, they wouldn't have come there. He always went to see people about his work, and he hadn't actually told anyone he was living with me. That's why he left his camper up the road.'

'Can you draw me a plan of where you buried him?' Roy asked, giving her a pen and a sheet of paper.

'You don't have to do that,' Steven said quickly.

'I want to,' she said, giving him a scathing look.

Steven and Roy exchanged glances as she bent over the desk, painstakingly drawing in the house and the river, a winding path going around flower beds, even marking out and naming certain trees.

'It's about twenty yards from the back door, there's a lilac bush on top of it,' she said, drawing a broken line which ran left at a forty-five-degree angle away from the house. 'The bush will be very big now, I expect,' she said. 'In case they can't recognize it as lilac now while there's no leaves, there's a holly bush about fifteen feet behind it.'

'Please sign and date that plan,' Roy said as she finished, his voice cracking because he hadn't wanted to believe this of her. He went on to question her about the day she left The Rookery and whether her brother Martin had come before she left.

'He was too cowardly to come again while I was still there,' she said, a gleam of triumph in her eyes. 'You see, the last time he came, he insisted I was to make an inventory of everything in the house, then mark which pieces I wanted to take with me. He said he would then decide which of them I could have. Liam came in while he was there, and he went mad at Martin. He said if Martin stopped me taking anything I wanted, he would not only call the national newspapers and tell them what a rat he was but he'd also give him a good hiding.'

'That stopped him, did it?' Steven asked, forgetting he wasn't supposed to make any comment except when reminding Susan of her rights. From his one meeting with Martin Wright, he didn't think the man would be easily intimidated.

'Martin was scared he'd be in trouble at his bank if his name was in the papers,' Susan said, and half smiled. 'Liam was wonderful that day. He sounded like he really meant it. Martin backed right down and he couldn't get out of the house fast enough. But then, I suppose he knew I wouldn't take everything, or start selling stuff. I'm sure he turned up again the moment I'd left, though, to check.'

She paused for a moment, then suddenly laughed.

'When I first got to Bristol, I used to hope someone would find Liam's body and Martin would be charged with the murder. Wouldn't that have been divine justice? No one would have suspected me. The whole village would have turned out to tell the court what a bastard he was.'

Steven couldn't help but snigger and Roy looked at him sharply. 'Sorry,' Steven said. 'But I have to agree with my client on that point.'

'Would you have stood by and let him stand trial for murder?' Roy asked Susan.

She smirked. 'Certainly. He deserved it after the way he treated me. I just wish it was him I stabbed, not Liam. If Martin hadn't been so nasty after our father died, if he'd given me some of the money for the house to buy a place of my own, I don't think I would be sitting here now.'

Roy looked at her, saw the sincerity in her face and felt a tug of sympathy. She had been brave and forthright in spilling it all out so clearly. He had no doubt that part of the reason why she had clung so desperately to Liam was because of the way her brother had treated her. Martin Wright had a great deal to answer for.

'Tell me about how it was after you buried Liam and before you moved,' Roy asked. 'It was another two weeks, wasn't it?'

'Do you mean how did I feel?' she asked.

Roy nodded.

'Like a sleep-walker, I suppose.' She sighed. 'The good weather broke, it rained for about three days solidly. I remember being glad about that because wherever Liam was supposed to be working, they wouldn't expect him to turn up in such heavy rain. I stayed in and began packing, though I kept going outside to check the grave. I could almost see the turf settling in and growing. I was very weepy. I couldn't eat or sleep. I was sick several times too.'

'Did you know you were pregnant then?' Roy asked.

'No. I didn't realize until the morning of the day the removal man was coming to collect me and my stuff. I'd put the sickness down to panic, but that morning my tummy felt different, my breasts were tender, and I suddenly realized that's what it was.'

'What was your reaction?' Roy asked.

'Reaction?' She frowned. 'I was glad of course. Really glad.'

'Really?' he said in disbelief. 'You'd just killed and buried your lover but you were glad you were carrying his child?'

'I was thirty-five,' she said as if that explained it. 'I had always wanted a baby. It didn't seem so awful to be leaving the house and starting over again somewhere else, not with that to look forward to.'

The interview was halted at that point because Susan said she needed to go to the toilet. Roy asked her if she wished to stop for the day and continue again the next morning, but she said she'd rather do it all today.

As Susan went off with the prison officer who had been waiting outside the room, Roy turned to Steven.

'Tell me, off the record, did you expect that?' he asked.

'No. I'm astounded,' Steven said sadly. 'When she said she had killed them and wanted to confess, I thought she just meant Reuben and Zoë. But it kind of makes sense of something that's cropped up several times.'

'Annabel's dying being punishment?' Roy asked.

Steven nodded. 'She used to go to church. Right up until she left Luddington. She's mentioned it several times in our interviews. I asked her once if she had Annabel christened, and she was a bit odd about it, she said she couldn't when she wasn't married. I didn't think anything of it at the time. But now –' he broke off, not sure what he actually meant.

Roy nodded. 'For someone religious that would have been troubling. I wouldn't know if it was the thought of entering God's house after murder that was the problem, or the lack of protection for the child. But I could see it could prey on someone's mind after the child had died.'

'I wonder what's going to come next.' Sergeant Bloom spoke up for the first time from his chair in the corner of the room. 'Reckon she's preparing her next bombshell right now.'

Susan wasn't preparing anything. As she washed her hands after using the lavatory, she was thinking about Martin. He was the only thing she was really afraid of, just the thought of seeing him in a court room made her quake inside.

Her earliest memories were all of him being cruel to her. Knocking her over in the garden, hiding or breaking her favourite toys, terrifying her with threats of nasty things he intended to do to her. He was clever with it too, nothing was ever done in front of anyone and any injuries to her looked accidental, so he was never punished.

When he got older and left home for university, his cruelty didn't stop, it just changed to the mental kind. Constant belittlement, caustic remarks about her appearance, her school work. He made her believe she was worthless. Yet perhaps the saddest thing of all was that she kept striving to make him like her.

When Martin came home to visit after Mother had the stroke, she would always cook something special, make his room and the whole house look nice. Just one word of praise would have been enough for her, but she never got it. He was so smart, handsome and sophisticated, and she thought for years that she deserved his contempt for being so mousy and ordinary. Her mother had said once that it was because he felt pushed out when she was born. But that had never made any sense to Susan because as she remembered, he was the one her parents always boasted about.

He was awful after their father died. He would come to the house unexpectedly, ordering her around and calling her a fat slag, because someone had told him about Liam. Even though he had all that money coming to him from the sale of the house, and she was looking after the house and garden for him, he wouldn't help her out, not even with at least part of the household bills. He coldly ordered her to sign on at the Job Centre and claim dole money, and said it was about time she entered the real world.

If Liam hadn't given her money every week for food, she would have been forced to break into the money left to her, and she needed that for advance rent and a deposit. It was only through the intervention of Mr Browning, Father's solicitor, that he let her take furniture with her when she left. And that was only because Mr Browning said if he didn't do this, he would encourage Susan to challenge the will.

In fact Mr Browning did actively encourage her to do so, but she couldn't go through with it because she was so afraid of Martin. That was why she chose to move to Bristol. She knew if she stayed around Stratford-upon-Avon he'd be keeping tabs on her. She even changed her name to Fellows, a name she'd picked at random out of the phone book, as she didn't want her unborn child to bear the same name as Martin.

She wished now she'd never relented and written to him about Annabel. She'd done it in the first flush of euphoria after Annabel was born, convinced it would make a difference. But he hadn't even replied to her letter.

Nor did she know now why she telephoned his office to tell him about Annabel's death and ask for a loan when she got back to Bristol from Wales. She might have known he wouldn't help. But that was what tipped her over the edge. It seemed to her at that moment that if even her own brother didn't care that her child had died, and she was destitute, there was no hope for her at all.

She straightened up in front of the mirror, smoothing down her hair. Perhaps now she was confessing everything, Martin wouldn't be called to her trial.

'Did you feel guilty about Liam after you moved into the house in Bristol?' Roy asked her when she'd come back and sat down. He had started the tape again.

'Not really,' she said. 'That sounds so awful, but it's true. I had so much to do making the new house nice, and all I could really think about was my baby inside me.'

'And after Annabel was born? You must have been reminded of Liam constantly then?'

Susan had been reminded. She could remember holding Annabel in her arms as she sat up in the hospital bed and seeing Liam's face so clearly in her daughter's. She looked like a little gypsy baby with her curly dark hair and olive skin. One of the nurses had asked if her father was Spanish or Greek.

Susan had felt deep pangs of remorse, thinking how if she hadn't fought with Liam they might have remained

412

friends and she could contact him now. But her real sorrow was that she wouldn't have him somewhere in the background to share her joy and pride in their child. Just the way Annabel's fingers gripped hers, her little head butting against her chest for more milk, was so sweet that she felt privileged to have been given her.

'Yes, she did remind me, but only of the good things.' She shrugged. 'She had his curly hair and olive skin, but she made me so happy and complete I just kind of blanked out what I'd done to him. It was like he died from natural causes really. I saw myself as a widow.'

'Four happy years?' Roy said.

Susan looked up at him, and the sympathy in his eyes brought a lump to her throat. She had never really been able to explain adequately to anyone just how happy those years had been: the rush of joy when Annabel held up her little arms to be lifted out of the cot, the sound of her laughter, the sheer jubilation she experienced when she took her first faltering steps. How could she make anyone understand the bliss she felt when, all rosy from a bath, Annabel fell asleep in her arms, or when her plump little arms were wound tightly round her mother's neck? It was a mother's thing, a state of grace too wonderful for mere words.

'Yes,' she said simply, looking down at her hands. 'But I paid a heavy price for those years, didn't I? When she died I was convinced it was God's judgment on me. I wanted to die too.' For the first time in the interview her eyes filled with tears, and Roy too found he had a lump in his throat.

413

'Then you met Reuben?' Roy prompted her after a few seconds of silence.

She looked up, her eyes swimming with tears. 'Yes, and he convinced me it was possible to find happiness again.'

Steven had already heard how Susan met Reuben, and about her life in Wales with him. Roy knew some of it from Beth and he'd gleaned more from the witnesses in Wales and things Susan had told him in previous interviews.

Both men had been left with the impression that it hadn't been a real love affair, more something born out of desperation. Yet as Susan began to talk about it, they both saw they were entirely wrong.

'I believed in Reuben,' she said forcefully. 'I don't mean just him loving and looking after me, but I believed in his philosophy of life, his truthfulness, his nobility. To me he stood head and shoulders above other men, he was above corruption. He was like the Good Shepherd, he rounded up damaged people who needed his guidance, strength and love and he made them whole again. I suppose I thought he had been sent to save me. I would have done anything for him.'

She paused, trembling with emotion. 'I gave him everything I had,' she said simply. 'Not just my worldly possessions, but my love, trust and all my skills. When I arrived at Hill House it was a grubby, disorganized place. I cleaned it up, made it comfortable and cosy. By planning meals in advance I reduced waste and made economies. Some of the people there couldn't cook, they had no idea of hygiene. I taught them those things. I mended clothes,

I nursed them when they were sick. I cared for the garden too.' She looked round at Steven. 'I know I told you that I knew what Reuben was long before he came home with Zoë, but that wasn't true. Yes, I found out how much money he got for my belongings, and that he was making more from the workshop than everyone supposed, but that didn't matter to me. He was sharing his home and his life with a bunch of people who would have been living on the streets but for him. That's how I saw it, and even when the others grumbled to me, I always took his part.'

'But then he turned up with Zoë?' Roy said, trying to nudge her along. 'Now, when was that?'

'A few days before Christmas of 1992,' she said haltingly.

Even after all this time, everything was so clear and sharp about that day. It was very cold, with a biting wind, but Susan had been in the kitchen all afternoon, making mince pies and icing the cake for Christmas. The others kept coming in and out, trying to steal the pies sitting cooling on the wire tray on the table.

It had been a happy day, everyone childishly looking forward to Christmas, swapping childhood stories and laughing a great deal. Susan remembered Megan was sitting in the corner of the kitchen folding coloured paper to make Chinese lanterns to hang on some branches she'd sprayed with gold paint. She had a tinsel crown on her head.

It was dark when they heard Reuben's van arrive back. The table was laid for dinner and everyone was waiting expectantly as Susan had made a rabbit pie and they were all starving.

Then Reuben walked in, rubbing his hands together with the cold, and just behind him was the girl.

She was tall, slender, with long blonde hair and azure-blue eyes. She wore a sheepskin coat, the soft, expensive kind, a red beret, jeans and long riding boots. She could have just stepped out of the pages of a fashion magazine.

'This is Zoë,' Reuben said, drawing her forward and keeping his arm around her. 'She's come to join us.'

Everyone looked surprised, but as he introduced Zoë to each of them, they recovered quickly, and someone went and found another chair and began squeezing it in at the already crowded table for her.

'Oh, don't put yourself out for me,' she said, waving her hand. Her long nails were painted black with a little glitter on each one. 'I can make do with a sandwich and sit anywhere.'

Susan had sensed just by the protective way Reuben was with her, that this young, pretty and confident girl was going to be trouble, but she felt she had to be welcoming. 'Of course you must join us, we always eat all together,' she said. 'It's an important part of our life here.'

Zoë's blue eyes fixed for a moment on Susan's face and slid down her plump body contemptuously, as if comparing her own to it. 'You must be the Earth Mother I've heard so much about,' she said with a smirk.

All through the meal Zoë charmed everyone but Susan. She tossed her hair with one hand as she spoke of bathing under a waterfall in Thailand, and it was obvious from the glow in all the men's eyes that they were imagining her firm young body naked. She said she'd got a tattoo, and stood up and unzipped her jeans to show a green gecko on her washing-board stomach.

Her cut-glass accent irritated Susan, especially when Zoë went on to speak scornfully of her stuffy parents in Bath. Daddy was a dentist. He wanted her to have a career. Mummy was a lady who lunched and raised money for charities. She said they knew nothing of the real world.

She held forth for some time on her philosophy of complete freedom, that youth shouldn't be spoiled by work, that pleasure was all. She said she had lived for a while with some 'freaks' in a squat in Bristol, but when Reuben told her about the set-up here, she'd thought she'd 'give it a stab', as she put it.

'I'm very artistic,' she said airily. 'I'm sure I could design something crafty we could sell for a fortune.'

Her arrogance astounded Susan. She remembered how on her first night she had hardly dared say a word to anyone. This girl looked set on taking control.

But even worse was watching Reuben's reaction to her. He couldn't take his eyes off her, he nodded in agreement at almost everything she said, however infantile. It was obvious he had fallen for her completely, and Susan suspected they were already lovers.

Yet however hurtful that was, Susan expected that Reuben would do the right thing and tell her himself when they were alone in their bedroom later that night. As she began the washing up, with everyone else still sitting around the table, she tried to squash her anger and jealousy and prepare herself for it. She hoped she could handle it with dignity, maybe ask that he take Zoë somewhere else until she could make plans to leave.

'Leave that, Sue,' Reuben said suddenly. 'Get on upstairs and change the sheets on my bed.'

She remembered letting a plate slip from her fingers back into the sink and break. 'Why?' she asked stupidly.

'Well, Zoë won't want to sleep in your sheets,' he said with a malicious grin. 'So hurry along, we're tired.'

It was impossible to believe that anyone could be so cruel, and in front of so many witnesses. Susan turned towards the others at the table, tears starting up in her eyes, expecting at least some of them to speak up for her. But Simon and Roger were grinning furtively, a kind of 'well-you-can't-blame-him' expression. Heather smirked, and everyone else looked away. Only young Megan looked as if she felt for her.

Later, Susan was to wonder why she didn't shout at Reuben, or at least tell him to do it himself, anything but obey meekly. But in that humiliating moment she thought it prudent to remove her own things from that room, rather than have Zoë going through them.

As she took her jumpers out of the chest of drawers, her hand made contact with her father's revolver, wrapped in a piece of soft cloth. She hadn't touched it since the day she'd moved into Hill House, but as she felt its heaviness, for a brief second she thought of turning it on Reuben right then.

There had been times since moving into Hill House

when it had crossed her mind that Reuben might tire of her one day. She had spoken of it once, and Reuben had said that if the day ever came he promised he'd tell her to her face, long before he embarked on a relationship with a new woman. She had believed him too, for he was always talking about honesty in relationships being all-important.

Now it seemed promises and loyalty meant nothing to him. The pain she felt was so terrible she wanted to scream it out, and if she had had anywhere to go, she would have gone then, walking right through the night, rather than stay under the same roof as them. But it was below freezing outside, she had no money, and there was no place to run to.

In many ways it was like Annabel's death all over again, the pain and the disbelief were all so similar. She could remember asking herself why she had to be punished again. And why it was when she had so much love in her heart, no one had any for her.

Relegated to the smallest, dampest room, with a sagging, lumpy bed, night after night she grew more angry. She could hear them making love across the landing, and it seemed to go on for hours. Then they'd wake her with it again in the mornings, and she would lie there rigid with hate, completely impotent even to flee from her tormentors.

They did torment her too, all over that Christmas. They cuddled and kissed in front of her, sniggering at her embarrassment and humiliating her further by getting her to wait on them.

On New Year's Eve they disappeared together for a few days, giving her a little respite, but they came back all too soon. All through the bitter weather of January and February, while the rest of them braved the cold to work in the craft room, they were either lolling in the kitchen, smoking dope, or up in the bedroom making love.

'Susan!' Roy said sharply, bringing her back to the present with a jolt. 'I asked you if Zoë and Reuben had already formed a relationship before he brought her to Hill House? Or did it start afterwards?'

'I'm sorry,' she said. 'I was thinking about the day he brought her there. I think they were already lovers.'

She explained what had happened, then went on to say that over Christmas and New Year they humiliated her in every possible way.

'They stuffed themselves with the food I'd prepared, drank the wine I made, and acted like I was just a half-witted housekeeper,' she said angrily. 'It was just like the way Father and Martin treated me all over again, only much worse because in the days when I was at home in Luddington I didn't know any different.'

'Why didn't you just leave?' Roy asked.

'How could I? I had no money, nowhere to go to.' She made a gesture of hopelessness with her hands. 'I begged Reuben to give me some money so I could leave, but he just laughed at me. He was so cruel, he said I didn't know how well off I was, and who else would give a home to a broken-down old crone like me?'

'So you saw what he really was then?' Roy said with some sympathy.

She nodded. 'All my belief in him turned to hatred. He'd clear off for a few days with Zoë, and each time he came back he was nastier because by then he really wanted me out. I saw how stupid he really was then. He thought Zoë could take my place in every way.' She gave a hollow laugh. 'As if! She had no interest in keeping house for him, that wasn't her scene. Reuben and his house were just a stop-gap till she got a better offer somewhere else.'

'So when did you start planning to kill them?' Roy asked.

'In March,' she said, crossing her arms defiantly. 'I knew Reuben would throw me out before long, but he still wouldn't give me any money. He said he didn't care if I starved on the streets, I could do with it because I was too fat.'

She paused for a moment and dabbed at her eyes. 'Then I overheard him telling Zoë that he had this secret place, and he'd take her there when the weather was better. I knew where he meant of course, and I decided then and there, that would be their graveyard. So each time I went out for a walk, I went there, taking a piece of camping equipment or tins of food with me. Then in early April they went off to North Wales – Reuben always had a stall at some craft market there. As soon as they'd gone I told the others I was leaving, and went, only I didn't leave Wales. I went on up to the glade in the woods to wait.'

She began to say something else, but her voice faded away and when Roy looked at her he saw she had gone chalky-white. He leapt up and went round the table, just in time to catch her as she fainted.

'Terminate the interview,' he rapped out to Bloom. 'And get her a drink of water.' As Bloom hastily did as he was ordered, Roy and Steven pulled out Susan's chair and put her head down between her knees.

'That's definitely enough for one day,' Steven said.

'It certainly is,' Roy sighed.

Chapter eighteen

Steven was deeply troubled as he drove away from the prison. According to the prison doctor, Susan had fainted as the result of a combination of stress and lack of food. She had been taken to the hospital wing for observation over the weekend, and Steven had said he would ring the prison on Monday morning to see how she was.

As he approached the Almondsbury interchange between the M4 and the M5, and saw the Friday evening traffic almost at a standstill, he felt even worse. He wanted to go back to the office and see Beth before he went home, but he had promised to take Polly and Sophie to Brownies that evening, and if he went to Clifton first, he wouldn't make it home again in time.

Wearily, he joined the queue of cars. It would be a long weekend having to hold Susan's partial confession inside him. Anna had never taken much interest in his cases, but since she'd stopped drinking she seemed almost jealous of his relationship with his clients, and Susan in particular, but that was probably because she'd picked up on his sympathy for her.

Anna was even more jealous of Beth. She'd sensed that she and Steven had become close friends and felt

423

threatened, so now it was safer for him to avoid mentioning her at all. But that meant he wouldn't go and see her this weekend, even a phone call was out of the question. Anna wouldn't need much of an excuse to start drinking again, for she had reached the stage where she had almost forgotten the bad aspects of her drinking, and the effect it had on the children. Now she really missed the pleasure of it and she was often snappy and depressed.

But with his mind on Susan, and still shocked by her frank confession, Steven hadn't got much sympathy left for Anna right now. She'd had it all, a secure and happy childhood, the career of her choice, a great deal of fun, and freedom to express herself, plus two pretty, healthy children and a husband who loved her and took care of her. It was a great deal more than Susan had.

Steven thought of Susan's revelations to Roy about Beth earlier that day, and wondered if he should at least make a quick call to her to warn her about it in case Roy contacted her this weekend. Yet it didn't seem right to blurt out something like that over the phone, or to tell her about the confession. Both were likely to distress her.

But then, everyone involved in this case was distressed by it – himself, Beth, Roy and not least Susan. Then there were the victims' families, and the present owners of The Rookery who were about to find out that their garden concealed a grave. That hardly bore thinking about.

He wondered what Susan was thinking about right now. He didn't entirely believe the doctor's verdict as to why she fainted. He thought it was more likely a panic attack brought on by what she knew she had yet to reveal.

Susan lay in her bed in the hospital wing, her head spinning with confused thoughts. It seemed to her she'd got herself into a situation which was a bit like climbing up on a big rock at low tide. The tide had turned and now she was cut off, watching the dark water swirl around her rock, knowing that before long the waters would rise to engulf her.

It hadn't seemed that difficult to admit to killing Liam because she knew she really hadn't meant to do it. But she soon found that knowing in her head what she had done was very different to relating it to someone else for the first time. She found she was almost standing back from herself and seeing the full horror of it as another person.

She couldn't understand now how she managed to stay so calm afterwards, or why she felt so little remorse or guilt. If Annabel hadn't died, how would she have coped with her questions about her father later on? She didn't remember ever considering that before.

But then she supposed she was guilty of never really considering anything properly in her entire life. She hadn't stopped to think what agreeing to take care of her mother would mean. She certainly hadn't stopped to think before embarking on a love affair with Liam. Maybe she could excuse both of those because her heart was ruling her head and she was naive. Yet she couldn't understand why she allowed herself to become entrapped by Reuben, for in many ways he was another Martin, every bit as cunning, cold-hearted, cruel and on the make.

Of course she didn't see that at the time. The way he talked about feelings, religion and psychology made him seem as opposite to Martin as it was possible to be. Then there was his unconventional appearance and that way he had of looking right into your eyes, as if you were the most fascinating person in the entire world.

Yet when she thought back to the way Reuben just took her off to the bedroom and stripped off his clothes, she realized she ought to have heard warning bells jangling. It was, in her vulnerable state, almost rape. Just the fact that he'd said he loved her shouldn't have made her believe he had a right to take complete control of every aspect of her life.

She did believe that though. She let him mould her into exactly what he wanted from his woman. He didn't like her ordinary clothes, she had to wear hippie-style long dresses. He wouldn't let her get her hair cut, or wear makeup. She had to learn to like New Age music and read David Eddings fantasy books instead of Catherine Cookson. She didn't dare admit to approving of Margaret Thatcher, she had to become a dyed-in-the-wool lefty.

She got so far into his power that she almost admitted to him once that she believed Annabel was taken from her because she'd killed Liam. It wasn't long after she'd arrived at Hill House.

With her eyes closed, she could see herself on that warm, sunny afternoon in early October. Reuben had taken her out for a walk, to what he said was a secret place which he'd never shared with anyone before. They walked across one of his fields, then through another, and skirted round a wooded hill and over a fence to a tiny rough path that went up into the woods.

The trees and bushes were so dense, the ground so rocky, steep and difficult to walk on that she didn't really want to go on. It was chilly in the shade of the trees, and brambles and twigs were snatching at her face and clothes. But Reuben kept saying it would be worth it when they got there.

It was indeed worth the hard slog to reach it, for once they'd fought their way through the last of the thick bushes they came into a little horseshoe-shaped glade, encircled by tall trees which almost met above their heads. The opening of the horseshoe was at an escarpment of rock, far too steep for anyone to climb up that way. The afternoon sun streamed down through the opening on to lush, mossy grass. Reuben led her over to the rocks, and there was Hill House far below, the village beyond, and a view all the way to the sea.

'This is your new kingdom,' he said, kissing her. 'And you are my queen.'

He had brought a blanket with him, and a bottle of wine, and he said they had to make love there for it would be like a marriage ceremony. It had seemed so sacred, not a sound except birdsong, the sun slanting in through the leaves which were just starting to change colour. Susan could remember thinking as she lay back on the rug that it was almost like being in a cathedral.

Reuben's love-making was the best ever that day, tender

and giving. She felt like Guinevere being seduced by Sir Lancelot, for she was wearing a medieval-looking, long russet-coloured crushed-velvet dress he'd bought for her from a second-hand clothes shop.

'You are so beautiful,' Reuben said, leaning up on his elbow to look at her, running one hand through her hair. 'There is purity in your face, despite the hurt in your eyes. That hurt will go when you have my baby in your arms. Nothing will ever harm you again.'

He looked handsome that day, his newly washed hair falling on to his lightly tanned shoulders, and his eyes so adoring. Susan felt he had rescued her and brought her to a new happy world and her heart filled with gratitude.

Reuben was always saying that people should share their inmost secrets, good and bad. In the evenings at the house they had sessions they called 'sharing', when each of them would tell the others something from their past. Susan had listened to so many shocking stories of prostitution, or stealing from family members to buy drugs. One of the men talked about his days as a pimp and how cruel he was to 'his girls'. All these things were so far removed from Susan's own experience that she listened in appalled astonishment.

So far, the only thing she had told the others about herself was Annabel's death. But in that moment there in the glade she was ready to tell Reuben why she thought it had happened.

She thought later that God or whatever power it was who took her child didn't want her to reveal it, for Reuben suddenly got up and began pulling on his clothes. He had remembered he had to collect some paints and other craft materials before five-thirty. The chance was gone, and she never had the desire to tell him again. Much later she was very glad she hadn't told him, he would almost certainly have used it against her.

In the ensuing months, Hill House turned her inside out and upside down. Although there were no prayers or formal religion, there was a strong leaning towards the spiritual. Astrology, I Ching, Tarot and meditation were common interests among the residents. Most of them had some experience of group therapy, they liked to dig into one another's minds, and discuss each other's problems. They saw themselves as a large family, to which Susan was the latest welcome addition, and in her bruised and battered state she found this immensely comforting.

Yet at the same time she felt like an orphaned child taken into a totally different world where she barely spoke the same language, and all the customs were the opposite of what she had learned previously. All the standards she'd been taught by her parents were challenged. No one at Hill House cared if the table was laid correctly for meals – they laughed at her when she first got there because she asked where the napkins were kept. Beds were never made, cleaning was minimal, nudity didn't raise so much as an eyebrow, and bodily functions were discussed openly.

One day she would be totally repelled by someone discussing homosexual acts in graphic detail, the next she would be mesmerized by exotic stories of travelling in

India or Africa. Reuben wouldn't have hard drugs in the house, but they all smoked cannabis. Some of the others changed sexual partners frequently. Roger liked to watch other people having sex, and the others seemed to welcome it. There were pornographic magazines all over the house.

Yet to balance the things she didn't like, there were so many that she did – Simon playing classical guitar, Megan's painting, the work in the craft room, the discussions and the laughter over the evening meal. And Reuben made her feel safe and protected because he called her 'his woman'.

She was happy there and her past became misty as she embraced a new way of living. No one ridiculed her for clearing up, cleaning windows or washing clothes, the way Liam had. They called her Mother Earth and said they loved her for it.

Yet it was her shooting that really impressed them. Father's revolver was tucked away, wrapped in a soft cloth, and she didn't tell anyone about it. But there was a shotgun in the house which Reuben said had been left by a previous resident. She cleaned it up and practised out in the fields until she got back the skill she'd had as a young girl.

Nothing made her happier than seeing their shock at her bagging a pheasant or a rabbit. She supposed the elation she got was much like the kid at school who always won the hundred-yards sprint on sports day. She liked being praised for her cooking and her ability to mend clothes, but shooting was something special. It set her apart, made up for her ignorance about sex, drugs and travel. It made people look up to her.

But the honeymoon period when everything seemed exciting, new and challenging was beginning to pall by the following spring. By then she'd heard everyone's stories several times. Being Mother Earth and cleaning up after everyone wasn't much fun when she had to do it day after day, without any real appreciation, and she was starting to doubt that Reuben was all she had first thought.

She had fully believed he set up the commune for the good of the members, that all the money made in the craft shop went straight back into the common purse to feed and clothe them all. But she had noticed he had a mercenary streak – he could never be drawn into admitting how much money came into the house. At times she had a sneaky feeling he was conning them all, and that the meagre pocket money he doled out from time to time was a mere fraction of what he pocketed himself.

The warmer weather brought the sparkle back. It was wonderful not to be cold all the time, to be able to work in the garden, to go out in the fields and woods, to watch the sun going down over the hills in the long light evenings. But as summer arrived, Reuben expected them to work harder still so he could sell more to the tourist shops, and he got angry if anyone was slacking in the workshop. Some of the others became rebellious, they wanted to go off to rock festivals or visit friends, and in whispers they would suggest that Reuben was making fools of them all.

When Susan found the bill from the auctioneers for her furniture, and saw it had raised over £7,000, she felt crushed. While she was happy to share all she had with Reuben, she felt he ought to have told her exactly what she had put in. But just as she had never confronted her father with his unfairness and duplicity, she remained silent and became an observer.

It was only then that she began to see what Hill House really was, a kind of working hostel for the damaged. Every single one of its occupants had problems, whether it was lack of self-esteem, laziness, selfishness, an addictive personality or even mental instability. All of them had been through traumas, ranging from being abused as children to prison and drink and drug addiction. Hill House had helped them all in as much as it had removed them from damaging environments and given them a kind of family life, but it failed in that it didn't prepare them to go back into the real world.

Yet Susan couldn't say she was disillusioned. Reuben had saved these people, and she still believed he truly loved her. He continued to make passionate love to her whenever he returned home from selling trips, and still said he wanted her to have his baby. She imagined that the day she told him she was pregnant, he'd want to persuade the others to leave so they could be alone. She even dreamed of running the place as a sort of bed and breakfast for hikers and those needing a retreat from city life.

Then Zoë arrived and everything, all her hopes and dreams, were shattered.

Susan supposed killing Reuben must have entered her

mind long before she was even aware of it, because one day she took the revolver out of its wrapping and cleaned and oiled it without knowing why. But it was weeks later, during March, that all her hurt, jealousy and anger bubbled up to the surface and spilled over.

She had gone for a walk that afternoon. It was a cold but sunny day, and as she walked down the track from Hill House she noticed the first signs of spring, green shoots on the hedgerows and a few clumps of primroses on the most sheltered banks. While she couldn't say she felt happy, these signs were a kind of salve to her hurt, and as she walked she thought perhaps she could pawn her mother's rings, catch the bus to Cardiff and stay in a cheap room until she found a job.

The further she walked, the more cheerful she felt, thinking perhaps she could apply for a position as a housekeeper, or even a nanny. She imagined a house near the sea, and her own comfortable, warm room. She thought that would be more than enough for her, she certainly didn't want any more men entering her life.

On the way back home, she gathered some primroses, but as she stepped into the kitchen, Zoë and Reuben were there. Zoë was wearing her usual tight jeans and a cardigan unbuttoned to show her cleavage and was in the process of painting her nails.

They looked startled, and she guessed they had been talking about her. The table she had left clear was strewn with dirty coffee mugs and plates, and she could smell cannabis over the nail varnish and the casserole in the oven.

'You were supposed to be in the workroom this afternoon,' Reuben said curtly.

'I went for a walk instead,' she retorted, and went over to a cupboard to find a vase for the primroses.

'If you don't work here, you don't eat or sleep here either,' he said. 'It's not a fucking holiday camp.'

He hadn't shaved or washed his long hair for several days and he looked like a tramp in his patched green cords and ancient sweater with frayed cuffs. Yet it was the venom in his voice and eyes which made Susan's anger rise. He had no right to treat her as if she was loathsome.

'I was working for at least three hours this morning before you even got up,' she snapped back at him. 'Who do you think made that casserole cooking in the oven?'

'No wonder you're so fat,' he sneered at her. 'All you think of is food.' Then, getting up from his chair, he snatched the primroses out of her hand and threw them down on the floor. 'You can stop all these bourgeois flower arrangements too, they make me want to throw up. The only thing I want you to do is to piss off for good.'

Zoë started to giggle. 'Yes, dear, why don't you?' she said in that superior tone of hers. 'You've outlived your usefulness.'

Susan was tempted to slap her, but she knew Reuben would have no compunction about knocking her out for that. 'What use are you?' she snarled at the girl. 'I've never seen you do a hand's turn around the place.'

'I don't need to,' Zoë said, tossing her blonde hair back

and smirking at Reuben. 'He likes me just the way I am.'

Susan knew she was in a completely defenceless position, much the same way she'd always been with Martin. They would deride her whatever she said, they might even throw her out of the house. Retreat was the only course open to her now.

That night she lay in bed crying, remembering the times when she and Reuben took walks together in the afternoons, when they'd lain awake in bed just talking and laughing for hours. He used to praise her cooking, admire her gentleness and calm. He said she had brought this house and the residents together in the way he had always hoped for.

She could possibly accept that he didn't want her as his woman any more, but she couldn't understand why he didn't still value her as a friend. Surely he could see that Zoë was just using him and that she'd be off as soon as something better came along?

It was just a few nights later that she heard Reuben say, 'Let's make a baby tonight,' as he came up the stairs with Zoë. That was the point when she flipped and began to want vengeance.

Every month since she'd been with him, she'd hoped she'd find herself pregnant, and every month she was disappointed. She was forty-two then, perhaps too old to conceive, and the thought that pretty, blonde Zoë might end up with Reuben's baby in her arms was like a knife through the heart.

She finally left Hill House when Reuben and Zoë went away for a few days in April. She said her goodbyes to everyone the night before, and found them sympathetic as each one of them had complaints about how everything had changed since Zoë arrived. Yet even as they said words which were intended to comfort her, Susan knew they weren't really sorry about her humiliation, they were only wondering who was going to cook and clean once she was gone.

She didn't catch the bus to the station though. Instead, she took a circuitous walk up to Reuben's glade. She had started to make her plans just after she'd heard Reuben mention a baby. Every dry afternoon she went for a walk and smuggled a camping item up there: a one-man tent, a sleeping bag and a small camping stove, along with food, a saucepan and a shovel. The planning eased the strain of still living under the same roof as Reuben and Zoë – every insult or sarcastic word from them added fuel to her fire.

Yet each time she revisited the glade, she was reminded painfully of the first time Reuben had shown it to her. It had been one of the most special moments in her life, a day when she had felt she was being launched into a whole new world where she was valued and would never feel unloved or alone ever again.

It was the only place Susan knew where she could go through with her plan. For the memories there fanned the anger inside her, keeping it white-hot. Spring had come now and she knew Reuben would bring Zoë up there before long, because she'd heard him telling her he had somewhere special to take her to. All she had to do was wait.

She pitched the tent right back in the woods, so it was invisible from the glade, and settled in. There was a small stream close by for water, she had several books and a lantern for the evenings. And by day she had their grave to dig. She didn't even feel lonely, it was good to be alone, to plan and savour her revenge.

It was on the fifth day, when she made her usual midday observation of Hill House from the escarpment, that she saw Reuben's van was back again. It was raining then, so she knew he wasn't likely to come up that day. But the bluebells and wild garlic were just beginning to flower, so she guessed it wouldn't be long.

The grave was proving hard to dig, for once she got through the top couple of feet of soft loam, it was rocky and full of tree roots. But that didn't matter much. The spot she'd selected was a natural hollow, and she could cover it with bracken and shovel leaf mould from elsewhere on to it. Besides, no one ever came up here anyway.

The next day was fine but cold, and Susan sat by the escarpment most of the day watching Hill House. She saw Megan pegging washing on the line, and at one point Reuben and Roger got up on to the roof to make some repairs. She didn't see Zoë.

It was around noon the day after, a much warmer day, that she saw Reuben and Zoë leaving the house. Reuben had a rolled-up blanket strapped to his back and a basket in his hand. She smiled bitterly at the way he was so predictable, thinking that he'd probably woken up that morning, seen the sunshine and told Zoë he was going to take her somewhere special, just as he had promised her.

She watched for a little while until there was no doubt that this was where they were coming. Then, after making a check that she'd left nothing in the glade to alert Reuben anyone had been there, she went back to the tent, got her gun and loaded it.

As well as practising with the gun, she had worked out some time ago exactly where she would wait. It had to be far enough back in the bushes so she was completely hidden, and any small movements wouldn't be heard by them. But it couldn't be too far back for she needed to watch them and almost certainly fire from her hiding place.

The spot she had chosen was right opposite the way into the glade, behind a thick evergreen bush. If they lay down in the same spot as she and Reuben had, they would be only twelve feet from her, a perfect range. She had cleared the ground behind the bush, a precaution against accidentally standing on a twig and alerting them, and as she got into her position she smiled to herself; she'd thought of everything.

She heard Zoë's braying voice long before they got anywhere near the glade.

'This had better be good, Reuben,' she said. 'I'm not really into woodland walks, I'm more of a city girl.'

'So you are,' Susan thought gleefully. 'But a wood is where you are going to remain for all eternity.'

Reuben was wearing a new dusky-pink sweatshirt, Susan noted as he came into the glade with his hands over Zoë's eyes. She supposed that he was upping his image for Zoë's benefit. She was wearing skin-tight black leather trousers and a short red sweater, her long hair loose and tousled.

Seeing them together again, unaware they were being watched, brought her hatred of them into sharp focus. She shivered, partly from fear of what she intended to do, yet from exhilaration too.

'One more step,' Reuben said, still covering Zoë's eyes and nudging her forward. 'There!' he exclaimed as he whipped his hand away.

'Wow!' Zoë said predictably, turning round a full circle to look at where she'd been brought. 'It's beautiful.'

Susan smiled. She could sense the girl wasn't that impressed, she made no secret of the fact that she wasn't the outdoors sort, and perhaps she was already tiring of her cranky, middle-aged lover who was never going to show her the kind of good times she hankered for.

He looked his age that day, despite the new sweatshirt. His long hair had grown almost white in the last two years, and it was receding fast at his forehead. But it was the gauntness of his face Susan noticed most. Time had caught up with him while he was trying to keep up with someone half his age, and his skin looked grey and his facial lines much deeper.

'You should have worn a dress,' Reuben said. 'You'd look like a wood nymph then. Why don't you take your clothes off?'

Zoë giggled. 'It's too cold for that,' she said. 'Let's have some of that whisky while you roll a joint.'

Susan could sense Reuben's disappointment that Zoë wasn't more ecstatic about his special place. She didn't go over to the escarpment to look at the view, nor did she gasp with pleasure at the bluebells under the trees. She just pulled the rug off his shoulder, saying her feet ached and she wanted to sit down.

Reuben unrolled the rug and laid it out almost exactly where Susan had thought he would. He sat down by her and passed a bottle of whisky to her from the basket. She unscrewed the top and took a long swig.

For Susan, it was like watching a film in slow motion. They weren't saying much, Reuben intent on rolling a joint, Zoë lying on her side, propped up on one elbow watching him.

'Where do you reckon the old bat's gone to then?' Zoë asked suddenly. Susan knew she was referring to her.

'Back to Bristol, I expect,' Reuben replied.

'I hope you don't think I'm going to do the cleaning and the cooking,' Zoë said petulantly. 'That's not my scene.'

'You're too beautiful for such menial tasks,' he said, passing her the lighted joint. 'I'll get someone else in to do it.'

'If it were me, I'd sell the place,' she said, taking a deep draw and exhaling slowly. 'Let's face it, Reub, they're a load of wankers, and with the money you got, we could live like royalty in Thailand.'

'I've got a good little business going,' he said defensively. 'Besides, I love it here.'

'Well, I can't promise I'll stay with you then,' she said with a toss of her hair. 'It's so remote. I like bars, clubs and shops.'

Susan began to feel a little sorry for Reuben then, for she knew just how much he loved Wales. He wasn't going to find happiness with Zoë after all. He would get punishment enough when she moved on, and Hill House collapsed around him. Perhaps she didn't need to do it, she found herself thinking. Maybe she should just wait for him to get his natural justice.

But she was stuck behind the bush. If she moved away they would hear her.

Zoë seemed to mellow after the joint and more whisky. She lay back on the rug and remarked on the sun coming through the bare branches above. Then, without any prompting from Reuben, she unzipped her leather trousers and began wriggling out of them.

'Give me some sexual healing, then,' she said with a giggle. 'A good hour of licking my fanny will do for starters.'

Susan found herself blushing as Zoë peeled off a pair of black knickers, opened her legs wide and parted the lips of her vagina. She couldn't believe that any woman could be so dirty and crude. It was worse than embarrassing, she found it deeply shaming. Liam had introduced her to oral sex, but it had taken her quite some time to overcome her shock that any man would want to do such a thing. She had come to love it eventually, for Liam was a persuasive and skilful lover. But even so, she could never bring herself to indulge in it in broad daylight, and she would certainly never have had the effrontery to demand it.

Something else took her over entirely as Reuben knelt between Zoë's knees and obliged all too willingly. Susan was squirming with embarrassment, yet rooted to the spot with horrified fascination. Reuben was slobbering over her, Susan could see his tongue running up and down the length of Zoë's vagina, and after a short while he had to unzip his jeans to release his penis, which was rock-hard.

Zoë was shouting out the most filthy things, she called him Daddy and urged him to finger-fuck her at the same time. It was disgusting, and Susan felt they were desecrating the beautiful glade where she had felt so happy and at peace. She watched in ever-increasing revulsion as Zoë got on to her knees, pushed Reuben down and then sat on his face, writhing herself into his mouth, at the same time massaging her own breasts.

All at once, the full force of Susan's anger came back, stronger than ever. She had lost her home, her friends and everything for the sake of this trollop. Incandescent with rage, she watched their indecent behaviour, incensed that Reuben had wanted that more than her loving support.

'I'm coming in your mouth, Daddy,' Zoë yelled out. 'Do it harder, fuck me with your tongue.'

Susan found herself almost robotic as she lifted the gun. Despite the shaking in her hand, she supported it calmly with her left hand and told herself to wait, for if she was to shoot now she would hit Zoë first and that might give Reuben time to get away.

At last Zoë rolled off him, murmuring stuff about him being the world's greatest lover, and Reuben leapt on to her, showering her face with kisses and telling her he had never loved anyone until he met her.

It was when he leaned back on his haunches, holding on to Zoë's hips as he thrust himself into her, that Susan fired at his back.

Even when she missed and caught his side, only winging him, she remained unfazed. He seemed to jump, and the birds surprised up out of the trees rose squawking in protest.

'What was that?' Zoë exclaimed, presumably too dim to realize that what she'd heard was a gunshot.

'I've been shot!' Reuben gasped out, clutching at his bleeding side and trying to get off her.

Zoë didn't scream, only made a daft sort of gasping noise.

At that point Susan stepped out from behind the bush, calmly took aim and fired again. She had the satisfaction of seeing Reuben mouth her name in shock just as the bullet hit him in the chest. A second later he slumped down on to Zoë.

Zoë screamed then, and tried to wriggle out from under him. Susan took a step or two closer, just as Zoë had managed to push him off her. 'It's your turn now, you slag,' Susan said.

In that moment as she stood over Zoë, she understood completely why people used the expression 'Revenge is sweet'. It was sweet to see Zoë's blue eyes wide with horror and terror, all her confidence and smart retorts gone.

'Yes, it's the old bat,' Susan said as she squeezed the trigger. 'You will stay here forever with him now,' she added maliciously as the bullet hit the girl in the chest. Zoë's mouth opened to scream, but no sound came out, only a soft plop as she fell backwards on to the rug.

Even though it was well over two years ago, Susan could still feel the satisfaction of that moment. The job was done. It was over. But that was the only emotion she felt, if it could be called that in her robotic state – no horror at what she'd done, not even a twinge of regret. It was as if someone else had done it and her role was only to check it out.

She walked over to them and looked down at them coldly, the gun still in her hand. Zoë's torso lay in one direction, Reuben's in another, joined only by their entangled legs. Their eyes were wide open, a look of astonishment on both their faces. She could smell their genitals even over the cordite and blood. She was glad they were dead, she wasn't even nervous someone might catch her before she could bury them.

That strange calm stayed with her even as she dragged their bodies to their grave. She bundled in Zoë first, without ceremony, pushing her down as if she were just a side of meat.

Reuben was much heavier. She had to wrap him in the blanket and pull him over the rough ground, and she was sweating profusely by the time she'd got him in on top of Zoë.

When she went back to pick up Zoë's leather trousers

and knickers, and Reuben's jeans, she found a bundle of £20 notes in one of his pockets. That made her smile. It was so like him to carry money around with him, he didn't trust anyone at Hill House.

There was over £300, not nearly as much as he'd taken from her, but it would help her put her life together again. She didn't mind stamping down the soil over their bodies one bit. She even did a little dance as she swigged at their whisky.

The silence in the darkness of the cell suddenly seemed menacing. She had grown used to the sounds of other people breathing, snoring and talking in their sleep. There was silence here in the hospital wing, and it was eerie, the way it used to be in her room at Belle Vue.

She realized then that rather than getting her life back together after leaving Wales, it had fallen apart completely.

Chapter nineteen

Steven paused outside the prison gates before ringing the bell, looking up at the tall wire fence and the razor wire topping it. The sky beyond was almost black, threatening snow later. He shuddered. It looked so bleak and forbidding.

It was Monday morning, and he expected that Susan would have got even less sleep than himself over the weekend. Yet he was glad she was well enough to resume the confession today, for the sooner it was done the sooner he might be able to regain some sense of normality.

He hadn't telephoned Beth and he had purposely turned off his car phone this morning in case she tried to contact him. He thought it kinder to leave her in ignorance until the whole confession had been completed, rather than stringing it out over a weekend. As for what Susan had told Roy about her, he had concluded that was no business of his. He would leave Roy to decide how to tackle it.

Anna had been impossible all weekend, crying, shouting at him and accusing him of not loving her enough. He supposed she had picked up on the fact that his mind

446

had been elsewhere recently and it was making her feel insecure. It didn't seem to occur to her that she had been making him feel insecure for most of their married life. Or that his job involved him looking after other people even more needy than her.

He rang the prison bell and as he waited for an officer to come to open the gate for him he wished he had gone in for some branch of the law that wasn't so exacting. Conveyancing was the one that sprang to mind.

'Are you really feeling up to continuing today?' Steven asked Susan once she was brought into the interview room.

She was very pale, with dark circles beneath her eyes. Her hair needed washing and she'd pinned it back un-flatteringly behind her ears.

'Yes, I'm fine,' she said, but glancing at her hands he noticed she'd been biting her nails over the weekend.

'The police will be here any minute,' he said. 'Is there anything you wish to discuss with me or ask before they get here?'

She shook her head. 'I just want to get it over with as quickly as possible,' she said curtly.

Longhurst and Bloom arrived within minutes, and Longhurst began by reminding Susan that on the previous Friday she had reached the point in her confession where she went up to the woods to wait for Reuben and Zoë to turn up there.

Longhurst started the tape with the date, time and

those present, then asked Susan if she would continue. She agreed she would.

'Did you go up to the woods with the intention of killing Reuben Moreland and Zoë Fremantle?' he asked first.

'Yes,' she agreed. 'I've told you that already. I put up the tent, got myself organized, then I began digging their grave.'

'So it was entirely premeditated?' Roy asked.

'Of course it was,' she snapped. 'I wouldn't camp out in a wood just for fun.'

Roy was well used to being surprised and shocked in his job, but as Susan related how she spent the next five days digging the grave, deciding exactly where she would hide to wait for her victims, and keeping a watch on Hill House, he felt sickened.

He could perfectly well understand her feeling murderous towards Reuben and Zoë. If she had gunned them down in the house while distraught, he might have been sympathetic. But the meticulous planning and the waiting put her crime into a different realm, one he found utterly repulsive. As she graphically described her preparations, the concealment of the tent and the grave-digging, he stopped seeing her as a short, dumpy woman on the wrong side of forty, but as a female Rambo on the loose, lurking behind trees waiting for her victims to come and make love in the glen so she could gun them down.

It was only when she got to the point where the couple arrived in the glen and Zoë lay down on the blanket that she began to show some emotion. Her voice shook as she related the conversation she'd overheard.

'I did have second thoughts then,' she admitted. 'You see, I sensed that Zoë would ditch Reuben if he didn't sell the house and go gallivanting around the world with her. I even felt a bit sorry for him getting tangled up with her. But she started being so dirty with him, I got angry all over again.'

'What do you mean by dirty?' Roy asked.

Susan blushed and couldn't look at him. 'I can't say all that,' she said. 'She took her trousers off and she was showing herself to him and stuff.'

Roy had a pretty good idea what she meant by this and decided he didn't need the graphic details. 'They were making love? And you were still behind the bush close by them?'

'Yes.'

'How close?'

'About twelve feet away.'

'Who did you shoot first?'

'Reuben,' she said. 'But I only winged him in the side with the first shot. I suppose I was shaking. So I came out of the bush round in front of him and shot him again, through the chest. Then I shot her.'

Roy had to make Susan explain with the aid of a diagram where she was, and the angle at which she fired all three shots.

'Did Zoë try to get away after you'd fired the first shot?' Roy asked.

'No, I don't think she knew what the sound was, she

449

only tried to get away once I'd come out from behind the bush and shot Reuben the second time, but she was half trapped beneath him. I shot her straight after Reuben.'

'Then what did you do?'

'I dragged Zoë to the hole I'd dug first, put her in, then went back for Reuben. I had to wrap him in the blanket and pull that because he was so heavy.'

There was complete silence for a moment, all three men looking stunned.

'Then you buried them?' Roy said, his voice cracking.

'Yes.'

He found it almost unbelievable that she'd stayed up in those woods for another two nights. That she'd been able to make herself something to eat and to sleep soundly only a few yards from the newly filled grave.

'It must have been cold up there at night,' he said. He wanted her to tell him she was sorry that she'd done it. Or say something that might prove she was mentally deranged. But she only smiled faintly.

'I had the rest of their whisky. That kept the chill out, and besides, I needed to stay a while to make sure they were well covered. The hole I dug wasn't very deep.'

Once again Roy asked her if she'd draw a plan of where the bodies were buried, and once again Steven reminded her there was no obligation to do so.

'I thought you wanted me to tell the whole truth?' she said scornfully. 'They've got the cake, they might as well have the icing too.'

Like before, she drew a very clear map, showing the way she entered the glade, and marked the place where her victims had been making love, and where she hid to shoot them.

She drew a small circle to the left of the glade. 'You would have found the camping equipment here. But that wasn't where I pitched camp, I moved it all before I left,' she said, putting a larger circle on the far side of the glade, close to the cross which marked the grave. 'That's where I originally pitched it. If you push through the undergrowth about another twelve or fifteen feet on from there, you'll come to a little spring. That's where I got my water from.'

'How much camping had you done before that time?' Roy asked. It didn't have any bearing on her statement, he was just curious.

'None since I was a child,' she said. 'I used to go with my father for weekends of shooting when I was about eight, up till when I was ten. Usually around Tintern, he liked forests and the whole survival thing. He taught me to cook on an open fire, dig holes for rubbish and stuff. He did all that when he was in the army.'

Roy remained silent for a few moments. 'Why, Susan?' he asked eventually. 'Why did you have to kill them?'

'Because they'd destroyed me,' she said, but it sounded as if she were asking a question rather than stating what she believed.

'But if you had just left, gone away and found a job, you could have rebuilt your life,' he said.

'Could I?' she retorted. 'With what? I had nothing left but their insults ringing in my ears, the humiliation burning inside me.'

*

Roy ended the interview then. He had all he needed, including the maps of where the bodies were. He got all those present to sign and date both the map and the tapes. He'd heard more than enough for one day.

As Susan was led away down the corridor by a prison officer to her wing, the men went in the opposite direction to leave, Sergeant Bloom some way ahead of Roy and Steven.

Roy paused for a moment and leaned against a window-sill. 'Were you satisfied at the way I conducted the interview?' he asked, his dark eyes grave and troubled.

'Perfectly,' Steven said. 'But then she gave it to you on a plate.' He sighed and rubbed his hand over his eyes. He guessed Roy felt just as he did, stunned and drained. 'That woman's got more layers than an onion.'

'Enough to make you wonder if there's any more bodies anywhere,' Roy said drily.

Steven's eyes widened, and Roy half smiled. 'That was meant to be a joke, in poor taste, I admit. I suppose it's to cover up how foolish I feel. I saw her as a weak little woman half mad with grief. But she's a one-woman commando raid.'

All at once Steven felt a surge of respect and real liking for this man. A great many policemen would be gloating at getting such a cut-and-dried result, in a tearing hurry to get back to the station to report on it. But Roy was too bright and compassionate not to sense that he had only really scratched the surface of what Susan had gone through mentally. She may have told them the facts about what she did, and when, but she hadn't given them more than a glimpse of her emotional state.

Looking at his watch, Steven saw it had just turned eleven. 'Too early to offer you a beer or even lunch,' he said regretfully.

'I could murder a large scotch,' Roy admitted. 'I'd like to chat a while with you too. But I've got to get back with these tapes and start the procedure for the searches. Perhaps another time?'

'I'll have to update Beth too.' Steven sighed. 'This is going to knock her for six.'

Roy reached out and grasped Steven's forearm. He said nothing, but Steven knew it was intended as a gesture of friendship and understanding.

'Beth's another one with more layers than an onion,' Steven said. 'Help her unpeel them.'

As it turned out, Steven didn't get to see Beth until late in the afternoon. The threatened snow started during the drive back to the office, reducing the traffic to a crawl, and by the time he got there, she was at court for the afternoon with a client.

He heard her voice out on the stairs at five, just as he was about to go home. But he had to tell her then, he couldn't stand another night of holding it in, so he went out and called down to her.

Ironically, he'd never seen her looking lovelier in the whole time they'd worked together. She was wearing a camel coat with a big furry collar and cuffs and matching hat. Her face was rosy from a walk back from the courts in the snow.

'What is it?' she called back up the stairwell. 'I was just going home to get warm.'

'About Susan,' he said abruptly, and went back into his office to wait for her.

'Bad news?' she asked as she came in.

Steven nodded. 'The worst, I'm afraid. She's made a full confession to the murders of Liam, Reuben and Zoë.'

Beth's face blanched and she covered her mouth with her hands. 'No!' she exclaimed. 'That can't be right.'

Steven went over to her and made her sit down, then got her a drink of brandy he kept for emergencies. Then he rapped it all out, as concisely as he could, how Susan had killed them and where the bodies were.

'I don't believe it,' she gasped out. 'I can't believe it.' Tears started up in her eyes.

'Neither could I,' he said, and explained how much of it had been confessed on Friday, and why he hadn't felt able to tell her then. 'But it's true, Beth. She wasn't coerced or tricked into talking, it was all of her own volition. The police will begin digging tomorrow, I expect. Then it will all be confirmed.'

She just sat there for a moment, her wide mouth trembling. 'I have to go home,' she said eventually, getting up a little unsteadily. 'I need to think this through on my own.'

Steven saw what real dignity and courage was then. Any other woman he'd ever known when faced with such shattering news would have crumbled. But Beth wouldn't, not in front of him or anyone else. She would go home and cry alone.

He wanted to hug her, but he sensed to do so might make things worse. He couldn't even suggest she phoned him later because that would start Anna off again.

'I'm so sorry, Beth,' he said simply. 'I'll come in early tomorrow if you like and we can talk more about it.'

'Okay,' she said, and with that walked out of the door. Steven watched as she made her way down the stairs, only a faint wobble in her walk showing she wasn't as composed as she looked.

Beth walked into her flat, turned up the heating, took her coat, hat and boots off, then drew the curtains before sitting down.

She was so shocked she felt numb. One word kept running through her mind. *Involvement*. Yet it was a word that until a few months ago had no real meaning for her.

But she had experienced it now. A dry mouth from anxiety, butterflies in her stomach, constant questions in her mind, her sleep being invaded.

She'd had cases before which other lawyers claimed would have given them nightmares. But they didn't affect her. She had listened dry-eyed to tragedies that would have made a strong man weep. She had always been able to listen to the verdict at a client's trial, and whether they were found guilty or innocent, her only concern was whether she'd played her part in the case to the best of her ability. It never concerned her how that same client would cope afterwards, whether in prison or going back to their normal life. Once her job was done, she shut herself off. Justice had been done, and that was that, to her.

Yet since the day Susan came back into her life unexpectedly, everything seemed to have changed. She wasn't sorry it had, but she still couldn't understand why one woman should have such an impact on her life.

So they were friends as children, but that was such a tenuous link. They spent one month a year, for five years, in each other's company, a mere five months in total. Beth had worked for years with some people, day in, day out. Would she have found it as distressing to find that one of them had become a serial killer? She very much doubted it. She'd hardly bothered to find out most of those people's birthdays, the names of their children, or even where they lived.

Steven was distressed too, she had heard it in his voice, seen it in his face, yet she knew much of that distress was for her, which was why she had to pretend she was fine. He was the opposite to her, he cared for everyone. He had almost certainly fallen in love with Anna because of her problems – caring people always did seem to find the lame dogs of this world to support. Once she would have found that funny, or pathetic, but not any more. Now it looked more like nobility.

She remembered how at sixteen she thought Susan was noble to stay at home and nurse her mother. Nothing would ever have persuaded Beth to do such a thing. Not even if her mother had been crippled and widowed, and begging her. But then Susan was tender-hearted in every way. When the Aberfan disaster happened in Wales, Beth could remember her sending all her saved pocket money to the relief fund. She looked out for ducks and swans on the river, always afraid they'd injure themselves on fishing lines. She sobbed through romantic films, she cried when the two of them parted at the end of August.

So how could such a sensitive and placid girl become a killer? Beth could understand her shooting the doctor, in a strange way it appeared righteous and clean. But not the others. That was just savagery.

Beth felt icy cold all evening, inside and out. She had two large brandies and a bath to try to warm herself up, yet she still felt chilled. As she sat at the dressing-table brushing her hair, she was still thinking about involvement. She had shunned it all her life and now she was ensnared by it. Susan, Roy and Steven had all made a place for themselves in her heart, which had once held nothing but a few valves and a great deal of blood.

Cold reason told her that Susan was Steven's client, and it was just Roy's job to bring her to trial. She could distance herself from it all.

But that wasn't possible, not now. Steven would need her support and guidance in preparing the defence. Roy would almost certainly get commendations for his work on this case, and she was going to be torn between pride in his work and remorse at betraying her old friend.

It was that feeling of betrayal that worried her the most. She had convinced herself that she only went digging into Susan's past to provide a watertight case of diminished responsibility. But was that her real motive? It seemed more like a case of insatiable curiosity about her old friend now. Surely Annabel's death alone was enough for a court to hear? If she hadn't wanted to know every last thing about Susan, it was doubtful the other three murders would ever have been discovered.

That was perhaps her real dilemma. Susan would get life, because of her. The whole world would say she deserved it, especially the relatives of her victims. They would applaud those who had brought her to justice. But Beth would always feel like a Judas.

She looked around her bedroom and saw for the first time how impersonal it was. Cream walls and carpet like the living room, the expensive brocade curtains a slightly darker shade. Wardrobes and cupboards all built in, the wood a light beech. It was like a hotel room, tasteful, comfortable, but there was not a shred of her personality in it.

'But then you don't have one,' she whispered to herself. 'You've spent your whole life squashing what you feel. If you died tomorrow, what could anyone say about you?'

She supposed someone would say she was an excellent solicitor, punctual, trustworthy, reliable. But that was about all. There would be no one to tell funny anecdotes, no friends weeping. Even Robert and Serena would be hard-pressed to give a reason why they loved her.

She got into bed and lay there looking at the ceiling. For twenty-eight years she'd let the rape dominate her life. She would have denied that just a few months ago, insisted that it had spurred her on to greater things than she would have achieved if it hadn't happened. She had even convinced herself that she was born with a frosty nature.

Then Susan turned up, bringing with her the memories of the days when she wasn't cold and aloof, and a thaw had begun to set in, melting the ice she'd packed around those secrets and feelings inside her.

Maybe it was Steven who chipped away the ice, and Roy blew warm air to speed the defrosting, but Susan started it.

She began to cry then, scalding-hot tears flowing down her cheeks unchecked.

Chapter twenty

Two days after Susan's confession, Roy stood in the Welsh woods, shoulders hunched, hands in pockets, watching as the team of men cleared another area of fallen leaves and undergrowth.

It was eleven-thirty in the morning and bitterly cold. Too cold for snow, someone had said earlier, as if that was a bonus. The men were all in good spirits, for usually when they were sent out searching an area for evidence of a crime or a missing person, they half expected a long and often fruitless task. But with a taped confession and a map of where the bodies were, everyone was expecting a quick result.

Yet Roy was very tense. He hadn't expected that when they arrived here at first light, they would find the spot marked on Susan's map immediately, but he hadn't imagined it would take this long.

Susan might have been very clear in her mind about where the grave was located, but without measurements from some kind of landmark – a big rock, an easily identified tree – it could be almost anywhere. They had nearly completed clearing the area Roy believed she meant, looking for a hump or an indentation which would suggest digging had taken place in recent years. But so far they had seen nothing unusual, and the ground was frozen solid all over.

Doubts had started to creep into his mind. Could Susan have made it up? It was he after all who suggested she'd killed them here. It wasn't unknown for someone held in custody to confess to other crimes out of some kind of mental sickness. Even while she'd been relating what she'd done, it hadn't sounded totally believable. And there was a large part of him which still couldn't believe she was capable of it anyway.

He supposed that in his heart he didn't want it to be true. Yet if it wasn't, and the search revealed nothing, he knew he'd be in hot water.

Roy wondered, too, what was going on in Luddington. The search of the garden at The Rookery was being handled by the Warwickshire murder squad, and it was only late yesterday that he'd heard they'd got the necessary order to go in and start digging.

'There's a lot of dead branches here, guv!' a young constable suddenly called out from a place on the fringe of the cleared area.

Roy's heart leapt and he raced over to the younger man.

The heap of branches uncovered beneath a mulch of dead leaves did look incongruous. They covered an area of some eight feet by four, and they were stacked at least a foot high.

'They couldn't have just fallen that way, could they?' the younger man asked.

'I doubt it,' Roy said, looking up at the nearest tree. It

was a fine healthy one, the branches couldn't belong to it. Besides, branches didn't fall into neat piles, this one had been made by hand. 'It could be that someone collected it up to burn it, but changed their mind. But we'll look under it anyway.'

As the constable began moving the heap, Roy had his fingers crossed inside his pocket. Some of the men were beginning to grouse about the cold, but if there was something here they'd get a new burst of energy.

'I've found something, guv!' another constable called out behind him. Roy turned in the direction of the small stream Susan had mentioned. The man was holding something on the end of a stick. 'Looks like a woman's boot,' he yelled.

Roy examined it before bagging it as evidence. It was the remains of a black leather, small-size ankle-length boot with a side zip. It appeared to have been chewed by an animal, and it was so thickly covered in mould that it could have lain there for years. He examined the site where the constable found it, but there was nothing further there.

Going back to the spot with the branches, he saw the men had now cleared it, and were tentatively putting spades in all around it, feeling for softer spots. 'Go on, dig,' he called out.

It took a pick-axe to penetrate the top layer of frozen soil, but once it was through, the digging suddenly became easier, with soft, dark loam beneath.

'I reckon this is it,' one of the men called out jubilantly. 'It's been dug before.'

It soon became obvious he was right, for the going was only easy within a rough rectangular shape. Outside this, the earth was rock-hard to a far greater depth.

The men's earlier lethargy vanished. The ones digging were putting their backs into it, their faces growing red with exertion, their breath like smoke in the frosty air. There was a palpable excitement, everyone's eyes on the ever-growing hole.

The sound of a spade hitting something solid made everyone move closer. 'Scrape around it now,' Roy ordered. 'It might be bone.'

A few minutes later, a skull was uncovered.

Men engaged elsewhere came running over as they heard the news. They crowded round the shallow grave to take a look and one man crossed himself. It looked like something from a horror film, for though the flesh had mostly been eaten away, the hair was still intact, long and grey. The empty eye sockets and the almost grinning open jaw looked very ghoulish.

Even with so many willing hands, it still took over an hour of patient and gentle scraping away with small trowels before the entire body was exposed. As Roy looked down at it, a lump came up in his throat, for the sight of a skeleton in just a rotting sweatshirt, boots still on the feet, was a sharp reminder that Susan had shot Reuben while he was making love.

'He seems to be intact,' someone said. 'And lying on some kind of blanket or ground sheet. That's handy, we can probably lift him out without disturbing anything.'

That initial jubilation faded as the day wore on, for the

pathologist had his work to do before the bones could be removed and photographs had to be taken at every stage. Searchlights had to be set up as it grew dark, the area was cordoned off and a tent erected over the grave. Zoë's body was only exposed in the early evening, and by then it was eerie working under the lights.

Although coffee and sandwiches had been brought up for the men throughout the day, they were all stiff with the cold, and the hanging around waiting for orders was tortuous.

'You must be on top of the world about this, boyo,' one of the senior Welsh police officers said to Roy just after Zoë's body was found.

This man had been making jocular and inappropriate remarks all day. Roy thought he was probably annoyed that he wasn't heading the investigation, and also embarrassed that it had taken someone from Bristol to uncover a double murder on his patch.

'I'll just be glad to go home,' Roy said. He wasn't on top of the world, in fact he felt sickened. Day after day his work brought him into contact with all the worst aspects of human behaviour. There was usually some satisfaction to be had when the guilty were caught and punished, but in this particular case there wasn't even that. Susan had been in a state of punishment for almost all her life.

'I won't lose any sleep over this duo,' the Welshman said, rubbing his hands gleefully. 'That bunch at Hill House have been like a stone in my boot for too long. Glad to be rid of the lot of 'em, I'll be. There's too many of these cranks, weirdos and druggies coming to live in Wales.'

Roy didn't bother to reply. He had disliked this Welshman at first sight, for he was a total bigot. The people living at Hill House now *were* undesirables, no one in their right mind would want their sort on their doorstep, but they certainly weren't representative of all newcomers to Wales. Yet this man clearly thought that every unconventionally dressed person he came across was on drugs. He wouldn't understand that sensitive people brought up in inner cities could get high just on the beauty of Wales. Or that the country desperately needed new blood, people who wanted to live peaceable and industrious lives and bring up their children in the country.

Roy left the murder scene at around nine to go down to the pub in the village where he'd booked a room for the night. He wanted a hot bath, bed and oblivion, nothing more.

But he couldn't sleep for thinking about Beth and wondering how she had reacted when Steven told her about Susan's confession. He knew from past experience what friends and relatives of murderers went through. Often it was far worse for them than for the criminal, sometimes they felt in some way responsible, love, anger, shame and pity all mixed up into a cocktail they couldn't cope with.

He wished he could phone her, but even if she was prepared to speak to him, what could he say? Susan had been right at the centre of their relationship. She had brought them together, and pushed them apart too.

Beth wouldn't want to hear about how sick he'd felt as he watched the bodies being uncovered, his admiration for the stoicism of the other men in the freezing wood, or his concerns as to how Zoë's parents were going to take the news that their only daughter was dead.

He remembered how it was this kind of thing which had driven a wedge between him and Meg after Peter died. Meg had no room in her mind for anything other than her own grief. She didn't understand that he still had a job to do, one that threw unpleasant and often traumatic things up on a regular basis. She wanted him to be as broken as she was, to think and talk of nothing but their son. He was devastated, but he knew he had to work through it. She never forgave him for that. She said he'd shrugged off Peter's death as if it were nothing.

Beth wasn't like Meg, of course. This situation was very different too, but Roy was only too aware that a rape victim would find it hard to trust anyone. And sadly, as he headed this investigation into Susan's further three murders, Beth must see him as being untrustworthy.

As he huddled in the bed, trying to get warm, he wished he was anything but a policeman. His work on this case wouldn't end tomorrow when the last of the bones were removed from the woods and taken away. It wouldn't be over until Susan was tried and convicted. By then the chances were Beth would have lost interest in him completely.

The following morning both Beth and Steven got into the office early so they could talk before their first clients arrived. The police had contacted Steven just before he left work the previous evening to tell him the two bodies in Wales had been found, and also the one at Luddington. Steven had rung Beth during the evening to tell her, knowing that it would be on the nine o'clock news and that by this morning it would be splashed across the front page of every newspaper.

'You couldn't blame anyone for thinking Susan is another Fred West,' Steven said, pointing to the front page of the *Mirror*, one of several papers he'd brought in with him. The headline read, 'The death count mounts'.

Beth read the page quickly. 'They've reported it as if more are expected,' she sighed.

'My old grandmother used to say, "There's nothing like a good murder to sell papers."' Steven half smiled. 'She was practically a world expert on murder trials, she used to read up about them all the time. Loved the psychology profile stuff. Maybe that's what influenced me to become a lawyer.'

Beth sighed dejectedly. 'I wonder what she would have made of our Susan?'

'I don't even know what to make of her myself,' Steven said. 'One moment I feel angry with her, the next sorry for her. I understand, yet I don't. I still keep thinking that there's something she hasn't told us. One thing that would make a huge difference.'

'Perhaps that's because we can't feel what she was going through as she did it?' Beth suggested. 'Maybe you should ask her to tell you that, Steven?'

467

'I'm not sure I want to know that.' He sighed. 'She's given me enough nightmares already.'

Beth got out of her chair and went over to him, putting one hand on his shoulder. 'I bet you wish I'd never handed her over to you,' she said. 'It's turned out to be a poisoned chalice, hasn't it?'

He smiled weakly. 'When I was at law school I used to imagine being a defence lawyer was mainly about saving the innocent from being sent down for crimes they didn't commit.'

Beth could see he was deeply troubled, and judging by the bags under his eyes he hadn't been sleeping any better than she had.

'I was the same,' she said. 'I thought I was going to be the champion of the oppressed. But do try to winkle out that one thing she hasn't told you. It probably won't change anything at all. But it might give us both a clearer understanding of her.'

'I'm going to see her tomorrow,' he said gloomily. 'I'll do my best, but don't be surprised if I get nothing.'

All the way to the prison the next day, Steven told himself he must be dispassionate about Susan. He couldn't afford to spend so much time thinking and worrying about her, he had other clients who needed him more. It was down to the psychiatrist to dig into her mental state, his role was only to see she got a fair trial.

He began well enough. 'You'll have been told the police found the bodies in Wales?' he said crisply. 'I got word this morning they've found the one in Luddington too.

Is there anything more you want to tell me? Or anything you want to know?'

'You look tired,' she said, looking hard at him. 'Is that because of me?'

He was thrown again, for it was so like her to show concern for others despite being in such deep trouble herself.

'No, of course not,' he said quickly. 'I've just been working hard lately and not getting to bed early enough.'

'Don't tell me lies,' she said quietly. 'I do understand what all this must have done to you.'

Steven looked into her greenish-blue eyes and saw real concern. It touched him, for he didn't get that concern at home. 'It's all part of my job.' He shrugged.

'Not any more it isn't,' she said. 'I'm going to dismiss you. I'd like a new solicitor.'

That was the last thing Steven expected. 'But why, Susan?' he asked. 'It's your right of course. But I'd like to be given a good reason after all we've been through together.'

She looked at him sadly, her lower lip trembling. 'Let's just say you are too involved now,' she said in a small voice. 'I want someone to defend me who doesn't care.'

'That's an absolutely ridiculous thing to say,' he retorted indignantly.

'Is it?' she asked, raising one eyebrow. 'You can't win now, Mr Smythe, I'm going to get life, whatever you try to do for me. I can accept that. But I don't believe you'll be able to. That's why I want someone else.'

Steven sighed. He was touched by her obvious sincerity

469

and he also felt a sense of relief, even though he'd come to see her today believing he wanted to defend her to the end. 'If that's what you really want, then that's what you shall have,' he said.

She smiled. 'It will be better for both of us,' she said, and her voice was lighter. 'You are a bit like me, Mr Smythe, you feel too much. If you are going to continue in criminal law, you'll have to grow a harder shell.'

'I'm not usually so affected by my clients,' Steven said defensively. 'You are a special case.'

'You want to understand, don't you?' she said, and smiled faintly. 'I wish I could help you, but I don't really understand it myself.'

'Could you try? For me?' he said.

She sighed. 'Liam's death is quite easy to explain, for it was just an accident. I'd been through so much, I was scared of losing him, and I struck out in desperation. I can only suppose that once you've seen a body lying dead on the floor, buried it, cleared up and got away with it, the taboo of killing is broken. And you can do it again.'

She paused, looking thoughtful.

'None of us ever know what we are really capable of, not until a moment of intense fear or anger. It's like there's another person inside of you that comes out at times like that. If I hadn't killed Liam, I would never have killed Reuben and Zoë. But then, if I hadn't killed Liam I wouldn't ever have fallen prey to Reuben in the first place.'

'What makes you think that?' Steven asked.

'I wouldn't have been so needy, all those guilt feelings about Annabel's death being punishment for Liam.'

She got to her feet suddenly, showing that her explanation and the visit were over. 'Thank you for everything you've done for me, Mr Smythe,' she said, holding out her hand. 'And you have done a great deal, even if you can't see it.'

Steven shook her hand. He thought in that moment that she was as regal as a duchess thanking her servants for taking care of her.

'Don't lose any more sleep over me,' she said. 'You've got a wife and family to think of.'

Steven didn't know what to say in the face of such dignity. 'I wish you luck' was all he could think of.

'I've written a letter to Beth,' she said, pulling an envelope out of her trouser pocket. 'Will you give it to her for me?'

Steven nodded. 'Look after yourself, Susan. I *will* be thinking about you, I can't help that.'

'I don't want another solicitor from your firm,' she said as she went to the door and signalled to the officer outside she wanted to be let out. 'I want someone completely unconnected.'

Beth hadn't been home more than five minutes when her door-bell rang.

She picked up the intercom phone and heard Steven's voice. 'I'm just putting a letter from Susan through the letter-box,' he said. 'Can't stop, I'm running late, but I thought you'd like it right away.'

Beth ran down the stairs two at a time, hoping to catch

him, but she was too late. He was gone, and the letter was lying on the mat. She opened it as she walked up the stairs.

Dear Beth, she read. *I don't know if you'll get to read this before Mr Smythe tells you I've dismissed him, but it doesn't really matter because I think you'll understand why, even if he doesn't.*

I don't want to see you again. Not ever. Please don't come to the trial, or try and visit me, or even write to me. It won't do either of us any good.

Beth paused in the reading of it as she got back upstairs. She shut her front door, went into her living room, sat down and continued.

What we had together as girls will always be precious to me. I want to keep those good memories intact for ever. Can you understand that? It was a cruel twist of fate that we should meet up again the way we did. You so successful, and me right down there in the gutter. But I believe there is always a good reason for everything, and perhaps in our case it was not just to make me ashamed of what I'd become, but so you too could face up to your past.

I told your policeman you'd been raped. Maybe you even know that by now. I told him purely to hurt him, and bring him down, I took pleasure in it.

I know you will be puzzled by that, just as you will have been by me confessing to the other murders. You wouldn't have believed I was capable of such cruelty and vindictiveness. But I am.

I can't pinpoint exactly when I began to change from the girl you knew, it was probably a gradual process over the years. I can remember getting very resentful towards both my father and brother in the last few years of my mother's life. I was being wound up like a spring, tighter each day. I told you about the moral blackmail, but it was more than that. I was frightened of them, especially Martin. He had intimidated me almost from birth, and as I grew older it got worse. So when my father left everything to him, I guess that was a bridge too far. If it hadn't been for Liam coming back into the picture, I know without any doubt it would have been Martin I killed, for the spring was at breaking-point at that time.

If only it had been Martin. I would have felt justified in ridding the world of someone so cruel and mean. I could have gone to the police right then and owned up, taken my punishment and felt justice had finally been done.

But I killed the man I loved. And then later I lost my Annabel and I was broken completely. Then along came Reuben, and I thought I was being offered a chance to redeem myself.

Sitting here writing this in my cell, I can't adequately explain why I felt I had to kill him and Zoë. But I do know that all the rage I felt towards Martin, and my father, the loss of Annabel, what I'd done to Liam was mingled with the humiliation and hurt Reuben and Zoë put me through. I had to show them they couldn't do that to me and get away with it.

Killing them haunted me, yet not in a guilty way as you'd expect. I felt a kind of jubilation that I'd done it. I felt powerful and in control for the first time in my life.

I thought that new power would stay with me back in Bristol. I had visions of finding a good job, and a nice home again. But my clothes were shabby. I had no money and I was back with all the memories of Annabel.

I was stuck in a hole. Without tidy clothes I couldn't get a decent job, without a job I didn't have any money to buy them. All the cleaning job brought in was the bare minimum to pay the rent and eat, no way out.

Maybe if I hadn't seen Dr Wetherall and that blonde bitch together up on the Downs, I might have found a ladder eventually. But seeing them together brought it all back that they were responsible for her death. All at once I was focused. It gave me a buzz stalking them, a whole new reason for living. I learned so much about them, and their daily routine. They used to walk up to the Adam and Eve pub in Hotwells for a drink after work. I would sit in the corner behind a newspaper and watch them, and marvel that they were so wrapped up in one another that they were unaware of me. I thought of so many different ways to hurt them, as varied as informing his wife and her husband what was going on, painting 'Adulterers' on the door of the medical centre, I even considered killing one of their children. People may have thought I was an alcoholic, but the only thing I was addicted to was revenge.

There was a small part of me however that was frightened of the feelings inside me. I knew I was out of control but I had no way of communicating with anyone, I didn't even pass the time of day with anyone at the house in Belle Vue. I let myself into the offices to do the cleaning. They left my money on a desk every Friday. I didn't even see anyone there, ever. It was almost like being a small nocturnal animal, living a life that was invisible to everyone. I was so lonely. When I took a bottle of drink with me to sit in the square at Hotwells, I suppose I was always hoping someone would eventually confront me, that I'd be arrested, or taken to a mental hospital. But no one cared enough to even speak to me.

A few days before I eventually shot them, I was ill. I lay shivering up in my bed in that horrible room, knowing that if I was to die it would be weeks before anyone even found my body, much less care that I was all alone. Prison suddenly seemed very much better than what I had, and so I gave up all ideas of a covert killing. Shooting them openly was simpler and more dramatic. Everyone would know who did it, and why. I didn't care what happened to me afterwards.

Had I been given any other solicitor I doubt if I'd have had one moment of remorse. But you turned up and all those memories, feelings, hopes and dreams I once had came flooding back. Enough to make me think what I had become. Because of you, Mr Smythe cared about me, and Detective Inspector Longhurst. All those years I'd wanted someone to care just a little, but when it came, too late for me to change anything, I found I couldn't cope with it.

Despite what I know you think, I am dangerous. I need to be locked away from other people. So forget me, Beth. Get on with your life, find happiness. I could be happy if I thought that in all my wickedness I was at least the catalyst that gave you the power to set yourself free from the pain in your past.

Remember how we used to joke about being wallflowers? We didn't really believe we would be, did we? I used to imagine that on my sixteenth birthday I'd be miraculously transformed into a slender, dainty beauty, that there'd be a queue of boys waiting to take me out. I used to picture a white wedding, with you as my chief bridesmaid, and then I'd project the dream even further to

475

seeing myself with several children and you coming to visit as their favourite aunt.

I don't know which was the sadder of us two, me too weak to insist on a life of my own, then one day turning killer.

Or you, with all your brains and beauty, allowing three brutes to prevent you from finding love and happiness.

It isn't too late for you to get down from that wall you've stayed on for so long. Get down from it now, join in, be part of it all. Do it for me, Beth.

My love and fondest memories
Susan

Beth was crying long before she got to the end of the letter, and as she finished it she went into her bedroom, flung herself down on the bed and cried the way she had as a teenager.

Maybe Susan's explanation wouldn't be enough for most people, but it was for her. Their lives might have been poles apart, yet at their core they were the same. Beth knew what it was to feel so alone that her mind turned in on itself, preventing anyone from breaking through. She knew how hurt and humiliation could wind someone up to breaking-point.

She had her hatred for her father. Susan had hers for her brother. There were incidents in both their lives which had never been resolved. Beth knew she was luckier in that her career had given her the ability to be entirely independent. But she was as tied to the past as Susan was with her sick mother.

Still crying an hour later, Beth heard the door-bell ring,

and thinking it might be Steven, she got up to answer it.

But it wasn't Steven, it was Roy.

She couldn't refuse to let him in. For all she knew he might have some urgent message.

By the time he'd come up the stairs she'd attempted to bathe her face, but she hadn't managed to get rid of the mascara streaks or the redness of her eyes.

He took one look at her, put his arms round her tightly and just held her there in the tiny hall.

'I had to come,' he murmured against her hair. 'I couldn't stand another day without seeing you.'

'I told you to stay away from me until all this was over,' she sobbed out, trying to push him away.

'I know you did,' he said, restraining her arms. 'But it looks to me as if you need a friend right now just as much as I do.'

Beth gave in, she had no strength left to fight with him, and handed him Susan's letter to read, so at least he would know why she was upset.

She watched his face as he read it. She told herself that if there was just a trace of cynicism on it, or if he sneered or made a sharp remark, she'd show him the door. But to her astonishment she saw a tear trickling down his cheek.

Her heart melted, for she knew that rugged face wasn't accustomed to feeling the wetness of tears.

He looked up at her, dark eyes swimming. 'She's very noble,' he said in a croaky voice. 'No self-pity, no wanting to cling to you like a life raft.'

'Nothing cynical to add?' Beth said, still struggling to hold back her own tears.

Roy reached out for her, took her hand and drew her down on to the settee beside him. 'How can I be cynical? She's written that straight from the heart. She was even honest enough to admit what she'd told me, and why.'

'But you arrested her. You've been there at the searches for the bodies. You've met Zoë's mother. I couldn't blame you if you were totally against her.'

'I don't like what she did, but that doesn't stop me from seeing what she is,' he said. 'Or what she might have been if fate hadn't conspired against her.'

'How long ago did she tell you about me?' Beth asked.

'It was last Friday morning. It broke up the interview. Then when we started again in the afternoon she said she wanted to confess.'

'I was going to tell you myself.' Beth began to cry again. 'I'm so ashamed you had to find out that way.'

Roy put his arms around her and held her tightly against his chest. 'There's no need for you to feel any shame. Lay that at the feet of the animals who did that terrible thing to you,' he said fiercely. 'Besides, I think I always knew it was something like that,' he murmured against her forehead. 'I think you should tell me all about it now, don't you?'

'But you're tired, you've had a miserable time for days now,' she said, trying to stall him.

'Not so tired I don't want to hear something you've kept locked away for years,' he said gently.

Beth told him then, described it in detail, and as she did so she knew she was able to put it behind her at last. His reaction of outrage and pain was the one she had always longed for from her father, and never got.

'No wonder you despise your father,' Roy burst out, clenching his fists and thumping them on the arm of the settee. 'What a bastard! If he wasn't so old now I could be tempted to go to his nursing home and shake him senseless.'

Beth gave a hollow laugh. 'He hasn't got much sense left,' she said. 'But there's something more, Roy, more important to you and me. It's left me frigid.'

Her words, ones she had never uttered to a living soul, seemed to echo round the room. She had to close her eyes because she didn't want to see his shock or disappointment.

She felt his big hand on her cheek, smoothing it gently, then he kissed her lips tenderly. 'Then we'll work on that,' he whispered. 'I've got all the patience in the world as far as you are concerned. If we could never have anything more than a platonic relationship, I'd settle for that rather than losing you.'

Roy went home later, after making them both an omelette and insisting Beth had a hot bath and went to bed early. She could see he was exhausted, yet he made light of it, saying he was used to it.

He hadn't made her dredge up more of the past, nor had he suggested she spoke to a psychiatrist as she'd expected and dreaded. He didn't speak of what he'd been doing in Wales, it was as though he'd decided the only way forward was to separate the past from the present and just look ahead.

The last thing he said as he left around nine was that he wanted to take her to his cottage on Saturday.

Beth woke from an erotic dream in which Roy was making love to her in a wood. It was so intense and real that her whole body was quivering and sticky with sweat. She had never had an orgasm, or even come close to it, but she sensed she'd had one then. She closed her eyes again, wanting to sink right back into it, but although she could see Roy's face and relive his kisses, it wasn't the same.

Unable to go back to sleep, she turned on the light and looked at the clock. It was five o'clock.

All at once she knew what she wanted to do. If she tried to suppress the instinct she might never do it. She leapt out of bed, pulled her coat on over her nightdress, put on her slippers, grabbed her keys and ran out down to her car.

It wasn't until Beth drove into the village of Queen Charlton that she realized she didn't know the name of Roy's cottage. She pulled up by a crossroads, wondering which way to go. It was still pitch dark, there was no street lighting and few of the cottages even had lights outside.

To her right was the church, the houses to her left looked too big, as did the ones she'd already passed, and she knew that the road straight ahead went to Keynsham. She thought Roy would have mentioned if it was that road he lived on. That left only the lane, which she knew was a cul-de-sac with fields at the end.

She drove down it very slowly, peering at each cottage. They all appeared very much grander than how she had imagined Roy's. It crossed her mind that if anyone should see her they might call the police, thinking she was a burglar. She smiled at the thought of being pulled up and found to be wearing her nightie, while she was looking for a policeman herself.

Then she saw Roy's car right at the end of the lane, outside a cottage which was bigger and, even in the dark, more attractive than Roy had led her to believe. She parked up behind his car and got out, closing the door very quietly, and tiptoed up the gravel to the front door.

Her eyes were growing used to the dark now. She could just make out the hedge around the garden which presumably led on to fields. It was so quiet compared to where she lived, almost as if the darkness was a blanket muffling her ears. But it was freezing cold, the wind whistling through her coat and up her bare legs.

There was no bell she could see, so she tried knocking on the door. But no light came on, and this was beginning to look like complete folly. She knocked again, louder this time, but there was still no response, so she walked round the side of the house, guessing that Roy would choose a bedroom with a view.

Only one room had drawn curtains, and she threw a handful of gravel at the window. No response. She tried again, but still no response.

She was about to go back to the car when she noticed the tree – probably an apple or cherry tree, judging by its size and shape. Although it wasn't close enough to the window for her to bang on it if she could climb it, she could shake a branch at the window.

She giggled to herself. As a girl she'd been the best in her village at climbing trees, but she hadn't attempted it for at least thirty years, and never in the dark before. But she felt as if she could do anything now – climb, fly, do a tap-dance on his doorstep. She had been liberated at last, she could do all the things now that she'd bypassed after the rape.

The lower part of the trunk had no hand- or footholds, but the lowest branch was only a couple of feet above her head. She jumped, managed to grab it, then swinging hand over hand she worked her way back towards the trunk. Her coat hindered her, her slippers fell off and the wind was icy on her bare legs and naked bottom, but the thought of Roy's surprise when he woke to find her in the tree outside his window kept her going. She reached the trunk, managed to find a foothold on it and hauled herself up into the main part of the tree.

She was only a few yards from the window now. She bounced tentatively on a thick branch which felt as though it would hold her weight, then she edged along it, holding on to another higher one. She was close enough to start banging on the window now, and reaching out she grabbed a slender branch above her, bashing it against the window.

'Roy!' she hissed. 'Roy!'

Although she was freezing, the ludicrousness of her position kept making her giggle. She could imagine newspaper headlines – 'Knickerless Solicitor Attempts to

Break into Policeman's House' or 'No Nicks for Policeman's Brief'.

She pulled the light branch right back and let it go so it made a far louder noise this time. A dog barked in a house somewhere nearby. She wondered what on earth she would do if someone came along.

Then suddenly Roy pulled back the curtain and looked out.

She laughed out loud at his astonishment, for she knew she must look like a witch with her white face and dark hair. But perhaps he heard her laugh, for he opened the window.

'Beth?' he said, as if unable to believe it was really her.

'Yes, it's me, trying to make an illegal entry,' she whispered, breaking into a fit of giggles.

'I've a good mind to leave you up there,' he whispered back.

'I'll scream if you do, then your neighbours will all come running out,' she said. 'And I warn you, I've only got a nightie on under this coat, nothing else.'

He disappeared from the window and suddenly he was below her, looking up, wearing a dressing-gown, his legs bare. 'How on earth did you get up there?' he whispered.

Beth shuffled back along the branch, then climbed down to the trunk and the branch she'd hauled herself along on. She sat down on it and held out her arms to Roy. 'Catch me!'

It wasn't more than ten feet, and he caught her effortlessly, hugging her tightly to him. 'What a crazy thing to do!' he exclaimed in a stage whisper. 'Why didn't you phone?'

He was carrying her indoors as if she weighed nothing. 'You wouldn't have done this if I'd warned you I was coming,' she giggled.

'You deserve to have your bottom smacked,' he said with mock sternness and put her down by the fire which he immediately switched on. 'It's not even warm in here because I've been away. I went to bed as soon as I got home.'

'Well, let's go and get in there, before it gets cold too,' Beth said, switching off the fire. She stood up and held out her hand.

His wide smile was a joy to see, and she was glad he didn't ask if she was sure about it. He grasped her hand, held it to his lips and kissed it. 'After me, Milady,' he said, pulling her behind him to the stairs.

Once in the still dark bedroom, he took off his dressing-gown, but Beth could see enough to know he was still wearing boxer shorts. Then he removed her coat and literally bundled her into the bed.

'You're like a block of ice,' he exclaimed as he got in beside her and pulled her into his arms, recoiling momentarily when he felt how cold she was. 'I shall have to give you not only the kiss of life but a brisk rub-down.'

There wasn't one moment of fear, dread or even apprehension, for the sure but gentle way he massaged warmth back into her limbs, bottom and back with his big warm hands felt so right. She could feel herself melting as he

484

kissed her, his body fitting against hers as if it was made specifically for it.

He didn't attempt to touch her breasts until she began to press them into his chest, but when his hand finally cupped round one of them it gave her the same thrill she remembered from when she was sixteen and got her first fondle from a boy in a hayfield.

It was such slow, tender and gradual love-making that Beth lost herself and entered into something so new, so beautiful that the past vanished, nothing mattered but his lips on hers, his caressing fingers. It was like her dream earlier, only hotter, more sensual and thrilling. There was no fear now, only the desire for it to go on for ever. She couldn't believe that at last she was with a man who was capable of awakening all those parts of her which had lain dormant for so long.

'Tell me what you like best,' Roy whispered.

'I can't, it's all so wonderful,' she sighed in rapture. 'But show me how to please you too.'

'It pleases me just to play with you,' he said, sucking at her breasts as he probed inside her with his fingers, making her gasp with pleasure. 'I love you, Beth, I want you beside me for ever.'

It seemed to Beth that she was being sucked from the real world into one of exquisite sensations, and her body was not her own any more but a pulsating organ which Roy was playing. The sensations built and built until suddenly she felt some kind of overwhelming, rushing, astounding feeling, and all at once she finally knew what an orgasm meant.

He entered her then as she clung to him, still drowning in the bliss of it all. She could hear herself calling out his name, bucking under him, urging him to drive deeper and deeper into her. It was just the most wonderful thing she had ever known.

Grey light was filtering through the curtains as they lay in each other's arms, sleepy, but too new to one another to sleep yet.

'I have to go to work,' Beth said sadly.

'No you don't,' Roy replied. 'Play ill and stay home with me.'

'But I've got appointments –'

Roy cut off her argument with a kiss. 'They are thieves and rogues, let them wait another day or two,' he said. 'Besides, you can't go home in your nightie in broad daylight.'

Beth hadn't considered that aspect. She couldn't possibly park her car and walk to her flat the way she'd come here.

'What will I do then?' she said.

'I'll phone in for you, I'm a good liar when I need to be,' he chuckled. 'We'll stay here in bed until lunch-time, then I'll go over to the supermarket and buy something for lunch and for you to wear.'

'I think I feel a really grave illness coming on.' She giggled and snuggled down further into the bed. 'I may take weeks to recover.'

'I'm bound to catch it too,' he said, pulling the duvet

over their heads. 'We might never be able to get out of this bed again.'

Steven smiled as he put the phone down after speaking to Roy. His story about Beth going down with a stomach upset after a meal at his house would have been entirely plausible to anyone else. But Steven knew Beth was the kind who would have insisted on being taken to her own home if she was ill. He guessed the only sickness in that house was love-sickness.

He was glad for Beth. Really glad that something good had come out of this whole sorry mess with Susan. But then, if it hadn't been for Susan he wouldn't have got to know Beth so well, and Anna would still be drinking, the girls unhappy.

He stood up. He had to go and tell Brendan about Susan dismissing him, and that Beth was ill. Brendan wouldn't like either, but Steven didn't really care. One thing they could be certain of in a criminal law practice was that they'd never be short of clients. He just hoped that if another Susan came along, she wouldn't get under his skin the way this one had.

Chapter twenty-one

'What are you looking so smug about, Fellows?'

Susan smiled at the woman unlocking the gate for her. Bagnell, or Baggy, as the girls called her, was one of the decent screws. She had a brusque manner but she wasn't a brute, and she wasn't gay either. In fact she often came along to Susan's cell for a chat. She liked gardening and was in charge of the prison greenhouses.

'Just got back from a chat with my brief,' Susan said. 'It looks as if my trial will be in early July.'

It was April now. Susan had been on remand in Oakwood Park for six months already.

'You know you won't get sent back here?' Baggy warned her. She was a big woman with tight curly fair hair, and a port wine birthmark on her cheek. Susan suspected she'd joined the prison service because it was a way of hiding herself away. 'You'll probably be sent to Durham, at least for a while. That's no picnic, I worked there for a time.'

'I'll be a good girl then, and get them to send me somewhere else,' Susan said lightly.

She wasn't afraid of prison any more. She knew how to handle herself now. After she'd finished her punishment on the block, she was given a cell on her own. Word had got round she'd knocked Frankie out, and all the teasing and nastiness stopped miraculously. Then Baggy got her work in the greenhouses, looking after the bedding plants they grew there, and being outside for a couple of hours a day had made all the difference to Susan. Plus she'd got some glasses now, and she could see to read at last.

'You are the only woman I've ever known who wasn't scared of being sentenced,' Baggy said with some degree of admiration.

'Why should I be scared when I already know what I'm going to get?' Susan asked. 'They're going to give me life, and that's all there is to it.'

'Doesn't that worry you?'

Susan shrugged. 'There's nothing outside for me. If I was let out tomorrow I wouldn't even know where to go. At least inside there's people who actually care whether I'm alive or dead. I'm warm, I'm fed, I've got people to talk to. I've even got used to the noise.'

'So what's this new brief you've got like?' Baggy asked as they walked along the corridor together. Steven Smythe was liked by many of the prison officers, and many of them were curious as to why Fellows had dismissed him. She wouldn't say why, of course, she rarely talked about herself, and they sensed a mystery as Smythe always made a point of asking how Fellows was when he called to see another client. Sometimes he brought in books or sweets for her too.

'Franklin's okay. Not likely to send your pulse racing

489

of course.' Susan giggled as she pictured the sixteen-stone solicitor with white hair and a round, jolly face. 'The best thing about him is that he accepts me as I am now. He doesn't keep making me talk about my past.'

'Well, he doesn't need to, I suppose,' Baggy said thoughtfully. 'What with you pleading guilty and all. Go on, tell me, why did you dismiss the other chap? He's a nice guy.'

'Too nice for his own good,' Susan said with a little chuckle. They were at the door of her cell now. 'I had this feeling if I stuck with him I'd end up in a place for the criminally insane.'

She smiled as she walked into her cell. Baggy often brought her in gardening magazines, and she had cut out some of the flower pictures and stuck them on the wall with toothpaste to brighten it up. She'd been told that in some prisons, lifers could have a duvet, a bedside lamp, and even their own television. With that in store for her she didn't mind having to leave here.

'I thought you must be insane when you first came here,' Baggy admitted. 'I don't mean you behaved as if you were, but –' She stopped suddenly.

'Because of what I'd done?' Susan finished for her. 'No, not insane, just pushed too far I suppose. If you look around in here, there's a lot more like me. Luckily for them they didn't do anything as bad as me though.'

'Tell me, Fellows,' Baggy said. 'Are you sorry now?'

'Truthfully?' Susan asked.

Baggy nodded. 'Just between ourselves.'

'No, I'm not. Well, I am about the first one, but then I

didn't mean to hurt him, it was an accident. But I'd be lying if I was to say I regretted the others.'

Baggy shook her head in bewilderment. 'You're a funny one,' she sighed. 'I think for your own good you'd better take to lying about it at your trial. And I've got to lock you up again now.'

Susan sat down on her bed as the door clanked shut. She thought she probably was a 'funny one', most of the women wouldn't even tell the truth about what they were in for. They said 'fraud' when it was shop-lifting. Or made out they'd attacked a man and were up for GBH, when in fact they'd really hurt their own child. Personally she couldn't see any point in telling lies, not because of the moral issue, but because once you'd owned up, it was sorted. You didn't have to spend any more time agonizing over when you were going to be found out.

Most of the remand prisoners who'd been here when she was first brought in were gone, Frankie included, but almost daily new ones arrived. She'd hear them crying at night and feel for them, especially the young ones. So many of them were still children at eighteen, dragged through children's homes, foster homes and ending up here emaciated from drug abuse. Many could barely read or write, they often had children themselves who had been taken from them, some were pregnant when they were brought in. That made Susan cry, but she couldn't cry about her own crimes.

It seemed to her that remorse for what she'd done was unnecessary. So instead she tried to help those who needed it in here. Helping them write letters, listening to their anxieties, and preventing others from bullying them, that was useful. Remorse wasn't going to bring anyone back from the dead, it didn't change anything for anyone.

Susan walked over to the window and stood up on the toilet so she could see out through the bars. Her cell overlooked the exercise yard. There was a flower bed up the far end, bright with red and yellow tulips. She hoped she'd get to see all those petunias and busy lizzies she'd pricked out into trays in flower before she left here.

She wondered then if Beth had got into gardening. Mr Franklin had given her a note from Mr Smythe on his previous visit. He'd said Beth spent most of her spare time now with her policeman at his cottage. He thought they would get married before long.

'I hope so, Beth,' Susan whispered to herself. 'Be happy. I am now.'

She wasn't fooling herself either. It was true she'd often looked back to the point when her parents died and wished she'd thought then of applying for a job in a boarding school, or tried to get into nursing. She would have been good at either job. But then, if it hadn't been for Liam she would never have had Annabel and all that joy of motherhood. Despite all the agony of losing her, those four years were still the golden ones, the best ones in her whole life.

Nothing could ever again give her the sheer bliss she'd experienced in those years, but she was contented now.

There was nothing to strive for in here, no real anxiety. She found she liked the orderliness of prison and the feeling of security. Looking back, she could see it was insecurity and perhaps the lack of rigid structure to her life that unhinged her slightly when her parents died. Clinging to Liam, hating Martin all added to it.

Maybe she would find a new prison tougher than this one, but she knew the ropes now and she could, by appealing to the right people, get herself moved to an easier one. Nothing was ever going to be as bad again as living in that cold, damp room in Belle Vue.

The cherry tree Beth had climbed in Roy's cottage garden was in full blossom in May. On a warm, sunny Sunday afternoon, Beth and Roy were sunbathing on a blanket on the lawn, discussing their wedding.

Roy had stripped off to a pair of shorts, and had tried to persuade Beth to take off her dress and put on her bikini, but she wouldn't because she was embarrassed at how lily-white her body was. She had however made up her mind to start going to a solarium in her lunch-hours, if only to reach the pale biscuit colour Roy was.

'We can't have a white wedding, it would be ridiculous,' Beth protested.

'Why?' Roy argued. 'Because of our ages, or because you don't think we're entitled to one?'

Since that night back in February when Beth had climbed the tree to wake him they had spent every moment of their spare time together. Roy's cottage had gradually become Beth's first home, she only stayed in her flat occasionally if she worked late at the office. Even when Roy worked nights or was called away for a couple of days, she preferred the tranquillity of the cottage. Looking out over fields might not be as spectacular as the view of Bristol from her flat, but to her it was far more appealing. They had been talking about getting married for some weeks now, and Beth was every bit as keen as Roy.

'I don't know exactly why I think it's ridiculous,' she admitted, looking up at the umbrella of pink blossom above them. 'Too much fuss, I suppose.'

'It doesn't have to be a big affair,' he said. 'We could have it at the church here, just your family, those of mine who can be trusted to behave, and a few friends.'

Beth laughed. Roy was always a little anxious about his family, but Beth liked his sisters. Perhaps they were a bit rough and ready, but they had good hearts. She knew Serena and Robert would like them too, for snobbishness was one thing none of them had inherited from their father.

She had taken Roy to meet her family back in March, and she still glowed at the memory of that wonderful weekend. Serena and Robert had welcomed him with open arms, and he'd been equally bowled over by them. To see Serena smiling fondly as Roy played football with Robert's boys, her two nieces asking breathlessly if they could be bridesmaids, was almost enough on its own. And suddenly Beth didn't feel she was the outsider looking in longingly at a happy family, it was as though she belonged to it.

'Go on, say yes,' Roy said, leaning over and kissing her. 'I want to be up at that altar and turning to see you coming up the aisle in a white dress and veil, your nieces holding your train. It's like a public declaration of how much I love you.'

Tears prickled Beth's eyes. Roy could be so soppy and romantic sometimes. She loved it, for it was all new to her, yet sometimes she felt she didn't really deserve it.

'What if the vicar won't marry us?' she asked. 'You've been divorced, remember!'

'She left me,' Roy reminded her. 'Besides, I've already asked the vicar, he's all for it.'

'Oh, have you now?' Beth playfully rolled him over and sat astride him. 'Going behind my back already! What else have you done in secret?'

'Tentatively arranged it for the first Saturday in August,' he admitted, pretending to look anxious. 'I said I'd ring him to confirm it tonight, if you were agreeable.'

'And what if I'm not?' she asked, pulling at his ears.

'Then I'll have to torture you till you do agree,' he said. 'I shall take you upstairs, handcuff you to the bed and roger you again and again until you submit.'

'Roger me!' she exclaimed. 'What sort of an expression is that?'

He didn't reply but caught hold of her round the middle and lifted her bodily off him in the same way he played aeroplanes with her nieces.

'Put me down,' she giggled, as she wavered in the air above him. 'I'm too big for this.'

'Maybe I won't roger you then, I'll just hold you here

495

all afternoon instead,' he laughed. 'It will start to hurt in a minute.'

'It already is,' she squealed. 'I'll take the rogering instead.'

He dropped her to the grass and bent over her to kiss her again. 'I love you, Beth. Let's do it all properly. It is for ever and ever, after all,' he said tenderly.

Beth got up a few minutes later and went into the cottage to get them both a drink. As she walked into the living room she stopped to look around her, reminding herself that once they were married this would really be her home.

Before she'd seen Roy's home, he had led her to believe that it was still something of a derelict hovel. Yet nothing could be farther from the truth. He had knocked several small rooms into a huge 'L'-shaped one so there were windows all round, and the ceiling was supported with beams. The part of the room nearest the front door and hall was the sitting end, the back part was the dining area, leading on to the kitchen. All the floors had been sanded smooth and varnished.

When Beth had first come here there was little furniture, just the white settee he'd told her about, a television and an old table. She had picked the material for the curtains herself, lovely heavy off-white wool with crewel embroidery in scarlet and soft greens.

Since then, they'd bought a big Indian rug which was remarkably like the curtains, a dining table and chairs, and the beech kitchen had been finished. Beth was intending to sell her flat and most of her furniture, for it was all too modern to bring here. But her paintings would fit in. That struck her as very significant, for they were the only things she really cared about, and Roy liked them as much as she did.

Sometimes she felt she ought to pinch herself to check this wasn't all a dream. She had found the kind of love she thought only existed in soppy romances, discovered she was far from frigid, and released the young girl who had been frozen deep inside her.

That was really the best part. It was wonderful to be spontaneous, to view each day ahead with optimism, to take an interest in other people and to let her own defences drop.

When Beth thought back to the night she'd climbed the tree to wake Roy, it always made her smile. It was so hare-brained and out of character. And as for the next few days! They had stayed in bed most of the time, hours and hours of love-making, talking, laughing. She would never forget either the dreadful clothes Roy bought her in Asda. Polyester slacks which were four inches too short, a ghastly striped sweater and a red and black bra with matching knickers.

'I can see you are a high-maintenance sort of woman,' Roy said with an ear-to-ear grin when she tried them on. 'Perhaps I should have tried Tesco.'

In those few days Beth felt as if she had shed her old skin and emerged a different woman. She was even afraid to go back to her flat in case the old Beth returned. But she needn't have worried, the new Beth was stronger. She wrinkled her nose at the so-called tasteful cream decor, and went straight on out and bought half a dozen brilliant-coloured cushions to jazz it up a bit. She got on the phone and told Serena she was in love.

Since then it had been one long round of new experiences. Weekends were spent in wellingtons and jeans, working on the garden. At night when Roy was working she decorated their bedroom. There were visits to his mother and sisters, helping Roy to tile the bathroom. Loneliness and time hanging on her hands were just a distant memory.

She had come to see that Roy had immersed himself in work for much the same reasons she had – a substitute for a loving relationship. He had his own guilt, for not being closer to his wife and perhaps for not being able to give her what she needed when their son died.

But work came second-place to them both now.

Susan was the only sadness in Beth's life. She knew perfectly well that she couldn't do anything to help her any more. She knew Susan wouldn't want her to either. But her affection for her remained, undiminished even in the face of the monstrousness of her crimes, for she knew it was her old friend who had opened up the door to this happy new life.

She and Steven had found a very able solicitor for Susan. Beth had met Thomas Franklin many times and she knew he was right for her friend. The trial was fixed for the start of July and as Susan was pleading guilty to all charges – four to murder and one of manslaughter in Liam's case – it wouldn't take too long.

Beth had sent Susan one last letter via Franklin on his last visit, reminding her that she would never forget her, and that if she needed anything she was to get in touch. Franklin had reported back that Susan had smiled as she read the letter and asked him to pass on a verbal message. It was simply: 'Stop being a wallflower.'

As Beth waited for the kettle to boil, she gazed out of the window by the sink and sighed with happiness. The window looked out on to more fields, with the boundary of the garden marked by a low hedge, and it faced west so it got the afternoon sun. She thought how good it would be on summer evenings to sit at the table eating dinner and watch the sun go down. Iris, Roy's mother, had commented that she wouldn't want so much open countryside so close, as any burglar could easily get through the hedge and rob them. Yet Beth felt more secure here than she'd ever felt in her third-floor flat with all its security systems.

'Where's that tea, wench?' Roy shouted from the front door.

'Just coming, sir,' she called back. 'While you wait you could call the vicar and tell him we're on for August.'

He leapt into the room, rucking up the rug as he ran to sweep her up in his arms. 'Great!' he exclaimed as he twirled her round. 'Now, you are sure, aren't you?' he added as he put her down, looking a little anxious. 'It might be a bit soon for you after Susan's trial?'

Beth was touched by his sensitivity. Roy had avoided talking about Susan since they became lovers; whatever

499

loose ends he'd had to tie up in the case he'd kept to himself. But clearly the trial was ever-present in his mind, along with the effect it was going to have on Beth.

'The wedding plans will take my mind off it,' she said positively. 'We know what the outcome will be anyway, don't we?'

He nodded gravely, then grinned irreverently. 'You'll be getting life too, remember?' he said.

'That's a joke in the worst possible taste, Roy,' she said in shocked tones.

'We can only joke about it,' he said, catching hold of her two arms. 'It's the best way to deal with it that I know. We can't change anything, Beth, or undo it. It's happened, that's all there is to it.'

Beth knew he was right. Almost everyone she knew involved with tragedy, be it firemen, police or lawyers, made jokes to ease the burden of it. It didn't mean they didn't care.

'Well, just don't refer to marriage as imprisonment then,' she said, giving him a sharp look.

He slid his arms around her and held her close. 'But at least it's an open prison and the governor loves you,' he said.

'Roy!' she exclaimed, but began to laugh anyway. 'You are incorrigible.'

'A council estate boy like me can't understand such big words.' He grinned. 'What does it mean?'

'Incurable,' she said. 'So I suppose I'm stuck with it.'